"I can help you," he said before he could let himself think about it, and he thrust out his hand. *"Massimo Valtieri. If you're ready to go, I can give you a lift to Siena now."*

He pronounced it Mah-*see*-mo, long and slow and drawn out, his Italian accent coming over loud and clear as he said his name, and she felt a shiver of something primeval down her spine. Or maybe it was just the cold. She smiled at her self-appointed knight in shining armour and held out her hand.

"I'm Lydia Fletcher—and if you can get us there before the others I'll love you forever."

His warm, strong and surprisingly slightly callused fingers closed firmly round hers, and she felt the world shift a little under her feet. And not just hers, apparently. She saw the shockwave hit his eyes, felt the recognition of something momentous passing between them, and in that crazy and insane instant she wondered if anything would ever be the same again....

CAROLINE ANDERSON

Valtieri's Bride

TORONTO NEW YORK LONDON
AMSTERDAM PARIS SYDNEY HAMBURG
STOCKHOLM ATHENS TOKYO MILAN MADRID
PRAGUE WARSAW BUDAPEST AUCKLAND

Recycling programs
for this product may
not exist in your area.

ISBN-13: 978-0-373-17808-7

VALTIERI'S BRIDE

First North American Publication 2012

A BRIDE WORTH WAITING
Copyright © 2006 by Caroline Anderson

Caroline Anderson has the mind of a butterfly. She's been a nurse, a secretary and a teacher, she ran her own soft furnishing business, and now she's settled on writing. She says, "I was looking for that elusive something. I finally realised it was variety, and now I have it in abundance. Every book brings new horizons and new friends, and in between books I have learned to be a juggler. My teacher husband, John, and I have two beautiful and talented daughters, Sarah and Hannah, umpteen pets and several acres of Suffolk that nature tries to reclaim every time we turn our backs!" Caroline also writes for the Harlequin Medical Romance™ series.

Books by Caroline Anderson

THE BABY SWAP MIRACLE
MOTHER OF THE BRIDE
TWO LITTLE MIRACLES

Other titles by this author available in ebook format.

If you would like to catch up with Caroline Anderson's other stories featuring the Valtieri family,
The Valtieri Marriage Deal
(from Harlequin Medical Romance) is available in ebook format from www.Harlequin.com.

And look out for *The Valtieri Baby*,
coming in September 2012!

VALTIERI'S BRIDE

Caroline Anderson

CHAPTER ONE

WHAT *on earth* was she doing?

As the taxi pulled up in front of the Jet Centre at London City Airport, he paused, wallet in hand, and stared spellbound across the drop-off point.

Wow. She was *gorgeous*.

Even in the crazy fancy-dress outfit, her beauty shone out like a beacon. Her curves—soft, feminine curves—were in all the right places, and her face was alight with laughter, the skin pale and clear, her cheeks tinged pink by the long blond curls whipping round her face in the cutting wind. She looked bright and alive and impossibly lovely, and he felt something squeeze in his chest.

Something that had been dormant for a very long time.

As he watched she anchored the curls absently with one hand, the other gesturing expressively as she smiled and talked to the man she'd stopped at the entrance. She was obviously selling something. Goodness knows what, he couldn't read the piece of card she was brandishing from this distance, but the man laughed and raised a hand in refusal and backed away, entering the building with a chuckle.

Her smile fading, she turned to her companion, more sensibly dressed in jeans and a little jacket. Massimo flicked his eyes over her, but she didn't hold his attention. Not like the blonde, and he found his eyes drawn back to her against his will.

Dio, she was exquisite. By rights she should have looked an utter tramp but somehow, even in the tacky low-cut dress and a gaudy plastic tiara, she was, quite simply, riveting. There was something about her that transcended all of that, and he felt himself inexplicably drawn to her.

He paid the taxi driver, hoisted his flight bag over his shoulder and headed for the entrance. She was busy again, talking to another man, and as the doors opened he caught her eye and she flashed a hopeful smile at him.

He didn't have time to pause, whatever she was selling, he thought regretfully, but the smile hit him in the solar plexus, and he set his bag down on the floor by the desk once he was inside, momentarily winded.

'Morning, Mr Valtieri. Welcome back to the Jet Centre. The rest of your party have arrived.'

'Thank you.' He cleared his throat and glanced over his shoulder at the woman. 'Is that some kind of publicity stunt?'

The official gave a quiet, mildly exasperated sigh and smiled wryly.

'No, sir. I understand she's trying to get a flight to Italy.'

Massimo felt his right eyebrow hike. 'In a *wedding dress*?'

He gave a slight chuckle. 'Apparently so. Some competition to win a wedding.'

He felt a curious sense of disappointment. Not that it made the slightest bit of difference that she was getting married; she was nothing to him and never would be, but nevertheless…

'We asked her to leave the building, but short of escorting her right back to the main road, there's little more we can do to get rid of her and she seems harmless enough. Our clients seem to be finding her quite entertaining, anyway.'

He could understand that. He was entertained himself—mesmerised, if he was honest. And intrigued—

'Whereabouts in Italy?' he asked casually, although the tightness in his gut was far from casual.

'I think I heard her mention Siena—but, Mr Valtieri, you really don't want to get involved,' he warned, looking troubled. 'I think she's a little…'

'Crazy?' he said drily, and the man's mouth twitched.

'Your word, sir, not mine.'

As they watched, the other man walked away and she gave her companion a wry little smile. She said something, shrugged her slender shoulders in that ridiculous meringue of a dress, then rubbed her arms briskly. She must be freezing! September was a strange month, and today there wasn't a trace of sunshine and a biting wind was whipping up the Thames estuary.

No! It was none of his business if she hadn't had the sense to dress for the weather, he told himself firmly, but then he saw another man approach the doors, saw the woman straighten her spine and go up to him, her face wreathed in smiles as she launched into a fresh charm offensive, and he felt his gut clench.

He knew the man slightly, more by reputation than anything else, and he was absolutely the last person this enchanting and slightly eccentric young woman needed to get involved with. And he would be flying to his private airfield, about an hour's drive from Siena. Close enough, if you were desperate…

He couldn't let it happen. He had more than enough on his conscience.

The doors parted with a hiss as he strode up to them, and he gave the other man a look he had no trouble reading. He told him—in Italian, and succinctly—to back off, and Nico shrugged and took his advice, smiling regretfully at the woman before moving away from her, and Massimo gave him a curt nod and turned to the woman, meeting her eyes again—vivid, startling blue eyes that didn't look at all happy with what he'd just done. There was no smile this time, just those eyes like blue ice chips skewering him as he stood there.

Stunning eyes, framed by long, dark lashes. Her mouth, even without the smile, was soft and full and kissable— No! He sucked in a breath, and found himself drawing a delicate and haunting fragrance into his lungs.

It rocked him for a second, took away his senses, and when they came back they *all* came back, slamming into him with the force of an express train and leaving him wanting in a way he hadn't wanted for years. Maybe ever—

'What did you *say* to him?' Lydia asked furiously, hardly able to believe the way he'd dismissed that man with a few choice words—not that she'd understood one of them, of course, but there was more to language than vocabulary and he'd been pretty explicit, she was sure. But she'd been so close to success and she was really, really cross and frustrated now. 'He'd just offered me a seat in his plane!'

'Believe me, you don't want to go on his plane.'

'Believe me, I do!' she retorted, but he shook his head.

'No. I'm sorry, I can't let you do it, it just isn't safe,' he said, a little crisply, and she dropped her head back and gave a sharp sigh.

Damn. He must be airport security, and a higher authority than the nice young man who'd shifted them outside. She sensed there'd be no arguing with him. There was a quiet implacability about him that reminded her of her father, and she knew when she was beaten. She met his eyes again, and tried not to notice that they were the colour of dark, bitter chocolate, warm and rich and really rather gorgeous.

And unyielding.

She gave up.

'I would have been perfectly safe, I've got a minder and I'm no threat to anyone and nobody's complained, as far as I know, but you can call the dogs off, I'm going.'

To her surprise he smiled, those amazing eyes softening and turning her bones to mush.

'Relax, I'm nothing to do with Security, I just have a social conscience. I believe you need to go to Siena?'

Siena? Nobody, she'd discovered, was flying to Siena but it seemed, incredibly, that he might be, or else why would he be asking? She stifled the little flicker of hope. 'I thought you said it wasn't safe?'

'It wasn't safe with *Nico*.'

'And it's safe with you?'

'Safer. My pilot won't have been drinking, and I—' He broke off, and watched her eyes widen as her mind filled in the blanks.

'And you?' she prompted a little warily, when he left it hanging there.

He sighed sharply and raked a hand through his hair, rumpling the dark strands threaded with silver at the temples. He seemed impatient, as if he was helping her against his better judgement.

'He has a—reputation,' he said finally.

She dragged her eyes off his hair. It had flopped forwards, and her fingers itched to smooth it back, to feel the texture…

'And you don't?'

'Let's just say that I respect women.' His mouth flickered in a wry smile. 'If you want a reference, my lawyer and doctor brothers would probably vouch for me, as would my three sisters—failing that, you could phone Carlotta. She's worked for the family for hundreds of years, and she delivered me and looks after my children.'

He had children? She glanced down and clocked the wedding ring on his finger, and with a sigh of relief, she thrust a laminated sheet at him and dug out her smile again. This time, it was far easier, and she felt a flicker of excitement burst into life.

'It's a competition to win a wedding at a hotel near Siena. There are two of us in the final leg, and I have to get to the hotel first to win the prize. This is Claire, she's from the radio station doing the publicity.'

Massimo gave Claire a cursory smile. He wasn't in the least interested in Claire. She was obviously the minder, and pretty enough, but this woman with the crazy outfit and sassy mouth...

He scanned the sheet, scanned it again, shook his head in disbelief and handed it back, frankly appalled. 'You must be mad. You have only a hundred pounds, a wedding dress and a passport, and you have to race to Siena to win this wedding? What on *earth* is your fiancé thinking of to let you do it?'

'Not my fiancé. I don't have a fiancé, and if I did, I wouldn't need his permission,' she said crisply, those eyes turning to ice again. 'It's for my sister. She had an accident, and they'd planned— Oh, it doesn't matter. Either you can help me or you can't, and if you can't, the clock's ticking and I really have to get on.'

She didn't have a fiancé? 'I can help you,' he said before he could let himself think about it, and he thrust out his hand. 'Massimo Valtieri. If you're ready to go, I can give you a lift to Siena now.'

He pronounced it Mah-*see*-mo, long and slow and drawn

out, his Italian accent coming over loud and clear as he said his name, and she felt a shiver of something primeval down her spine. Or maybe it was just the cold. She smiled at her self-appointed knight in shining armour and held out her hand.

'I'm Lydia Fletcher—and if you can get us there before the others, I'll love you forever.'

His warm, strong and surprisingly slightly calloused fingers closed firmly round hers, and she felt the world shift a little under her feet. And not just hers, apparently. She saw the shockwave hit his eyes, felt the recognition of something momentous passing between them, and in that crazy and insane instant she wondered if anything would ever be the same again.

The plane was small but, as the saying goes, perfectly formed.

Very perfectly, as far as she was concerned. It had comfortable seats, lots of legroom, a sober pilot and a flight plan that without doubt would win her sister the wedding of her dreams.

Lydia could hardly believe her luck.

She buckled herself in, grabbed Claire's hand and hung on tight as the plane taxied to the end of the runway. 'We did it. We got a flight straight there!' she whispered, and Claire's face lit up with her smile, her eyes sparkling.

'I know. Amazing! We're going to do it. We can't fail. I just know you're going to win!'

The engines roared, the small plane shuddering, and then it was off like a slingshot, the force of their acceleration pushing her back hard into the leather seat as the jet tipped and climbed. The Thames was flying past, dropping rapidly below them as they rose into the air over London, and then they were heading out over the Thames estuary towards France, levelling off, and the seat belt light went out.

'Oh, this is so exciting! I'm going to update the diary,' Claire said, pulling out her little notebook computer, and Lydia turned her head and met Massimo's eyes across the narrow aisle.

He unclipped his seat belt and shifted his body so he was facing her, his eyes scanning her face. His mouth tipped into a smile, and her stomach turned over—from the steep ascent, or from the warmth of that liquid-chocolate gaze?

'All right?'

'Amazing.' She smiled back, her mouth curving involuntarily in response to his, then turning down as she pulled a face. 'I don't know how to thank you. I'm so sorry I was rude.'

His mouth twitched. 'Don't worry. You weren't nearly as rude to me as I was to Nico.'

'What *did* you say to him?' she asked curiously, and he gave a soft laugh.

'I'm not sure it would translate. Certainly not in mixed company.'

'I think I got the gist—'

'I hope not!'

She gave a little laugh. 'Probably not. I don't know any street Italian—well, no Italian at all, really. And I feel awful now for biting your head off, but…well, it means a lot to me, to win this wedding.'

'Yes, I gather. You were telling me about your sister?' he said.

'Jennifer. She had an accident a few months ago and she was in a wheelchair, but she's getting better. She's on crutches now, but her fiancé had to give up his job to help look after her. They're living with my parents and Andy's working with Dad at the moment for their keep. My parents have got a farm—well, not really a farm, more of a smallholding, really—but they get by, and they could always have the wedding there. There's a vegetable packing barn they could dress up for the wedding reception, but—well, my grandmother lived in Italy for a while and Jen's always dreamed of getting married there, and now they haven't got enough money even for a glass of cheap bubbly and a few sandwiches. So when I heard about this competition I just jumped at it, but I never in my wildest dreams imagined we'd get this far, never mind get a flight to exactly the right place. I'm just so grateful I don't know where to start.'

She was gabbling. She stopped, snapped her mouth shut and gave him a rueful grin. 'Sorry. I always talk a lot when the adrenaline's running.'

He smiled and leant back, utterly charmed by her. More than charmed…

'Relax. I have three sisters and two daughters, so I'm quite used to it, I've had a lot of practice.'

'Gosh, it sounds like it. And you've got two brothers as well?'

'*Sì*. Luca's the doctor and he's married to an English girl called Isabelle, and Gio's the lawyer. I also have a son, and two parents, and a million aunts and uncles and cousins.'

'So what do you do?' she asked, irresistibly curious, and he gave her a slightly lopsided grin.

'You could say I'm a farmer, too. We grow grapes and olives and we make cheese.'

She glanced around at the plane. 'You must make a heck of a lot of cheese,' she said drily, and he chuckled, soft and low under his breath, just loud enough for her to hear.

The slight huff of his breath made an errant curl drift against her cheek, and it was almost as if his fingertips had brushed lightly against her skin.

'Not that much,' he said, his eyes still smiling. 'Mostly we concentrate on our wine and olive oil—Tuscan olive oil is sharper, tangier than the oil from southern Italy because we harvest the olives younger to avoid the frosts, and it gives it a distinctive and rich peppery flavour. But again, we don't make a huge amount, we concentrate on quality and aim for the boutique market with limited editions of certified, artisan products. That's what I was doing in England—I've been at a trade fair pushing our oil and wine to restaurateurs and gourmet delicatessens.'

She sat up straighter. 'Really? Did you take samples with you?'

He laughed. 'Of course. How else can I convince people that our products are the best? But the timing was bad, because we're about to harvest the grapes and I'm needed at home. That's why we chartered the plane, to save time.'

Chartered. So it wasn't his. That made him more approachable, somehow and, if it was possible, even more attractive. As did the fact that he was a farmer. She knew about farming, about aiming for a niche market and going for quality rather than quantity. It was how she'd been brought up. She relaxed, hitched one foot up under her and hugged her knee under the voluminous skirt.

'So, these samples—do you have any on the plane that I could try?'

'Sorry, we're out of wine,' he said, but then she laughed and shook her head.

'That's not what I meant, although I'm sure it's very good. I was talking about the olive oil. Professional interest.'

'You grow olives on your farm in England?' he asked incredulously, and she laughed again, tightening his gut and sending need arrowing south. It shocked him slightly, and he forced himself to concentrate.

'No. Of course not. I've been living in a flat with a pot of basil on the window sill until recently! But I love food.'

'You mentioned a professional interest.'

She nodded. 'I'm a—' She was going to say chef, but could you be a chef if you didn't have a restaurant? If your kitchen had been taken away from you and you had nothing left of your promising career? 'I cook,' she said, and he got up and went to the rear of the plane and returned with a bottle of oil.

'Here.'

He opened it and held it out to her, and she sniffed it slowly, drawing the sharp, fruity scent down into her lungs. 'Oh, that's gorgeous. May I?'

And taking it from him, she tipped a tiny pool into her hand and dipped her finger into it, sucking the tip and making an appreciative noise. Heat slammed through him, and he recorked the bottle and put it away to give him something to do while he reassembled his brain.

He never, *never* reacted to a woman like this! What on earth was he thinking of? Apart from the obvious, but he didn't want to think about that. He hadn't looked at a woman in that way for years, hadn't thought about sex in he didn't know how long. So why now, why this woman?

She wiped up the last drop, sucking her finger again and then licking her palm, leaving a fine sheen of oil on her lips that he really, really badly wanted to kiss away.

'Oh, that is so good,' she said, rubbing her hands together to remove the last trace. 'It's a shame we don't have any bread or balsamic vinegar for dunking.'

He pulled a business card out of his top pocket and handed it to her, pulling his mind back into order and his eyes out of her cleavage. 'Email me your address when you get home, I'll send you some of our wine and oil, and also a traditional *aceto balsamico* made by my cousin in Modena. They only make a little, but it's the best I've ever tasted. We took some with us, but I haven't got any of that left, either.'

'Wow. Well, if it's as good as the olive oil, it must be fabulous!'

'It is. We're really proud of it in the family. It's nearly as good as our olive oil and wine.'

She laughed, as she was meant to, tucking the card into her bag, then she tipped her head on one side. 'Is it a family business?'

He nodded. 'Yes, most definitely. We've been there for more than three hundred years. We're very lucky. The soil is perfect, the slopes are all in the right direction, and if we can't grow one thing on any particular slope, we grow another, or use it for pasture. And then there are the chestnut woods. We export a lot of canned chestnuts, both whole and puréed.'

'And your wife?' she asked, her curiosity getting the better of her. 'Does she help with the business, or do you keep her too busy producing children for you?'

There was a heartbeat of silence before his eyes clouded, and his smile twisted a little as he looked away. 'Angelina died five years ago,' he said softly, and she felt a wave of regret that she'd blundered in and brought his grief to life when they'd been having a sensible and intelligent conversation about something she was genuinely interested in.

She reached across the aisle and touched his arm gently. 'I'm so sorry. I wouldn't have brought it up if...'

'Don't apologise. It's not your fault. Anyway, five years is a long time.'

Long enough that, when confronted by a vivacious, dynamic and delightful woman with beautiful, generous curves and a low-cut dress that gave him a more than adequate view of those curves, he'd almost forgotten his wife...

Guilt lanced through him, and he pulled out his wallet and showed her the photos—him and Angelina on their wedding day, and one with the girls clustered around her and the baby in her arms, all of them laughing. He loved that one. It was the last photograph he had of her, and one of the best. He carried it everywhere.

She looked at them, her lips slightly parted, and he could see the sheen of tears in her eyes.

'You must miss her so much. Your poor children.'

'It's not so bad now, but they missed her at first,' he said gruffly. And he'd missed her. He'd missed her every single day, but missing her didn't bring her back, and he'd buried himself in work.

He was still burying himself in work.

Wasn't he?

Not effectively. Not any more, apparently, because suddenly he was beginning to think about things he hadn't thought about for years, and he wasn't ready for that. He couldn't deal with it, couldn't think about it. Not now. He had work to do, work that couldn't wait. Work he should be doing now.

He put the wallet away and excused himself, moving to sit with the others and discuss how to follow up the contacts they'd made and where they went from here with their marketing strategy, with his back firmly to Lydia and that ridiculous wedding dress that was threatening to tip him over the brink.

Lydia stared at his back, regret forming a lump in her throat.

She'd done it again. Opened her mouth and jumped in with both feet. She was good at that, gifted almost. And now he'd pulled away from her, and must be regretting the impulse that had made him offer her and Claire a lift to Italy.

She wanted to apologise, to take back her stupid and trite and intrusive question about his wife—Angelina, she thought, remembering the way he'd said her name, the way he'd almost tasted it as he said it, no doubt savouring the precious memories. But life didn't work like that.

Like feathers from a burst cushion, it simply wasn't possible to gather the words up and stuff them back in without trace. She just needed to move on from the embarrassing lapse, to keep out of his personal life and take his offer of a lift at face value.

And stop thinking about those incredible, warm chocolate eyes...

'I can't believe he's taking us right to Siena!' Claire said quietly, her eyes sparkling with delight. 'Jo will be so miffed when we get there first, she was so confident!'

Lydia dredged up her smile again, not hard when she thought about Jen and how deliriously happy she'd be to have her Tuscan wedding. 'I can't believe it, either. Amazing.'

Claire tilted her head on one side. 'What was he showing you? He looked sort of sad.'

She felt her smile slip. 'Photos of his wife. She died five years ago. They've got three little children—ten, seven and five, I think he said. Something like that.'

'Gosh. So the little one must have been tiny—did she die giving birth?'

'No. No, she couldn't have. There was a photo of her with two little girls and a baby in her arms, so no. But it must have been soon after.'

'How awful. Fancy never knowing your mother. I'd die if I didn't have my mum to ring up and tell about stuff.'

Lydia nodded. She adored her mother, phoned her all the time, shared everything with her and Jen. What would it have been like never to have known her?

Tears welled in her eyes again, and she brushed them away crossly, but then she felt a light touch on her arm and looked up, and he was staring down at her, his face concerned.

He frowned and reached out a hand, touching the moisture on her cheek with a gentle fingertip.

'Lydia?'

She shook her head. 'I'm fine. Ignore me, I'm a sentimental idiot.'

He dropped to his haunches and took her hand, and she had a sudden and overwhelming urge to cry in earnest. 'I'm sorry. I didn't mean to distress you. You don't need to cry for us.'

She shook her head and sniffed again. 'I'm not. Not really. I was thinking about my mother—about how I'd miss her— and I'm twenty-eight, not five.'

He nodded. 'Yes. It's very hard.' His mouth quirked in a fleeting smile. 'I'm sorry, I've neglected you. Can I get you a drink? Tea? Coffee? Water? Something stronger?'

'It's a bit early for stronger,' she said, trying for a light note, and he smiled again, more warmly this time, and straightened up.

'Nico would have been on the second bottle of champagne by now,' he said, and she felt a wave of relief that he'd saved her from what sounded more and more like a dangerous mistake.

'Fizzy water would be nice, if you have any?' she said, and he nodded.

'Claire?'

'That would be lovely. Thank you.'

He moved away, and she let her breath out slowly. She hadn't really registered, until he'd crouched beside her, just how big he was. Not bulky, not in any way, but he'd shed his jacket and rolled up his shirtsleeves, and she'd been treated to the broad shoulders and solid chest at close range, and then his narrow hips and lean waist and those long, strong legs as he'd straightened up.

His hands, appearing in her line of sight again, were clamped round two tall glasses beaded with moisture and fizzing gently. Large hands, strong and capable, no-nonsense.

Safe, sure hands that had held hers and warmed her to the core.

Her breasts tingled unexpectedly, and she took the glass from him and tried not to drop it. 'Thank you.'

'*Prego*, you're welcome. Are you hungry? We have fruit and pastries, too.'

'No. No, I'm much too excited to eat now,' she confessed, sipping the water and hoping the cool liquid would slake the heat rising up inside her.

Crazy! He was totally uninterested in her, and even if he wasn't, she wasn't in the market for any more complications in her life. Her relationship with Russell had been fraught with complications, and the end of it had been a revelation. There was no way she was jumping back into that pond any time soon. The last frog she'd kissed had turned into a king-sized toad.

'How long before we land?' she asked, and he checked his watch, treating her to a bronzed, muscular forearm and strong-boned wrist lightly scattered with dark hair. She stared at it and swallowed. How ridiculous that an arm could be so sexy.

'Just over an hour. Excuse me, we have work to do, but please, if you need anything, just ask.'

He turned back to his colleagues, sitting down and flexing his broad shoulders, and Lydia felt her gut clench. She'd never, *never* felt like that about anyone before, and she couldn't believe she was reacting to him that way. It must just be the adrenaline.

One more hour to get through before they were there and they could thank him and get away—hopefully before she disgraced herself. The poor man was still grieving for his wife. What was she thinking about?

Ridiculous! She'd known him, what, less than two hours altogether? Scarcely more than one. And she'd already put her foot firmly in it.

Vowing not to say another thing, she settled back in her seat and looked out of the window at the mountains.

They must be the Alps, she realised, fascinated by the jagged peaks and plunging valleys, and then the mountains fell away behind them and they were moving over a chequered landscape of forests and small, neat fields. They were curiously ordered and disciplined, serried ranks of what must be olive trees and grape vines, she guessed, planted with geometric precision, the pattern of the fields interlaced with narrow winding roads lined with avenues of tall, slender cypress trees.

Tuscany, she thought with a shiver of excitement.

The seat belt light came on, and Massimo returned to his seat across the aisle from her as the plane started its descent.

'Not long now,' he said, flashing her a smile. And then they were there, a perfect touchdown on Tuscan soil with the prize almost in reach.

Jen was going to get her wedding. Just a few more minutes...

They taxied to a stop outside the airport building, and after a moment the steps were wheeled out to them and the door was opened.

'We're really here!' she said to Claire, and Claire's eyes were sparkling as she got to her feet.

'I know. I can't believe it!'

They were standing at the top of the steps now, and Massimo smiled and gestured to them. 'After you. Do you have the address of the hotel? I'll drive you there.'

'Are you sure?'

'I'd hate you not to win after all this,' he said with a grin.

'Wow, thank you, that's really kind of you!' Lydia said, reaching for her skirts as she took another step.

It happened in slow motion.

One moment she was there beside him, the next the steps had disappeared from under her feet and she was falling, tumbling end over end, hitting what seemed like every step until finally her head reached the tarmac and she crumpled on the ground in a heap.

Her scream was cut off abruptly, and Massimo hurled himself down the steps to her side, his heart racing. No! Please, she couldn't be dead…

She wasn't. He could feel a pulse in her neck, and he let his breath out on a long, ragged sigh and sat back on his heels to assess her.

Stay calm, he told himself. She's alive. She'll be all right.

But he wouldn't really believe it until she stirred, and even then…

'Is she all right?'

He glanced up at Claire, kneeling on the other side of her, her face chalk white with fear.

'I think so,' he said, but he didn't think any such thing. Fear was coursing through him, bringing bile rising to his throat. Why wasn't she moving? This couldn't be happening again.

Lydia moaned. Warm, hard fingers had searched for a pulse in her neck, and as she slowly came to, she heard him snap out something in Italian while she lay there, shocked and a little stunned, wondering if it was a good idea to open her eyes. Maybe not yet.

'Lydia? Lydia, talk to me! Open your eyes.'

Her eyes opened slowly and she tried to sit up, but he pressed a hand to her shoulder.

'Stay still. You might have a neck injury. Where do you hurt?'

Where didn't she? She turned her head and winced. 'Ow... my head, for a start. What happened? Did I trip? Oh, I can't believe I was so stupid!'

'You fell down the steps.'

'I know that—ouch.' She felt her head, and her hand came away bloodied and sticky. She stared at it. 'I've cut myself,' she said, and everything began to swim.

'It's OK, Lydia. You'll be OK,' Claire said, but her face was worried and suddenly everything began to hurt a whole lot more.

Massimo tucked his jacket gently beside her head to support it, just in case she had a neck injury. He wasn't taking any chances on that, but it was the head injury that was worrying him the most, the graze on her forehead, just under her hair. How hard had she hit it? Hard enough to...

It was bleeding faster now, he realised with a wave of dread, a red streak appearing as she shifted slightly, and he stayed beside her on his knees, holding her hand and talking to her comfortingly in between snapping out instructions.

She heard the words '*ambulanza*' and '*ospedale*', and tried to move, wincing and whimpering with pain, but he held her still.

'Don't move. The ambulance is coming to take you to hospital.'

'I don't need to go to hospital, I'm fine, we need to get to the hotel!'

'No,' Massimo and Claire said in unison.

'But the competition.'

'It doesn't matter,' he said flatly. 'You're hurt. You have to be checked out.'

'I'll go later.'

'No.' His voice was implacable, hard and cold and somehow strange, and Lydia looked at him and saw his skin was colourless and grey, his mouth pinched, his eyes veiled.

He obviously couldn't stand the sight of blood, Lydia realised, and reached out her other hand to Claire.

She took it, then looked at Massimo. 'I'll look after her,' she said. 'You go, you've got lots to do. We'll be all right.'

His eyes never left Lydia's.

'No. I'll stay with you,' he insisted, but he moved out of the way to give her space.

She looked so frail suddenly, lying there streaked with blood, the puffy layers of the dress rising up around her legs and making her look like a broken china doll.

Dio, he felt sick just looking at her, and her face swam, another face drifting over it. He shut his eyes tight, squeezing out the images of his wife, but they refused to fade.

Lydia tried to struggle up again. 'I want to go to the hotel,' she said to Claire, and his eyes snapped open again.

'No way.'

'He's right. Don't be silly. You just lie there and we'll get you checked out, then we'll go. There's still plenty of time.'

But there might not be, she realised, as she lay there on the tarmac in her ridiculous charity shop wedding dress with blood seeping from her head wound, and as the minutes ticked by her joy slid slowly away...

CHAPTER TWO

The ambulance came, and Claire went with Lydia.

He wanted to go with her himself, he felt he ought to, felt the weight of guilt and worry like an elephant on his chest, but it wasn't his place to accompany her, so Claire went, and he followed in his car, having sent the rest of the team on with a message to his family that he'd been held up but would be with them as soon as he could.

He rang Luca on the way, in case he was there at the hospital in Siena that day as he sometimes was, and his phone was answered instantly.

'Massimo, welcome home. Good flight?'

He nearly laughed. 'No. Where are you? Which hospital?'

'Siena. Why?'

He did laugh then. Or was it a sob of relief? 'I'm on my way there. I gave two girls a lift in the plane, and one of them fell down the steps as we were disembarking. I'm following the ambulance. Luca, she's got a head injury,' he added, his heart pounding with dread, and he heard his brother suck in his breath.

'I'll meet you in the emergency department. She'll be all right, Massimo. We'll take care of her.'

He grunted agreement, switched off the phone and followed the ambulance, focusing on facts and crushing his fear

and guilt down. It couldn't happen again. Lightning didn't
strike twice, he told himself, and forced himself to follow the
ambulance at a sensible distance while trying desperately to
put Angelina firmly out of his mind...

Luca was waiting for him at the entrance.

He took the car away to park it and Massimo hovered by
the ambulance as they unloaded Lydia and whisked her inside, Claire holding her hand and reassuring her. It didn't
sound as if it was working, because she kept fretting about
the competition and insisting she was all right when anyone
could see she was far from all right.

She was taken away, Claire with her, and he stayed in the
waiting area, pacing restlessly and driving himself mad with
his imagination of what was happening beyond the doors. His
brother reappeared moments later and handed him the keys,
giving him a keen look.

'You all right?'

Hardly. 'I'm fine,' he said, his voice tight.

'So how do you know this woman?' Luca asked, and he
filled him in quickly with the bare bones of the accident.

'Oh—she's wearing a wedding dress,' he warned. 'It's a
competition, a race to win a wedding.'

A race she'd lost. If only he'd taken her arm, or gone in
front, she would have fallen against him, he could have saved
her...

'Luca, don't let her die,' he said urgently, fear clawing at
him.

'She won't die,' Luca promised, although how he could
say that without knowing—well, he couldn't. It was just a
platitude, Massimo knew that.

'Let me know how she is.'

Luca nodded and went off to investigate, leaving him there

to wait, but he felt bile rise in his throat and got abruptly to his feet, pacing restlessly again. How long could it take?

Hours, apparently, or at least it felt like it.

Luca reappeared with Claire.

'They're taking X-rays of her leg now but it looks like a sprained ankle. She's just a little concussed and bruised from her fall, but the head injury doesn't look serious,' he said.

'Nor did Angelina's,' he said, switching to Italian.

'She's not Angelina, Massimo. She's not going to die of this.'

'Are you sure?'

'Yes. Yes, I'm sure. She's had a scan. She's fine.'

It should have reassured him, but Massimo felt his heart still slamming against his ribs, the memories crowding him again.

'She's all right,' Luca said quietly. 'This isn't the same.'

He nodded, but he just wanted to get out, to be away from the hospital in the fresh air. Not going to happen. He couldn't leave Lydia, no matter how much he wanted to get away. And he could never get away from Angelina...

Luca took him to her.

She was lying on a trolley, and there was blood streaked all over the front of the hideous dress, but at least they'd taken her off the spinal board. 'How are you?' he asked, knowing the answer but having to ask anyway, and she turned her head and met his eyes, her own clouded with worry and pain.

'I'm fine, they just want to watch me for a while. I've got some bumps and bruises, but nothing's broken, I'm just sore and cross with myself and I want to go to the hotel and they won't let me leave yet. I'm so sorry, Massimo, I've got Claire, you don't need to wait here with me. It could be ages.'

'I do.' He didn't explain, didn't tell her what she didn't need to know, what could only worry her. But he hadn't taken

Angelina's head injury seriously. He'd assumed it was nothing. He hadn't watched her, sat with her, checked her every
few minutes. If he had—well, he hadn't, but he was damned
if he was leaving Lydia alone for a moment until he was sure
she was all right.

Luca went back to work, and while the doctors checked
her over again and strapped her ankle, Massimo found some
coffee for him and Claire and they sat and drank it. Not a
good idea. The caffeine shot was the last thing his racing
pulse needed.

'I need to make a call,' Claire told him. 'If I go just outside, can you come and get me if there's any news?'

He nodded, watching her leave. She was probably phon-
ing the radio station to tell them about Lydia's accident. And
she'd been so close to winning…

She came back, a wan smile on her face. 'Jo's there.'

'Jo?'

'The other contestant. Lydia's lost the race. She's going to
be so upset. I can't tell her yet.'

'I think you should. She might stop fretting if it's too late,
let herself relax and get better.'

Claire gave a tiny, slightly hysterical laugh. 'You don't
know her very well, do you?'

He smiled ruefully. 'No. No, I don't.' And it was ridiculous that he minded the fact.

Lydia looked up as they went back in, and she scanned Claire's
face.

'Did you ring the radio station?'

'Yes.'

'Has…' She could hardly bring herself to ask the question,
but she took another breath and tried again. 'Has Jo got there
yet?' she asked, and then held her breath. It was possible she'd

been unlucky, that she hadn't managed to get a flight, that any one of a hundred things could have happened.

They hadn't. She could see it in Claire's eyes, she didn't need to be told that Jo and Kate, her minder, were already there, and she felt the bitter sting of tears scald her eyes.

'She's there, isn't she?' she asked, just because she needed confirmation.

Claire nodded, and Lydia turned her head away, shutting her eyes against the tears. She was so, *so* cross with herself. They'd been so close to winning, and if she'd only been more careful, gathered up the stupid dress so she could see the steps.

She swallowed hard and looked back up at Claire's worried face. 'Tell her well done for me when you see her.'

'I will, but you'll see her, too. We've got rooms in the hotel for the night. I'll ring them now, let them know what's happening. We can go there when they discharge you.'

'No, I could be ages. Why don't you go, have a shower and something to eat, see the others and I'll get them to ring you if there's any change. Or better still, if you give me back my phone and my purse, I can call you and let you know when I'm leaving, and I'll just get a taxi.'

'I can't leave you alone!'

'She won't be alone, I'll stay with her. I'm staying anyway, whether you're here or not,' Massimo said firmly, and Lydia felt a curious sense of relief. Relief, and guilt.

And she could see the same emotions in Claire's face. She was dithering, chewing her lip in hesitation, and Lydia took her hand and squeezed it.

'There, you see? And his brother works here, so he'll be able to pull strings. It's fine, Claire. Just go. I'll see you later.' And she could get rid of Massimo once Claire had gone…

Claire gave in, reluctantly. 'OK, if you insist. Here, your things. I'll put them in your bag. Where is it?'

'I have no idea. Is it under the bed?'

'No. I haven't seen it.'

'It must have been left on the ground at the airport,' Massimo said. 'My men will have picked it up.'

'Can you check? My passport's in it.'

'*Sì.*' He left them briefly, and when he came back he confirmed it had been taken by the others. 'I'll make sure you get it tonight,' he promised.

'Thanks. Right, Claire, you go. I'm fine.'

'You will call me and let me know what's going on as soon as you have any news?'

'Yes, I promise.'

Claire gave in, hugging Lydia a little tearfully before she left them.

Lydia swallowed. Damn. She was going to join in.

'Hey, it's all right. You'll be OK.'

His voice was gentle, reassuring, and his touch on her cheek was oddly comforting. Her eyes filled again.

'I'm causing everyone so much trouble.'

'That's life. Don't worry about it. Are you going to tell your family?'

Oh, cripes. She ought to phone Jen, but she couldn't. Not now. She didn't think she could talk to her just yet.

'Maybe later. I just feel so sleepy.'

'So rest. I'll sit with you.'

Sit with her and watch her. Do what he should have done years ago.

She shut her eyes, just for a moment, but when she opened them again he'd moved from her side. She felt a moment of panic, but then she saw him. He was standing a few feet away reading a poster about head injuries, his hands rammed in his pockets, tension radiating off him.

Funny, she'd thought it was because of the blood, but there was no sign of blood now apart from a dried streak on her dress. Maybe it was hospitals generally. Had Angelina been ill for a long time?

Or maybe hospitals just brought him out in hives. She could understand that. After Jen's accident, she felt the same herself, and yet he was still here, still apparently labouring under some misguided sense of obligation.

He turned his head, saw she was awake and came back to her side, his dark eyes searching hers.

'Are you all right?'

She nodded. 'My head's feeling clearer now. I need to ring Jen,' she said quietly, and he sighed and cupped her cheek, his thumb smoothing away a tear she hadn't realised she'd shed.

'I'm sorry, *cara*. I know how much it meant to you to win this for your sister.'

'It doesn't matter,' she said dismissively, although of course it would to Jen. 'It was just a crazy idea. They can get married at home, it's really not an issue. I really didn't think I'd win anyway, so we haven't lost anything.'

'Claire said Jo's been there for ages. She would probably have beaten you to it anyway,' he said. 'She must have got away very fast.'

She didn't believe it. He was only trying to make it better, to take the sting out of it, but before she had time to argue the doctor came back in, checked her over and delivered her verdict.

Massimo translated.

'You're fine, you need to rest for a few days before you

fly home, and you need watching overnight, but you're free to go.'

She thanked the doctor, struggled up and swung her legs over the edge of the trolley, and paused for a moment, her head swimming.

'All right?'

'I'm fine. I need to call a taxi to take me to the hotel.'

'I'll give you a lift.'

'I can't take you out of your way! I've put you to enough trouble as it is. I can get a taxi. I'll be fine.'

But as she slid off the edge of the trolley and straightened up, Massimo caught the sheen of tears in her eyes.

Whatever she'd said, the loss of this prize was tearing her apart for her sister, and he felt guilt wash over him yet again. Logically, he knew he had no obligation to her, no duty that extended any further than simply flying her to Siena as he'd promised. But somehow, somewhere along the way, things had changed and he could no more have left her there at the door of the hospital than he could have left one of his children. And they were waiting for him, had been waiting for him far too long, and guilt tugged at him again.

'Ouch!'

'You can't walk on that ankle. Stay here.'

She stayed, wishing her flight bag was still with her instead of having been whisked away by his team. She could have done with changing out of the dress, but her comfy jeans and soft cotton top were in her bag, and she wanted to cry with frustration and disappointment and pain.

'Here.'

He'd brought a wheelchair, and she eyed it doubtfully.

'I don't know if the dress will fit in it. Horrible thing! I'm going to burn it just as soon as I get it off.'

'Good idea,' he said drily, and they exchanged a smile.

He squashed it in around her, and wheeled her towards the exit. Then he stopped the chair by the door and looked down at her.

'Do you really want to go to the hotel?' he asked.

She tipped her head back to look at him, but it hurt, and she let her breath out in a gusty sigh. 'I don't have a choice. I need a bed for the night, and I can't afford anywhere else.'

He moved so she could see him, crouching down beside her. 'You do have a choice. You can't fly for a few days, and you don't want to stay in a strange hotel on your own for all that time. And anyway, you don't have your bag, so why don't you come back with me?' he said, the guilt about his children growing now and the solution to both problems suddenly blindingly obvious.

'I need to get home to see my children, they've been patient long enough, and you can clean up there and change into your own comfortable clothes and have something to eat and a good night's sleep. Carlotta will look after you.'

Carlotta? Lydia scanned their earlier conversations and came up with the name. She was the woman who looked after his children, who'd worked for them for a hundred years, as he'd put it, and had delivered him.

Carlotta sounded good.

'That's such an imposition. Are you sure you don't mind?'

'I'm sure. It's by far the easiest thing for me. The hotel's the other way, and it would save me a lot of time I don't really have, especially by the time I've dropped your bag over there. And you don't honestly want to be there on your own for days, do you?'

Guilt swamped her, heaped on the disappointment and the worry about Jen, and she felt crushed under the weight of it all. She felt her spine sag, and shook her head. 'I'm so sorry. I've wasted your entire day. If you hadn't given me a lift…'

'Don't go there. What-ifs are a waste of time. Yes or no?'

'Yes, please,' she said fervently. 'That would be really kind.'

'Don't mention it. I feel it's all my fault anyway.'

'Rubbish. Of course it's not your fault. You've done so much already, and I don't think I've even thanked you.'

'You have. You were doing that when you fell down the steps.'

'Was I?' She gave him a wry grin, and turned to look up at him as they arrived at the car, resting her hand on his arm lightly to reassure him. 'It's really not your fault, you know.'

'I know. You missed your step. I know this. I still…'

He was still haunted, because of the head injury, images of Angelina crowding in on him. Angelina falling, Angelina with a headache, Angelina slumped over the kitchen table with one side of her face collapsed. Angelina linked up to a life support machine…

'Massimo?'

'I'm all right,' he said gruffly, and pressing the remote, he opened the door for her and settled her in, then returned the wheelchair and slid into the driver's seat beside her. 'Are you OK?'

'I'm fine.'

'Good. Let's go.'

She phoned Claire and told her what was happening, assured her she would be all right and promised to phone her the next day, then put the phone down in her lap and rested her head back.

Under normal circumstances, she thought numbly, she'd be wallowing in the luxury of his butter-soft leather, beautifully supportive car seats, or taking in the picture-postcard countryside of Tuscany as the car wove and swooped along the narrow winding roads.

As it was she gazed blankly at it all, knowing that she'd have to phone Jen, knowing she should have done it sooner, that her sister would be on tenterhooks, but she didn't have the strength to crush her hopes and dreams.

'Have you told your sister yet?' he asked, as if he'd read her mind.

She shook her head. 'No. I don't know what to say. If I hadn't fallen, we would have won. Easily. It was just so stupid, so clumsy.'

He sighed, his hand reaching out and closing over hers briefly, the warmth of it oddly comforting in a disturbing way. 'I'm sorry. Not because I feel it was my fault, because I know it wasn't, really, but because I know how it feels to let someone down, to have everyone's hopes and dreams resting on your shoulders, to have to carry the responsibility for someone else's happiness.'

She turned towards him, inhibited by the awful, scratchy dress that she couldn't wait to get out of, and studied his profile.

Strong. Clean cut, although no longer clean-shaven, the dark stubble that shadowed his jaw making her hand itch to feel the texture of it against her palm. In the dusk of early evening his olive skin was darker, somehow exotic, and with a little shiver she realised she didn't know him at all. He could be taking her anywhere.

She closed her eyes and told herself not to be ridiculous. He'd followed them to the hospital, got his brother in on the act, a brother she'd heard referred to as *il professore*, and now he was taking her to his family home, to his children, his parents, the woman who'd delivered him all those years ago. Forty years? Maybe. Maybe more, maybe less, but give or take.

Someone who'd stayed with the family for all that time, who surely wouldn't still be there if they were nasty people?

'What's wrong?'

She shrugged, too honest to lie. 'I was just thinking, I don't know you. You could be anyone. After all, I was going in the plane with Nico, and you've pointed out in no uncertain terms that that wouldn't have been a good idea, and I just don't think I'm a very good judge of character.'

'Are you saying you don't trust me?'

She found herself smiling. 'Curiously, I do, or I wouldn't be here with you.'

He flashed her a look, and his mouth tipped into a wry grin. 'Well, thanks.'

'Sorry. It wasn't meant to sound patronising. It's just been a bit of a whirlwind today, and I'm not really firing on all cylinders.'

'I'm sure you're not. Don't worry, you're safe with me, I promise, and we're nearly there. You can have a long lazy shower, or lie in the bath, or have a swim. Whatever you choose.'

'So long as I can get out of this horrible dress, I'll be happy.'

He laughed, the sound filling the car and making something deep inside her shift.

'Good. Stand by to be happy very soon.'

He turned off the road onto a curving gravelled track lined by cypress trees, winding away towards what looked like a huge stone fortress. She sat up straighter. 'What's that building?'

'The house.'

'House?' She felt her jaw drop, and shut her mouth quickly. That was their *house*?

'So…is this your land?'

'*Sì.*'

She stared around her, but the light was fading and it was hard to tell what she was looking at. But the massive edifice ahead of them was outlined against the sunset, and as they drew closer she could see lights twinkling in the windows.

They climbed the hill, driving through a massive archway and pulling up in front of a set of sweeping steps. Security lights came on as they stopped, and she could see the steps were flanked by huge terracotta pots with what looked like olive trees in them. The steps rose majestically up to the biggest set of double doors she'd ever seen in her life. Strong doors, doors that would keep you safe against all invaders.

She had to catch her jaw again, and for once in her life she was lost for words. She'd thought, foolishly, it seemed, that it might shrink as they got closer, but it hadn't. If anything it had grown, and she realised it truly was a fortress.

An ancient, impressive and no doubt historically significant fortress. And it was his family home?

She thought of their modest farmhouse, the place she called home, and felt the sudden almost overwhelming urge to laugh. What on earth did he think of her, all tarted up in her ludicrous charity shop wedding dress and capering about outside the airport begging a lift from any old stranger?

'Lydia?'

He was standing by her, the door open, and she gathered up the dress and her purse and phone and squirmed off the seat and out of the car, balancing on her good leg and eyeing the steps dubiously.

How on earth—?

No problem, apparently. He shut the car door, and then to her surprise he scooped her up into his arms.

She gave a little shriek and wrapped her arms around his neck, so that her nose was pressed close to his throat in the open neck of his shirt. Oh, God. He smelt of lemons and musk and warm, virile male, and she could feel the beat of his heart against her side.

Or was it her own? She didn't know. It could have been either.

He glanced down at her, concerned that he might be hurting her. There was a little frown creasing the soft skin between her brows, and he had the crazy urge to kiss it away. He almost did, but stopped himself in time.

She was a stranger, nothing more, and he tried to ignore the feel of her against his chest, the fullness of her breasts pressing into his ribs and making his heart pound like a drum. She had her head tucked close to his shoulder, and he could feel the whisper of her breath against his skin. Under the antiseptic her hair smelled of fresh fruit and summer flowers, and he wanted to bury his face in it and breathe in.

He daren't look down again, though. She'd wrapped her arms around his neck and the front of the dress was gaping slightly, the soft swell of those beautiful breasts tempting him almost beyond endurance.

Crazy. Stupid. Whatever was the matter with him? He gritted his teeth, shifted her a little closer and turned towards the steps.

Lydia felt his body tense, saw his jaw tighten and she wondered why. She didn't have time to work it out, though, even if she could, because as he headed towards the house three children came tumbling down the steps and came to a sliding halt in front of them, their mouths open, their faces shocked.

'Papà?'

The eldest, a thin, gangly girl with a riot of dark curls and her father's beautiful eyes, stared from one of them to the other, and the look on her face was pure horror.

'I think you'd better explain to your children that I am *not* your new wife,' she said drily, and the girl glanced back at her and then up at her father again.

'Papà?'

He was miles away, caught up in a fairy-tale fantasy of carrying this beautiful woman over the threshold and then peeling away the layers of her bridal gown...

'Massimo? I think you need to explain to the children,' Lydia said softly, watching his face at close range. There was a tic in his jaw, the muscle jumping. Had he carried Angelina up these steps?

'It's all right, Francesca,' he said in English, struggling to find his voice. 'This is Miss Fletcher. I met her today at the airport, and she's had an accident and has to rest for a few days, so I've brought her here. Say hello.'

She frowned and asked something in Italian, and he smiled a little grimly and shook his head. 'No. We are *not* married. Say hello to Miss Fletcher, *cara.*'

'Hello, Miss Fletcher,' Francesca said in careful English, her smile wary but her shoulders relaxing a little, and Lydia smiled back at her. She felt a little awkward, gathered up in his arms against that hard, broad chest with the scent of his body doing extraordinary things to her heart, but there was nothing she could do about it except smile and hope his arms didn't break.

'Hello, Francesca. Thank you for speaking English so I can understand you.'

'That's OK. We have to speak English to Auntie Isabelle. This is Lavinia, and this is Antonino. Say hello,' she prompted.

Lydia looked at the other two, clustered round their sister.

Lavinia was the next in line, with the same dark, glorious curls but mischief dancing in her eyes, and Antonino, leaning against Francesca and squiggling the toe of his shoe on the gravel, was the youngest. The baby in the photo, the little one who must have lost his mother before he ever really knew her.

Her heart ached for them all, and she felt a welling in her chest and crushed it as she smiled at them.

'Hello, Lavinia, hello, Antonino. It's nice to meet you,' she said, and they replied politely, Lavinia openly studying her, her eyes brimming over with questions.

'And this is Carlotta,' Massimo said, and she lifted her head and met searching, wise eyes in a wizened face. He spoke rapidly to her in Italian, explaining her ridiculous fancy-dress outfit no doubt, and she saw the moment he told her that they'd lost the competition, because Carlotta's face softened and she looked at Lydia and shook her head.

'Sorry,' she said, lifting her hands. 'So sorry for you. Come, I help you change and you will be happier, *Sì*?'

'*Sì*,' she said with a wry chuckle, and Massimo shifted her more firmly against his chest and followed Carlotta puffing and wheezing up the steps.

The children were tugging at him and questioning him in Italian, and he was laughing and answering them as fast as he could. Bless their little hearts, she could see they were hanging on his every word.

He was the centre of their world, and they'd missed him, and she'd kept him away from them all these hours when they must have been desperate to have him back. She felt another shaft of guilt, but Carlotta was leading the way through the big double doors, and she looked away from the children and gasped softly.

They were in a cloistered courtyard, with a broad covered

walkway surrounding the open central area that must cast a welcome shade in the heat of the day, but now in the evening it was softly lit and she could see more of the huge pots of olive trees set on the old stone paving in the centre, and on the low wall that divided the courtyard from the cloistered walkway geraniums tumbled over the edge, bringing colour and scent to the evening air.

But that wasn't what had caught her attention. It was the frescoed walls, the ancient faded murals under the shelter of the cloisters that took her breath away.

He didn't pause, though, or give her time to take in the beautiful paintings, but carried her through one of the several doors set in the walls, then along a short hallway and into a bedroom.

He set her gently on the bed, and she felt oddly bereft as he straightened up and moved away.

'I'll be in the kitchen with the children. Carlotta will tell me when you're ready and I'll come and get you.'

'Thank you.'

He smiled fleetingly and went out, the children's clamouring voices receding as he walked away, and Carlotta closed the door.

'Your bath,' she said, pushing open another door, and she saw a room lined with pale travertine marble, the white suite simple and yet luxurious. And the bath—she could stick her bandaged leg up on the side and just wallow. Pure luxury.

'Thank you.' She couldn't wait. All she wanted was to get out of the dress and into water. But the zip…

'I help you,' Carlotta said, and as the zip slid down, she was freed from the scratchy fabric at last. A bit too freed. She clutched at the top as it threatened to drift away and smiled at Carlotta.

'I can manage now,' she said, and Carlotta nodded.

'I get your bag.'

She went out, and Lydia closed the bedroom door behind her, leaning back against it and looking around again.

It was much simpler than the imposing and impressive entrance, she saw with relief. Against expectations it wasn't vast, but it was pristine, the bed made up with sparkling white linen, the rug on the floor soft underfoot, and the view from the French window would be amazing in daylight.

She limped gingerly over to the window and stared out, pressing her face against the glass. The doors opened onto what looked like a terrace, and beyond—gosh, the view must be utterly breathtaking, she imagined, because even at dusk it was extraordinary, the twinkling lights of villages and scattered houses sparkling in the twilight.

Moving away from the window, she glanced around her, taking in her surroundings in more detail. The floor was tiled, the ceiling beamed, with chestnut perhaps? Probably, with terracotta tiles between the beams. Sturdy, simple and homely—which was crazy, considering the scale of the place and the grandeur of the entrance! But it seemed more like a farm now, curiously, less of a fortress, and much less threatening.

And that established, she let go of the awful dress, kicked it away from her legs, bundled it up in a ball and hopped into the bathroom.

The water was calling her. Studying the architecture could wait.

CHAPTER THREE

WHAT was that noise?

Lydia lifted her head, water streaming off her hair as she surfaced to investigate.

'Signorina? Signorina!'

Carlotta's voice was desperate as she rattled the handle on the bathroom door, and Lydia felt a stab of alarm.

'What is it?' she asked, sitting up with a splash and sluicing the water from her hair with her hands.

'Oh, *signorina*! You are all right?'

She closed her eyes and twisted her hair into a rope, squeezing out the rest of the water and suppressing a sigh. 'I'm fine. I'm OK, really. I won't be long.'

'I wait, I help you.'

'No, really, there's no need. I'll be all right.'

'But Massimo say I no leave you!' she protested, clearly worried for some reason, but Lydia assured her again that she was fine.

'OK,' she said after a moment, sounding dubious. 'I leave your bag here. You call me for help?'

'I will. Thank you. *Grazie.*'

'Prego.'

She heard the bedroom door close, and rested her head back down on the bath with a sigh. The woman was kindness itself, but Lydia just wanted to be left alone. Her head ached, her ankle throbbed, she had a million bruises all over her body and she still had to phone her sister.

The phone rang, almost as if she'd triggered it with her thoughts, and she could tell by the ringtone it was Jen.

Oh, rats. She must have heard the news.

There was no getting round it, so she struggled awkwardly out of the bath and hobbled back to the bed, swathed in the biggest towel she'd ever seen, and dug out her phone and rang Jen back.

'What's going on? They said you'd had an accident! I've been trying to phone you for ages but you haven't been answering! Are you all right? We've been frantic!'

'Sorry, Jen, I was in the bath. I'm fine, really, it was just a little slip on the steps of a plane and I've twisted my ankle. Nothing serious.'

Well, she hoped it wasn't. She crossed her fingers, just to be on the safe side, and filled in a few more details. She didn't tell her the truth, just that Jo had got there first.

'I'm so sorry, we really tried, but we probably wouldn't have made it even without the accident.'

There was a heartbeat of hesitation, then Jen said, 'Don't worry, it really doesn't matter and it's not important. I just need you to be all right. And don't go blaming yourself, it's not your fault.'

Why did *everyone* say that? It *was* her fault. If she'd looked where she was going, taken a bit more care, Jen and Andy would have been having the wedding of their dreams in a few months' time. As it was, well, as it was they wouldn't, but she wasn't going to give Jen anything to beat herself up about, so she told her she was fine, just a little twinge—and nothing at all about the head injury.

'Actually, since I'm over here, I thought I'd stay on for a

few days. I've found a farm where I can get bed and break-fast, and I'm going to have a little holiday.'

Well, it wasn't entirely a lie. It *was* a farm, she had a bed, and she was sure they wouldn't make her starve while she recovered.

'You do that. It sounds lovely,' Jen said wistfully, and Lydia screwed her face up and bit her lip.

Damn. She'd been so close, and the disappointment that Jen was trying so hard to disguise was ripping Lydia apart.

Ending the call with a promise to ring when she was com-ing home, she dug her clean clothes out of the flight bag and pulled her jeans on carefully over her swollen, throbbing ankle. The soft, worn fabric of the jeans and the T-shirt were comforting against her skin, chafed from her fall as well as the boning and beading in the dress, and she looked around for the offending article. It was gone. Taken away by Carlotta? She hoped she hadn't thrown it out. She wanted the pleasure of that for herself.

She put her trainers on, managing to squeeze her bandaged foot in with care, and hobbled out of her room in search of the others, but the corridor outside didn't seem to lead any-where except her room, a little sitting room and a room that looked like an office, so she went back through the door to the beautiful cloistered courtyard and looked around for any clues.

There were none.

So now what? She couldn't just stand there and yell, nor could she go round the courtyard systematically opening all the doors. Not that there were that many, but even so.

She was sitting there on the low wall around the central courtyard, studying the beautiful frescoes and trying to work out what to do if nobody showed up, when the door nearest to her opened and Massimo appeared. He'd showered and changed out of the suit into jeans and a soft white linen shirt stark against his olive skin, the cuffs rolled back to reveal those tanned forearms which had nearly been her undoing on the plane, and her heart gave a tiny lurch.

Stupid.

He caught sight of her and smiled, and her heart did another little jiggle as he walked towards her.

'Lydia, I was just coming to see if you were all right. I'm sorry, I should have come back quicker. How are you? How's the head?'

'Fine,' she said with a rueful smile. 'I'm just a bit lost. I didn't want to go round opening all the doors, it seemed rude.'

'You should have shouted. I would have heard you.'

'I'm not in the habit of yelling for help,' she said drily, and he chuckled and came over to her side.

'Let me help you now,' he said, and offered her his arm. 'It's not far, hang on and hop, or would you rather I carried you?'

'I'll hop,' she said hastily, not sure she could cope with being snuggled up to that broad, solid chest again, with the feel of his arms strong and safe under her. 'I don't want to break you.'

He laughed at that. 'I don't think you'll break me. Did you find everything you needed? How's your room?'

She slipped her arm through his, conscious of the smell of him again, refreshed now by his shower and overlaid with soap and more of the citrusy cologne that had been haunting her nostrils all day. She wanted to press her nose to his chest, to breathe him in, to absorb the warmth and scent and maleness of him.

Not appropriate. She forced herself to concentrate.

'Lovely. The bath was utter bliss. I can't tell you how won-

derful it was to get out of that awful dress. I hope Carlotta
hasn't burned it, I want to do it myself.'

He laughed again, a warm, rich sound that echoed round
the courtyard, and scanned her body with his eyes. 'It really
didn't do you justice,' he said softly, and in the gentle light
she thought she caught a glimpse of whatever it was she'd
seen in his eyes at the airport.

But then it was gone, and he was opening the door and
ushering her through to a big, brightly lit kitchen. Carlotta
was busy at the stove, and the children were seated at a large
table in the middle of the room, Antonino kneeling up and
leaning over to interfere with what Lavinia was doing.

She pushed him aside crossly, and Massimo intervened
before a fight could break out, diffusing it swiftly by split-
ting them up. While he was busy, Carlotta came and helped
her to the table. She smiled at her gratefully.

'I'm sorry to put you to so much trouble.'

'Is no trouble,' she said. 'Sit, sit. Is ready.'

She sniffed, and smiled. 'It smells wonderful.'

'*Buono*. You eat, then you feel better. Sit!'

She flapped her apron at Lydia, and she sat obediently at
the last place laid at the long table. It was opposite Francesca,
and Massimo was at the end of the table on her right, brack-
eted by the two younger ones who'd been split up to stop them
from squabbling.

They were fractious—overtired, she thought guiltily—and
missing their father. But Francesca was watching her warily.
She smiled at the girl apologetically.

'I'm sorry I kept your father away from you for so long.
He's been so kind and helpful.'

'He is. He helps everybody. Are you better now?'

'I'm all right. I've just got a bit of a headache but I don't
think it's much more than that. I was so stupid. I tripped over

the hem of my dress and fell down the steps of the plane and hit my head.'

Behind her, there was a clatter, and Francesca went chalk white, her eyes huge with horror and distress.

'*Scusami,*' she mumbled, and pushing back her chair, she ran from the room, her father following, his chair crashing over as he leapt to his feet.

'Francesca!' He reached the door before it closed, and she could hear his voice calling as he ran after her. Horrified, uncertain what she'd done, she turned to Carlotta and found her with her apron pressed to her face, her eyes above it creased with distress.

'What did I say?' she whispered, conscious of the little ones, but Carlotta just shook her head and picked up the pan and thrust it into the sink.

'Is nothing. Here, eat. Antonino!'

He sat down, and Lavinia put away the book he'd been trying to tug away from her, and Carlotta picked up Massimo's overturned chair and ladled food out onto all their plates.

There was fresh bread drizzled with olive oil, and a thick, rich stew of beans and sausage and gloriously red tomatoes. It smelt wonderful, tasted amazing, but Lydia could scarcely eat it. The children were eating. Whatever it was she'd said or done had gone right over their heads, but something had driven Francesca from the room, and her father after her.

The same something that had made Massimo go pale at the airport, as he'd knelt on the tarmac at her side? The same something that had made him stand, rigid with tension, staring grimly at a poster when he thought she was asleep in the room at the hospital?

She pushed back her chair and hopped over to the sink, where Carlotta was scrubbing furiously at a pot. 'I'm sorry, I can't eat. Carlotta, what did I say?' she asked under her breath, and those old, wise eyes that had seen so much met hers, and she shook her head, twisting her hands in the dishcloth and biting her lips.

She put the pot on the draining board, and Lydia automatically picked up a tea towel and dried it, her hip propped against the edge of the sink unit as she balanced on her good leg. Another pot followed, and another, and finally Carlotta stopped scouring the pots as if they were lined with demons and her hands came to rest.

She hobbled over to the children, cleared up their plates, gave them pudding and then gathered them up like a mother hen.

'Wait here. Eat. He will come back.'

They left her there in the kitchen, their footsteps echoing along a corridor and up stairs, and Lydia sank down at the table and stared blankly at the far wall, going over and over her words in her head and getting nowhere.

Carlotta appeared again and put Francesca's supper in a microwave.

'Is she coming down again? I want to apologise for upsetting her.'

'No. Is all right, *signorina*. Her *papà* look after her.' And lifting the plate out of the microwave, she carried it out of the room on a tray, leaving Lydia alone again.

She poked at her food, but it was cold now, the beans congealing in the sauce, and she ripped up a bit of bread and dabbed it absently in the stew. What had she said, that had caused such distress?

She had no idea, but she couldn't leave the kitchen without finding out, and there was still a pile of washing up to do. She didn't know where anything lived, but the table was big enough to put it all on, and there was a dishwasher sitting there empty.

Well, if she could do nothing else while she waited, she

could do that, she told herself, and pushing up her sleeves, she hopped over to the dishwasher and set about clearing up the kitchen.

He had to go down to her—to explain, or apologise properly, at the very least.

His stomach growled, but he ignored it. He couldn't eat, not while his daughter was just settling into sleep at last, her sobs fading quietly away into the night.

He closed his eyes. Talking to Lydia, dredging it all up again, was the last thing he wanted to do, the very last, but he had no choice. Leaning over Francesca, he pressed a kiss lightly against her cheek, and straightened. She was sleeping peacefully now; he could leave her.

Leave her, and go and find Lydia, if she hadn't had the sense to pack up her things and leave. It seemed unlikely, but he couldn't blame her.

He found her in the kitchen, sitting with Carlotta over a cup of coffee, the kitchen sparkling. He stared at them, then at the kitchen. Carlotta had been upstairs until a short while ago, settling the others, and the kitchen had been in chaos, so how…?

'She's OK now,' he said in Italian. 'Why don't you go to bed, Carlotta? You look exhausted and Roberto's worried about you.'

She nodded and got slowly to her feet, then rested her hand on Lydia's shoulder and patted it before leaving her side. 'I *am* tired,' she said to him in Italian, 'but you need to speak to Lydia. I couldn't leave her. She's a good girl, Massimo. Look at my kitchen! A good, kind girl, and she's unhappy. Worried.'

He sighed. 'I know. Did you explain?'

'No. It's not my place, but be gentle with her—and yourself.' And with that pointed remark, she left them alone together.

Lydia looked up at him and searched his eyes. 'What did she say to you?'

He gave her a fleeting smile. 'She told me you were a good, kind girl. And she told me to be gentle with you.'

Her eyes filled, and she looked away. 'I don't know what I said, but I'm so, so sorry.'

His conscience pricked him. He should have warned her. He sighed and scrubbed a hand through his hair.

'No. I should be apologising, not you. Forgive us, we aren't normally this rude to visitors. Francesca was upset.'

'I know that. Obviously I made it happen. What I don't know is why,' she said, looking up at him again with grief-stricken eyes.

He reached for a mug, changed his mind and poured himself a glass of wine. 'Can I tempt you?'

'Is it one of yours?'

'No. It's a neighbour's, but it's good. We could take it outside. I don't know if it's wise, though, with your head injury.'

'I'll take the risk,' she said. 'And then will you tell me what I said?'

'You know what you said. What you don't know is what it meant,' he said enigmatically, and picking up both glasses of wine, he headed for the door, glancing back over his shoulder at her. 'Can you manage, or should I carry you?'

Carry her? With her face pressed up against that taunting aftershave, and the feel of his strong, muscled arms around her legs? 'I can manage,' she said hastily, and pushing back her chair, she got to her feet and limped after him out into the still, quiet night.

She could hear the soft chirr of insects, the sound of a motorbike somewhere in the valley below, and then she saw a

single headlight slicing through the night, weaving and turning as it followed the snaking road along the valley bottom
and disappeared.

He led her to a bench at the edge of the terrace. The ground
fell away below them so it felt as if they were perched on the
edge of the world, and when she was seated he handed her
the glass and sat beside her, his elbows propped on his knees,
his own glass dangling from his fingers as he stared out over
the velvet blackness.

For a while neither of them said anything, but then the tension got to her and she broke the silence.

'Please tell me.'

He sucked in his breath, looking down, staring into his
glass as he slowly swirled the wine before lifting it to his lips.

'Massimo?' she prompted, and he turned his head and met
her eyes. Even in the moonlight, she could see the pain etched
into his face, and her heart began to thud slowly.

'Angelina died of a brain haemorrhage following a fall,'
he began, his voice expressionless. 'Nothing serious, nothing much at all, just a bit of a bump. She'd fallen down the
stairs and hit her head on the wall. We all thought she was
all right, but she had a bit of a headache later in the day, and
we went to bed early. I woke in the night and she was missing, and I found her in the kitchen, slumped over the table,
and one side of her face had collapsed.'

Lydia closed her eyes and swallowed hard as the nausea
threatened to choke her. What had she *done*? Not just by
saying what she had at the table—the same table?—but by
bringing this on all of them, on Claire, on him, on the children—most especially little Francesca, her eyes wide with
pain and shock, fleeing from the table. The image would stay
with her forever.

'It wasn't your fault,' he said gently. 'You weren't to know.

I probably should have told you—warned you not to talk about it in that way, and why. I let you walk right into it.'

She turned back to him, searching his face in the shadows. She'd known something was wrong when he was bending over her on the tarmac, and again later, staring at the poster. And yet he'd said nothing.

'Why didn't you *tell* me? I knew something was wrong, something else, something more. Luca seemed much more worried than my condition warranted, even I knew that, and he kept looking at you anxiously. I thought he was worried about me, but then I realised it was you he was worried about. I just didn't know why. You should have told me.'

'How could I? You had a head injury. How could I say to you, "I'm sorry, I'm finding this a bit hard to deal with, my wife died of the same thing and I'm a bit worried I might lose you, too." How could I say that?'

He'd been worried he could lose her?

No. Of course he hadn't meant that, he didn't know her. He meant he was worried she might be about to die, too. Nothing more than that.

'You should have left us there instead of staying and getting distressed. I had no business tangling you all up in this mess—oh, Massimo, I'm so sorry.'

She broke off, clamping her teeth hard to stop her eyes from welling over, but his warm hand on her shoulder was the last straw, and she felt the hot, wet slide of a tear down her cheek.

'*Cara*, no. Don't cry for us. It was a long time ago.'

'But it still hurts you, and it'll hurt you forever,' she said unevenly.

'No, it just brought the memories back. We're all right, really. We're getting there. Francesca's the oldest, she remembers Angelina the most clearly, and she's the one who bears the brunt of the loss, because when I'm not there the little ones turn to her. She has to be mother to them, and she's been so strong, but she's just a little girl herself.'

He broke off, his jaw working, and she laid her hand gently against it and sighed.

'I'm so sorry. It must have been dreadful for you all.'

'It was. They took her to hospital, and she died later that day—she was on life support and they tested her brain but there was nothing. No activity at all. They turned off the machine, and I came home and told the children that their mother was gone. That was the hardest thing I've ever had to do in my life.'

His voice broke off again, turning away this time, and Lydia closed her eyes and swallowed the anguished response. There was nothing she could say that wouldn't be trite or meaningless, and so she stayed silent, and after a moment he let out a long, slow breath and sat back against the bench.

'So, now you know,' he said, his voice low and oddly flat.

Wordlessly, she reached out and touched his hand, and he turned it, his fingers threading through hers and holding on tight.

They stayed like that for an age, their hands lying linked between them as they sipped their wine, and then he turned to her in the dim light and searched her face. He'd taken comfort from her touch, felt the warmth of her generous spirit seeping into him, easing the ache which had been a part of him for so long.

How could she do that with just a touch?

No words. Words were too hard, would have been trite. Did she know that?

Yes. He could see that she did, that this woman who talked too much actually knew the value of silence.

He lifted her hand and pressed it to his lips, then smiled at her sadly. 'Did you eat anything?'

She shook her head. 'No. Not really.'

'Nor did I. Shall we see what we can find? It's a very, very long time since breakfast.'

It wasn't exactly *haute cuisine*, but the simple fare of olive bread and ham and cheese with sweetly scented baby plum tomatoes and a bowl of olive oil and balsamic vinegar just hit the spot.

He poured them another glass of wine, but it didn't seem like a good idea and so she gave him the second half and he found some sparkling water for her. She realised she'd thought nothing of handing him her glass of wine for him to finish, and he'd taken it without hesitation and drunk from it without turning a hair.

How odd, when they'd only met a scant twelve hours ago. Thirteen hours and a few minutes, to be more exact.

It seemed more like a lifetime since she'd watched him getting out of the taxi, wondered if he'd be The One to make it happen. The guy she'd been talking to was funny and seemed nice enough, but he wasn't about to give her a lift and she knew that. But Massimo had looked at her as he'd gone into the Jet Centre foyer, his eyes meeting hers and locking...

She glanced up, and found him watching her with a frown.

'Why are you frowning?' she asked, and his mouth kicked up a fraction in one corner, the frown ironed out with a deliberate effort.

'No reason. How's your head now?'

She shrugged. 'OK. It just feels as if I fell over my feet and spent the day hanging about in a hospital.' It was rather worse than that, but he didn't need to know about every ache and pain. The list was endless.

She reached out and covered his hand. 'Massimo, I'm all right,' she said softly, and the little frown came back.

'Sorry. It's just a reflex. I look after people—it's part of my job description. Everyone comes to me with their problems.'

She smiled at him, remembering her conversation with Francesca.

'I'm sorry I kept your father away from you for so long. He's been so kind and helpful.'

'He is. He helps everybody.'

'You're just a fixer, aren't you? You fix everything for everybody all the time, and you hate it when things can't be fixed.'

His frown deepened for a moment, and then he gave a wry laugh and pulled his hand away, swirling the wine in her glass before draining it. 'Is it so obvious?'

She felt her lips twitch. 'Only if you're on the receiving end. Don't get me wrong, I'm massively grateful and just so sorry I've dragged you into this awful mess and upset everyone. I'm more than happy you're a fixer, because goodness only knows I seemed to need one today. I think I need a guardian angel, actually. I just have such a gift for getting into a mess and dragging everybody with me.'

She broke off, and he tipped his head on one side and that little crease between his eyebrows returned fleetingly. 'A gift?'

She sighed. 'Jen's accident was sort of my fault.'

He sat back, his eyes searching hers. 'Tell me,' he said softly, so she did.

She told him about Russell, about their trip to her parents' farm for the weekend, because Jen and Andy were going to be there as well and she hadn't seen them for a while. And she'd shown him the farm, and he'd seen the quad bike, and suggested they go out on it so she could show him all the fields.

'I didn't want to go with him. He was a crazy driver, and I knew he'd want to go too fast, so I said no, but then Jen offered to show him round. She wanted to get him alone, to threaten him with death if he hurt me, but he hurt her instead. He went far too fast, and she told him to stop but he thought she was just being chicken and she wasn't, she knew about the fallen tree hidden in the long grass, and then they hit it and the quad bike cartwheeled through the air and landed on her.'

He winced and closed his eyes briefly. 'And she ended up in a wheelchair?'

'Not for a few weeks. She had a fractured spine, and she was in a special bed for a while. It wasn't displaced, the spinal cord wasn't severed, but it was badly bruised and it took a long time to recover and for the bones to heal. She's getting better now, she's starting to walk again, but she lost her job and so did Andy so he could look after her. He took away everything from them, and if I'd gone with him, if it had been me, then I might have been able to stop him.'

'You really think so? He sounds like an idiot.'

'He is an idiot,' she said tiredly. 'He's an idiot, and he was my boss, so I lost my job, too.'

'He sacked you?'

She gave him a withering look. 'I walked…and then his business folded without me, and he threatened to sue me if I didn't go back. I told him to take a flying hike.'

'What business was he in?'

'He had a restaurant. I was his chef.'

Hence the tidy kitchen, he realised. She was used to working in a kitchen, used to bringing order to chaos, used to the utensils and the work space and the arrangement of them that always to him defied logic. And his restaurant had folded without her?

'You told me you were a cook,' he rebuked her mildly. 'I didn't realise you were a chef.'

She quirked an eyebrow at him mockingly. 'You told me you were a farmer and you live in a flipping fortress! I think that trumps it,' she said drily, and he laughed and lifted his glass to her.

'Touché,' he said softly, and her heart turned over at the wry warmth in his eyes. 'I'm sorry,' he went on. 'Sorry about this man who clearly didn't deserve you, sorry about your sister, sorry about your job. What a mess. And all because he was a fool.'

'Absolutely.'

'Tell me more about him.'

'Like what?'

'Like why your sister felt she needed to warn him not to hurt you. Had you been hurt before?'

'No, but she didn't really like him. He wasn't always a nice man, and he took advantage of me—made me work ridiculous hours, treated me like a servant at times, and yet he could be a charmer, too. He was happy enough to talk me into his bed once he realised I was a good chef—sorry, you really didn't need to know that.'

He smiled slightly. 'Maybe you needed to say it,' he suggested, and her laugh was a little brittle.

'There are so many things I could tell you about him. I said I was a lousy judge of character. I think he had a lot in common with Nico, perhaps.'

He frowned. 'Nico?'

'The guy at the airport?'

'Yes, I know who you mean. In what way? Was he a drinker?'

'Yes. Definitely. But not just a drinker. He was a nasty drunk, especially towards the end of our relationship. He seemed to change. Got arrogant. He used to be quite charming at first, but it was just a front. He— Well, let's just say he didn't respect women either.'

His mouth tightened. 'I'm sorry. You shouldn't have had to tolerate that.'

'No, I shouldn't. So—tell me about your house,' she said, changing the subject to give them both a bit of a break. She reached out and tore off another strip of bread, dunking it in the oil that she couldn't get enough of, and looked up to see a strange look on his face. Almost—tender?

Nonsense. She was being silly. 'Well, come on, then,' she mumbled round the bread, and he smiled, the strange look disappearing as if she'd imagined it.

'It's very old. We're not sure of the origins. It seems it might have been a Medici villa, but the history is a little cloudy. It was built at the time of the Florentine invasion.'

'So how come your family ended up with it?'

His mouth twitched. 'One of our ancestors took possession of it at the end of the seventeenth century.'

That made her laugh. 'Took possession?'

The twitch again, and a wicked twinkle in his eye. 'We're not quite sure how he acquired it, but it's been in the family ever since. He's the one who renamed the villa *Palazzo Valtieri.*'

Palazzo? She nearly laughed at that. Not just a fortress, then, but a proper, full-on palace. Oh, boy.

'I'll show you round it tomorrow. It's beautiful. Some of the frescoes are amazing, and the formal rooms in the part my parents live in are fantastic.'

'Your parents live here?' she asked, puzzled, because

there'd been no mention of them. Not that they'd really had time, but—

'*Sì*. It's a family business. They're away at the moment, snatching a few days with my sister Carla and her new baby before the harvest starts, but they'll be back the day after tomorrow.'

'So how many rooms are there?'

He laughed. 'I have no idea. I've never counted them, I'm too busy trying not to let it fall down. It's crumbling as fast as we can patch it up, but so long as we can cheat time, that's fine. It's quite interesting.'

'I'm sure it is. And now it's your turn to run it?'

His mouth tugged down at the corners, but there was a smile in his eyes. '*Sì*. For my sins. My father keeps trying to interfere, but he's supposed to be retired. He doesn't understand that, though.'

'No. It must be hard to hand it over. My father wouldn't be able to do it. And the harvest is just starting?'

He nodded. 'The grape harvest is first, followed by the chestnuts and the olives. It's relentless now until the end of November, so you can see why I was in a hurry to get back.'

'And I held you up.'

'*Cara*, accidents happen. Don't think about it any more.' He pushed back his chair. 'I think it's time you went to bed. It's after midnight.'

Was it? When had that happened? When they were outside, sitting in the quiet of the night and watching the twinkling lights in the villages? Or now, sitting here eating bread and cheese and olive oil, drinking wine and staring into each other's eyes like lovers?

She nodded and pushed back her chair, and he tucked her arm in his so she could feel the solid muscle of his forearm under her hand, and she hung on him and hopped and hobbled her way to her room.

'Ring me if you need anything. You have my mobile number on my card. I gave it to you on the plane. Do you still have it?'

'Yes—but I won't need you.'

Well, not for anything she'd dream of asking him for...

His brows tugged together. 'Just humour me, OK? If you feel unwell in the night, or want anything, ring me and I'll come down. I'm not far away. And please, don't lock your door.'

'Massimo, I'm feeling all right. My headache's gone, and I feel OK now. You don't need to worry.'

'You can't be too careful,' he said, and she could see a tiny frown between his brows, as if he was still waiting for something awful to happen to her.

They reached her room and he paused at the door, staring down into her eyes and hesitating for the longest moment. And then, just when she thought he was going to kiss her, he stepped back.

'Call me if you need me. If you need anything at all.'

'I will.'

'Good. *Buonanotte*, Lydia,' he murmured softly, and turned and walked away.

CHAPTER FOUR

WHAT was she *thinking* about?

Of course he hadn't been about to kiss her! That bump on the head had obviously been more serious than she'd realised. Maybe a blast of fresh air would help her think clearly?

She opened the French doors onto the terrace and stood there for a moment, letting the night air cool her heated cheeks. She'd been so carried along on the moment, so lured by his natural and easy charm that she'd let herself think all sorts of stupid things.

Of course he wasn't interested in her. Why would he be? She'd been nothing but a thorn in his side since the moment he'd set eyes on her. And even if he hadn't, she wasn't interested! Well, that was a lie, of course she was interested, or she wouldn't even be thinking about it, but there was no way it was going anywhere.

Not after the debacle with Russell. She was sworn off men now for life, or at least for a good five years. And so far, it hadn't been much more than five months!

Leaving the doors open, she limped back to the bed and pulled her pyjamas out of her flight bag, eyeing them dubiously. The skimpy top and little shorts she'd brought for their weightlessness had seemed fine when she was going to be sharing a hotel room with Claire, but here, in this ancient historic house—*palazzo*, even, for heaven's sake!—she wondered what on earth he'd make of them.

Nothing. Nothing at all, because he wasn't going to see her in her nightclothes! Cross with herself, her head aching and her ankle throbbing and her bruises giving her a fair amount of grief as well, she changed into the almost-pyjamas, cleaned her teeth and crawled into bed.

Oh, bliss. The pillows were cloud-soft, the down quilt light and yet snuggly, and the breeze from the doors was drifting across her face, bringing with it the scents of sage and lavender and night-scented stocks.

Exhausted, weary beyond belief, she closed her eyes with a little sigh and drifted off to sleep...

Her doors were open.

He hesitated, standing outside on the terrace, questioning his motives.

Did he *really* think she needed checking in the night? Or was he simply indulging his—what? Curiosity? Fantasy? Or, perhaps...need?

He groaned softly. There was no doubt that he *needed* her, needed the warmth of her touch, the laughter in her eyes, the endless chatter and the brilliance of her smile.

The silence, when she'd simply held his hand and offered comfort.

Thinking about that moment brought a lump to his throat, and he swallowed hard. He hadn't allowed himself to need a woman for years, but Lydia had got under his skin, penetrated his defences with her simple kindness, and he wanted her in a way that troubled him greatly, because it was more than just physical.

And he really wasn't sure he was ready for that—would ever be ready for that again. But the need...

He'd just check on her, just to be on the safe side. He couldn't let her lie there alone all night.

Not like Angelina.

Guilt crashed over him again, driving out the need and leaving sorrow in its wake. Focused now, he went into her room, his bare feet silent on the tiled floor, and gave his eyes a moment to adjust to the light.

Had she sensed him? Maybe, because she sighed and shifted, the soft, contented sound drifting to him on the night air. When had he last heard a woman sigh softly in her sleep?

Too long ago to remember, too soon to forget.

It would be so easy to reach out his hand, to touch her. To take her in his arms, warm and sleepy, and make love to her.

Easy, and yet impossibly wrong. What was it about her that made him feel like this, that made him think things he hadn't thought in years? Not since he'd lost Angelina.

He stood over her, staring at her in the moonlight, the thought of his wife reminding him of why he was here. Not to watch Lydia sleep, like some kind of voyeur, but to keep her safe. He focused on her face. It was peaceful, both sides the same, just as it had been when he'd left her for the night, and she was breathing slowly and evenly. As he watched she moved her arms, pushing the covers lower. Both arms, both working.

He swallowed. She was fine, just as she'd told him, he realised in relief. He could go to bed now, relax.

But it was too late. He'd seen her sleeping, heard that soft, feminine sigh and the damage was done. His body, so long denied, had come screaming back to life, and he wouldn't sleep now.

Moving carefully so as not to disturb her, he made his way back to the French doors and out onto the terrace. Propping his hands on his hips, he dropped his head back and sucked in a lungful of cool night air, then let it out slowly before dragging his hand over his face.

He'd swim. Maybe that would take the heat out of his blood. And if it was foolish to swim alone, if he'd told the children a thousand times that no one should ever do it—well, tonight was different.

Everything about tonight seemed different.

He crossed the upper terrace, padded silently down the worn stone steps to the level below and rolled back the thermal cover on the pool. The water was warm, steam billowing from the surface in the cool night air, and stripping off his clothes, he dived smoothly in.

Something had woken her.

She opened her eyes a fraction, peeping through the slits between her eyelids, but she could see nothing.

She could hear something, though. Not loud, just a little, rhythmic splash—like someone swimming?

She threw off the covers and sat up, wincing a little as her head pounded and the bruises twinged with the movement. She fingered the egg on her head, and sighed. *Idiot*. First thing in the morning she was going to track down that dress and burn the blasted thing.

She inched to the edge of the bed, and stood up slowly, her ankle protesting as she put weight through it. Not as badly as yesterday, though, she thought, and limped out onto the terrace to listen for the noise.

Yes. Definitely someone swimming. And it seemed to be coming from straight ahead. As she felt her way cautiously across the stone slabs and then the grass, she realised that this was the terrace they'd sat on last night, or at least a part of it. They'd been further over, to her left, and straight ahead of her were railings, the top edge gleaming in the moonlight.

She made her way slowly to them and looked down, and there he was. Well, there someone was, slicing through the water with strong, bold strokes, up and down, up and down, length after length through the swirling steam that rose from the surface of the pool.

Exorcising demons?

Then finally he slowed, rolled to his back and floated spread-eagled on the surface. She could barely make him out because the steam clouded the air in the moonlight, but she knew instinctively it was him.

And as if he'd sensed her, he turned his head and as the veil of mist was drawn back for an instant, their eyes met in the night. Slowly, with no sense of urgency, he swam to the side, folded his arms and rested on them, looking up at her.

'You're awake.'

'Something woke me, then I heard the splashing. Is it sensible to swim on your own in the dark?'

He laughed softly. 'You could always come in. Then I wouldn't be alone.'

'I haven't got any swimming things.'

'Ah. Well, that's probably not very wise then because neither have I.'

She sucked in her breath softly, and closed her eyes, suddenly embarrassed. Amongst other things. 'I'm sorry. I didn't realise. I'll go away.'

'Don't worry, I'm finished. Just close your eyes for a second so I don't offend you while I get out.'

She heard the laughter in his voice, then the sound of him vaulting out of the pool. Her eyes flew open, and she saw him straighten up, water sluicing off his back as he walked calmly to a sun lounger and picked up an abandoned towel. He dried himself briskly as she watched, unable to look away, mesmerised by those broad shoulders that tapered down to lean hips and powerful legs.

In the magical silver light of the moon, the taut, firm globes of his buttocks, paler than the rest of him, could have been carved from marble, like one of the statues that seemed to litter the whole of Italy. Except they'd be warm, of course, alive...

Her mouth dry, she snapped her eyes shut again and made herself breath. In, out, in, out, nice and slowly, slowing down, calmer.

'Would you like a drink?'

She jumped and gave a tiny shriek. 'Don't creep up on people like that!' she whispered fiercely, and rested her hand against the pounding heart beneath her chest.

Yikes. Her all but bare chest, in the crazily insubstantial pyjamas...

'I'm not really dressed for entertaining,' she mumbled, which was ridiculous because the scanty towel twisted round his hips left very little to the imagination.

His fingers, cool and damp, appeared under her chin, tilting her head up so she could see his face instead of just that tantalising towel. His eyes were laughing.

'That makes two of us. I tell you what, I'll go and put the kettle on and pull on my clothes, and you go and find something a little less...'

'Revealing?'

His smile grew crooked. 'I was going to say alluring.'

Alluring. Right.

'I'll get dressed,' she said hastily, and limped rather faster than was sensible back towards her room, shutting the doors firmly behind her.

* * *

He watched her hobble away, his eyes tracking her progress across the terrace in the skimpiest of pyjamas, the long slender legs that had been hidden until now revealed by those tiny shorts in a way that did nothing for his peace of mind.

Or the state of his body. He swallowed hard and tightened his grip on the towel.

So much for the swimming cooling him down, he thought wryly, and went into the kitchen through the side door, rubbed himself briskly down with the towel again and pulled on his clothes, then switched on the kettle. Would she be able to find him? Would she even know which way to go?

Yes. She was there, in the doorway, looking deliciously rumpled and sleepy and a little uncertain. She'd pulled on her jeans and the T-shirt she'd been wearing last night, and her unfettered breasts had been confined to a bra. Pity, he thought, and then chided himself. She was a guest in his house, she was injured, and all he could do was lust after her. He should be ashamed of himself.

'Tea, coffee or something else? I expect there are some herbal teabags or something like that.'

'Camomile?' she asked hopefully.

Something to calm her down, because her host, standing there in bare feet, a damp T-shirt clinging to the moisture on his chest and a pair of jeans that should have had a health warning on them, hanging on his lean hips, was doing nothing for her equilibrium.

Not now that she knew what was underneath those clothes.

He poured boiling water into a cup for her, then stuck another cup under the coffee maker and pressed a button. The sound of the grinding beans was loud in the silence, but not loud enough to drown out the sound of her heartbeat.

She should have stayed in her room, kept out of his way.

'Here, I don't know how long you want to keep the tea-bag in.'

He put the mug down on the table and turned back to the coffee maker, and as she stirred the teabag round absently she watched him. His hands were deft, his movements precise as he spooned sugar and stirred in a splash of milk.

'Won't that keep you awake?' she asked, but he just laughed softly.

'It's not a problem, I'm up now for the day. After I've drunk this I'll go and tackle some work in my office, and then I'll have breakfast with the children before I go out and check the grapes in each field to see if they're ripe.'

'Has the harvest started?'

'La Vendemmia?' He shook his head. 'No. If the grapes are ripe, it starts tomorrow. We'll spend the rest of the day making sure we're ready, because once it starts, we don't stop till it's finished. But today—today should be pretty routine.'

So he might have time to show her round…

'Want to come with me and see what we do? If you're interested, of course. Don't feel you have to.'

If she was interested? She nearly laughed. *The farm*, she told herself firmly. He was talking about the *farm*.

'That would be great, if I won't be in your way?'

'No, of course not. It might be dull, though, and once I leave the house I won't be back for hours. I don't know if you're feeling up to it.'

Was he trying to get out of it? Retracting his invitation, thinking better of having her hanging around him all day like a stray kitten that wouldn't leave him alone?

'I can't walk far,' she said, giving him a get-out clause, but he shook his head.

'No, you don't have to. We'll take the car, and if you don't feel well I can always bring you back, it's not a problem.'

That didn't sound as if he was trying to get out of it, and she was genuinely interested.

'It sounds great. What time do you want to leave?'

'Breakfast is at seven. We'll go straight afterwards.'

It was fascinating.

He knew every inch of his land, every nook and cranny, every slope, every vine, almost, and as he stood on the edge of a little escarpment pointing things out to her, his feet planted firmly in the soil, she thought she'd never seen anyone who belonged so utterly to their home.

He looked as if he'd grown from the very soil beneath his feet, his roots stretching down into it for three hundred years. It was a part of him, and he was a part of it, the latest guardian in its history, and it was clear that he took the privilege incredibly seriously.

As they drove round the huge, sprawling estate to check the ripeness of the grapes on all the slopes, he told her about each of the grape varieties which grew on the different soils and orientations, lifting handfuls of the soil so she could see the texture, sifting it through his fingers as he talked about moisture content and pH levels and how it varied from field to field, and all the time his fingers were caressing the soil like a lover.

He mesmerised her.

Then he dropped the soil, brushed off his hands and gave her a wry smile.

'I'm boring you to death. Come on, it's time for lunch.'

He helped her back to the car, frowning as she trod on some uneven ground and gave a little cry as her ankle twisted.

'I'm sorry, it's too rough for you. Here.' And without hesitating he scooped her off her feet and set her back on the passenger seat, shut the door and went round and slid in behind the wheel.

He must have been mad to bring her out here on the rough ground in the heat of the day, with a head injury and a sprained ankle. He hadn't been thinking clearly, what with the upset of yesterday and Francesca's scene at the table and then the utter distraction of her pyjamas—even if he'd been intending to go back to bed, there was no way he would have slept. In fact, he doubted if he'd ever sleep again!

He put her in the car, drove back to the villa and left her there with Carlotta. He'd been meaning to show her round the house, but frankly, even another moment in her company was too dangerous to contemplate at the moment.

He made a work-related excuse, and escaped.

He had a lot to do, he'd told her as he'd hurried off, because *La Vendemmia* would start the following day.

So much for her tour of the house, she thought, but maybe it was as well to keep a bit of distance, because her feelings for him were beginning to confuse her.

Roberto brought the children home from school at the end of the afternoon, and she heard them splashing in the pool. She'd been contemplating the water herself, but without a suit it wasn't a goer, so she'd contented herself with sitting in the sun for a while and relaxing.

She went over to the railings and looked down, and saw all three of them in the water, with Carlotta and Roberto sitting in the shade watching them and keeping order. Carlotta glanced up at her and waved her down, and she limped down the steps and joined them.

It looked so inviting. Was her face a giveaway? Maybe, because Carlotta got to her feet and went to a door set in the wall of the terrace, under the steps. She emerged with a sleek

black one-piece and offered it to her. 'Swim?' she said, en-
couragingly.

It was so, so tempting, and the children didn't seem to
mind. Lavinia swam to the edge and grinned at her, and
Antonino threw a ball at her and missed, and then gig-
gled because she threw it back and bounced it lightly off
his head. Only Francesca kept her distance, and she could
understand why. It was the first time she'd seen her since
supper last night, and maybe now she'd find a chance to
apologise.

She changed in the cubicle Carlotta had taken the costume
from, and sat on the edge of the pool to take off her elastic
ankle support.

'Ow. It looks sore.'

She glanced up, and saw Francesca watching her warily,
her face troubled.

'I'm all right,' she assured her with a smile. 'I was really
stupid to fall like that. I'm so sorry I upset you last night.'

She shrugged, and returned the smile with a tentative one
of her own. 'Is OK. I was just tired, and *Papà* had been away
for days, and—I'm OK. Sometimes, I just remember...'

She nodded, trying to understand what it must be like to be
ten and motherless, and coming up with nothing even close,
she was sure.

'I'm sorry.' She slipped into the water next to Francesca,
and reached out and touched her shoulder gently. Then she
smiled at her. 'I wonder, would you teach me some words of
Italian?'

'Sure. What?'

'Just basic things. Sorry. Thank you. Hello, goodbye—just
things like that.'

'Of course. Swim first, then I teach you.'

And she smiled, a dazzling, pretty smile like the smile of her mother in the photograph, and it nearly broke Lydia's heart.

He came into the kitchen as she was sitting there with the children, Francesca patiently coaching her.

'No! *Mee dees-pya-che*,' said Francesca, and Lydia repeated it, stretching the vowels.

'That's good. *Ciao, bambini!*'

'*Ciao, Papà!*' the children chorused, and he came over and sat down with them.

'I'm teaching Lydia *Italiano*,' Francesca told him, grinning at him.

He smiled back, his eyes indulgent. '*Mia bella ragazza,*' he said softly, and her smile widened, a soft blush colouring her cheeks.

'So what do you know?' he asked Lydia, and she laughed ruefully.

'*Mi dispiace*—I thought sorry was a word I ought to master pretty early on, with my track record,' she said drily, and he chuckled.

'Anything else?'

'*Grazie mille*—I seem to need that a lot, too! And *per favore*, because it's rude not to say please. And *prego*, just in case I ever get the chance to do something that someone thanks me for. And that's it, so far, but I think it's the most critical ones.'

He laughed. 'It's a good start. Right, children, bedtime. Say goodnight.'

'*Buonanotte*, Lydia,' they chorused, and she smiled at them and said, '*Buonanotte,*' back.

And then she looked at Francesca, and added, '*Grazie mille*, Francesca,' her eyes soft, and Francesca smiled back.

'*Prego.* We do more tomorrow?'

'*Sì.*'

She grinned, and then out of the blue she came over to Lydia and kissed her on both cheeks. 'Goodnight.'

'Goodnight, Francesca.'

He ushered them away, although Francesca didn't really need to go to bed this early, but she'd lost sleep the night before and she was always happy to lie in bed and read.

He chivvied them through the bathroom, checked their teeth, redid Antonino's and then tucked them up. As he bent to kiss Francesca goodnight, she slid her arms round his neck and hugged him. 'I like Lydia,' she said. 'She's nice.'

'She is nice,' he said. 'Thank you for helping her.'

'It's OK. How long is she staying?'

'I don't know. A few days, just until she's better. You go to sleep, now.'

He turned off her top light, leaving the bedside light on so she could read for a while, and went back down to the kitchen.

Lydia was sitting there studying an English-Italian dictionary that Francesca must have lent her, and he poured two glasses of wine and sat down opposite her.

'She's a lovely girl.'

'She is. She's very like her mother. Kind. Generous.'

Lydia nodded. 'I'm really sorry you lost her.'

He smiled, but said nothing. What was there to say? Nothing he hadn't said before.

'So, the harvest starts tomorrow,' Lydia said after a moment.

'*Sì.* You should come down. Carlotta brings lunch for everyone at around twelve-thirty. Come with her, I'll show you what we do.'

* * *

Massimo left before dawn the following morning, and she found Carlotta up to her eyes in the kitchen.

'How many people are you feeding?' she asked.

Carlotta's face crunched up thoughtfully, and she said something in Italian which was meaningless, then held up her outspread hands and flashed them six times. Sixty. *Sixty?*

'Wow! That's a lot of work.'

'*Sì.* Is lot of work.'

She looked tired at the very thought, and Lydia frowned slightly and began to help without waiting to be asked. They loaded the food into a truck at twelve, and Roberto, Carlotta's husband, drove them down to the centre of operations.

They followed the route she'd travelled with Massimo the day before, bumping along the gravelled road to a group of buildings. It was a hive of activity, small tractors and pickup trucks in convoy bringing in the grapes, a tractor and trailer with men and women crowded on the back laughing and joking, their spirits high.

Massimo met them there, and helped her down out of the truck with a smile. 'Come, I'll show you round,' he said, and led her to the production line.

Around the tractors laden with baskets of grapes, the air was alive with the hum of bees. Everyone was covered in sticky purple grape juice, the air heavy with sweat and the sweet scent of freshly pressed grapes, and over the sound of excited voices she could hear the noise of the motors powering the pumps and the pressing machines.

'It's fascinating,' she yelled, and he nodded.

'It is. You can stay, if you like, see what we do with the grapes.'

'Do you need me underfoot?' she asked, and his mouth quirked.

'I'm sure I'll manage. You ask intelligent questions. I can live with that.'

His words made her oddly happy, and she smiled. 'Thank you. They seem to be enjoying themselves,' she added, gesturing to the laughing workers, and he grinned.

'Why wouldn't they be? We all love the harvest. And anyway, it's lunchtime,' he said pragmatically as the machines fell silent, and she laughed.

'So it is. I'm starving.'

The lunch was just a cold spread of bread and cheese and ham and tomatoes, much like their impromptu supper in the middle of the first night, and the exhausted and hungry workers fell on it like locusts.

'Carlotta told me there are about sixty people to feed. Does she do this every day?'

'Yes—and an evening meal for everyone. It's too much for her, but she won't let anyone else take over, she insists on being in charge and she's so fussy about who she'll allow in her kitchen it's not easy to get help that she'll accept.'

She nodded. She could understand that. She'd learned the art of delegation, but you still had to have a handle on everything that was happening in the kitchen and that took energy and physical resources that Carlotta probably didn't have any more.

'How old is she?'

Massimo laughed. 'It's a state secret and more than my life's worth to reveal it. Roberto's eighty-two. She tells me it's none of my business, which makes it difficult as she's on the payroll, so I had to prise it out of Roberto. Let's just say there's not much between them.'

That made her chuckle, but it also made her think. Carlotta hadn't minded her helping out in the kitchen this morning, or the other night—in fact, she'd almost seemed grateful. Maybe she'd see if she could help that afternoon. 'I think I'll head back with them,' she told him. 'It's a bit hot out here for me now anyway, and I could do with putting my foot up for a while.'

It wasn't a lie, none of it, but she had no intention of putting her foot up if Carlotta would let her help. And it would be a way to repay them for all the trouble she'd caused.

It was an amazing amount of work.

It would have been a lot for a team. For Carlotta, whose age was unknown but somewhere in the ballpark of eighty-plus, it was ridiculous. She had just the one helper, Maria, who sighed with relief when Lydia offered her assistance.

So did Carlotta.

Oh, she made a fuss, protested a little, but more on the lines of 'Oh, you don't really want to,' rather than 'No, thank you, I don't need your help.'

So she rolled up her sleeves and pitched in, peeling and chopping a huge pile of vegetables. Carlotta was in charge of browning the diced chicken, seasoning the tomato-based sauce, tasting.

That was fine. This was her show. Lydia was just going along for the ride, and making up for the disaster of her first evening here, but by the time they were finished and ready to serve it on trestle tables under the cherry trees, her ankle was paying for it.

She stood on one leg like a stork, her sore foot hooked round her other calf, wishing she could sit down and yet knowing she was needed as they dished up to the hungry hordes.

They still looked happy, she thought. Happy and dirty and smelly and as if they'd had a good day, and there was a good deal of teasing and flirting going on, some of it in her direction.

She smiled back, dished up and wondered where Massimo was. She found herself scanning the crowd for him, and told herself not to be silly. He'd be with the children, not here, not eating with the workers.

She was wrong. A few minutes later, when the queue was thinning out and she was at the end of her tether, she felt a light touch on her waist.

'You should be resting. I'll take over.'

And his firm hands eased her aside, took the ladle from her hand and carried on.

'You don't need to do that. You've been working all day.'

'So have you, I gather, and you're hurt. Have you eaten?'

'No. I was waiting till we'd finished.'

He ladled sauce onto the last plate and turned to her. 'We're finished. Grab two plates, we'll go and eat. And you can put your foot up. You told me you were going to do that and I hear you've been standing all day.'

They sat at the end of a trestle, so she was squashed between a young girl from one of the villages and her host, and the air was heady with the scent of sweat and grape juice and the rich tomato and basil sauce.

He shaved cheese over her pasta, his arm brushing hers as he held it over her plate, and the soft chafe of hair against her skin made her nerve-endings dance.

'So, is it a good harvest?' she asked, and he grinned.

'Very good. Maybe the best I can remember. It'll be a vintage year for our Brunello.'

'Brunello? I thought that was only from Montalcino?'

'It is. Part of the estate is in the Montalcino territory. It's very strictly regulated, but it's a very important part of our revenue.'

'I'm sure.' She was. During the course of her training and apprenticeships she'd learned a lot about wines, and she knew that Brunellos were always expensive, some of them extremely so. Expensive, and exclusive. Definitely niche market.

Her father would be interested. He'd like Massimo, she realised. They had a lot in common, in so many ways, for all the gulf between them.

Deep in thought, she ate the hearty meal, swiped the last off the sauce from her plate with a chunk of bread and licked her lips, glancing up to see him watching her with a smile on his face.

'What?'

'You. You really appreciate food.'

'I do. Carlotta's a good cook. That was delicious.'

'Are you making notes?'

She laughed. 'Only mental ones.'

He glanced over her head, and a smile touched his face. 'My parents are back. They're looking forward to meeting you.'

Really? Like this, covered in tomato sauce and reeking of chopped onions? She probably had an orange tide-line round her mouth, and her hair was dragged back into an elastic band, and—

'Mamma, *Papà*, this is Lydia.'

She scrambled to her feet, wincing as her sore ankle took her weight, and looked up into the eyes of an elegant, beautiful, immaculately groomed woman with clear, searching eyes.

'Lydia. How nice to meet you. Welcome to our home. I'm Elisa Valtieri, and this is my husband, Vittorio.'

'Hello. It's lovely to meet you, too.' Even if she did look a fright.

She shook their hands, Elisa's warm and gentle, Vittorio's rougher, his fingers strong and hard, a hand that wasn't afraid of work. He was an older version of his son, and his eyes were kind. He reminded her of her father.

'My son tells me you've had an accident?' Elisa said, her eyes concerned.

'Yes, I was really stupid, and he's been unbelievably kind.'

'And so, I think, have you. Carlotta is singing your praises.'

'Oh.' She felt herself colour, and laughed a little awkwardly. 'I didn't have anything else to do.'

'Except rest,' Massimo said drily, but his smile was gentle and warmed her right down to her toes.

And then she glanced back and found his mother looking at her, curiosity and interest in those lively brown eyes, and she excused herself, mumbling some comment about them having a lot to catch up on, and hobbled quickly back to Carlotta to see if there was anything she could do to help.

Anything, other than stand there while his mother eyed her speculatively, her eyes asking questions Lydia had no intention of answering.

If she even knew the answers…

CHAPTER FIVE

'You ran away.'

She was sitting outside her room on a bench with her foot up, flicking through a magazine she'd found, and she looked up guiltily into his thoughtful eyes.

'I had to help Carlotta.'

'And it was easier than dealing with my mother,' he said softly, a fleeting smile in his eyes. 'I'm sorry, she can be a little…'

'A little…?'

He grinned slightly crookedly. 'She doesn't like me being on my own. Every time I speak to a woman under fifty, her radar picks it up. She's been interrogating me for the last three hours.'

Lydia laughed, and she put the magazine down, swung her foot to the ground and patted the bench. 'Want to hide here for a while?'

His mouth twitched. 'How did you guess? Give me a moment.'

He vanished, then reappeared with a bottle of wine and two glasses. 'Prosecco?'

'Lovely. Thanks.' She took a glass from him, sniffing the bubbles and wrinkling her nose as she sipped. 'Mmm, that's really nice. So, how was the baby?'

'Beautiful, perfect, amazing, the best baby in the world—oh, apart from all their other grandchildren. This is the sixth, and Luca and Isabelle are about to make it seven. Their second is due any time now.'

'Wow. Lots of babies.'

'Yes, and she loves it. Nothing makes her happier. Luca and Isabelle and my brother Gio are coming over tomorrow for dinner with some neighbours, by the way. I'd like you to join us, if you can tolerate it.'

She stared at him. 'Really? I'm only here by default, and I feel such a fraud. I really ought to go home.'

'How's your head now?'

She pulled a face. 'Better. I'm still getting the odd headache, but nothing to worry about. It's my ankle and the other bruises and scrapes that are sorest. I think I hit every step.'

He frowned. 'I'm sorry. I didn't really think about the things I can't see.'

Well, that was a lie. He thought about them all the time, but there was no way he was confessing that to Lydia. 'So—will you join us?'

She bit her lip, worrying it for a moment with her teeth, which made him want to kiss her just to stop her hurting that soft, full mouth that had been taunting him for days. *Dio*, the whole damn woman had been taunting him for days—

'Can I think about it?'

A kiss? No. No! Not a kiss!

'Of course,' he said, finally managing to unravel his tongue long enough to speak. 'Of course you may. It won't be anything impressive, Carlotta's got enough to do as it is, but my mother wanted to see Isabelle and Luca before the baby comes, and Gio's coming, and so my mother's invited Anita and her parents, and so it gets bigger—you know how it is.'

She laughed softly. 'I can imagine. Who's Anita?'

'The daughter of our neighbours. She and Gio had a thing a while back, and my mother keeps trying to get them together again. Can't see it working, really, but she likes to try.'

'And how do they feel?'

He laughed abruptly. 'I wouldn't dare ask Gio. He has a fairly bitter and twisted attitude to love. Comes from being a lawyer, I suppose. His first line of defence is always a pre-nuptial agreement.'

She raised an eyebrow. 'Trust issues, then. I can understand that. I have a few of my own after Russell.'

'I'm sure. People like that can take away something precious, a sort of innocence, a naivety, and once it's gone you can never get it back. Although I have no idea what happened to Gio. He won't talk about it.'

'What about Anita? What's she like?'

His low chuckle made her smile. 'Anita's a wedding planner. What do you think?'

'I think she might like to plan her own?'

'Indeed. But Gio can't see what's under his nose, even if Mamma keeps putting her there.' He tipped his head on one side. 'It could be an interesting evening. And if you're there, it might take the heat off Gio, so he'll probably be so busy being grateful he'll forget to quiz me about you, so it could be better all round!'

She started to laugh at that, and he joined in with another chuckle and topped up her glass.

'Here's to families and their politics and complications,' he said drily, and touched his glass to hers.

'Amen to that,' she said, remembering guiltily that she'd meant to phone Jen again. 'I heard from Claire, by the way— she's back home safely, and she said Jo's ecstatic about winning.'

'How's your sister about it?'

She pulled a face. 'I'm not sure. She was putting on a brave face, but I think she's gutted. I know none of us expected me to win but, you know, it would have been so nice.'

He nodded. 'I'm sorry.'

'Don't be. You've done more than enough.' She drained her glass and handed it to him. 'I'm going to turn in. I need to rest my leg properly, and tomorrow I need to think about arranging a flight back home.'

'For tomorrow?' He sounded startled, and she shook her head.

'No. I thought maybe the next day? I probably ought to phone the hospital and get the go-ahead to fly.'

'I can take you there if you want a check-up.'

'You've got so much to do.'

'Nothing that's more important,' he said, and although it wasn't true, she knew that for him there was nothing more important than making sure there wasn't another Angelina.

'I'll see what they say,' she compromised. There was always the bus, surely? She'd ask Carlotta in the morning.

She got to her feet, and he stood up and took her hand, tucking it in the crook of his arm and helping her to the French doors. Quite unnecessarily, since she'd been hobbling around without help since the second day, really, but it was still nice to feel the strength of his arm beneath her hand, the muscles warm and hard beneath the fine fabric of his shirt.

Silk and linen, she thought, sampling the texture with her fingertips, savouring it.

He hesitated at the door, and then just when she thought he was going to walk away, he lowered his head and touched his lips to hers, sending rivers of ice and fire dancing over her skin.

It was a slow kiss, lingering, thoughtful, their mouths the only point of contact, but then the velvet stroke of his tongue against her lips made her gasp softly and part them for him, and everything changed.

He gave a muffled groan and deepened the kiss, searching the secret recesses of her mouth, his tongue finding hers and dancing with it, retreating, tangling, coaxing until she thought her legs would collapse.

Then he eased away, breaking the contact so slowly so that for a tiny second their lips still clung.

'*Buonanotte*, Lydia,' he murmured unevenly, his breath warm against her mouth, and then straightening slowly, he took a step back and turned briskly away, gathering up the glasses and the bottle as he went without a backwards glance.

She watched him go, then closed the curtains and undressed, leaving the doors open. The night was warm still, the light breeze welcome, and she lay there in the darkness, her fingertips tracing her lips, and thought about his kiss...

He must have been mad to kiss her!

Crazy. Insane. If he hadn't walked away, he would have taken her right there, standing on the terrace in full view of anyone who walked past.

He headed for the stairs, but then hesitated. He wouldn't sleep—but what else could he do? His office was next to her room, and he didn't trust himself that close to her. The pool, his first choice of distraction for the sheer physical exertion it offered, was too close to her room, and she slept with her doors open. She'd hear him, come and investigate, and...

So not the pool, then.

Letting out a long, weary sigh, he headed slowly up the stairs to his room, and sat on the bed, staring at the photograph of Angelina on his bedside table.

He'd loved her—really, deeply and enduringly loved her. But she was gone, and now, as he looked at her face, another face seemed superimposed on it, a face with laughing eyes and a soft, full bottom lip that he could still taste.

He groaned and fell back against the pillows, staring up at the ceiling. The day after tomorrow, she'd be gone, he told himself, and then had to deal with the strange and unsettling sense of loss he felt at the thought that he was about to lose her.

She didn't sleep well.

Her dreams had been vivid and unsettling, and as soon as she heard signs of life, she got up, showered and put on her rinsed-out underwear, and then sat down on the edge of the bed and sighed thoughtfully as she studied her clothes.

She couldn't join them for dinner—not if their neighbours were coming. She'd seen Elisa, seen the expensive and elegant clothes she'd worn for travelling back home from her daughter's house, and the only things she had with her were the jeans and top she'd been wearing now for two days, including all the cooking she'd done yesterday.

No way could she wear them to dinner, even if she'd earn Gio's undying gratitude and give Elisa something else to think about! She put the clothes on, simply because she had absolutely no choice apart from the wedding dress Carlotta had stuffed in a bag for her and which she yet had to burn, and went outside and round the corner to the kitchen.

Carlotta was there, already making headway on the lunch preparations, and the children were sitting at the table eating breakfast. For a slightly crazy moment, she wondered if they could tell what she'd been dreaming about, if the fact that she'd kissed their father was written all over her face.

She said good morning to them, in her best Italian learned yesterday from Francesca, asked them how they were and then went over to Carlotta. '*Buongiorno*, Carlotta,' she said softly, and Carlotta blushed and smiled at her and patted her cheek.

'*Buongiorno, signorina,*' she said. 'Did you have good sleep?'

'Very good,' she said, trying not to think of the dreams and blushing slightly anyway. 'What can I do to help you?'

'No, no, you sit. I can do it.'

'You know I can't do that,' she chided softly. She stuck a mug under the coffee machine, pressed the button and waited, then added milk and went back to Carlotta, sipping the hot, fragrant brew gratefully. 'Oh, that's lovely. Right. What shall I do first?'

Carlotta gave in. 'We need to cut the meat, and the bread, and—'

'Just like yesterday?'

'*Sì.*'

'So I'll do that, and you can make preparations for tonight. I know you have dinner to cook for the family as well as for the workers.'

Her brow creased, looking troubled, and Lydia could tell she was worried. Exhausted, more like. 'Look, let me do this, and maybe I can give you a hand with that, too?' she offered, but that was a step too far. Carlotta straightened her gnarled old spine and plodded to the fridge.

'I do it,' she said firmly, and so Lydia gave in and concentrated on preparing lunch for sixty people in the shortest possible time, so she could move on to cooking the pasta sauce for the evening shift with Maria. At least that way Carlotta would be free to concentrate on dinner.

Massimo found her in the kitchen at six, in the throes of draining gnocchi for the workers, and she nearly dropped the pan. Crazy. Ridiculous, but the sight of him made her heart pound and she felt like a gangly teenager, awkward and confused because of the kiss.

'Are you in here again?' he asked, taking the other side of the huge pan and helping her tip it into the enormous strainer.

'Looks like me,' she said with a forced grin, but he just frowned and avoided her eyes, as if he, too, was feeling awkward and uncomfortable about the kiss.

'Did you speak to the hospital?' he asked, and she realised he would be glad to get rid of her. She'd been nothing but trouble for him, and she was unsettling the carefully constructed and safe status quo he'd created around them all.

'Yes. I'm fine to travel,' she said, although it wasn't quite true. They'd said they needed to examine her, and when she'd said she was too busy, they'd fussed a bit but what could they do? So she'd booked a flight. 'I've got a seat on a plane at three tomorrow afternoon from Pisa,' she told him, and he frowned again.

'Really? You didn't have to go so soon,' he said, confusing her even more.

'It's not soon. It'll be five days—that's what they said, and I've been under your feet long enough.'

And any longer, she realised, and things were going to happen between them. There was such a pull every time she was with him, and that kiss last night—

She thrust the big pot at him. 'Here, carry the *gnocci* outside for me. I'll bring the sauce.'

He followed her, set the food down for the workers and stood at her side, dishing up.

'So can I persuade you to join us for dinner?' he asked, but she shook her head.

'I've got nothing to wear,' she said, feeling safe because he couldn't argue with that, but she was wrong.

'You're about the same size as Serena. I'm sure she

wouldn't mind if you borrowed something from her wardrobe. She always leaves something here. Carlotta will show you.'

'Carlotta's trying to prepare a meal for ten people this evening, Massimo. She doesn't have time to worry about clothes for me.'

'Then I'll take you,' he said, and the moment the serving was finishing, he hustled her back into the house before she could argue.

He was right. She and Serena were about the same size, something she already knew because she'd borrowed her costume to swim in, and she found a pair of black trousers that were the right length with her flat black pumps, and a pretty top that wasn't in the first flush of youth but was nice enough.

She didn't want to take anything too special, but she didn't think Serena would mind if she borrowed that one, and it was good enough, surely, for an interloper?

She went back to the kitchen, still in her jeans and T-shirt, and found Carlotta sitting at the table with her head on her arms, and Roberto beside her wringing his hands.

'Carlotta?'

'She is tired, *signorina*,' he explained worriedly. 'Signora Valtieri has many people for dinner, and my Carlotta…'

'I'll do it,' she said quickly, sitting down and taking Carlotta's hands in hers. 'Carlotta, tell me what you were going to cook them, and I'll do it.'

'But Massimo said…'

'Never mind what he said. I can cook and be there at the same time. Don't worry about me. We can make it easy. Just tell me what you're cooking, and Roberto can help me find things. We'll manage, and nobody need ever know.'

Her eyes filled with tears, and Lydia pulled a tissue out of a box and shoved it in her hand. 'Come on, stop that, it's all right. We've got cooking to do.'

Well, it wasn't her greatest meal ever, she thought as she sat with the others and Roberto waited on them, but it certainly didn't let Carlotta down, and from the compliments going back to the kitchen via Roberto, she knew Carlotta would be feeling much less worried.

As for her, in her borrowed top and trousers, she felt under-dressed and overawed—not so much by the company as by the amazing dining room itself. Like her room and the kitchen, it opened to the terrace, but in the centre, with two pairs of double doors flung wide so they could hear the tweeting and twittering of the swallows swooping past the windows.

But it was the walls which stunned her. Murals again, like the ones in the cloistered walkway around the courtyard, but this time all over the ornate vaulted ceiling as well.

'Beautiful, isn't it?' Gio said quietly. 'I never get tired of looking at this ceiling. And it's a good way to avoid my mother's attention.'

She nearly laughed at that. He was funny—very funny, very quick, very witty, very dry. A typical lawyer, she thought, used to brandishing his tongue in court like a rapier, slashing through the opposition. He would be formidable, she realised, and she didn't envy the woman who was so clearly still in love with him.

Anita was lovely, though. Strikingly beautiful, but warm and funny and kind, and Lydia wondered if she realised just how often Gio glanced at her when she'd looked away.

Elisa did, she was sure of it.

And then she met Massimo's eyes, and realised he was studying her thoughtfully.

'Excuse me, I have to go and do something in the kitchen,'

she murmured. 'Carlotta very kindly let me experiment with the dessert, and I need to put the finishing touches to it.'

She bolted, running along the corridor and arriving in the kitchen just as Carlotta had put out the bowls.

'Roberto say you tell them I cook everything!' she said, wringing her hands and hugging her.

Lydia hugged her back. 'You did, really. I just helped you. You told me exactly what to do.'

'You *know* what to do. You such good *cuoca*—good cook. Look at this! So easy—so beautiful. *Bellisima!*'

She spread her hands wide, and Lydia looked. Five to a tray, there were ten individual gleaming white bowls, each containing glorious red and black frozen berries fogged with icy dew, and in the pan on the stove Roberto was gently heating the white chocolate sauce. Sickly sweet, immensely sticky and a perfect complement to the sharp berries, it was her favourite no-frills emergency pud, and she took the pan from Roberto, poured a swirl around the edge of each plate and then they grabbed a tray each and went back to the dining room.

'I hope you like it,' she said brightly. 'If not, please don't blame Carlotta, I made her let me try it!'

Elisa frowned slightly, but Massimo just gave her a level look, and as she set the plate down in front of him, he murmured, 'Liar,' softly, so only she could hear.

She flashed him a smile and went back to her place, between Gio and Anita's father, and opposite Isabelle. 'So, tell me, what's it like living in Tuscany full-time?' she asked Isabelle, although she could see that she was blissfully contented and the answer was going to be biased.

'Wonderful,' Isabelle said, leaning her head against Luca's shoulder and smiling up at him. 'The family couldn't have been kinder.'

'That's not true. I tried to warn you off,' Gio said, and Luca laughed.

'You try and warn everybody off,' he said frankly, 'but luckily for me she didn't listen to you. Lydia, this dessert is amazing. Try it, *cara*.'

He held a spoonful up to Isabelle's lips, and Lydia felt a lump rise in her throat. Their love was so open and uncomplicated and genuine, so unlike the relationship she'd had with Russell. Isabelle and Luca were like Jen and Andy, unashamedly devoted to each other, and she wondered with a little ache what it must feel like to be the centre of someone's world, to be so clearly and deeply loved. *That* would be amazing.

She glanced across the table, and found Massimo watching her, his eyes thoughtful. He lifted his spoon to her in salute.

'Amazing, indeed.'

She blinked. He was talking about the dessert, not about love. Nothing to do with love, or with her, or him, or the two of them, or that kiss last night.

'Thank you,' she said, a little breathlessly, and turned her attention to the sickly, sticky white chocolate sauce. If she glued her tongue up enough with that, maybe it would keep it out of trouble.

'So how much of that was you, and how much was Carlotta?'

It was midnight, and everyone else had left or gone to bed. They were alone in the kitchen, putting away the last of the serving dishes that she'd just washed by hand, and Massimo was making her a cup of camomile tea.

'Honestly? I gave her a hand.'

'And the dessert?'

'Massimo, she was tired. She had all the ingredients for my quick fix, so I just improvised.'

'Hmm,' he said, but he left it at that, to her relief. She

sensed he didn't believe her, but he had no proof, and Carlotta had been so distraught.

'Right, we're done here,' he said briskly. 'Let's go outside and sit and drink this.'

They went on her bench, outside her room, and sat in companionable silence drinking their tea. At least, it started out companionable, and then last night's kiss intruded, and she felt the tension creep in, making the air seem to fizz with the sparks that passed between them.

'You don't have to go tomorrow, you know,' he said, breaking the silence after it had stretched out into the hereafter.

'I do. I've bought a ticket.'

'I'll buy you another one. Wait a few more days.'

'Why? So I can finish falling for you? That's not a good idea, Massimo.'

He laughed softly, and she thought it was the saddest sound she'd ever heard. 'No. Probably not. I have nothing to offer you, Lydia. I wish I did.'

'I don't want anything.'

'That's not quite true. We both want something. It's just not wise.'

'Is it ever?'

'I don't know. Not for us, I don't think. We've both been hurt enough by the things that have happened, and I don't know about you but I'm not ready to try again. I have so many demands on me, so many calls on my time, so much *duty*.'

She put her cup down very carefully and turned to face him. 'We could just take tonight as it comes,' she said quietly, her heart in her mouth. 'No strings, just one night. No duty, no demands. Just a little time out from reality, for both of us.'

The silence was broken only by the beating of her heart, the roaring in her ears so loud that she could scarcely hear herself think. For an age he sat motionless, then he lifted a hand and touched her cheek.

'Why, *cara*? Why tonight?'

'Because it's our last chance?'

'Why me?'

'I don't know. It just seems right.'

Again he hesitated, then he took her hand and pressed it to his lips. 'Give me ten minutes. I need to check the children.'

She nodded, her mouth dry, and he brushed her lips with his and left her there, her fingers resting on the damp, tingling skin as if to hold the kiss in place.

Ten minutes, she thought. Ten minutes, and my life will change forever.

He didn't come back.

She gave up after half an hour, and went to bed alone, humiliated and disappointed. How stupid, to proposition a man so far out of her league. He was probably still laughing at her in his room.

He wasn't. There was a soft knock on the door, and he walked in off the terrace. 'Lydia? I'm sorry I was so long. Are you still awake?'

She propped herself up on one elbow, trying to read his face, but his back was to the moonlight. 'Yes. What happened? I'd given up on you.'

'Antonino woke. He had a nightmare. He's all right now, but I didn't want to leave him till he was settled.'

He sat on the edge of the bed, his eyes shadowed in the darkness, and she reached for the bedside light. He caught her hand. 'No. Leave it off. Let's just have the moonlight.'

He opened the curtains wide, but closed the doors—for privacy? She didn't know, but she was grateful that he had because she felt suddenly vulnerable as he stripped off his clothes and turned back the covers, lying down beside her and taking her into his arms.

The shock of that first contact took their breath away, and he rested his head against hers and gave a shuddering sigh. 'Oh, Lydia, *cara*, you feel so good,' he murmured, and then after that she couldn't understand anything he said, because his voice deepened, the words slurred and incoherent. He was speaking Italian, she realised at last, his breath trembling over her body with every groaning sigh as his hands cupped and moulded her.

She arched against him, her body aching for him, a need like no need she'd ever felt swamping her common sense and turning her to jelly. She ran her hands over him, learning his contours, the feel of his skin like hot silk over the taut, corded muscles beneath, and then she tasted him, her tongue testing the salt of his skin, breathing in the warm musk and the lingering trace of cologne.

He seemed to be everywhere, his hands and mouth caressing every part of her, their legs tangling as his mouth returned to hers and he kissed her as if he'd die without her.

'Please,' she whispered, her voice shaking with need, and he paused, fumbling for something on the bedside table.

Taking care of her, she realised, something she'd utterly forgotten, but not him. He'd remembered, and made sure that she was safe with him.

No strings. No repercussions.

Then he reached for her, taking her into his arms, and as he moved over her she stopped thinking altogether and just *felt*.

He woke to the touch of her hand on his chest, lying lightly over his heart.

She was asleep, her head lying on his shoulder, her body

silvered by the moonlight. He shifted carefully, and she sighed and let him go, so he could lever himself up and look down at her.

There was a dark stain over one hip bone. He hadn't noticed it last night, but now he did. A bruise, from her fall. And there was another, on her shoulder, and one on her thigh, high up on the side. He kissed them all, tracing the outline with his lips, kissing them better like the bruises of a child.

It worked, his brother Luca told him, because the caress released endorphins, feel-good hormones, and so you really could kiss someone better, but only surely if they were awake—

'Massimo?'

He turned his head and met her eyes. 'You're hurt all over.'

'I'm all right now.'

She smiled, reaching up and cradling his jaw in her hand, and he turned his face into her hand and kissed her palm, his tongue stroking softly over the sensitive skin.

'What time is it?'

He glanced at his watch and sighed. 'Two. Just after.'

Two. Her flight was in thirteen hours.

She swallowed hard and drew his face down to hers. 'Make love to me again,' she whispered.

How could he refuse? How could he walk away from her, even though it was madness?

Time out, she'd said, from reality. He needed that so badly, and he wasn't strong enough to resist.

Thirteen hours, he thought, and as he took her in his arms again, his heart squeezed in his chest.

Saying goodbye to the children and Carlotta and Roberto was hard. Saying goodbye to Massimo was agony.

He'd parked at the airport, in the short stay carpark, and

they'd had lunch in the café, sitting outside under the trailing pergola. She positioned herself in the sun, but it didn't seem to be able to warm her, because she was cold inside, her heart aching.

'Thank you for everything you've done for me,' she said, trying hard not to cry, but it was difficult and she felt a tear escape and slither down her cheek.

'Oh, *bella*.' He sighed, and reaching out his hand, he brushed it gently away. 'No tears. Please, no tears.'

'Happy tears,' she lied. 'I've had a wonderful time.'

He nodded, but his eyes didn't look happy, and she was sure hers didn't. She tried to smile.

'Give my love to the children, and thank Francesca again for my Italian lessons.'

He smiled, his mouth turning down at the corners ruefully. 'They'll miss you. They had fun with you.'

'They'll forget me,' she reassured him. 'Children move on very quickly.'

But maybe not if they'd been hurt in the past, he thought, and wondered if this had been so safe after all, so without consequences, without repercussions.

Maybe not.

He left her at the departures gate, standing there with his arms round her while she hugged him tight. She let him go, looked up, her eyes sparkling with tears.

'Take care,' she said, and he nodded.

'You, too. Safe journey.'

And without waiting to see her go through the gate, he walked away, emotions raging through him.

Madness. He'd thought he could handle it, but—

He'd got her address from her, so he could send her a crate of wine and oil.

That was all, he told himself. Nothing more. He certainly wasn't going to contact her, or see her again—

He sucked in a breath, surprised by the sharp stab of loss. Ships in the night, he told himself more firmly. They'd had a good time but now it was over, she was gone and he could get on with his life.

How hard could it be?

CHAPTER SIX

'Why don't you just go and see her?'

Massimo looked up from the baby in his arms and forced himself to meet his brother's eyes.

'I don't know what you mean.'

'Of course you do. You've been like a grizzly bear for the last two weeks, and even your own children are avoiding you.'

He frowned. Were they? He hadn't noticed, he realised in horror, and winced at the wave of guilt. But...

'It's not a crime to want her, you know,' Luca said softly.

'It's not that simple.'

'Of course not. Love never is.'

His head jerked up again. 'Who's talking about love?' he snapped, and Luca just raised an eyebrow silently.

'I'm *not* in love with her.'

'If you say so.'

He opened his mouth to say, 'I do say so,' and shut it smartly. 'I've just been busy,' he said instead, making excuses. 'Carlotta's been ill, and I've been trying to juggle looking after the children in the evenings and getting them ready for school without neglecting all the work of the grape harvest.'

'But that's over now—at least the critical bit. And you're wrong, you know, Carlotta isn't ill, she's old and tired and she needs to stop working before she becomes ill.'

Massimo laughed out loud at that, startling his new nephew and making him cry. He shushed him automatically, soothing the fractious baby, and then looked up at Luca again. 'I'll let you tell her that.'

'I have done. She won't listen because she thinks she's indispensable and she doesn't want to let anybody down. And she's going to kill herself unless someone does something to stop her.'

And then it dawned on him. Just the germ of an idea, but if it worked…

He got to his feet, wanting to get started, now that the thought had germinated. He didn't know why he hadn't thought of it before, except he'd been deliberately putting it—her—out of his mind.

'I think I'll take a few days off,' he said casually. 'I could do with a break. I'll take the car and leave the children here. Mamma can look after them. It'll keep her off Gio's back for a while and they can play with little Annamaria while Isabelle rests.'

Luca took the baby from him and smiled knowingly.

'Give her my love.'

He frowned. 'Who? I don't know what you're talking about. This is a business trip. I have some trade samples to deliver.'

His brother laughed and shut the door behind him.

'Do you know anyone with a posh left-hand-drive Mercedes with a foreign number plate?'

Lydia's head jerked up. She did—but he wouldn't be here. There was no way he'd be here, and certainly not without warning—

'Tall, dark-haired, uber-sexy. Wow, in fact. Very, *very* wow!'

Her mouth dried, her heart thundering. No. Surely not—not when she was just getting over him—

'Let me see.'

She leant over Jen's shoulder and peeped through the doorway, and her heart, already racing, somersaulted in her chest. Over him? Not a chance. She'd been fooling herself for over two weeks, convincing herself she didn't care about him, it had just been a holiday romance, and one sight of him and all of it had come slamming back. She backed away, one hand on her heart, trying to stop it vaulting out through her ribs, the other over her mouth holding back the chaotic emotions that were threatening to erupt.

'It's him, isn't it? Your farmer guy. You never said he was that hot!'

No, she hadn't. She'd said very little about him because she'd been desperately trying to forget him and avoid the inevitable interrogation if she so much as hinted at a relationship. But—farmer? Try millionaire. More than that. Try serious landowner, old-money, from one of Italy's most well-known and respected families. Not a huge brand name, but big enough, she'd discovered when she'd checked on the internet in a moment of weakness and aching, pathetic need.

And try lover—just for one night, but the most magical, memorable and relived night of her life.

She looked down at herself and gave a tiny, desperate scream. She was cleaning tack—old, tatty tack from an even older, tattier pony who'd finally met his maker, and they were going to sell it. Not for much, but the saddle was good enough to raise a couple of hundred pounds towards Jen's wedding.

'He's looking around.'

So was she—for a way to escape from the tack room and back to the house without being seen, so she could clean up and at least look slightly less disreputable, but there was no other way out, and…

'He's seen me. He's coming over. Hi, there. Can I help?'

'I hope so. I'm looking for Lydia Fletcher.'

His voice made her heart thud even harder, and she backed into the shadows, clutching the filthy, soapy rag in a desperate fist.

'She's here,' Jen said, dumping her in it and flashing him her most charming smile. 'I'm her sister, Jen—and she's rather grubby, so she probably doesn't want you to see her like that, so why don't I take you over to the house and make you a cup of tea—'

'I don't mind if she's grubby. She's seen me looking worse, I'm sure.'

And before Jen could usher him away, he stepped past her into the tack room, sucking all the air out of it in that simple movement.

'Ciao, bella,' he said softly, a smile lurking in his eyes, and she felt all her resolve melt away to nothing.

'Ciao,' she echoed, and then toughened up. 'I didn't expect to see you again.'

She peered past him at Jen, hovering in the doorway. 'Why don't you go and put the kettle on?' she said firmly.

With a tiny, knowing smile, Jen took a step away, then mouthed, 'Be nice!'

Nice? She had no intention of being anything *but* nice, but she also had absolutely no intention of being anything more accommodating. He'd been so clear about not wanting a relationship, and she'd thought she could handle their night together, thought she could walk away. Well, she wasn't letting him in again, because she'd never get over it a second time.

'You could have warned me you were coming,' she said when Jen had gone, her crutches scrunching in the gravel.

'And don't tell me you lost my phone number, because it was on the same piece of paper as my address, which you clearly have or you wouldn't be here.'

'I haven't lost it. I didn't want to give you the chance to avoid me.'

'You thought I would?'

'I thought you might want to, and I didn't want you to run away without hearing me out.' He looked around, studying the dusty room with the saddle racks screwed to the old beams, the saddle horse in the middle of the room with Bruno's saddle on it, half-cleaned, the hook dangling from the ceiling with his bridle and stirrup leathers hanging from it, still covered in mould and dust and old grease.

Just like her, really, smeared in soapy filth and not in any way dressed to impress.

'Evocative smell.' He fingered the saddle flap, rubbing his fingertips together and sniffing them. 'It takes me back. I had a friend with horses when I was at boarding school over here, and I stayed with him sometimes. We used to have to clean the tack after we rode.'

He smiled, as if it was a good memory, and then he lifted his hand and touched a finger to her cheek. 'You've got dirt on your face.'

'I'm sure. And don't you dare spit on a tissue and rub it off.'

He chuckled, and shifting an old riding hat, he sat down on a rickety chair and crossed one foot over the other knee, his hands resting casually on his ankle as if he really didn't care how dirty the chair was.

'Well, don't let me stop you. You need to finish what you're doing—at least the saddle.'

She did. It was half-done, and she couldn't leave it like

that or it would mark. She scrunched the rag in her fingers and nodded. 'If you don't mind.'

'Of course not. I didn't know you had a horse,' he added, after a slight pause.

'We don't—not any more.'

His eyes narrowed, and he leant forwards. 'Lydia?' he said softly, and she sniffed and turned away, reaching for the saddle soap.

'He died,' she said flatly. 'We don't need the tack, so I'm going to sell it. It's a crime to let it rot out here when someone could be using it.'

'I'm sorry.'

'Don't be. He was ancient.'

'But you loved him.'

'Of course. That's what life's all about, isn't it? Loving things and losing them?' She put the rag down and turned back to him, her heart aching so badly that she was ready to howl her eyes out. 'Massimo, why are you here?'

'I promised you some olive oil and wine and balsamic vinegar.'

She blinked, and stared at him, dumbfounded. 'You drove all this way to deliver me *olive oil*? That's ridiculous. Why are you really here, in the middle of harvest? And what was that about not wanting me to run away before hearing you out?'

He smiled slowly—reluctantly. 'OK. I have a proposition for you. Finish the saddle, and I'll tell you.'

'Tell me now.'

'I'll tell you while you finish,' he compromised, so she picked up the rag again and reapplied it to the saddle, putting on rather more saddle soap than was necessary. He watched her, watched the fierce way she rubbed the leather, the pucker in her brow as she waited for him to speak.

'So?' she prompted, her patience running out.

'So—I think Carlotta is unwell. Luca says not, and he's the doctor. He says she's just old, and tired, and needs to stop before she kills herself.'

'I agree. She's been too old for years, probably, but I don't suppose she'll listen if you tell her that.'

'No. She won't. And the trouble is she won't allow anyone else in her kitchen.' He paused for a heartbeat. 'Anyone except *you*.'

She dropped the rag and spun round. 'Me!' she squeaked, and then swallowed hard. 'I—I don't understand! What have I got to do with anything?'

'We need someone to feed everybody for the harvest. After that, we'll need someone as a housekeeper. Carlotta won't give that up until she's dead, but we can get her local help, and draft in caterers for events like big dinner parties and so on. But for the harvest, we need someone she trusts who can cater for sixty people twice a day without getting in a flap—someone who knows what they're doing, who understands what's required and who's available.'

'I'm not available,' she said instantly, and he felt a sharp stab of disappointment.

'You have another job?'

She shook her head. 'No, not really, but I'm helping with the farm, and doing the odd bit of outside catering, a bit of relief work in the pub. Nothing much, but I'm trying to get my career back on track and I can't do that if I'm gallivanting about all over Tuscany, however much I want to help you out. I have to earn a living—'

'You haven't heard my proposition yet.'

She stared at him, trying to work out what he was getting at. What he was offering. She wasn't sure she wanted to know, because she had a feeling it would involve a lot of heart-ache, but—

'What proposition? I thought that was your proposition?'

'You come back with me, work for the harvest and I'll give your sister her wedding.'

She stared at him, confused. She couldn't have heard him right. 'I don't understand,' she said, finding her voice at last.

'It's not hard. The hotel was offering the ceremony, a reception for—what, fifty people?—a room for their wedding night, accommodation for the night before for the bridal party, a food and drink package— Anything I've missed?'

She shook her head. 'Flowers, maybe?'

'OK. Well, we can offer all that. There's a chapel where they can marry, if they're Catholic, or they could have a blessing there and marry in the Town Hall, or whatever they wanted, and we'll give them a marquee with tables and chairs and a dance floor, and food and wine for the guests. And flowers. And if they don't want to stay in the guest wing of the villa, there's a lodge in the woods they can have the use of for their honeymoon.'

Her jaw dropped, and her eyes suddenly filled with tears. 'That's ridiculously generous! Why would you do this for them?'

'Because if I hadn't distracted you on the steps, you wouldn't have fallen, and your sister would have had her wedding.'

'No! Massimo, it wasn't your fault! I don't need your guilt as well as my own! This is not your problem.'

'Nevertheless, you would have won if you hadn't fallen, and yet when I took you back to my home that night you just waded in and helped Carlotta, even though you were hurt and disappointed. You didn't need to do that, but you saw she was struggling, and you put your own worries and injuries out of

your mind and just quietly got on with it, even though you
were much more sore than you let on.'

'What makes you say that?'

He smiled tenderly. 'I saw the bruises, cara. All over your
body.'

She blushed furiously, stooping to pick the rag up off the
floor, but it was covered in dust and she put it down again.
The saddle was already soaped to death.

'And that dinner party—I know quite well that all of those
dishes were yours. Carlotta doesn't cook like that, and yet
you left an old woman her pride, and for that alone, I would
give you this wedding for your sister.'

The tears spilled down her cheeks, and she scrubbed them
away with the backs of her hands. Not a good idea, she realised instantly, when they were covered in soapy filth, but
he was there in front of her, a tissue in his hand, wiping the
tears away and the smears of dirt with them.

'Silly girl, there's no need to cry,' he tutted softly, and she
pushed his hand away.

'Well, of course I'm crying, you idiot!' she sniffed, swallowing the tears. 'You're being ridiculously generous. But I
can't possibly accept.'

'Why not? We need you—and that is real and genuine. I knew you'd refuse the wedding if I just offered it, but
we really need help with the harvest, and it's the only way
Carlotta will allow us to help her. If we do nothing, she'll
work herself to death, but she'll be devastated if we bring in
a total stranger to help out.'

'I was a total stranger,' she reminded him.

He gave that tender smile again, the one that had unrav-
elled her before. 'Yes—but now you're a friend, and I'm asking you, as a friend, to help her.'

She swallowed. 'And in return you'll give Jen this amazing wedding?'

'*Sì.*'

'And what about us?'

Something troubled flickered in his eyes for a second until the shutters came down. 'What about us?'

'We agreed it was just for one night.'

'Yes, we did. No strings. A little time out from reality.'

'And it stays that way?'

He inclined his head. '*Sì.* It stays that way. It has to.'

Did it? She felt—what? Regret? Relief? A curious mixture of both, probably, although if she was honest she might have been hoping...

'Can I think about it?'

'Not for long. I have to return first thing tomorrow morning. I would like to take you with me.'

She nodded. 'Right. Um. I need to finish this—what are you *doing*?'

He'd taken off his jacket, slung it over the back of the chair and was rolling up his sleeves. 'Helping,' he said, and taking a clean rag from the pile, he buffed the saddle to a lovely, soft sheen. 'There. What else?'

It took them half an hour to clean the rest of Bruno's tack, and then she led him back to the house and showed him where he could wash his hands in the scullery sink.

'Don't mention any of this to Jen, not until I've made up my mind,' she warned softly, and he nodded.

Her sister was in the kitchen, and she pointed her in the direction of the kettle and ran upstairs to shower. Ten minutes later, she was back down in the kitchen with her hair in soggy rats' tails and her face pink and shiny from the steam, but at least she was clean.

He glanced up at her and got to his feet with a smile. 'Better now?'

'Cleaner,' she said wryly. 'Is Jen looking after you?'

Jen was, she could see that. The teapot was on the table, and the packet of biscuits they'd been saving for visitors was largely demolished.

'She's been telling me all about you,' he said, making her panic, but Jen just grinned and helped herself to another biscuit.

'I've invited him to stay the night,' she said airily, dunking it in her tea while Lydia tried not to panic yet again.

'I haven't said yes,' he told her, his eyes laughing as he registered her reaction. 'There's a pub in the village with a sign saying they do rooms. I thought I might stay there.'

'You can't stay there. The pub's awful!' she said without thinking, and then could have kicked herself, because realistically there was nowhere else for miles.

She heard the door open, and the dogs came running in, tails wagging, straight up to him to check him out, and her mother was hard on their heels.

'Darling? Oh!'

She stopped in the doorway, searched his face as he straightened up from patting the dogs, and started to smile. 'Hello. I'm Maggie Fletcher, Lydia's mother, and I'm guessing from the number plate on your car you must be her Italian knight in shining armour.'

He laughed and held out his hand. 'Massimo Valtieri—but I'm not sure I'm any kind of a knight.'

'Well, you rescued my daughter, so I'm very grateful to you.'

'She hurt herself leaving my plane,' he pointed out, 'so really you should be throwing me out, not thanking me!'

'Well, I'll thank you anyway, for trying to get her there

in time to win the competition. I always said it was a crazy idea.'

'Me, too.' He smiled, and Lydia ground her teeth. The last thing she needed was him cosying up to her mother, but it got worse.

'I promised her some produce from the estate, and I thought, as I had a few days when I could get away, I'd deliver it in person. I'll bring it in, if I may?'

'Of course! How very kind of you.'

It wasn't kind. It was an excuse to bribe her into going back there to feed the troops by dangling a carrot in front of her that he knew perfectly well she'd be unable to resist. Two carrots, really, because as well as Jen's wedding, which was giving her the world's biggest guilt trip, there was the problem of the aging and devoted Carlotta, who'd become her friend.

'I'll help you,' she said hastily, following him out to the car so she could get him alone for a moment.

He was one step ahead of her, though, she realised, because as he popped the boot open, he turned to her, his face serious. 'Before you say anything, I'm not going to mention it to your family. This is entirely your decision, and if you decline, I won't say any more about it.'

Well, damn. He wasn't even going to *try* to talk her into it! Which, she thought with a surge of disappointment, could only mean that he really wasn't interested in picking up their relationship, and was going to leave it as it stood, as he'd said, with just that one night between them.

Not that she wanted him to do anything else. She really didn't want to get involved with another man, not after the hatchet job Russell had done on her self-esteem, and not when she was trying to resurrect her devastated career, but...

'Here. This is a case of our olive oils. There are three types, different varietals, and they're quite distinctive. Then this is a case of our wines—including a couple of bottles of vintage Brunello. You really need to save them for an important occasion, they're quite special. There's a nice *vinsanto* dessert wine in there, as well. And this is the *aceto balsamico* I promised you, from my cousin in Modena.'

While she was still standing there open-mouthed, he reached into a cool box and pulled out a leg of lamb and a whole Pecorino cheese.

'Something for your mother's larder,' he said with a smile, and without any warning she burst into tears.

'Hey,' he said softly, and wrapping his arms around her, he drew her up against his chest. He could feel the shudders running through her, and he cradled her against his heart and rocked her, shushing her gently. 'Lydia, please, *cara*, don't cry.'

'I'm not,' she lied, bunching her fists in his shirt and burrowing into his chest, and he chuckled and hugged her.

'I don't think that's quite true,' he murmured. 'Come on, it's just a few things.'

'It's nothing to do with the things,' she choked out. Her fist hit him squarely in the chest. 'I didn't think I'd ever see you again, and I was trying to move on, and then you just come back into my life and drop this bombshell on me about the wedding, and of all the times to choose, when I'm already...'

Realisation dawned, and he stroked her hair, gentling her. 'Oh, *cara*, I'm sorry. When did he die, the pony?'

She sniffed hard and tried to pull away, but he wouldn't let her, he just held her tight, and after a moment she went still, unyielding but resigned. 'Last week,' she said, her voice clogged with tears. 'We found him dead in the field.'

'And you haven't cried,' he said.

She gave up fighting and let her head rest against his chest. 'No. But he was old.'

'We lost our dog last year. She was very, very old, and she'd been getting steadily worse. After she died, I didn't cry for weeks, and then one day it suddenly hit me and I disintegrated. Luca said he thought it was to do with Angelina. Sometimes grief is like that. We can't acknowledge it for the things that really hurt, and then something else comes along, and it's safe then to let go, to let out the hurt that you can't face.'

She lifted her head and looked up at him through her tears. 'But I don't hurt.'

'Don't you? Even after Russell treated you the way he did? For God's sake, Lydia, he was supposed to be your lover, and yet when he'd crippled your sister, his only reaction was anger that you'd left him and his business was suffering! What kind of a man is that? Of course you're hurting.'

She stared at him, hearing her feelings put into words somehow making sense of them all at last. She eased away from him, needing a little space, her emotions settling now.

'You know I can't say no, don't you? To your proposition?'

His mouth quirked slightly and he nodded slowly and let her go. 'Yes. I do know, and I realise it's unfair to ask this of you, but—I need help for Carlotta, and you need the wedding. This way, we both win.'

Or lose, depending on whether or not he could keep his heart intact, seeing her every day, working alongside her, knowing she'd be just there in the room beside his office, taunting him even in her sleep.

She met his eyes, her own troubled. 'I don't want an affair. I can't do it. One night was dangerous enough. I'm not ready, and I don't want to hurt your children.'

He nodded. 'I know. And I agree. If I wanted an affair, it would be with a woman my children would never meet, someone they wouldn't lose their hearts to. But I would like to be your friend, Lydia. I don't know if that could work but I would like to try.'

No. It couldn't work. It was impossible, because she was already more than half in love with him, but—Jen needed her wedding, and she'd already had it snatched away from her once. This was another chance, equally as crazy, equally as dangerous, if not more so.

It was a chance she had to take.

'OK, I'll do it,' she said, without giving herself any further time to think, and his shoulders dropped slightly and he smiled.

'*Grazie, cara. Grazie mille.* And I know you aren't doing it for me, but for your sister and also for Carlotta, and for that, I thank you even more.'

He hugged her—just a gentle, affectionate hug between friends, or so he told himself as she slid her arms round him and hugged him back, but the feel of her in his arms, the soft pressure of her breasts, the smell of her shampoo and the warmth of her body against his all told him he was lying.

He was in this right up to his neck, and if he couldn't hold it together for the next two months—but he had to. There was no choice. Neither of them was ready for this.

He let her go, stepped back and dumped the lamb and the cheese in her arms. 'Let's go back in.'

'Talk to me about your dream wedding,' he said to Jen, after they'd taken all the things in from the car.

Her smile tugged his heartstrings. 'I don't dream about my wedding. The last time I did that, it turned into a nightmare for Lydia, so I'm keeping my feet firmly on the ground from now on, and we're going to do something very simple and quiet from here, and it'll be fine.'

'What if I was to offer you the *palazzo* as a venue?' he suggested, and Jen's jaw dropped.

'What?' she said, and then shook her head. 'I'm sorry, I don't understand.'

'The same deal as the hotel.'

She stared, looking from Lydia to Massimo and back again, and shook her head once more. 'I don't...'

'They need me,' Lydia explained. 'Carlotta's not well, and if I cook for the harvest season, you can have your wedding. I don't have another job yet, and it's good experience and an interesting place to work, so I thought it might be a good idea.'

'I've brought a DVD of my brother's wedding so you can see the setting. It might help you to decide.'

He handed it to her, and she handed it straight back.

'There's a catch,' she said, her voice strained. 'Lydia?'

'No catch. I work, you get the wedding.'

'But—that's so generous!'

'Nonsense. We'd have to pay a caterer to do the job, and it would cost easily as much.'

'But—Lydia, what about you? You were looking for another job, and you were talking about setting up an outside catering business. How can you do that if you're out of the country? No, I can't let you do it!'

'Tough, kid,' she said firmly, squashing her tears again. Heavens, she never cried, and this man was turning her into a fountain! 'I'm not doing it just for you, anyway. This is a job—a real job, believe me. And you know what I'm like. I'd love to know more about Italian food—real, proper country food—and this is my chance, so don't go getting all soppy on me, all right? My catering business will keep. Just say thank you and shut up.'

'Thank you and shut up,' she said meekly, and then burst into tears.

Lydia cooked the leg of lamb for supper and served it with rosemary roast potatoes and a redcurrant *jus*, and carrots and runner beans from the garden, and they all sat round at the battered old kitchen table with the dogs at their feet and opened one of the bottles of Brunello.

'It seems wrong, drinking it in here,' she said apologetically, 'but Andy's doing the accounts on the dining table at the moment and it's swamped.'

'It's not about the room, it's about the flavour. Just try it,' he said, watching her closely.

So she swirled it, sniffed it, rolled it round on her tongue and gave a glorious sigh. 'That is *the* most gorgeous wine I have ever tasted,' she told him, and he inclined his head and smiled.

'Thank you. We're very proud of it, and it's a perfect complement to the lamb. It's beautifully cooked. Well done.'

'Thank you. Thank you for trusting me with it.' She smiled back, suddenly ridiculously happy, and then the men started to talk about farming, and Jen quizzed her about the *palazzo*, because she'd hardly said anything about it since she'd come home.

'It sounds amazing,' Jen said, wide-eyed. 'We'll have to look at that video.'

'You will. It's great. The frescoes are incredible, and the view is to die for, especially at night, when all you can see is the twinkling lights in the distance. It's just gorgeous, and really peaceful. I know it'll sound ridiculous, but it reminded me of home, in a way.'

'I don't think that's ridiculous,' Massimo said, cutting in with a smile. 'It's a home, that's all, just in a beautiful setting, and that's what you have here—a warm and loving family home in a peaceful setting. I'm flattered that you felt like that about mine.'

The conversation drifted on, with him telling them more about the farm, about the harvest and the soil and the weather patterns, and she could have sat there for hours just listening to his voice, but she had so much to do before they left in the morning, not least gathering together her clothes, so she left them all talking and went up to her room.

Bearing in mind she'd be flying back after the harvest was over, she tried to be sensible about the amount she took, but she'd need winter clothes as well as lighter garments, and walking boots so she could explore the countryside, and something respectable in case he sprang another dinner on her—

'You look lost.'

She looked up from her suitcase and sighed. 'I don't know what to take.'

'Your passport?'

'Got that,' she said, waggling it at him with a smile. 'It's clothes. I want enough, but not too much. I don't know what the weather will be like.'

'It can get cold. Bring warm things for later, but don't worry. You can buy anything you don't have.'

'I'm trying to stick to a sensible baggage allowance for when I come back.'

'Don't bother. I'll pay the excess. Just bring what you need.'

'What time are we leaving?'

'Seven.'

'Seven?' she squeaked, and he laughed.

'That's a concession. I would have left at five, or maybe six.'

'I'll be ready whenever you tell me. Have you been shown to your room?'

'*Sì*. And the bathroom is opposite?'

'Yes. I'm sorry it doesn't have an *en suite* bathroom—'

'Lydia, stop apologising for your home,' he said gently. 'I'm perfectly capable of crossing a corridor. I'll see you at six for breakfast, OK?'

'OK,' she said, and for a heartbeat she wondered if he'd kiss her goodnight.

He didn't, and she spent a good half-hour trying to convince herself she was glad.

They set off in the morning shortly before seven, leaving Jen and Andy still slightly stunned and busy planning their wedding, and she settled back in the soft leather seat and wondered if she'd completely lost her mind.

'Which way are we going?' she asked as they headed down to Kent.

'The quickest route—northern France, across the Alps in Switzerland, past Lake Como and onto the A1 to Siena. We'll stay somewhere on the way. I don't want to drive through the Alps when I'm tired, the mountain roads can be a little tricky.'

Her heart thudded. They were staying somewhere overnight?

Well, of course they were, he couldn't possibly drive whatever distance it was from Suffolk to Tuscany in one day, but somehow she hadn't factored an overnight stop into her calculations, and the journey, which until now had seemed simple and straightforward, suddenly seemed fraught with the danger of derailing their best intentions.

CHAPTER SEVEN

'LYDIA?'

She stirred, opened her eyes and blinked.

He'd pulled up in what looked like a motorway service area, and it was dark beyond the floodlit car park. She yawned hugely and wrapped her hand around the back of her neck, rolling her head to straighten out the kinks.

'Oh, ow. What time is it? I feel as if I've been asleep for hours!'

He gave her a wry, weary smile. 'You have. It's after nine, and I need to stop for the night before I join you and we have an accident.'

'Where are we?'

'A few miles into Switzerland? We're getting into the mountains and this place has rooms. It's a bit like factory farming, but it's clean and the beds are decent. I'd like to stop here if they have any vacancies.'

'And if they don't?'

He shrugged. 'We go on.'

But he must be exhausted. They'd only stopped twice, the last time at two for a late lunch. What if they only have one room? she thought, and her heart started to pound. How strong was her resolve? How strong was his?

She never found out. They had plenty of space, so he

booked two rooms and carried her suitcase for her and put it down at the door. 'We should eat fairly soon, but I thought you might want to freshen up. Ten minutes?'

'Ten minutes is fine,' she said, and let herself into her lonely, barren motel room. It was clean and functional as he'd promised, just another generic hotel room like all the rest, and she wished that for once in her life she had the courage to go after the thing she really wanted.

Assuming the thing—the person—really wanted her, of course, and he'd made it clear he didn't.

She stared at herself in the bathroom mirror. What was she *thinking* about? She didn't want him! She wasn't ready for another relationship. Not really, not if she was being sensible. She wanted to get her career back on track, to refocus her life and remember where she was going and what she was doing. She certainly didn't need to get her heart broken by a sad and lonely workaholic ten years her senior, with three motherless children and a massively demanding business empire devouring all his time.

Even if he was the most fascinating and attractive man she'd ever met in her life, and one of the kindest and most thoughtful. He was hurting, too, still grieving for his wife, and in no way ready to commit to another relationship, no matter how deeply she might fall in love with him. He wouldn't hurt her intentionally, but letting herself get close to him— that was a recipe for disaster if nothing else was.

'Lydia?'

There was a knock at the bedroom door, and she turned off the bathroom light and opened it. Massimo was standing there in the corridor, in a fresh shirt and trousers, his hair still damp from the shower. He looked incredible.

'Are you ready for dinner?'

She conjured up a smile. 'Give me ten seconds.'

She picked up her bag, gave her lips a quick swipe of translucent colour as a concession to vanity and dragged a comb through her hair. And then, just out of defiance, she added a spritz of scent.

She might be travel weary, and she might not be about to get involved with him, but she still had her pride.

The dinner was adequate. Nothing more, nothing less.

He was tired, she was tired—and yet still they lingered, talking for an hour over their coffee. She asked about Isabelle and Luca's baby, and how the children were, and he asked her about Jen's progress and if she'd be off the crutches by the time of the wedding, whenever it would be.

They talked about his time at boarding school, and she told him about her own schooling, in a village just four miles from where she lived.

And then finally they both fell silent, and he looked at his watch in disbelief.

'It's late and tomorrow will be a hard drive,' he said. 'We should go to bed.'

The word *bed* reverberated in the air between them, and then she placed her napkin on the table and stood up a little abruptly. 'You're right. I'm sorry, you should have told me to shut up.'

He should. He should have cut it short and gone to bed, instead of sitting up with her and hanging on her every word. He paid the bill and escorted her back to her room, leaving a clear gap between them as he paused at her door.

Not because he wanted to, but because he didn't, and if he got any closer, he didn't trust himself to end it there.

'Buonanotte, bella,' he said softly. 'I'll wake you at five thirty.'

She nodded, and without looking back at him, she opened

the door of her room, went in and closed it behind her. He stared at it for a second, gave a quiet, resigned laugh and let himself into his own room.

This was what he'd wanted, wasn't it? For her to keep her distance, to enable him to do the same?

So why did he suddenly feel so lonely?

It was like coming home.

This time, when she saw the fortress-like building standing proudly on the hilltop, she felt excitement and not trepidation, and when the children came tumbling down the steps to greet them, there was no look of horror, but shrieks of delight and hugs all round.

Antonino just wanted his father, but Francesca hugged her, and Lavinia hung on her arm and grinned wildly. 'Lydia!' she said, again and again, and then Carlotta appeared at the top of the steps and welcomed her—literally—with open arms.

'*Signorina!* You come back! Oh!'

She found herself engulfed in a warm and emotional hug, and when Carlotta let her go, her eyes were brimming. She blotted them, laughing at herself, and then taking Lydia by the hand, she led her through the courtyard to her old room.

This time there were flowers on the chest of drawers, and Roberto brought in her luggage and put it down and hugged her, too.

'*Grazie mille, signorina,*' he said, his voice choked. 'Thank you for coming back to help us.'

'Oh, Roberto, it's my pleasure. There's so much Carlotta can teach me, and I'm really looking forward to learning.'

'I teach,' she said, patting her hand. 'I teach you everything!'

She doubted it. Carlotta's knowledge of traditional dishes was a rich broth of inheritance, and it would take more than a few experiments to capture it, but it would still be fascinating.

They left her to settle in, and a moment later there was a tap at the French doors.

'The children and I are going for a swim. Want to join us?'

She was so tempted. It was still warm here, much warmer than in England, although she knew the temperature would drop once it was dark. The water in the pool would be warm and inviting, though, and it would be fun playing with the children, but she felt a shiver of danger, and not just from him.

'I don't think so. I'm a bit tired. I might rest for a little while.'

He nodded, smiled briefly and walked away, and she closed the door and shut the curtains, just to make the point.

The children were delightful, but they weren't why she was here, and neither was he. And the more often she reminded herself of that, the better, because she was in serious danger of forgetting.

She didn't have time to think about it.

The harvest season was in full swing, and from first thing the following morning, she was busy. Carlotta still tried to do too much, but she just smiled and told her she was allowed to give orders and that was all, and after the first two days she seemed happy to do that.

She even started taking a siesta in the middle of the day, which gave Lydia time to make a lot of the preparations for the evening without prodding Carlotta's conscience.

And every evening, she dished up the food to the workers and joined them for their meal.

They seemed pleased to see her, and there was a bit of flirting and whistling and nudging, but she could deal with that. And then Massimo appeared at her side, and she heard a ripple of laughter and someone said something she'd heard a few times before when he was about. She'd also heard him say it to Francesca on occasions.

'What does *bella ragazza* mean?' she asked in a quiet moment as they were finishing their food, and he gave a slightly embarrassed laugh.

'Beautiful girl.'

She studied his face closely, unconvinced. 'Are you sure? Because they only say it when you're near me.'

He pulled a face. 'OK. It's usually used for a girlfriend.'

'They think I'm your *girlfriend*?' she squeaked, and he cleared his throat and pushed the food around his plate.

'Ignore them. They're just teasing us.'

Were they? Or could they see the pull between them? Because ignore it as hard as she liked, it wasn't going away, and it was getting stronger with every day that passed.

A few days later, while she was taking a breather out on the terrace before lunch, Isabelle appeared. She was pushing a pram, and she had a little girl in tow.

'Lydia, hi. I was hoping to find you. Mind if we join you?'

She stood up, pleased to see her again, and hugged her. 'Of course I don't mind. Congratulations! May I see?'

'Sure.'

She peered into the pram, and sighed. 'Oh, he's gorgeous. So, so gorgeous! All that dark hair!'

'Oh, yes, he's his daddy's boy. Sometimes I wonder where my genes went in all of this.' She laughed, and Lydia smiled and reached out to touch the sleeping baby's outstretched hand.

It clenched reflexively, closing on her fingertip, and she gave a soft sigh and swallowed hard.

He looked just like the picture of Antonino with his mother in the photo frame in the kitchen. Strong genes, indeed, she thought, and felt a sudden, shocking pang low down in her abdomen, a need so strong it was almost visceral.

She eased her finger away and straightened up. 'Can I get you a drink? And what about your little girl?'

'Annamaria, do you want a drink, darling?'

'Juice!'

'Please.'

'P'ees.'

'Good girl. I'd love a coffee, if you've got time? And anything juice-related with a big slosh of water would be great. We've got a feeder cup.'

They went into the kitchen, and she found some biscuits and took them out into the sun again with the drinks, and sat on the terrace under the pergola, shaded by the jasmine.

'Are you completely better now, after your fall?' Isabelle asked her, and she laughed and brushed it aside.

'I'm fine. My ankle was the worst thing, really, but it's much better now. It still twinges if I'm careless, but it's OK. How about you? Heavens, you've had a baby, that's much worse!'

Isabelle laughed and shook her head. 'No. It was harder than when Annamaria was born, but really very straightforward, and you know Luca's an obstetrician?'

'Yes, I think so. I believe Massimo mentioned it. I know he's a doctor, he met us at the hospital when I had the fall and translated everything for me. So did he deliver him? What's he called, by the way?'

'Maximus—Max for short, after his uncle. Maximus and Massimo both mean the greatest, and my little Max was huge, so he really earned it. And yes, Luca did help deliver him, but at home with a midwife. Not like last time. He nearly missed

Annamaria's birth, and I was at home on my own, so this time he kept a very close eye on me!'

'I'll bet. Wow. You're very brave having them at home.'

'No, I just have confidence in the process. I'm a midwife.'

'Is that how you met?'

She laughed. 'No. We met in Florence, in a café. We ended up together by a fluke, really.' She tipped her head on one side. 'So what's the story with you and Massimo?'

She felt herself colour and pretended to rearrange the biscuits. 'Oh, nothing, really. There is no story. He gave me a lift, I had an accident, he rescued me, and now I'm doing Carlotta's job so she doesn't kill herself.'

Isabelle didn't look convinced, but there was no way Lydia was going into details about her ridiculous crush or their one-night stand! But Luca's wife wasn't so easily put off. She let the subject drop for a moment, but only long enough to lift the now-crying baby from the pram and cradle him in her arms as she fed him.

Spellbound, Lydia watched the baby's tiny rosebud mouth fasten on his mother's nipple, saw the look of utter contentment on Isabelle's face, and felt a well of longing fill her chest.

'He's a good man, you know. A really decent guy. He'd be worth the emotional investment, but only if you're serious. I'd hate to see him hurt.'

'He won't get hurt. We're not getting involved,' she said firmly. 'Yes, there's something there, but neither of us want it.'

Isabelle's eyes were searching, and Lydia felt as if she could see straight through her lies.

Lies? Were they?

Oh, yes. Because she did want it, even though it was crazy, even though she'd get horribly badly hurt. And she'd thought

Russell had hurt her? He didn't even come close to what Massimo could do if she let him into her heart.

'He's not interested in an emotional investment,' she said, just in case there was any misunderstanding, but Isabelle just raised a brow slightly and smiled.

'No. He doesn't *think* he is, but actually he's ready to love again. He just hasn't realised it.'

'No, he isn't. We've talked about it—'

'Men don't talk. Not really. It's like pulling teeth. He's telling you what he thinks he ought to feel, not what he feels.'

She glanced up, at the same time as Lydia heard crunching on the gravel.

'Talk of the devil, here they are,' Isabelle said, smiling at her husband and his brother, and not wanting to get involved any deeper in this conversation, Lydia excused herself and went back to the kitchen.

Seconds later Massimo was in there behind her. 'I've come to tell you we've almost finished. The last of the vines are being stripped now and everyone's having the afternoon off.'

'So no lunch?'

He raised an eyebrow. 'I don't think you'll get away with that, but no evening meal, certainly. Not today. And tomorrow we're moving on to the chestnut woods. So tonight I'm taking you out for dinner, to thank you.'

'You don't need to do that. You're paying for my sister's wedding. That's thanks enough.'

He brushed it aside with a flick of his hand, and smiled. 'Humour me. I want to take you out to dinner. There's a place we eat from time to time—fantastic food, Toscana on a fork. The chef is Carlotta's great-nephew. I think you'll find it interesting. Our table's booked for eight.'

'What if I want an early night?'

'Do you?'

She gave in and smiled. 'No, not really. It sounds amazing. What's the dress code?'

'Clean. Nothing more. It's where the locals eat.'

'Your mother's a local,' she said drily, and he chuckled.

'My mother always dresses for the occasion. I'll wear jeans and a jacket, no tie. Does that help?'

She smiled. 'It does. Thank you. Help yourselves to coffee, I need to get on with lunch.'

Jeans and a jacket, no tie.

So what did that mean for her? Jeans? Best jeans with beaded embroidery on the back pockets and a pretty top?

Black trousers and a slinky top with a cardi over it?

A dress? How about a long skirt?

Clean. That was his first stipulation, so she decided to go with what was comfortable. And by eight, it would be cool, and they'd be coming back at about eleven, so definitely cooler.

Or maybe...

She'd just put the finishing touches to her makeup, not too much, just enough to make her feel she'd made the effort, when there was a tap on her door.

'Lydia? I'm ready to go when you are.'

She opened the door and scanned him. Jeans—good jeans, expensive jeans, with expensive Italian leather loafers and a handmade shirt, the leather jacket flung casually over his shoulder hanging from one finger.

He looked good enough to eat, and way up the scale of clean, so she was glad she'd changed her mind at the last minute and gone for her one decent dress. It wasn't expensive, but it hung like a dream to the asymmetric hem and made her feel amazing, and from the way he was scanning her, he wasn't disappointed.

'Will I do?' she asked, twirling slowly, and he said nothing for a second and then gave a soft huff of laughter.

'Oh, yes. I think so.'

His eyes were still trailing over her, lingering on the soft swell of her breasts, the curve of her hip, the hint of a thigh—

He pulled himself together and jerked his eyes back up to meet hers. 'You look lovely,' he said, trying not to embarrass himself or her. 'Are you ready to go?'

'I just need a wrap for later.' She picked up a pretty pashmina the same colour as her eyes, and her bag, and shut the door behind her. 'Right, then. Let's go get Toscana on a fork!'

It was a simple little building on one side of a square in the nearby town.

From the outside it looked utterly unpretentious, and it was no different inside. Scrubbed tables, plain wooden chairs, simple décor. But the smell was amazing, and the place was packed.

'Massimo, *ciao*!'

He shook hands with a couple on the way in, introduced her as a friend from England, and ushered her past them to the table he'd reserved by the window.

'Is it always this busy?'

His lips twitched in a smile. 'No. Sometimes it's full.'

She looked around and laughed. 'And these are all locals?'

'Mostly. Some will be tourists, people who've bothered to ask where they should eat.'

She looked around again. 'Is there a menu?'

'No. He writes it on a board—it's up there. Tonight it's a casserole of wild boar with plums in a red wine reduction.'

'And that's it?'

'No. He cooks a few things every night—you can choose

from the board, but the first thing up is always his dish of the day, and it's always worth having.'

She nodded. 'Sounds great.'

He ordered a half-carafe of house wine to go with it—again, the wine was always chosen to go with the meal and so was the one to go for, he explained—and then they settled back to wait.

'So—are you pleased with the harvest?' she asked to fill the silence, and he nodded.

'*Sì*. The grapes have been exceptional this year, it should be an excellent vintage. We need that. Last year was not so good, but the olives were better, so we made up for it.'

'And how are the olives this year?'

'Good so far. It depends on the weather. We need a long, mild autumn to let them swell and ripen before the first frosts. We need to harvest early enough to get the sharp tang from the olives, but not so early that it's bitter, or so late that it's sweet and just like any other olive oil.'

She smiled. 'That's farming for you. Juggling the weather all the time.'

'*Sì*. It can be a disaster or a triumph, and you never know. We're big enough to weather it, so we're fortunate.'

'We're not. We had a dreadful year about three years ago, and I thought we'd go under, but then the next year we had bumper crops. It's living on a knife edge that's so hard.'

'Always. Always the knife edge.'

Her eyes met his, and the smile that was hovering there was driven out by an intensity that stole her breath away. 'You look beautiful tonight, *cara*,' he said softly, reaching out to touch her hand where it lay on the table top beside her glass.

She withdrew it, met his eyes again warily. 'I thought we weren't going to do this?'

'We're not doing anything. It was a simple compliment. I would say the same to my sister.'

'No, you wouldn't. Not like that.' She picked up her glass of water and drained the last inch, her mouth suddenly dry. 'At least, I hope not.'

His mouth flicked up briefly at the corners. 'Perhaps not quite like that.'

He leant back as the waiter appeared, setting down bread and olive oil and balsamic vinegar, and she tore off a piece of bread and dunked it, then frowned thoughtfully as the taste exploded on her tongue. 'Is this yours?'

He smiled. 'Yes. And the *balsamico* is from my cousin.'

'And the wild boar?'

'I have no idea. If it's from our estate, I don't know about it. The hunting season doesn't start until November.'

She smiled, and the tension eased a little, but it was still there, simmering under the surface, the compliment hovering at the fringes of her consciousness the whole evening. It didn't spoil the meal. Rather, it heightened the sensations of taste and smell and texture, as if somehow his words had brought her alive again and set her free.

'This casserole is amazing,' she said after the first mouthful. 'I want the recipe.'

He laughed at that. 'He won't give it to you. Women offer to sleep with him, but he never reveals his secrets.'

'Does he sleep with them anyway?'

He chuckled again. 'I doubt it. His wife would skin him alive.'

'Good for her. She needs to keep him. He's a treasure. And I've never been that desperate for a recipe.'

'I'm glad to hear it.' He was. He didn't even want to think about her sleeping with anybody else, even if she wasn't sleeping with him. And she wasn't.

She really, really wasn't. He wasn't going to do that again, it was emotional suicide. It had taken him over a week before he could sleep without waking aroused and frustrated in a tangle of sheets, aching for her.

He returned his attention to the casserole, mopping up the last of the sauce with a piece of bread until finally the plate was clean and he had no choice but to sit back and look up and meet her eyes.

'That was amazing,' she said. 'Thank you so much.'

'Dessert?'

She laughed a little weakly. 'I couldn't fit it in. Coffee, though—I could manage coffee.'

He ordered coffee, and they lingered over it, almost as if they daren't leave the safety of the little *trattoria* for fear of what they might do. But then they ran out of words, out of stalling tactics, and their eyes met and held.

'Shall we go?'

She nodded, getting to her feet even though she knew what was going to happen, knew how dangerous it was to her to leave with him and go back to her room—because they would end up there, she was sure of it, just as they had before, and all their good intentions would fall at the first hurdle...

CHAPTER EIGHT

THEY didn't speak on the way back to the *palazzo*.

She sat beside him, her heart in her mouth, the air between them so thick with tension she could scarcely breathe. They didn't touch. All the way to her bedroom door, there was a space between them, as if they realised that the slightest contact would be all it took to send them up in flames.

Even when he shut the door behind them, they still hesitated, their eyes locked. And then he closed his eyes and murmured something in Italian. It could have been a prayer, or a curse, or just a 'what the hell am I doing?'

She could understand that. She was doing it herself, but she was beyond altering the course of events. She'd been beyond it, she realised, the moment he'd walked into the tack room at home and smiled at her.

He opened his eyes again, and there was resignation in them, and a longing that made her want to weep. He lifted his hand and touched her cheek, just lightly, but it was enough.

She turned her face into his hand, pressing her lips to his palm, and with a ragged groan he reeled her in, his mouth finding hers in a kiss that should have felt savage but was oddly tender for all its desperation.

His jacket hit the floor, then his shirt, stripped off over his head, and he spun her round, searching for the zip on her dress and following its progress with his lips, scorching a trail of fire down her spine. It fell away, and he unclipped her bra and turned her back to face him, easing it away and sighing softly as he lowered his head to her breasts.

She felt the rasp of his stubble against the sensitised skin, the heat of his mouth closing over one nipple, then the cold as he blew lightly against the dampened flesh.

She clung to his shoulders, her legs buckling, and he scooped her up and dropped her in the middle of the bed, stripping off the rest of his clothes before coming down beside her, skin to skin, heart to heart.

There was no foreplay. She would have died if he'd made her wait another second for him. Incoherent with need, she reached for him, and he was there, his eyes locking with hers as he claimed her with one long, slow thrust.

His head fell against hers, his eyes fluttering closed, a deep groan echoing in her ear. Her hands were on him, sliding down his back, feeling the powerful muscles bunching with restraint, the taut buttocks, the solid thighs bracing him as he thrust into her, his restraint gone now, the desperation overwhelming them, driving them both over the edge into frenzy.

She heard a muffled groan, felt his lips against her throat, his skin like hot, wet silk under her hands as his hard body shuddered against hers. For a long time he didn't move, but then, his chest heaving, he lifted his head to stare down into her eyes.

'Oh, *cara*,' he murmured roughly, and then gathering her against his heart he rolled to his side and collapsed against the pillows, and they lay there, limbs entangled, her head on his chest, and waited for the shockwaves to die away.

* * *

'I thought we weren't going to do that.'

He glanced down at her, and his eyes were filled with regret and despair. 'It looks like we were both wrong.'

His eyes closed, as if he couldn't bear to look at her, and easing away from her embrace he rolled away and sat up on the edge of the bed, elbows braced on his knees, dropping his head into his hands for a moment. Then he raked his fingers through his hair and stood up, pulling on his clothes.

'I have to check the children,' he said gruffly.

'We need to talk.'

'Yes, but not now. Please, *cara*. Not now.'

He couldn't talk to her now. He had to get out of there, before he did something stupid like make love to her again.

Make love? Who was he kidding? He'd slaked himself on her, with no finesse, no delicacy, no patience. And he'd promised her—promised himself, but promised *her*—that this wouldn't happen again.

Shaking his head in disgust, he pushed his feet into his shoes, slung his jacket over his shoulder and then steeled himself to look at her.

She was still lying there, curled on her side on top of the tangled bedding, her eyes wide with hurt and confusion.

'Massimo?'

'Later. Tomorrow, perhaps. I have to go. If Antonino wakes—'

She nodded, her eyes closing softly as she bit her lip. Holding back the tears?

He was despicable. All he ever did was make this woman cry.

He let himself out without another word, and went through to his part of the house, up the stairs to the children to check that they were all in bed and sleeping peacefully.

They were. Antonino had kicked off the covers, and he

eased them back over his son and dropped a kiss lightly on his forehead. He mumbled in his sleep and rolled over, and he went out, leaving the door open, and checked the girls.

They were both asleep, Francesca's door closed, Lavinia's open and her nightlight on.

He closed the landing door that led to his parents' quarters, as he always did when he was in the house, and then he made his way back down to the kitchen and poured himself a glass of wine.

Why? Why on earth had he been so stupid? After all his lectures to himself, how could he have been so foolish, so weak, so self-centred?

He'd have to talk to her, he realised, but he had no idea what he would say. He'd promised her—promised! And yet again he'd failed.

He propped his elbows on the table and rested his face in his hands. Of all the idiotic things—

'Massimo?'

Her voice stroked him like a lover's touch, and he lifted his head and met her eyes.

'What are you doing here?' he asked, his voice rough.

'I came to get a drink,' she said uncertainly.

He shrugged. 'Go ahead, get it.'

She stayed there, her eyes searching his face. 'Oh, Massimo, don't beat yourself up. We were deluded if we thought this wouldn't happen. It was so obvious it was going to and I can't believe we didn't realise. What we need to work out is what happens now.'

He gave a short, despairing laugh and pushed back his chair. 'Nothing, but I have no idea how to achieve that. All I know that whenever I'm with you, I want you, and I can't just have what I want. I'm not a tiny child, I understand the word no, I just can't seem to use it to myself. Wine?'

She shook her head. 'Tea. I'll make it.'

He watched her as she took out a mug from the cupboard, put a teabag in it, poured on boiling water, her movements automatic. She was wearing a silky, figure-hugging dressing gown belted round her waist, and he'd bet his life she had those tiny little pyjamas on underneath.

'Just tell me this,' she said at last, turning to face him. 'Is there any reason why we can't have an affair? Just—discreetly?'

'Here? In this house? Are you crazy? I have children here and they have enough to contend with without waking in the night from a bad dream and finding I'm not here because I'm doing something stupid and irresponsible for my own gratification.'

She sat down opposite him, cradling the tea in her hands and ignoring his stream of self-hatred. 'So what do you normally do?'

Normally? *Normally?* he thought.

'Normally, I don't have affairs,' he said flatly. 'I suppose if I did, it would be elsewhere.' He shrugged. 'Arranged meetings—afternoon liaisons when the children are at school, lunchtimes, coffee.'

'And does it work?'

He laughed a little desperately. 'I have no idea. I've never tried.'

She stared at him in astonishment. 'What? In five years, you've never had an affair?'

'Not what you could call an affair, no. I've had the odd liaison, but nothing you could in any way call a relationship.' He sighed shortly, swirled his wine, put it down again.

'You have to see it from my point of view. I have obligations, responsibilities. I would have to be very, very circumspect in any relationship with a woman.'

'Because of the children.'

'Mostly, but because of all sorts of things. Because of my duties and responsibilities, the position I hold within the family, the business—any woman I was to become involved with would have to meet a very stringent set of criteria.'

'Not money-grabbing, not lying, not cheating, not looking for a meal ticket or an easy family or status in the community.'

'Exactly. And it's more trouble than it's worth. I don't need it. I can live without the hassle. But it's more than that. If I make a mistake, many people could suffer. And besides, I don't have the time to invest in a relationship, not to do it justice. And nor do you, not if you're going to reinvent yourself and relaunch your career.'

He'd be worth the emotional investment, but only if you're serious.

Oh, Isabelle, you're so right, she thought. But was she serious? Serious enough? Could she afford to dedicate the emotional energy needed, to a man who was so clearly focused on his family life and business that women weren't considered necessary?

If she felt she stood the slightest chance, then yes, she realised, she could be very, very serious indeed about this man. But he wasn't ever going to be serious about her. Not serious enough to let her into all parts of his life, and there was no way she'd pass his stringent criteria test.

No job, for a start. No independent wealth—no wealth of any sort. And besides, he was right, she needed to get her career back on track. It had been going so well...

'So what happens now? We can't have an affair here, because of the children, and yet we can't seem to stick to that. So what do we do? Because doing nothing doesn't seem to work for us, Massimo. We need a plan.'

He gave a wry laugh and met her eyes again, his deadly serious. 'I have no idea, *cara*. I just know I can't be around you.'

'So we avoid each other?'

'We're both busy. It shouldn't be so hard.'

They were busy, he was right, but she felt a pang of loss even though she knew it made sense.

'OK. I'll keep out of your way if you keep out of mine.'

He inclined his head, then looked up as she got to her feet.

'You haven't finished your tea.'

'I'll take it with me,' she said, and left him sitting there wondering why he felt as if he'd just lost the most precious thing in the world, and yet didn't quite know what it was.

Nice theory, she thought later, when her emotions had returned to a more even keel. It just didn't have a hope of working in practice.

How could they possibly avoid each other in such an intimate setting?

Answer—they couldn't. He was in and out of the kitchen all the time with the children, and she was in and out of his workspace twice a day at least with food for the team of workers.

They were gathering chestnuts this week, in the *castagneti*, the chestnut woods on the higher slopes at the southern end of the estate. Carlotta told her all about it, showed her the book of chestnut recipes she'd gathered, many handed down from her mother or her grandmother, and she wanted to experiment.

So she asked Massimo one lunchtime if she could have some for cooking.

'Sure,' he said briskly. 'Help yourself. Someone will give you a basket.'

She shouldn't have been hurt. It was silly. She knew why he was doing it, why he hadn't met her eyes for more than a fleeting second, because in that fleeting second she'd seen something in his eyes that she recognised.

A curious mixture of pain and longing, held firmly in check.

She knew all about that.

She gathered her own chestnuts, joining the workforce and taking good-natured and teasing advice, most of which she didn't understand, because her Italian lessons with Francesca hadn't got that far yet—and in any case, she was very conscious of not getting too close to his children, for fear of them forming an attachment to her that would only hurt them when she went home again, so she hadn't encouraged it.

But she understood the gist. Sign language was pretty universal, and she learned how to split open the cases without hurting her fingers and remove the chestnuts—huge chestnuts, *marrone*, apparently—and that night after she'd given them all their evening meal, she went into the kitchen to experiment.

And he was there, sitting at the kitchen table with a laptop and a glass of wine.

'Oh,' she said, and stood there stupidly for a moment.

'Problem?'

'I was going to try cooking some of the chestnuts.'

His eyes met hers, and he shut the laptop and stood up. 'It's fine. I'll get out of your way.'

She looked guarded, he thought, her sunny smile and open friendliness wiped away by his lack of control and this overwhelming need that stalked him hour by hour. It saddened him. Greatly.

'You don't have to go.'

'I do,' he said wearily. 'I can't be around you, *cara*. It's too difficult. I thought I could do this, but I can't. The only way is to keep my distance.'

'But you can't. We're falling over each other all the time.'

'There's no choice.'

There was, she thought. They could just go with the flow, make sure they were discreet, keep it under control, but he didn't seem to think they could do that successfully, and he'd left the kitchen anyway.

She sat down at the table, in the same chair, feeling the warmth from his body lingering in the wood, and opened Carlotta's recipe book. Pointless. It was in Italian, and she didn't understand a word.

Frustration getting the better of her, she dropped her head into her hands and growled softly.

'Lydia, don't.'

'Don't what? I thought you'd gone,' she said, lifting her head.

'I had.' He sat down opposite her and took her hand in his, the contact curiously disturbing and yet soothing all at once.

'This is driving me crazy,' he admitted softly.

'Me, too. There must be another way. We can't avoid each other successfully, so why don't we just work alongside each other and take what comes? We know it's not long-term, we know you're not looking for commitment and I'm not ready to risk it again, and I have to go back and try and relaunch my career in some direction.'

He let go of her hand and sat back. 'Any ideas for that?' he said, not running away again as she'd expected, but staying to have a sensible conversation, and she let herself relax and began to talk, outlining her plans, such as they were.

'I've been thinking more and more about outside catering, using produce from my parents' farm. There are plenty of people with money living in the nearby villages, lots of second homes with people coming up for the weekend and bringing friends. I'm sure there would be openings, I just have to be there to find them.'

'It could be a bit seasonal.'

'Probably. Easter, summer and winter—well, Christmas and New Year, mostly. There's always lots of demand around Christmas, and I need to be back by then. Will the olive harvest be over?'

'Almost certainly. If it's not, we can manage if you need to return.' He stood up and put the kettle on. 'I was thinking we should invite your sister and her fiancé over to meet Anita so she can start the ball rolling.'

'Anita?'

'*Sì*. They'll need a wedding planner.'

'They can't afford a wedding planner!'

'It's part of the package. I'm not planning it, I simply don't have the time or the expertise, and Jen can't plan a wedding in a strange place from a distance of two thousand kilometres, so we need Anita.'

'I could do it. I'm here.'

'But do you have the necessary local contacts? No. And besides, you're already busy.'

'Can I do the catering?'

He smiled tolerantly. 'Really? Wouldn't you rather enjoy your sister's wedding?'

'No. I'd rather cut down the cost of it to you. I feel guilty enough—'

'Don't feel guilty.'

'But I do. I know quite well what cooks get paid, and it doesn't stack up to the cost of a wedding in just three months!'

He smiled again. 'We pay our staff well.'

She snorted rudely, and found a mug of tea put down in front of her.

'Don't argue with me, *cara*,' he said quietly. 'Just ask your sister when she could come over, and arrange the flights and check that Anita is free to see them.'

'Only if you'll let me do the catering.'

He rolled his eyes and laughed softly. 'OK, you can do the catering, but Anita will give you menu options.'

'No. I want to do the menus.'

'Why are you so stubborn?'

'Because it's my job!'

'To be stubborn?'

'To plan menus. And don't be obtuse.'

His mouth twitched and he sat down opposite her again, swirling his wine in the glass. 'I thought you were going to cook chestnuts?'

'I can't read the recipe book. My Italian is extremely limited so it's a non-starter.'

He took it from her, opened it and frowned. 'Ah. Well, some of it is in a local dialect anyway.'

'Can you translate?'

'Of course. But you'd need to know more than just classic Italian to understand it. Which recipe did you want to try?'

She raised an eyebrow. 'Well, how do I know? I don't know what they are.'

'I'll read them to you.'

'You know what? I'll do it in the morning, with Carlotta. She'll be able to tell me which are her favourites.'

'I can tell you that. She feeds them to us regularly. She does an amazing mousse for dessert, and stuffing for roast boar which is incredible. You should get her to teach you those if nothing else. Anyway, tomorrow won't work. There's a fair in the town.'

'Carlotta said there was a day off, but nobody told me why.'

'To celebrate the end of *La Vendemmia*. They hold one

every year. Then in a few weeks there's the chestnut fair, and then after *La Raccolta*, the olive harvest, there's another one. It's a sort of harvest festival gone mad. You ought to go tomorrow, it's a good day out.'

'Will you be there?'

He nodded. 'All of us will be there.'

'I thought we were avoiding each other?'

He didn't smile, as she'd expected. Instead he frowned, his eyes troubled. 'We are. I'll be with my children. Roberto and Carlotta will be going. I'm sure they'll give you a lift.'

And then, as if she'd reminded him of their unsatisfactory arrangement, he stood up. 'I'm going to do some work. I'll see you tomorrow.'

She did see him, but only because she kept falling over him.

Why was it, she thought, that if you lost someone in a crowd of that size you'd never be able to find them again, and yet every time she turned round, he was there?

Sometimes he didn't see her. Equally, probably, there were times when she didn't see him. But there were times when their eyes met, and held. And then he'd turn away.

Well, this time she turned away first, and made her way through the crowd in the opposite direction.

And bumped into Anita.

'Lydia! I was hoping I'd see you. Come, let's find a quiet corner for a coffee and a chat. We have a wedding to plan!'

She looked around at the jostling crowd and laughed. 'A quiet corner?'

'There must be one. Come, I know a café bar on a side street. We'll go there.'

They had to sit outside, but the sunshine was lovely and it was relatively quiet away from the hubbub and festival atmosphere of the colourful event.

'So—this wedding. Massimo tells me your sister's coming over soon to talk about it. Do you know what she wants?'

Lydia shrugged, still uncomfortable about him spending money on Anita's services. 'The hotel was offering a fairly basic package,' she began, and Anita gave a soft laugh.

'I know the hotel. It would have been basic, and they would have talked it up to add in all sorts of things you don't really need.'

'Well, they wouldn't, because she hasn't got any money, which is why I'm working here now.'

Anita raised an eyebrow slightly. 'Is that the only reason?' she asked softly. 'Because I know these Valtieri men. They're notoriously addictive.'

Poor Anita. Lydia could see the ache in her eyes, knew that she could understand. Maybe, for that reason, she let down her guard.

'No. It's not the only reason,' she admitted quietly. 'Maybe, subconsciously, it gave me an excuse to spend time with him, but trust me, it's not going to come to anything.'

'Don't be too sure. He's lonely, and he's a good man. He can be a bit of a recluse—he shuts himself away and works rather than dealing with his emotions, but he's not alone in that. It's a family habit, I'm afraid.'

She shook her head. 'I *am* sure nothing will come of it. We've talked about it,' she said, echoing her conversation with Isabelle and wondering if both women could be wrong or if it was just that they were fond of him and wanted him to be happy.

'He needs someone like you,' Anita said, 'someone honest and straightforward who isn't afraid of hard work and understands the pressures and demands of an agricultural lifestyle. He said your family are lovely, and he felt at home there with them. He said they were refreshingly unpretentious.'

She laughed at that. 'We've got nothing to be pretentious about,' she pointed out, but Anita just smiled.

'You have to understand where he's coming from. He has women after him all the time. He's a very, very good catch, and Gio is worried that some money-seeking little tart will get her claws into him.'

'Not a chance. He's much too wary for that, believe me. He has strict criteria. Anyway, I thought we were talking about the wedding?'

Anita smiled wryly and let it go, but Lydia had a feeling that the subject was by no means closed…

'What are you doing?'

A pair of feet appeared in her line of sight, slender feet clad in beautiful, soft leather pumps. She straightened up on her knees and looked up at his mother, standing above her on the beautiful frescoed staircase.

'I'm helping Carlotta.'

'It's not your job to clean. She has a maid for that.'

'But the maid's sick, so I thought I'd help her.'

Elisa frowned. 'I didn't know that. Why didn't Carlotta tell me?'

'Because she doesn't?' she suggested gently. 'She just gets on with it.'

'And so do you,' his mother said softly, coming down to her level. 'Dear girl, you shouldn't be doing this. It's not part of your job.'

'I don't have a job, Signora Valtieri. I have a bargain with your son. I help out, my sister gets her wedding, which is incredibly generous, so if there's some way I can help, I just do it.'

'You do, don't you, without any fuss? You are a quite remarkable girl. It's a shame you have to leave.'

'I don't think he thinks so.'

'My son doesn't know what's good for him.'

'And you do?'

'Yes, I do, and I believe you could be.'

She stared at Elisa, stunned. 'But—I'm just a chef. A no-body.'

'No, you are not a nobody, Lydia, and we're just farmers like your people.'

'No.' She laughed at that and swept an arm around her to underline her point. 'No, you're not just farmers, *signora*. My family are just farmers. You own half of Tuscany and a *palazzo*, with incredibly valuable frescoes on the walls painted by Old Masters. There is a monumental difference.'

'I think not—and please stop calling me *signora*. My name, as you well know, is Elisa. Come. Let's go and get some coffee and have a chat.'

She shook her head. 'I can't. I have work to do—lunch to prepare for everyone in a minute. I was just giving the stairs a quick sweep.'

'So stop now, and come, just for a minute. Please? I want to ask you something.'

It was a request, but from his mother it was something on the lines of an invitation to Buckingham Palace. You didn't argue. You just went.

So she went, leaving the ornate and exquisitely painted staircase hall and following her into the smaller kitchen which served their wing of the house.

'How do you take your coffee? Would you like a cappuccino?'

'That would be lovely. Thank you.'

Bone china cups, she thought, and a plate with little Amaretti biscuits. Whatever this was about, it was not going to be a quick anything, she realised.

'So,' Elisa said, setting the tray down at a low table between two beautiful sofas in the formal *salon* overlooking the terrace. 'I have a favour to ask you. My son tells me you're contemplating starting a catering business. I would like to commission you.'

Lydia felt her jaw drop. 'Commission?' she echoed faintly. 'For what?'

'I'm having a meeting of my book group. We get together every month over dinner and discuss a book we've read, and this time it's my turn. I would like you to provide the meal for us. There will be twenty people, and we will need five courses.'

She felt her jaw sag again. 'When?'

'Wednesday next week. The chestnuts should be largely harvested by then, and the olive harvest won't have started yet. So—will you do it?'

'Is there a budget?'

Elisa shrugged. 'Whatever it takes to do the job.'

Was it a test? To see if she was good enough? Or a way to make her feel valued and important enough to be a contender for her son? Or was it simply that she needed a meal provided and Carlotta was too unwell?

It didn't matter. Whatever the reason, she couldn't refuse. She looked into Elisa's eyes.

'Yes. Yes, I'll do it,' she said. 'Just so long as you'll give me a reference.'

Elisa put her cup down with a satisfied smile. 'Of course.'

CHAPTER NINE

THE book club dinner seemed to be going well.

She was using her usual kitchen—the room which historically had always been the main kitchen in the house, although it was now used by Massimo and his children, and for preparing the harvest meals.

She needed the space. Twenty people were quite hard to cater for if the menu was extravagant, and she'd drafted in help in the form of Maria, the girl who'd been helping her with the meals all along.

The *antipasti* to start had been a selection of tiny canapés, all bite-sized but labour intensive. Massimo had dropped in and tasted them, and she'd had to send him away before he'd eaten them all.

Then she'd served penne pasta with crayfish in a sauce of cream with a touch of fresh chilli, followed by a delicate lemon sorbet to cleanse the palette.

For the main, she'd sourced some wild boar with Carlotta's help, and she'd casseroled it with fruit and lots of wine and garlic, reducing it to a rich, dark consistency. Massimo, yet again, had insisted on tasting it, dipping his finger in the sauce and sucking it, and said it was at least as good as Carlotta's great-nephew's. Carlotta agreed, and asked her for the recipe, which amazed her.

She'd served it on a chestnut, apple and sweet potato mash, with fresh green beans and fanned Chantenay carrots. And now it was time for the dessert, individual portions of perfectly set and delicate pannacotta under a spun sugar cage, with fresh autumn raspberries dusted with vanilla sugar and drizzled with dark chocolate. If that didn't impress them, nothing would, she thought with satisfaction.

She carried them through with Maria's help, set them down in front of all the guests and then left them to it. She put the coffee on to brew in Elisa's smaller kitchen, with homemade *petit fours* sitting ready on the side, and then headed back to her kitchen to start the massive clean-up operation.

But Massimo was in there, up to his wrists in suds, scrubbing pans. The dishwasher was sloshing quietly in the background, and there was no sign of Maria.

'I sent her home,' he said in answer to her question. 'It's getting late, and she's got a child.'

'I was going to pay her.'

'I've done it. Roberto's taken her home. Why don't you make us both a coffee while I finish this?'

She wasn't going to argue. Her head was aching, her feet were coming out in sympathy and she hadn't sat down for six hours. More, probably.

'Are they happy?'

She shrugged. 'They didn't say not and they seemed to eat it all, mostly.'

'Well, that's a miracle. There are some fussy women amongst them. I don't know why my mother bothers with them.'

He dried his hands and sat down opposite her, picking up his coffee. 'Well done,' he said, and the approval in his voice warmed her.

'I'll reserve judgement until I get your mother's verdict,' she said, because after all he hadn't been her client.

'Don't bother. It was the best food this house has seen in decades. You did an amazing job.'

'I loved it,' she confessed with a smile. 'It was great to do something a bit more challenging, playing with flavours and presentation and just having a bit of fun. I love it. I've always loved it.'

He nodded slowly. 'Yes, I can see that. And you're very good at it. I don't suppose there's any left?'

She laughed and went to the fridge. 'There's some of the boar casserole, and a spare pannacotta. Haven't you eaten?'

He pulled a face. 'Kid's food,' he admitted. 'My father and I took them out for pizza. There didn't seem to be a lot of room in here.'

She plated him up some of the casserole with the vegetables, put it in the microwave and reheated it, then set it down in front of him and watched him eat. It was the best part of her job, to watch people enjoying the things she'd created, and he was savouring every mouthful.

She felt a wave of sadness and regret that there was no future for them, that she wouldn't spend the rest of her life creating wonderful, warming food and watching him eat it with relish.

She'd had the girls in with her earlier in the day, and she'd let them help her make the *petit fours* from homemade marzipan. That, too, had given her pangs of regret and a curious sense of loss. Silly, really. She'd never had them, so how could she feel that she'd lost them?

And after he'd eaten so much marzipan she was afraid he'd be sick, Antonino had stood up at the sink on an upturned box and washed up the plastic mixing bowls, soaking himself and the entire area in the process and having a great time with the bubbles. Such a sweet child, and the spitting image of his father. He was going to be a good-looking man one day, but she wouldn't be there to see it.

Or watch his father grow old.

She took away his plate, and replaced it with the pannacotta. He pressed the sugar cage with his fingertip, and frowned as it shattered gently onto the plate. 'How did you make it?' he asked, fascinated. 'I've never understood.'

'Boil sugar and water until it's caramelised, then trail it over an oiled mould. It's easy.'

He laughed. 'For you. I can't even boil an egg. Without Carlotta my kids would starve.'

'No. They'd eat pizza,' she said drily, and he gave a wry grin.

'Probably.' He dug the spoon into the pannacotta and scooped up a raspberry with it, then sighed as it melted on his tongue. 'Amazing,' he mumbled, and scraped the plate clean.

Then he put the spoon down and pushed the plate away, leaning back and staring at her. 'You really are an exceptional chef. If there's any justice, you'll do well in your catering business. That was superb.'

'Thank you.' She felt his praise warm her, and somehow that was more important than anyone else's approval. She washed his plate and their coffee cups, then turned back to him, her mind moving on to the real reason she was here.

'Massimo, I need to talk to you about Jen and the wedding. They'll be here in two days, and I need to pick them up from the airport somehow.'

'I'll do it,' he offered instantly. 'My mother's preparing the guest wing for them, but she wanted to know if they needed one room or two.'

'Oh, one. Definitely. She needs help in the night some-times. Is there a shower?'

'A wet room. That was one of the reasons for the choice. And it's got French doors out to the terrace around the other side. Come. I'll show you. You can tell me which room would be the best for them.'

She went, and was blown away by their guest suite. Two bedrooms, both large, twin beds in one and a huge double in the other, with a wet room between and French doors out onto the terrace. And there was a small sitting room, as well, a pri-vate retreat, with a basic kitchen for making drinks and snacks.

'This will be just perfect. Give them the double room. She wakes in the night quite often, having flashbacks. They're worse if Andy's not beside her.'

'Poor girl.'

She nodded, still racked with guilt. She always would be, she imagined. It would never go away, just like his guilt over Angelina slumped over the kitchen table, unable to summon help.

She felt his finger under her chin, tilting her face up to his so he could look into her eyes.

'It was not your fault,' he said as if he could read her mind.

Her eyes were steady, but sad. 'Any more than Angelina's death was your fault. Bad things happen. Guilt is just a natu-ral human reaction. Knowing it and believing it are two dif-ferent things.'

He felt his mouth tilt into a smile, but what kind of a smile it was he couldn't imagine. It faded, as he stared into her eyes, seeing the ache in them, the longing, the emptiness.

He needed her. Wanted her like he had never wanted any-one, but there was too much at stake to risk upsetting the sta-tus quo, for any of them.

He dropped his hand. 'What time do they arrive?' he asked, and the tension holding them eased.

For now.

They collected Jen and Andy from Pisa airport at midday on Friday, and they were blown away by their first view of the *palazzo*. By the time they'd pulled up at the bottom of the steps, Jen's eyes were like saucers, but all Lydia could think about was how her sister would get up the steps.

She hadn't even thought about it, stupidly, and now—

'Come here, gorgeous,' Andy said, unfazed by the sight of them, and scooping Jen up, he grinned and carried her up the steps to where Roberto was waiting with the doors open.

Massimo and Lydia followed, carrying their luggage and the crutches, and as they reached the top their eyes met and held.

The memory was in her eyes, and it transfixed him. The last woman to be carried up those steps had been her in that awful wedding dress—the dress that was still hanging on the back of his office door, waiting for her to ask for it and burn it.

He should let her. Should burn it himself, instead of staring at it for hour after hour and thinking of her.

He dragged his eyes away and forced himself to concentrate on showing them to their rooms.

'I'll leave you with Lydia. If you need anything, I'll be in the office.'

And he walked away, crossing the courtyard with a firm, deliberate stride. She dragged her eyes off him and closed the door, her heart still pounding from that look they'd exchanged at the top of the steps.

Such a short time since he'd carried her up them, and yet so much had happened. Nothing obvious, nothing apparently momentous, and yet nothing would ever be quite the same as it had been before.

Starting with her sister's wedding.

'Wow—this is incredible!' Jen breathed, leaning back on Andy and staring out of the French doors at the glorious view. 'So beautiful! And the house—my God, Lydia, it's fantastic! Andy, did you see those paintings on the wall?'

Lydia gave a soft laugh. 'Those are the rough ones. There are some utterly stunning frescoes in the main part of the house, up the stairwell, for instance, and in the dining room. Absolutely beautiful. The whole place is just steeped in history.'

'And we're going to get married from here. I can't believe it.'

'Believe it.' She glanced at her watch. 'Are you hungry? There's some soup and cheese for lunch, and we'll eat properly tonight. Anita's coming over before dinner to talk to you and show you where the marquee will go and how it all works—they've had Carla's wedding and Luca's here, so they've done it all before.'

'Not Massimo's?'

She had no idea. It hadn't been mentioned. 'I don't know. Maybe not. So—lunch. Do you want a lie down for a while, or shall I bring you something over?'

'Oh, I don't want to make work for you,' Jen said, but Lydia could see she was flagging, and she shook her head.

'I don't mind. I'll bring you both something and you can take it easy for a few hours. Travelling's always exhausting.'

Anita arrived at five, and by six Gio had put in an appearance, rather as she'd expected.

He found Lydia in the kitchen, and helped himself to a glass of Prosecco from the fridge and a handful of canapés.

'Hey,' she said, slapping his wrist lightly when he went back for more. 'I didn't know you were involved in the wedding planning.'

'I'm not,' he said with a cocky grin. 'I'm just here for the food.'

And Anita, she thought, but she didn't say that. She knew he'd turn from the smiling playboy to the razor-tongued lawyer the instant she mentioned the woman's name. Instead she did a little digging on another subject.

'So, how many weddings have there been here recently?' she asked.

'Two—Carla and Luca.'

'Not Massimo?'

'No. He got married in the *duomo* and they went back to her parents' house. Why?'

She shrugged. 'I just didn't want to say anything that hit a nerve.'

'I think you hit a nerve,' he said, 'even without speaking. You unsettle him.'

Was it so obvious? Maybe only to someone who was looking for trouble.

'Relax, Gio,' she said drily. 'You don't need to panic and get out your pre-nup template. This is going nowhere.'

'Shame,' he said, pulling a face, 'you might actually be good for him,' and while she was distracted he grabbed another handful of canapés.

She took the plate away and put it on the side. 'Shame?' she asked, and he shrugged.

'He's lonely. Luca likes you, so does Isabelle. And so does our mother, which can't be bad. She's a hard one to please.'

'Not as hard as her son,' she retorted. 'And talking of Massimo, why don't you go and find him and leave me in peace to cook? You're distracting me.'

'Wouldn't want to do that. You might ruin the food, and I've come all the way from Florence for it.'

And he sauntered off, stealing another mouthful from the plate in passing.

The dinner went well, and Anita came back the following day to go through the plans in detail, after talking to Jen and Andy the night before.

'She's amazing,' Jen said later. 'She just seems to know what I want, and she's got the answers to all of my questions.'

'Good,' she said, glad they'd got on well, because hearing the questions she'd realised there was no way someone without in-depth local knowledge could have answered them.

They were getting married the first weekend in May, in the town hall, and coming back to the *palazzo* for the marquee reception. They talked food, and she asked Anita for the catering budget and drew a blank. 'Whatever you need,' she was told, and she shook her head.

'I need to know.'

'I allow between thirty and eighty euros a head for food. Do whatever you want, he won't mind. Just don't make it cheap. That would insult him.'

'What about wine?'

'Prosecco for reception drinks, estate red and white for the meal, estate vinsanto for the dessert, champagne for toasts— unless you'd rather have prosecco again?'

'Prosecco would be fine. I prefer it,' Jen said, looking slightly stunned. 'Lydia, this seems really lavish.'

'Don't worry, Jen, she's earned it,' Anita said. 'He's been working her to the bone over the harvest season, and it's not finished yet.'

It wasn't, and there was a change in the weather. Saturday night was cold and clear, and there was a hint of frost on the railings. Winter was coming, and first thing on Monday morning Roberto, not Massimo, took Jen and Andy to the airport because *La Raccolta*, the olive harvest, was about to begin.

Jen hugged her goodbye, her eyes welling. 'It's going to be amazing. I don't know how to thank you.'

'You don't need to thank me. Just go home and concentrate on getting better, and don't buy your wedding dress until I'm there. I don't want to miss that.'

'What, with your taste in wedding dresses?' Massimo said, coming up behind them with a teasing smile that threatened to double her blood pressure.

'It was five pounds!'

'You were cheated,' he said, laughing, and kissed Jen goodbye, slapping Andy on the back and wishing them a safe journey. 'I have to go—I'm needed at the plant. We have a problem with the olive press. I'll see you in May.'

She waved them off, feeling a pang of homesickness as they went, but she retreated to the kitchen where Carlotta was carving bread.

'Here we go again, then,' she said with a smile, and Carlotta smiled back and handed her the knife.

'I cut the prosciutto,' she said, and turned on the slicer.

He was late back that night—more problems with the *frantoio*, so Roberto told her, and Carlotta was exhausted.

Elisa and Vittorio were out for dinner, and so apart from Roberto and Carlotta, she was alone in the house with the children. And he was clearly worried for his wife.

'Go on, you go and look after her. Make her have an early night. I'll put the children to bed and look after them.'

'Are you sure?'

'Of course. They don't bite.'

He smiled gratefully and went, and she found the children in the sitting room. Antonino and Lavinia were squabbling again, and Francesca was on the point of tears.

'Who wants a story?' she asked, and they stopped fighting and looked up at her.

'Where's *Papà*?' Lavinia asked, looking doubtful.

'Working,' she said, because explaining what he was doing when she didn't really understand was beyond her. But they seemed to accept it, and apart from tugging his sister's hair again, even Antonino co-operated.

More or less. There was some argument about whether or not they needed a bath, but she was pretty sure no child had died from missing a single bath night, so she chivvied them into their pyjamas, supervised the teeth cleaning and ushered them into Antonino's bedroom.

It was a squeeze, but they all fitted on the bed somehow, and he handed her his favourite story book.

It was simple enough, just about, that she could fudge her way through it, but her pronunciation made them all laugh, and Francesca coached her. Then she read it again, much better this time, and gradually Antonino's eyelids began to wilt.

She sent the girls out, tucked him up and, on impulse, she kissed him goodnight.

He was already asleep by the time she reached the door, and Lavinia was in bed. Francesca, though, looked unhappy still, so after she'd settled her sister, she went into the older girl's room and gave her a hug.

She wasn't surprised when she burst into tears. She'd been on the brink of it before, and Lydia took her back downstairs and made her a hot drink and they curled up on the sofa in the sitting room next to the kitchen and talked.

'He's always working,' she said, her eyes welling again. 'He's never here, and Nino and Vinia always fight, and then

Carlotta gets cross and upset because she's tired, and it's always me to stop them fighting, and—'

She broke off, her thin shoulders racked with sobs, and Lydia pulled her into her arms and rocked her, shushing her gently as she wept.

'—she's the one who bears the brunt of the loss, because when I'm not there the little ones turn to her. She has to be mother to them, and she's been so strong, but she's just a little girl herself—'

Poor, poor little thing. She was so stoic, trying to ease the burden on her beloved *papà*, and he was torn in half by his responsibilities. It was a no-win situation, and there was nothing she could do to change it, but maybe, just this one night, she'd made it a little easier.

She cradled Francesca in her arms until the storm of weeping had passed, and then they put on a DVD and snuggled up together to watch it.

Lydia couldn't understand it, but it didn't matter, and after a short while Francesca dropped off to sleep on Lydia's shoulder. She shifted her gently so she was lying with her head on her lap, and she stroked her hair as she settled again.

Dear, sweet child. Lydia was falling for her, she realised. Falling for them all. For the first time in her life she felt truly at home, truly needed, as if what she did really made a difference.

She sifted the soft, dark curls through her fingers and wondered what the future held for her and for her brother and sister.

She'd never know. Her time here was limited, they all knew that, and yet she'd grown to love them all so much that to leave them, never to know what became of them, how their lives panned out—it seemed unthinkable. She felt so much a part of their family, and it would be so easy to imagine living here with them, maybe adding to the family in time.

She squeezed her eyes shut and bit her lips.

No. It was never going to happen. She was going, and she had to remember that.

But not yet, she thought, a fine tendril of hair curled around her finger. Not now. For now, she'd just sit there with Francesca, and they'd wait for Massimo to return.

It was so late.

His mother would have put the children to bed, he thought, but yet again he'd missed their bedtime story, yet again he'd let them down.

The lights were on in the sitting room, and he could hear the television. Odd. He paused at the door, thinking the children must have left everything on, and he saw Lydia asleep on the sofa, Francesca sprawled across her lap.

Why Lydia? And why wasn't Francesca in bed?

He walked quietly over and looked down at them. They were both sound asleep, and Lydia was going to have a dreadful crick in her neck, but he was filthy, and if he was to carry Francesca up to bed, he needed a shower.

He backed out silently, went upstairs and showered, then threw on clean clothes and ran lightly downstairs.

'Lydia?' he murmured softly, touching her on the shoulder, and she stirred slightly and winced.

'Oh—you're home,' she whispered.

'*Sì*. I'll take her.'

He eased her up into his arms, and Francesca snuggled close.

'She missed you,' Lydia said. 'The little ones were tired and naughty.'

'I'm sorry.'

'Don't be. It's not your fault.'

'Why are you here? My mother should be putting them to bed. I sent her a text.'

'They're out for dinner.'

He dropped his head back with a sigh. 'Of course. Oh, Lydia, I'm so sorry.'

'It's fine. Put her to bed.'

He did, settling her quickly, earning a sleepy smile as he kissed her goodnight. But by the time he got downstairs again, the television was off and the sitting room was in darkness.

It was over.

La Raccolta was finished, the olive oil safely in the huge lidded terracotta urns where it would mature for a while before being bottled.

The fresh olive oil, straight from the press, was the most amazing thing she'd ever tasted, and she'd used it liberally in the cooking and on *bruschetta* as an appetiser for the family's meals.

Of all the harvests, she'd found the olive harvest the most fascinating. The noise and smell in the pressing room was amazing, the huge stone wheels revolving on edge in the great stainless steel bowl of the *frantoio*, the olive press, crushing the olives to a purple paste. It was spread on circular felt discs and then stacked and pressed so that the oily juice dribbled out and ran into a vat, where it separated naturally, the bright green oil floating to the top.

Such a simple process, really, unchanged for centuries, and yet so very effective.

Everything in there had been covered in oil, the floor especially, and she knew that every time she smelt olive oil now, she'd see that room, hear the sound of the *frantoio* grinding the olives, see Massimo tossing olives in the palm of his hand, or checking the press, or laughing with one of the workers.

It would haunt her for the rest of her life, and the time had come so quickly.

She couldn't believe she was going, but she was. She'd grown to love it, not just because of him, but because of all his family, especially the children.

They were sad she was leaving, and on her last night she cooked them a special meal of their own, with a seafood risotto for their starter, and a pasta dish with chicken and pesto, followed by the dessert of frozen berries with hot white chocolate sauce that was always everyone's favourite.

'I don't want you to go,' Francesca said sadly as they finished clearing up.

Massimo, coming into the room as she said it, frowned. 'She has to go, *cara*. She has a business to run.'

'No, she doesn't. She has a job here, with us.'

Her heart squeezed. 'But I don't, sweetheart,' she said gently. 'I was only here to help Carlotta with the harvest. It's finished now. I can't just hang around and wait for next year. I have to go and cook for other people.'

'You could cook for us,' she reasoned, but Lydia shook her head.

'No. Carlotta would feel hurt. That's her job, to look after you. And your *papà* is right, I have to go back to my business.'

'Not go,' Lavinia said, her eyes welling. '*Papà, no!*' She ran to him, begging him in Italian, words she couldn't understand.

'What's she saying?' she asked, and Lavinia turned to look at her, tugging at her father and pleading, and he met her eyes reluctantly.

'She wants you to stay. She said—'

He broke off, but Francesca wouldn't let him stop.

'Tell her what Lavinia said, *Papà*,' she prompted, and he closed his eyes briefly and then went on.

'*Papà* is unhappy when you aren't here,' he said grudgingly, translating directly as Lavinia spoke. 'Please don't go. We missed you when you went home before.' He hesitated, and she nudged him. 'It's lovely when you're here,' he went on, his bleak eyes locked with hers, 'because you make *Papà* laugh. He never laughs when you're not here.'

A tear slipped over and slid down her cheek, but she didn't seem to notice. Their eyes were locked, and he could see the anguish in them. He swallowed hard, his arm around Lavinia's skinny little shoulders holding her tight at his side.

Was it true? Was he unhappy when she wasn't there, unhappy enough that even the children could see it? Did he really not laugh when she wasn't there?

Maybe.

Lydia pressed her fingers to her lips, and shook her head. 'Oh, Lavinia. I'm sorry. I don't want to make your *papà* unhappy, or any of you, but I have to go home to my family.'

She felt little arms around her hips, and looked down to find Antonino hugging her, his face buried in her side. She laid a hand gently on his hair and stroked it, aching unbearably inside. She'd done this, spent so much time with them that she was hurting them now by leaving, and she never meant to hurt them. 'I'm sorry,' she said to him, *'mi dispiace.'* And his little arms tightened.

'Will you read us a story?' Francesca asked.

She'd be leaving for the airport before three in the morning, long before the children were up, so this was her last chance to read to them. Her last chance ever? 'Of course I will,' she said, feeling choked. She'd done it a few times since the night of the *frantoio* breakdown, and she loved it. Too much.

They were already in their pyjamas, and she ushered them up to bed, supervised the teeth cleaning as she'd done before, and then they settled down on Antonino's bed, all crowded round while she read haltingly to them in her awful, amateurish Italian.

She could get the expressions right, make it exciting—that was the easy bit. The pronunciation was harder, but it was a book they knew, so it didn't really matter.

What mattered was lying propped up against the wall, with Antonino under one arm and Lavinia under the other, and Francesca curled up by her knees leaning against the wall and watching her with wounded eyes.

She was the only one of them to remember her mother, and for a few short weeks, Lydia realised, she'd slipped into the role without thinking, unconsciously taking over some of the many little things a mother did. Things like making cupcakes, and birthday cards for Roberto. She'd stopped the two little ones fighting, and hugged them when they'd hurt themselves, and all the time she'd been playing happy families and ignoring the fact that she'd be going away soon, going back to her real life at home.

And now she had to go.

She closed the book, and the children snuggled closer, stretching out the moment.

Then Massimo's frame filled the doorway, his eyes shadowed in the dim light.

'Come on. Bedtime now. Lydia needs to pack.'

It was a tearful goodnight, for all of them, and as soon as she could she fled to her room, stifling the tears.

She didn't have to pack. She'd done it ages ago, been round all the places she might have left anything, and there was nothing to do now, nothing to distract her.

Only Lavinia's words echoing in her head.

He never laughs when you're not here.

The knock was so quiet she almost didn't hear it.

'Lydia?'

She opened the door, unable to speak, and met his tortured eyes.

And then his arms closed around her, and he held her hard against his chest while she felt the shudders run through him.

They stayed like that for an age, and then he eased back and looked down at her.

His eyes were raw with need, and she led him into the room and closed the door.

Just one last time…

CHAPTER TEN

'Is IT true?'

He turned his head and met her eyes in the soft glow of the bedside light, and his face was shuttered and remote.

'Is what true?'

'That you don't laugh when I'm not here?'

He looked away again. 'You don't want to listen to what the children say.'

'Why not, if it's true? Is it?'

He didn't answer, so she took it as a yes. It made her heart ache. If only he'd believe in them, if only he'd let her into his heart, his life, but all he would say was no.

'Talk to me,' she pleaded.

He turned his head back, his eyes unreadable.

'What is there to say?'

'You could tell me how you really feel. That would be a good start.'

He laughed, a harsh, abrupt grunt full of pain. 'I can't,' he said, his accent stronger than she'd ever heard it. 'I can't find the words, I don't have the language to do this in English.'

'Then tell me in Italian. I won't understand, but you can say it then out loud. You can tell me whatever you like, and I can't hold you to it.'

He frowned, but then he reached out and stroked her face,

his fingers trembling. His mouth flickered in a sad smile, and then he started to speak, as if she'd released something inside him that had been held back for a long, long time.

She didn't understand it, but she understood the tone—the gentleness, the anguish, the pain of separation.

And then, his eyes locked with hers, he said softly, *'Ciao, mia bella ragazza. Te amo...'*

She reached out and cradled his jaw, her heart breaking. *Ciao* meant hello, but it also meant goodbye.

'It doesn't have to be goodbye,' she said softly. 'I love you, too—so much.'

He shook his head. 'No. No, *cara*, please. I can't let you love me. I can't let you stay. You'll be hurt.'

'No!'

'Yes. I won't let you.'

'Would you stop that?' she demanded, angry now. 'The first time I met you, you said I couldn't go in the plane with Nico because it wasn't safe. Now you're telling me I can't love you because I'll get hurt! Maybe I want to take the risk, Massimo? Maybe I *need* to take the risk.'

'No. You have a life waiting for you, and one day there will be some lucky man...'

'I don't want another man, I want you.'

'No! I have nothing to give you. I'm already pulled in so many ways. How can I be fair to you, or the children, or my work, my family? How can I do another relationship justice?'

'Maybe I could help you. Maybe I could make it easier. Maybe we could work together?'

'No. You love your family, you have your career. If I let you give it all up for me, what then? What happens when we've all let you into our hearts and then you leave?'

'I won't leave!'

'You don't know that. You've been here less than three

months. What happens in three years, when we have another child and you decide you're unhappy and want to go? I don't have time for you, I can't give you what you need. I don't even have enough time now to sleep! Please, *cara*. Don't make it harder. You'll forget me soon.'

'No. I'll never forget you. I'll never stop loving you.'

'You will. You'll move on. You'll meet someone and marry him and have children of your own in England, close to your family, and you'll look back and wonder what you saw in this sad and lonely old man.'

'Don't be ridiculous, you're not old, and you're only sad and lonely because you won't let anybody in!'

His eyes closed, as if he couldn't bear to look at her any longer. 'I can't. The last time I let anyone into my life, she lost her own, and it was because I was too busy, too tired, too overstretched to be there for her.'

'It wasn't your fault!'

'Yes, it was! I was *here*! I was supposed to be looking after her, but I was lying in my bed asleep while she was dying.'

'She should have woken you! She should have told you she was sick. It was not your fault!'

'No? Then why do I wake every night hearing her calling me?'

He threw off the covers and sat up, his legs over the edge of the bed, his head in his hands, his whole body vibrating with tension. 'I can't do this, Lydia! Please, don't ask me to. I can't do it.'

Why do I wake every night hearing her calling me?

His words echoing in her head, her heart pounding, she knelt up behind him, her arms around him, her body pressed to his in comfort.

'It wasn't your fault,' she said gently. 'You weren't responsible, but you're holding yourself responsible, and you have to forgive yourself. It wasn't my fault Jen had her accident, but I've blamed myself, and it has taken months to accept that it wasn't my fault and to forgive myself for not stopping him. You have to do the same. You have to accept that you weren't at fault—'

'But I was! I should have checked on her.'

'You were asleep! What time of year was it?'

'Harvest,' he admitted, his voice raw. 'The end of *La Raccolta*.'

Right at the end of the season. Now, in fact. Any time now. Her heart contracted, and she sank back down onto her feet, her hands against his back.

'You were exhausted, weren't you? Just as you're exhausted now. And she didn't want to disturb you, so she went down to the kitchen for painkillers.'

He sucked in a breath, and she knew she was right.

'She probably wasn't thinking clearly. Did she suffer from headaches?'

'Yes. All the time. They said she had a weakness in the vessels.'

'So it could have happened at any time?'

'*Sì*. But it happened when I was there, and it happened slowly, and if I'd realised, if I hadn't thought she was with the baby, if I'd known...'

'If you'd been God, in fact? If you'd been able to see inside her head?'

'They could have seen inside her head. She'd talked of going to the doctor about her headaches, but we were too busy, and she'd just had the baby, and it was the harvest, and...'

'And there was just no time. Oh, Massimo. I'm so sorry, but you know it wasn't your fault. You can't blame yourself.'

'Yes, I can. I can, and I have to, because my guilt and my grief is all I have left to give her! I can't even love her any more because you've taken that from me!' he said harshly, his voice cracking.

The pain ran through her like a shockwave.

How could he tell her that he loved her, and yet cling to his guilt and grief so that he could hold onto Angelina?

He couldn't. Not if he really loved her. Unless...

'Why are you doing this to me?' she asked quietly. 'To yourself? To your children? You wear your grief and your guilt like a hair shirt to torture yourself with, but it's not just you you're torturing, you're torturing me, as well, and your children. And they don't deserve to be tortured just because you're too much of a coward to let yourself love again!'

'I am not a coward!'

'Then prove it!' she begged. 'Let yourself love again!'

He didn't answer, his shoulders rigid, unmoving, and after what felt like forever, she gave up. She'd tried, and she could do no more.

Shaking, she eased away from him and glanced at her watch.

'We have to leave in half an hour. I'm going to shower,' she said, as steadily as she could.

And she walked into the bathroom, closed the door and let the tears fall...

He didn't come into the airport building this time.

He gave her a handful of notes to pay for her excess baggage, put her luggage on the pavement at the drop-off point and then hesitated.

'I'll see you in May,' he said, his voice clipped and harsh.

His eyes were raw with pain, and she wanted to weep for him, and for herself, and for the children, but now wasn't the time.

'Yes. I'll be in touch.'

'Anita will email you. She's in charge. I'll be too busy.'

Of course he would.

'Take care of yourself,' she said softly. And going up on tiptoe, she pressed her lips to his cheek.

His arms came round her, and for the briefest moment he rested his head against hers. *'Ciao, bella,'* he said softly, so softly that she scarcely heard him, and then he was straightening up, moving back, getting into the car.

He started the engine and drove away, and she watched his tail lights until they disappeared. Then she gathered up her luggage and headed for the doors.

It was the worst winter of her life.

The weather was glorious, bright winter sunshine that seemed to bounce right off her, leaving her cold inside. She found work in the pub down the road, and she created a website and tried to promote her catering business.

It did well, better than she'd expected, but without him her life was meaningless.

Jen found her one day in mid-January, staring into space.

'Hey,' she said softly, and came and perched beside her on the back of the sofa, staring out across the valley.

'Hey yourself. How are you doing?'

'OK. We've had another email from Anita. She wants to know about food.'

She could hardly bring herself to think about food. For a while she'd thought she was pregnant she'd felt so sick, but she wasn't. The test said no, her body said no and her heart grieved for a child that never was and never would be. And still she felt sick.

'What does she want to know? I've given her menu plans.'

'Something about the carpaccio of beef?'

She sighed. 'OK. I'll contact her.'

It was nothing to do with the beef. It was about Massimo.

'He's looking awful,' Anita said. 'He hasn't smiled since you left.'

Nor have I, she thought, *but there's nothing I can do, either for him or me.*

She didn't reply to the email. Two hours later her phone rang.

'I can't help you, Anita,' she said desperately. 'He won't listen to me.'

'He won't listen to anyone—Luca, Carlotta, his mother— even Gio's on your side, amazingly, but he just says he doesn't want to talk about it. And we're all worried. We're really worried.'

'I'm sorry, I can't do any more,' she said again, choked, and hung up.

Jen found her in her room, face down on the bed sobbing her heart out, and she lay down beside her and held her, and gradually it stopped hurting and she was numb again.

Better, in a strange kind of way.

January turned into February, and then March, and finally Jen was able to walk without the crutches.

'That's amazing,' Lydia said, hugging her, her eyes filling with tears. 'I'm so glad.'

'So am I.' Jen touched her cheek gently. 'I'm all right now, Lydia. I'm going to be OK. Please stop hurting yourself about it.'

'I'm not,' she said, and realised it was true, to an extent. Oh, it would always hurt to know that she'd been part of the sequence of events that had led to Jen's accident, but she'd stopped taking the blame for it, and now she could share in the joy of Jen's recovery. If only Massimo…

'You need to buy your wedding dress, we're leaving it awfully late,' she said, changing the subject before her mind dragged her off down that route.

'I know. There's a shop in town that does them to take away, so they don't need to be ordered. Will you come with me?'

She ignored the stab of pain, and hugged her sister. 'Of course I will.'

It was bittersweet.

They all went together—Lydia, Jen and their mother, and she found a dress that laced up the back, with an inner elasticated corset that was perfect for giving her some extra back support.

'Oh, that's so comfy!' she said, and then looked in the mirror and her eyes filled.

'Oh…'

Lydia grabbed her mother's hand and hung on. It was definitely The Dress, and everybody's eyes were filling now.

'Oh, darling,' her mother said, and hugged her, laughing and crying at the same time, because it might never have come to this. They could have lost her, and yet here she was, standing on her own two feet, unaided, and in her wedding dress. Their tears were well and truly earned.

After she'd done another twirl and taken the dress off, the manageress of the little wedding shop poured them another glass of Prosecco to toast Jen's choice.

As the bubbles burst in her mouth, Lydia closed her eyes and thought of him.

Sitting on the terrace outside her bedroom, sipping Prosecco and talking into the night. They'd done it more than once, before the weather had turned. Pre-dinner drinks when Jen and Andy had come to visit. Sitting in the *trattoria* waiting for their food to come, the second time they'd made love.

'Lydia?'

She opened her eyes and dredged up a smile. 'You looked stunning in it, Jen. Absolutely beautiful. Andy'll be bowled over.'

'What about you?'

'I don't need a wedding dress!' she said abruptly, and then remembered she was supposed to be Jen's bridesmaid, and suddenly it was all too much.

'Can we do this another day?' she asked desperately, and Jen, seeing something in her eyes, nodded.

'Of course we can.'

She went back on her own a few days later, and flicked through the rails while she was waiting. And there, on a mannequin in the corner, was the most beautiful dress she'd ever seen.

The softest, heaviest silk crepe de Chine, cut on the cross and hanging beautifully, it was exquisite. So soft, she thought, fingering it with longing, such a far cry from the awful thing she'd worn for the competition, and she wondered, stupidly, if she'd worn it instead, would she have fallen? And if not, would she have known what it was to love him? Maybe, if he'd seen her wearing a dress like that...

'It's a beautiful dress, isn't it? Why don't you try it on?'

'I don't need a wedding dress,' she said bluntly, dropping her hand to her side. 'I'm here for a bridesmaid's dress.'

'You could still try it on. We're quiet today, and I'd love to see it on you. You've got just the figure for it.'

How on earth had she let herself be talked into it? Because, of course, it fitted like a dream on her hourglass figure, smoothing her hips, showing off her waist, emphasising her bust.

For a moment—just a moment—she let herself imagine

his face as he saw her in it. She'd seen that look before, when he'd been making love to her—

'This is silly,' she said, desperate to take it off now. 'I'm not getting married.'

Not ever…

The awful wedding dress was still hanging on the back of his door.

He stared at it numbly. It still had her blood on it, a dark brown stain on the bodice where she'd wiped her fingers after she'd touched the graze on her head.

He missed her. The ache never left him, overlying the other ache, the ache that had been there since Angelina died.

Their wedding photo was still on his desk, and he picked it up and studied it. Was Lydia right? Was her wearing a metaphorical hair shirt, punishing himself for what was really not his fault?

Rationally, he knew that, but he couldn't let it go.

Because he hadn't forgiven himself? Or because he was a coward?

It's not just you you're torturing, you're torturing me, as well, and your children. And they don't deserve to be tortured just because you're too much of a coward to let yourself love again!

Getting up from the desk, he went and found Carlotta and told her he was going out. And then he did what he should have done a long time ago.

He went to the place where she was buried, and he said goodbye, and then he went home and took off his wedding ring. There was an inscription inside. It read *'Amor vincit omnia'.*

Love conquers everything.

Could it? Not unless you gave it a chance, he thought, and

pressing the ring to his lips, he nestled it in Angelina's jewellery box, with the lock of her hair, the first letter she'd ever sent him, a rose from her bouquet.

And then he put the box away, and went outside into the garden and stood at the railings, looking out over the valley below. She'll be here soon, he thought, and then I'll know.

Jen and Andy saw her off at the airport.

She put on a bright face, but in truth she was dreading this part of the wedding.

She was going over early to finalise the menu and meet the people who were going to be helping her. Carlotta's nephew, the owner of the *trattoria*, had loaned her one of his chefs and sourced the ingredients, and the waiting staff were all from local families and had worked for Anita before, but the final responsibility for the menu and the food was hers.

None of that bothered her. She was confident about the menu, confident in the ability of the chef and the waiting staff, and the food she was sure would be fine.

It was seeing Massimo that filled her with dread.

Dread, and longing.

She was thinner.

Thinner, and her face was drawn. She looked as if she'd been working too hard, and he wondered how her business was going. Maybe she'd been too successful?

He hoped not—no! That was wrong. If it was going well, if it was what she wanted, then he must let her go.

Pain stabbed through him and he sucked in a breath. For the past few weeks he'd put thoughts of failure out of his mind, but now—now, seeing her there, they all came rushing to the fore.

He walked towards her, and as if she sensed him there she

turned her head and met his eyes. All the breath seemed to be sucked out of his body, and he had to tell his feet how to move.

'Ciao, bella,' he said softly, and her face seemed to crumple slightly.

'Ciao,' she said, her voice uneven, and then he hugged her, because she looked as if she'd fall down if he didn't.

'Is this everything?'

She nodded, and he took the case from her and wheeled it out of the airport to his car.

He was looking well, she thought. A little thinner, perhaps, but not as bad as she'd thought from what Anita had said. Because he was over her?

She felt a sharp stab of pain, and sucked in her breath. Maybe he'd been right. Maybe he couldn't handle it, and he'd just needed to get back onto an even keel again.

And then he came round and opened the car door for her, and she noticed his wedding ring was missing, and her heart began to thump.

Was it significant?

She didn't know, and he said nothing, just smiled at her as he got into the car and talked about what the children had been up to and how the wedding preparations were going, all the way back to the *palazzo*.

It was like coming home, she thought.

The children were thrilled to see her, especially Francesca who wrapped her arms around her and hugged her so hard she thought her ribs might break.

'Goodness, you've all grown so tall!' she said, her eyes filling. Lavinia's arms were round her waist, and Antonino was hanging on her arm and jumping up and down. It made getting up the steps a bit of a challenge, but they managed it, and Massimo just chuckled softly and carried her luggage in.

'I've put you in the same room,' he said, and she felt a shiver of dread. The last time she'd been in here, he'd broken her heart. She wasn't sure she wanted to be there again, but it felt like her room now, and it would be odd to be anywhere else.

'So, what's the plan?' she asked as he put her case down.

He smiled wryly. 'Anita's coming over. I've told her to give you time to unwind, but she said there was too much to do. Do you want a cup of tea?'

'I'd love a cup of tea,' she said fervently. 'But don't worry. I'll make it.'

He nodded. 'In that case, I'll go and get on. You know my mobile number—ring me if you need me.'

She didn't have time to need him, which was perhaps just as well. The next few days were a whirlwind, and by the time the family arrived, she was exhausted.

Anita was brilliant. She organised everything, made sure everyone knew what they were to do and kept them all calm and focused, and the day of the wedding went without a hitch.

Lydia's involvement in the food was over. She'd prepared the starters and the deserts, the cold buffet was in the refrigerated van beside the marquee, and all she had to do was dress her sister and hold her bouquet.

And catch it, apparently, when it was all over.

Jen wasn't subtle. She stood just a few feet from her, with everyone standing round cheering, and threw it straight at Lydia.

It hit her in the chest and she nearly dropped it, but then she looked up and caught Massimo's eye, and her heart began to pound slowly.

He was smiling.

Smiling? Why? Because he was glad it was all over? Or because the significance of her catching it wasn't lost on him?

She didn't know. She was too tired to care, and after Andy scooped his glowing, blushing bride up in his arms and carried her off at the end of the reception in a shower of confetti and good wishes, she took the chance and slipped quietly away.

There was so much to do—a mountain of clearing up in the kitchen in the *palazzo*, never mind all the catering equipment which had been hired in and had to be cleaned and returned.

Plates, cutlery, glasses, table linen.

'I thought I might find you in here.'

She looked up.

'There's a lot to do.'

'I know.'

He wasn't smiling. Not now. He was thoughtful. Maybe a little tense?

He took off his suit jacket and rolled up his sleeves and pitched in alongside her, and for a while they worked in silence. He changed the washing up water three times, she used a handful of tea towels, but finally the table was groaning with clean utensils.

'Better. The guests are leaving. Do you want to say goodbye?'

She smiled slightly and shook her head. 'They're not my guests. Let my parents do it. I've got enough to do.'

'I'll go and clear up outside,' he said, and she nodded. There was still a lot to do in there, and she worked until she was ready to drop.

Her feet hurt, her shoes were long gone and she wanted

to lie down. The rest, she decided, would keep, and turning off the light, she headed back to her room.

She passed her parents in the colonnaded walkway around the courtyard, on their way in with Massimo's parents.

They stopped to praise the food yet again, and Elisa hugged her. 'It was wonderful. I knew it would be. You have an amazing talent.'

'I know,' her mother said. 'We're very proud of her.'

She was hugged and kissed again, and then she excused herself and finally got to her room, pausing in surprise in the doorway.

The door was open, the bedside light was on, and the bed was sprinkled with rose petals.

Rose petals?

She picked one up, lifting it to her nose and smelling the delicately heady fragrance.

Who—?

'May I come in?'

She spun round, the rose petal falling from her fingers, and he was standing there with a bottle of sparkling water and two glasses. 'I thought you might be thirsty,' he said.

'I don't know what I am,' she said. 'Too tired to know.'

He laughed softly, and she wondered—just briefly, with the small part of her brain that was still functioning—how often he'd done that since she went away.

'Lie down before you fall.'

She didn't need telling twice. She didn't bother to take the dress off. It was probably ruined anyway, and realistically when would she wear it again? She didn't go to dressy events very often. She flopped onto the bed, and he went round the other side, kicked off his shoes and settled himself beside her, propped up against the headboard.

'Here, drink this,' he said, handing her a glass, and she drained the water and handed the glass back.

'More.'

He laughed—again?—and refilled it, then leant back and sighed.

'Good wedding.'

'It was. Thank you. Without you, it wouldn't have happened.'

'It might have been at the hotel.'

'No. Nobody was giving me a lift—well, only Nico, and we both know how that might have ended.'

'Don't.' He took the empty glass from her again, put them both down and slid down the bed so he was lying flat beside her. His hand reached out, and their fingers linked and held.

'How are you, really?' he asked softly.

He wasn't talking about tonight, she realised, and decided she might as well be honest. It was the only thing she had left.

'All right, I suppose. I've missed you.'

'I've missed you, too. I didn't know I could hurt as much as that, not any more. Apparently I can.'

She rolled to her side to face him, and he did the same, his smile gone now, his eyes serious.

'Massimo,' she said, cutting to the chase, 'where's your wedding ring?'

'Ah, *cara*. So observant. I took it off. I didn't need it any more. You were right, it was time to let the past go and move on with my life.'

'Without guilt?'

His smile was sad. 'Without guilt. With regret, perhaps. The knowledge that things probably wouldn't have been very different whatever I'd done. I'd lost sight of that. And you?' he added. 'Are you moving on with your life?'

She tried to laugh, but she was too tired and too hurt to make it believable. 'No. My business is going well, but I don't care. It's all meaningless without you.'

'Oh, *bella*,' he said softly, and reached for her. 'My life is the same. The only thing that's kept me going the last few weeks has been the knowledge that I'd see you again soon. Without that I would have gone insane. I nearly did go insane.'

'I know. Anita rang me. They were all worried about you.'

He eased her up against his chest, so that her face lay against the fine silk shirt, warm from his skin, the beat of his heart echoing in her ear, slow and steady.

'Stay with me,' he said. 'I have no right to ask you, after I sent you away like that, but I can't live without you. No. That's not true. I can. I just don't want to, because without you, I don't laugh. Lavinia was right. I don't laugh because there's nothing to laugh at when you're not here. Nothing seems funny, everything is cold and colourless and futile. The days are busy but monotonous, and the nights—the nights are so lonely.'

She swallowed a sob, and lifted her hand and cradled his stubbled jaw. 'I know. I've lain awake night after night and missed you. I can fill the days, but the nights…'

'The nights are endless. Cold and lonely and endless. I've tried working, but there comes a time when I have to sleep, and then every time I close my eyes, I see you.'

'Not Angelina?'

'No. Not Angelina. I said goodbye to her. I hadn't done it. I hadn't grieved for her properly, I'd buried myself in work and I thought I was all right, but then I met you and I couldn't love you as you deserved because I wasn't free. And instead of freeing myself, I sent you away.'

'I'm sorry. It must have been hard.'

His eyes softened, and he smiled and shook his head. 'No. It was surprisingly easy. I was ready to do it—more than ready. And I'm ready to move on. I just need to know that you're ready to come with me.'

She smiled and bit her lip. 'Where are we going?'

'Wherever life takes us. It will be here, because this is who I am and where I have to be, but what we do with that life is down to us.'

He took her hand from his cheek and held it, staring intently into her eyes. 'Marry me, Lydia. You've set me free, but that freedom is no use to me without you. I love you, *bella. Te amo.* If you still love me, if you haven't come to your senses in all this time, then marry me. Please.'

'Of course I'll marry you,' she breathed, her heart overflowing. 'Oh, you foolish, silly, wonderful man, of course I'll marry you! Just try and stop me. And I'll never, never stop loving you.'

'I've still got the dress,' he told her some time later, his eyes sparkling with mischief. 'It's hanging on my office door. I thought I'd keep it, just in case you said yes.'

Did the woman in the wedding dress shop have second sight? 'I think I might treat myself to a new one,' she said, and smiled at him.

They were married in June, in the town hall where Jen and Andy had been married.

It had been a rush—she'd had to pack up all her things in England and ship them over, and they'd moved, on his parents' insistence, into the main part of the *palazzo*.

A new start, a clean slate.

It would take some getting used to, but as Massimo said, it was a family home and it should have children in it. It was where he and his brothers and sisters had been brought up, and it was family tradition for the eldest son to take over the formal rooms of the *palazzo*. And hopefully, there would be other children to fill it.

She held onto that thought. She'd liked the simplicity of the other wing, but there was much more elbow room in the central part, essential if they were to have more children, and the views were, if anything, even more stunning. And maybe one day she'd grow into the grandeur.

But until their wedding night, she was still using the room she'd always had, and it was in there that Jen and her mother helped her put on the beautiful silk dress. It seemed woefully extravagant for such a small and simple occasion, but she was wearing it for him, only for him, and when she walked out to meet him, her heart was in her mouth.

He was waiting for her in the frescoed courtyard, and his eyes stroked slowly over her. He said nothing, and for an endless moment she thought he hated it. But then he lifted his eyes to hers, and the heat in them threatened to set her on fire.

She looked stunning.

He'd thought she was beautiful in the other wedding dress, much as he'd hated it. In this, she was spectacular. It hugged her curves like a lover, and just to look at her made him ache.

She wasn't wearing a veil, and the natural curls of her fine blond hair fell softly to her shoulders. It was the way he liked it. Everything about her was the way he liked it, and at last he found a smile.

'*Mia bella ragazza,*' he said softly, and held out his hand to her.

It was a beautiful, simple ceremony.

Their vows, said by both of them in both English and Italian, were from the heart, and they were witnessed by their closest family and friends. Both sets of parents, his three sisters, Jen and Andy, Luca and Isabelle, Gio, Anita, Carlotta and Roberto, and of course the children.

Francesca and Lavinia were bridesmaids, and Antonino was the ring bearer. There was a tense moment when he wobbled and the rings started to slide, but it was all right, and with a smile of encouragement for his son, Massimo took her ring from the little cushion and slid it onto her finger, his eyes locked with hers.

He loved her. When he'd lost Angelina, he'd thought he could never love again, but Lydia had shown him the way. There was always room for love, he realised, always room for another person in your heart, and his heart had made room for her. How had he ever thought it could do otherwise?

She slid the other ring onto his finger, her fingers firm and confident, and he cupped her shoulders in his hands and bent his head and kissed her.

'Te amo,' he murmured, and then his words were drowned out by the clapping and cheering of their family.

Afterwards they went for lunch to the little *trattoria* owned by Carlotta's nephew. He did them proud. They drank Prosecco and ate simple, hearty food exquisitely cooked, and when it was over, they drove back to the *palazzo*. The others were going back to Luca and Isabelle's for the rest of the day, to give them a little privacy, and Massimo intended to take full advantage of it.

He drove up to the front door, scooped her up in his arms and carried her up the steps. The last time he'd done this she'd been bloodstained and battered. This time—this time she was his wife, and he felt like the luckiest man alive.

Pausing at the top he turned, staring out over the valley

spread out below them. Home, he thought, his heart filled with joy, and Lydia rested her head on his shoulder and sighed.

'It's so beautiful.'

'Not as beautiful as you. And that dress...' He nuzzled her neck, making her arch against him. 'I've been wanting to take it off you all day.'

'Don't you like it? I wasn't sure myself. I thought maybe I should have stuck to the other one,' she teased, and he laughed, the sound carrying softly on the night air.

It was a sound she'd never tire of, she thought contentedly as he turned, still smiling, and carried his bride over the threshold.

* * * * *

A BRIDE WORTH WAITING FOR
Caroline Anderson

PROLOGUE

'It's over.'

For a moment he didn't move, just stood there and let it sink in. Then he turned slowly round and scanned her face.

'They've got him?'

Ruth nodded. 'They caught up with him in a villa just outside Antibes. He'd got sloppy—maybe he thought we'd given up.'

He grunted. 'Fat chance after what that bastard's done. So he's finally going to be put away—well, I hope they throw the book at him. They will if I have anything to do with it. Never mind the other things he's done and the countless lives he's ruined, that animal owes me nine years.'

Ruth—his researcher and friend, his ex-colleague and the woman who'd kept him sane for all that time—shook her head. 'Sorry, Michael. He's dead.'

He swore quietly and succinctly and with considerable feeling. 'What happened?'

'There was a girl there with him. Frank didn't say what he'd done to her, but I'm sure we can fill in the details. She shot him after they stormed the house—they were cuffing him, and she just shot him through the head with his own gun at point-blank range. Said he deserved it.'

'Is that the official version?'

Ruth shook her head and smiled. 'Oh, no. I gather his gun went off in the confusion. Conveniently.'

He nodded, glad the girl wouldn't be punished for what amounted to a public service. 'Good for her,' he said softly. 'I would have liked ten minutes alone with him, though, before she did it.'

'Absolutely. You and all the others. It was too good for him, but whatever. It's over—that's all that matters really.'

It was. And that meant they'd all be safe—him, Ruth, Annie and the son he had yet to get to know. The threat hanging over them was gone, finally, after all these years.

And now it was time for the last act.

He felt the rush of adrenaline, the nerves, the anticipation—like the start of an operation, but worse, because he was personally involved in this one. It wasn't something he could remain detached about. No way.

'What about the others?' he asked, his voice rough—rougher even than usual, rusty with emotion and lack of use.

'They were picking them up when Frank rang me. They've been closing in for days, had everyone under surveillance. They did a dawn swoop. It's massive. It'll be on the news.'

'So it's official?'

Ruth nodded. 'Yes—just about. I expect someone will come and see you. Frank rang me this morning—I'm surprised he hasn't called you.'

'He may have done. The phone rang when I was in the shower. I ignored it. I'll call him now.'

And then he could get things in motion. He'd been on ice for eight, nearly nine years, and now the waiting was over.

'Fancy living here?' he asked quietly. 'Swapping houses? Just for a while. I could use the flat as an excuse to be there.'

There was a silence, and as it stretched out he turned and studied her thoughtfully.

'Am I missing something?' he asked, and she gave a wry little smile.

'If you don't need me, there's somewhere else I'd rather be.'

'Tim?'

She nodded. 'He's asked me to marry him—again. And somehow, with this finally over, I feel free at last—as if the debt's paid and I can move on. And I do love him.'

He closed his eyes, let out his breath on a short huff of laughter before the emotion choked him. 'Ruth—that's great. Wonderful. I'm really glad for you. It's about time—and of course I don't need you. Not that much—not enough to get in the way of this. You know I'd never stand in your way. I've asked too much from you for too long as it is—'

'No. It's been fine. I needed your support every bit as much as you needed mine. You kept me safe, gave me a reason to live when it all fell apart, and I'll be eternally grateful for that, but…'

'But you don't need me any more,' he prompted.

'Not now.' She smiled gently at him. 'I'll always need your friendship, and you'll always have mine. You know that. But Tim's there for me now. I need to be with him.'

'How much does he know?'

She shrugged. 'Enough. I never thought I could ever trust a man again after what happened. And I certainly never thought I'd love again after David died. But—with Tim, it's all fallen into place, and I feel I can start again. Draw a line under this, get on with my life.'

'I'm so glad for you,' he said softly.

'Thank you. I'll still work for you,' she added. 'If you want me to.'

His grin was crooked. 'I don't know. This changes things, doesn't it? I don't need to write for a living. Not any more. I might try something different. Grow grapes or something. We'll talk about it. Why don't you have a holiday—six months? I'll take a break from my writing. That should give us both time to sort out the future.'

'Sounds perfect.'

'I'll still pay you, of course, in the meantime. Put you on a retainer or something—and don't argue.'

She opened her mouth, shut it again and smiled. 'So when do you want me to move out—if you still do?'

He felt the lick of adrenaline in his veins. 'Please—if you feel you can. I can use the excuse of refurbishing the building—that should give me plenty of opportunities to talk to her. How soon could you move?'

'The weekend? I don't know—the sooner the better, really. I can't imagine not being with Tim now. I'll talk to him when I see him.'

'You seeing him today?'

Ruth nodded. 'I'll go back at lunchtime—he's off today.'

'Go now. I've got things to do as well—people to talk to. We'll meet up again later in the week.'

She nodded again, then hugged him, the unprecedented physical contact taking him by surprise. In nine years he'd always kept his distance, giving her space, careful to preserve her comfort zone because of what had happened to her. Now it seemed she didn't need it any more.

'I hope it works out for you with Annie and Stephen,' she said a little unevenly. 'You deserve to be happy. It's been far, far too long—for all of us.'

And for ever for David. He put away that thought, shaking his head slightly to clear it. It was time for the living, now. Time to move on.

Time for the last and maybe most important op of his life. He'd planned it meticulously over the past year, and thrown out each plan. He was going to have to fly this one by the seat of his pants, but he was going to succeed. He had to. The stakes were too high for him to fail.

'You take care, babe. Tell Tim from me he's a lucky man.'

He watched Ruth go, then sat down, staring blindly out over the gently rolling fields. He could see a tractor working in the distance, the gulls wheeling in its wake, dots against the vivid blue of the sky.

It was still warm during the day, even though it was September. It reminded him of France. That late September had been just like this, with glorious sunny days and then later, moving into October, clear, starry nights when the temperature would fall and their breath would fog on the cold night air as they walked hand in hand between the vines.

He shut his eyes, seeing her again, young and vibrant and full of laughter, her eyes bubbling over with joy. She'd tasted so sweet, so eager and passionate—so utterly irresistible. He hadn't been able to resist—not that night, knowing things were coming to a head. He'd lost himself in her, and she'd given him everything. Her ring. Her heart.

And a son who didn't know him.

Yet.

His fingers closed over the ring. He'd worn it on a chain around his neck for so many years now the chain had worn a groove in the band. She'd given it to him that night to keep him safe, after they'd made love, and he'd treasured it all this time. It was almost as if he'd survive as long as he had it on him. He'd never taken it off, but he would now. He'd have to, or she'd see it and know, before he was ready.

He took it off, slipped it into his wallet, fingering the lump it made in the soft leather.

Maybe soon he could tell her the truth. Not yet, though.

First, she had to get to know him again, get to know the real man, the man he was now. And he had to get to know her.

At least they were free now—him free to woo her, her free to love him if she would. That was by no means certain, but he wouldn't allow the thought of failure. Not now, not at this stage.

He moved away from the window, his eyes no longer focusing on the tractor in the distance, but on his reflection in the mirror. Dispassionately, with clinical detachment, he studied the man who stared back at him.

Would he get away with it?

He didn't look like the man Annie had fallen in love with. Time and the surgery that had saved his life had seen to that. The results were passable—battered, but passable. He wasn't actively ugly, at least; he should be grateful for that. He wondered if his own parents would have recognised him. At least they'd been spared seeing him at his worst. It would have killed his mother. It had damn nearly killed him.

He turned away, reached for the phone, dialled a long-familiar number.

'It's me,' he said economically.

He could almost hear the smile at the other end.

'Michael. Welcome back to the real world.'

CHAPTER ONE

'HIYA.'

Annie was just about to close when she heard Ruth's voice behind her. 'Hiya yourself, stranger,' she said, turning with a grin. 'I missed you over the weekend. How are you?'

'Better than you, apparently. You look tired, Annie.'

She flapped her hand. 'I'm always tired. I've been tired for years,' she said, dismissing it. 'Don't worry about me, I'm used to it. What can I get you? Coffee? Tea?'

'Nothing. I don't want to stop you, you're about to close.'

'I have done,' she said, shutting the door and flipping the sign in the window. 'There's half a pot of coffee left and it's only going down the drain if we don't drink it. Want to share it with me?'

'If you're sure you've got time. What about Stephen?'

'He's got chess club.' She reached for the cups. 'So, how are you? I haven't seen you for days.' Annie scanned Ruth's face, checking out the slightly heightened colour in her cheeks, the sparkle in her eyes, as if something was bottled up inside her and threatening to spill over. She'd be a lousy poker player, she thought with a grin.

'OK, come on, spit it out. What's going on? Where have you been?'

Ruth gave a self-conscious chuckle. 'At Tim's. Actually, I've got something to tell you.'

'I'd never have guessed!' Annie teased, plonking the full cups on the round table by the window and pulling up a chair. 'Come on, then—tell away.'

Ruth laughed softly and sat, making a production of opening the creamer and tipping it into the cup, stirring it unnecessarily long until Annie was ready to scream.

'Ruth?' she prompted.

'Sorry.' Her smile was—good heavens—shy? 'I'm getting married.'

Annie's heart squeezed tight, and she leant over and hugged Ruth, pressing her eyes firmly shut to hold back the unexpected prickle of tears. 'Ruth, that's fantastic!' she said, her voice choked. 'When did he ask you? I take it we're talking about your gorgeous policeman, since you spent the weekend with him?'

Ruth sniffed and sat back, her cheeks pink. 'Of course it's Tim. And he's asked me over and over again. I said yes this morning. I'm going to move in with him.'

'Well, of course you will.' She listened to herself in dismay. Did she really sound so bereft? How silly. She injected a little enthusiasm and interest into her voice. 'Will you be far away? Where does he live?'

'Not far. Only three miles. He's been asking me endlessly to move in with him, dropping hints for ages before he began proposing—and I've finally decided to do it.'

'Oh, Ruth, I'm so pleased for you! I wondered what was going on—you've been looking so much happier since you met him.'

'I have been. I am.'

'It shows.' Annie smiled wistfully. 'Lucky old you. You know, I did wonder at one point, when there didn't seem to be a man in your life at all, if you'd got some kind of thing going on with Michael—'

'Michael? Good grief, no!' She laughed and shook her head. 'Hardly.'

'Is he so bad?'

Ruth chuckled. 'No, he's not bad at all. Far from it. I suppose if he was your type, you'd think he was very sexy in a rather brooding sort of way. I don't know. You can judge for yourself on Monday.'

'Monday?'

'Mmm. He's coming over then—I'm moving out at the weekend, and he's going to start tearing the place apart. He's jumped at the chance to get in there. He wants to refurbish the whole building, in fact; says it's long overdue, which it is.'

Annie blinked in surprise. 'Does he have time?'

Ruth nodded. 'He's going to have a break from writing, and he's told me to take a holiday, so I am. I think he's planning a little physical work to free up his thoughts and, let's face it, the place could do with a hefty dose of TLC. I think he's looking forward to pushing his sleeves up and getting stuck in.'

Her heart thudded unexpectedly. 'Wow. So I get to meet the great man at last.'

She chewed her lip absently. She'd never met her landlord, not in the seven years since he'd bought the Ancient House. Ruth had been the go-between, working for him as his researcher and living here in the flat that occupied the whole of the top floor, but curiously Michael himself had never darkened her door, so she knew little about him except that he was a writer—a hugely successful one, if the best seller lists were to be believed.

That was probably why she'd never met him. Too busy and

important to trouble himself with some trifling investment property—or so she'd thought. He certainly didn't need her contribution to his income if the rumours of his advances were true.

Roger had loved his books—he'd even met him once, but she'd been out when he called and so she'd missed him, to her disappointment. But he hadn't described him as broodingly sexy—

'I wonder if he'll use the refurb as an excuse to put my rent up?' she murmured, dragging herself back to practical matters and the here and now.

Ruth shrugged. 'Dunno. I doubt it. You'll have to ask him.' She pulled a face. 'It'll be odd not living here after so long.'

'Seven years. It'll be weird without you. I'll miss you.' Unaccountably she felt herself tearing up again and looked away crossly. 'Sorry, I'm being an idiot. I'm delighted for you, I really am. It's just—'

'You'll miss me. I know. I'll miss you, too.' Ruth patted her arm awkwardly. 'You'll be fine. You've got my mobile number—perhaps we could go out for a drink one evening, if Stephen's with a friend or something?'

'That would be lovely,' she said, knowing quite well it was unlikely to happen but grateful to Ruth for suggesting it. 'Thank you for all you've done for me in the past few years, especially since Roger died. You've been a star.'

'My pleasure. You've been a good friend to me, too, Annie. There were times when I couldn't have got through without you.'

That unexpected frankness was nearly her undoing. Annie swallowed and gave a little shrug. 'What are friends for? I'm glad you've found someone. You deserve to be happy.'

Ruth nodded and turned her attention to her coffee, looking at it rather than at Annie, stirring it with meticulous care. 'I just wish you could be as happy,' she said quietly after a moment. 'I know you and Roger were very fond of each other, but you weren't exactly soul mates, were you? You've never really told me about Stephen's father, but I get the feeling you're still a little in love with him. Is there any chance—?'

Annie felt her smile slip. 'No. He's dead—years ago, before I started running this place. The way I felt—well, it was a one-off, crazy thing. I don't know if it was the real thing, but it certainly felt like it at the time. He was French, and such a charmer—I just fell for that broken English and gorgeous, sexy accent hook, line and sinker. I adored him, but you can't base a marriage on it. At least we didn't have time to get bored with each other. I don't know. It might have worked given time, who knows, but I doubt it. We just didn't get the chance to find out.'

'But maybe now—if the right man came along—?'

She shook her head. 'No. I don't need any more heartache, and nor does Stephen. He's lost two fathers, although he only ever knew Roger. I think that's enough for anyone.'

Ruth was quiet for a moment, then she looked up and searched Annie's face. 'Do you think Stephen's suffered for not knowing his real father?'

Annie shook her head slowly. 'No—not really. I know we had an unconventional marriage, but Roger was a good father to all the children. Stephen adored him, and I would have been horribly lost without him—even if I could never compete with his first wife.'

'Ah, yes. The amazing Liz. Ghosts are always the hardest. She was a bit of a legend, by all accounts. They still talk about her, you know.'

Annie nodded. 'She was certainly loved in the village. Her death was an awful shock to everyone. I couldn't believe it. She'd been my college lecturer, you know—taught me everything I knew about catering, but she was more than that, even then. She was a friend, a real friend, and I was lost when she died, but at least we'd set this place up by then, so she saw her dream become reality. Still. Time moves on, and they're together again now. And you've got your Tim. I really, really hope you're happy together.'

'We will be. Do keep in touch. Can I come and have coffee still?'

Annie laughed. 'Of course. I run a coffee shop—what else would you do?'

'But you're busy.'

'Never too busy for a friend. Please come. Don't be a stranger. I couldn't bear to lose you, too.'

'You won't lose me—promise.'

Ruth hugged her again, and then went out, running up the stairs to the flat above to start her packing, and Annie scrubbed the kitchen until it sparkled, determined not to let the stupid tears fall. It wasn't as if Ruth was a bosom buddy, but as busy as she was, Ruth was probably one of her closest friends. Bringing up the children and working the hours she did didn't leave a lot of time for socialising.

She straightened up, threw the tea towel she'd used for polishing the worktops into a bag to take home, and looked round, checking to make sure she was ready for the morning.

What would her landlord make of it? she wondered. And how would he want to change it? Refurb covered a multitude of sins. A shiver of apprehension went down her spine. The Ancient House was Grade II listed, so there were restrictions on what he could do to it—she hoped. She didn't want it to change. She'd had enough change recently. But what if he wanted to throw her out and turn it back into a house? That was always a possibility now she was the only tenant.

It was old, very old, a typical low Tudor house, stretching

all across one side of the square, with a big heavy door in the centre that led to a small rectangular entrance hall. There was a door straight ahead that led to the flat above, another door leading to Miller's, her little tearoom that ran front to back on the right of the door, and one opening into the left-hand end that was occupied by the little antique shop.

Ex-antique shop, she reminded herself, now that Mary had wound down her business and closed the door finally for the last time only a week ago, so what better time for him to move in and make changes?

More changes. Heavens, her life was full of them recently. Roger's death in June last year had been the first. Even though they'd been waiting for it, it had still been a shock when it came. Still, they'd got through somehow, comforting each other, and it hadn't been all bad.

Kate, Roger's younger daughter, had got the grades she needed for uni, and there had been tears, of course, because her father hadn't been there to see her success. And Annie, telling her how proud he would have been, had reduced them all to tears again.

In September the girls had gone away—Vicky, the eldest, back to Leicester for her second year and Kate to Nottingham to start her degree—and the house had seemed unnaturally silent and empty. Stephen was back at school, and without the tearoom Annie would have gone crazy.

She'd grown used to the silence, though, and the holidays since had seemed almost too noisy. Much as she loved them, she'd been glad this September when the girls had gone away again and taken their chaos and untidiness with them, but without them, and with Ruth moving on, it would be very quiet. Probably too quiet.

She laughed softly to herself.

'You are perverse. One minute it's too noisy, the next it's too quiet. Nothing's ever right.'

Still, from Monday things would liven up with the refurb starting. And she'd finally get to meet her landlord, the broodingly sexy Michael Harding. Whatever that implied.

Well, she hoped it turned out right and he didn't have an ulterior motive. Here she was trying to work out what broodingly sexy might mean, when all the time he might be going to give her notice or put up her rent. It wouldn't be unreasonable if he did, but it would be the last straw.

Roger's pension kept the girls in uni. The tearoom provided the means to keep her and Stephen and run the house, but the balance was fine and she didn't need anything unexpected thrown into the equation.

There was always the trust fund, but she had no intention of touching that, even if she could. It was Stephen's, from some unknown distant cousin who'd died intestate; it had been passed down to him as the man's youngest living relative, which was apparently how the law worked. She wasn't going to argue, and as only one of the trustees she wasn't sure she could get access to it, even to provide for her son. Still, to know it was there was like a safety net, carefully invested for the future.

Whatever that might hold. Maybe Monday would bring some answers.

She went home, cutting the corner to where their pretty Georgian house stood at right angles to the tearoom, centred on the left-hand side of the square. Like the Ancient House, Beech House occupied a prominent position in the centre of the village, its elegant, symmetrical façade set back behind a low wall enclosing the pretty front garden.

The fact that it was so lovely hardly ever registered with Annie, though. For her, the main feature was its convenience.

It was handy being so close. That was why Liz had chosen to open the tearoom there, of course, and its proximity had been a godsend while the children were young.

It didn't feel like home, though. It never really had. She was like a caretaker, and with Roger gone and the girls flying the nest she wondered what on earth she was going to do with it. Keep it for ever, so the girls felt they could always come home? Or just until Stephen was eighteen?

Another nine years. Heavens. The thought of another nine years of this was enough to send her over the brink.

She closed the door behind her, leant back on it and listened to the silence. She was right, it was too quiet, and Stephen with his bubbly chatter wouldn't be home until eight. God, the house was so *empty*.

She made herself a cup of tea, then settled down on the sofa in the little sitting room to watch the news for company. She kicked off her shoes, tucked her feet under her bottom and flicked on the TV with the remote control.

And then she froze, riveted by the commentary and the picture she saw unfolding before her eyes.

'—a vineyard in the Rhône valley, high up on the steeply terraced hillside where only the most exclusive wines can justify the exorbitant labour costs for handpicking the grapes—unless, like Claude Gaultier, you use a migrant workforce.'

The reporter waved an arm behind him at the serried ranks of vines, bursting with fruit just starting to ripen. 'For the past eleven years, the vines here have been worked by what amounts to slave labour, the workers kept in very basic accommodation and forced to work hugely long hours in appalling conditions on these steep mountainsides to bolster Gaultier's extortionate profit.'

The picture scanned over the familiar scenery, the bunkhouse, the farmhouse where she'd cooked, the winery, the terraces where they'd walked hand in hand—

'All the workers were young men, most of whose parents had paid extraordinary sums to give them an opportunity to escape from countries such as Albania to the riches of Western Europe. They were lied to, cheated for the sake of money, but at least these young men were only forced to work hard. The young women, on the other hand, were shipped all over Europe and sold into prostitution, many of them in London and Manchester, and the fate of these innocent girls has been far worse. The dawn raid today, the culmination of a decade of work by the security services of several countries, has seen many of Gaultier's accomplices arrested. Gaultier himself, the mastermind behind this hideous empire trafficking in innocent lives, died resisting arrest when his house in Antibes was stormed this morning, and it must be said there will be few tears shed for this most evil and wanted of men.'

The picture returned to the newsroom, and Annie stared blankly at the screen.

Dear God. She'd always known the conditions there were dreadful, but she'd had no idea they were that bad. People-trafficking? Slave labour? She'd not really been involved with the labour force, more with the managers. Like Etienne. And Etienne had taken her mind off anything but him, from the moment she'd set eyes on him...

'*Bonjour.*'

She looked up, her heart hitching into her throat at the slow, lazy lilt of his voice. Blue eyes, a smile that started gradually and kicked up both corners of his mouth to reveal perfect, even teeth—no. Not perfect. Not quite. One of them was chipped, and his nose was nothing to write home about, but the smouldering eyes and the lazy smile were enough to counteract that in spades.

'*Bonjour,*' she replied, her hand hovering over a steaming dish of lamb casserole. '*Desirez-vous un peu de ragout?*'

The smile widened. '*Tu,*' he murmured. '*Vous* is too—how you say—formal?—for me.'

She felt herself colouring. 'Oh. Sorry. I thought it was correct.'

He grinned. 'It is—but we do not need to be correct, *hein*, you and me?'

She found herself smiling back, her heart fluttering against her ribs like a thing demented. Her hand still hovered over the casserole, her eyes trapped by his. 'How did you know I was English?' she said breathlessly.

'Your delightful accent,' he replied, in a delightful accent of his own, and her heart melted into a puddle at his feet. He held out his hand. 'Etienne Duprés—at your service, *mademoiselle.*'

'Annie Shaw,' she said breathlessly, and he took her hand, wrapping it in warm, hard fingers. His thumb slid over the back of it, grazing it gently, sending shivers up her spine while his eyes locked with hers.

'*Enchanté, mademoiselle,*' he murmured, then after an age he bent to press his lips to her hand—but not the back. Oh, no. He turned it over and pressed his lips firmly and devastatingly to the palm, then folded her fingers over to enclose the kiss and straightened up to meet her eyes again, a slow, sexy grin teasing at his mouth.

He wasn't the only one who was enchanted. Annie could hardly think straight for the rest of the meal, dishing up for the family and the skilled staff. The grape-pickers had their own catering arrangements in the bunkhouse, and her job was to help Madame Chevallier to cook for the permanent staff who ran the vineyard. And if she didn't want to lose her job, she'd better concentrate on what she was doing.

Finally they were all served and seated, and she took her own meal and went and sat in the only space left. Which just happened, by a curious coincidence, to be next to Etienne Duprés.

'You must be new here; I haven't seen you,' she said, but he shook his head.

'I have been away—*en vacances*. On holiday?'

She nodded. 'I wondered.'

'So you have been thinking about me. *Bon*,' he said with satisfaction. 'And you must be new here.'

She nodded again. 'I'm here for the harvest. I'm sorry, my French is dreadful—'

He waved a hand dismissively. 'I'm sure we understand what is necessary,' he said, and his eyes locked with hers again, their message unmistakeable.

'You're outrageous,' she told him, blushing, and he laughed, not a discreet chuckle but the real thing, throwing back his head and letting out a deep rumble of a belly-laugh that had all the others smiling and nodding and ribbing him.

'No, *mademoiselle*, I only tell the truth.'

And he was right, of course. She could understand enough of the muddle of his French and English to know precisely what he was trying to say to her, and he seemed to be able to understand English better than he could speak it, so between them they managed.

After all, it didn't take much facility with the language to walk side by side along the rows of vines in the setting sun, and to pause under the spreading branches of an old oak tree and exchange slow, lingering kisses.

That was all they ever did, and then he'd sigh and turn back to the path and wrap his arm around her, tucking her into his side and shortening his stride to hers as they strolled back to the farmhouse. On her nights off he took her to the village and they sat in the bar and talked in their halting French and English until late, then he walked her home, pausing to kiss her under the tree.

She learned that he was an estate manager, that he'd trained in Australia and California, that he had been brought in to supervise the production of the exclusive and very expensive wine produced here. She told him she had trained as a cook, but was going to run a tearoom—a café—called Miller's, with a friend in a village in Suffolk on her return.

He seemed interested, so she told him about Liz Miller, and about their plans and how Liz was getting it off the ground now and how they'd share it when she got home, and he grinned and promised to come and visit her. 'To take tea— in Miller's, a very English tearoom. I shall look forward to this. After the harvest,' he promised, and she believed him.

She learned to tease him, and he teased her back. One evening as they sat in the bar she reached out a hand and ran her fingertip down the bumpy and twisted length of his nose. 'What happened to it?' she asked, and he laughed.

'I was—*pouf*!' he said, making a fist and holding it to his nose and grinning.

'You had a fight?'

He nodded, blue eyes laughing.

'Don't tell me—over a woman?'

The grin widened. '*Mais oui!* What else is there to fight about?'

She chuckled. 'And did you win?'

'*Bien sur!* Of course. I always win the lady.'

'And was she married, this lady?' she asked, suddenly needing the answer to be no, and he frowned, serious for once.

'*Non.* Of course not. I would not do that. I am— How do you say it? A gentleman.'

And he was. He walked her home, kissed her lingeringly, sighed and handed her in through the door like the gentleman he said he was, then wandered off, whistling softly under his breath.

A week later, one cold October night, he seemed different. Distracted, somehow, and for once not focusing on her with that strange intensity, as if she was the centre of his world. At least not then, not in the bar, but later on the way home he drew her off the path, away from the farm buildings and up into a little wood, then he turned her into his arms and kissed her in a way he'd never kissed her before.

His body was strong and lean and full of coiled energy, warm and hard under her hands, his heart pounding against her chest, a strange urgency about him. He'd always been playful before, but that night there was no time for play. He kissed her as if he'd die without her, touched her as if she was the most precious thing in the universe. They made love then for the first and last time, on a bed of fallen leaves under the stars, and in his arms she found a happiness she'd never even dreamed of.

She'd been totally innocent, but he'd been so gentle, so thorough, so—incredible—that she'd felt no pain, only joy and an unbelievable rightness.

Afterwards he walked her back, kissing her once more as he left her at the door of the farmhouse, his touch lingering.

Struck suddenly by some sense of evil, she pulled off her ring and gave it to him, pressing it into his hand.

'Here—have this. It was my grandmother's. It's a St Christopher. It will keep you safe.' And she reached up and kissed him again. 'Take care, my love,' she whispered, and his arms tightened for a second before he let her go.

He murmured something. She didn't really catch it. It sounded curiously like *'Au revoir'*, but why would he be saying goodbye? So final, so irrevocable. It sent a shiver through her, and after she went to bed she lay and thought about it.

She must have misheard. It could have been *'Bonsoir'*, although even she knew that meant good evening and not goodnight. And anyway, he usually told her to sleep well. But *'Au revoir'*? Until we meet again? That seemed too final—not at all like goodnight. It puzzled her, but she convinced herself she must have heard it wrong, until the following day when she went down to make breakfast and found Madame Chevallier in tears.

A chill ran over her, and she hurried to her side, putting her arm around the woman who'd become her friend. *'Madame?'*

'Oh, Annie, *ma petite—je suis desolée.* I'm so sorry.'

'Pardon? Madame, what is it? What's happened?'

'Oh, *mon Dieu. C'est terrible.* Etienne—*il est mort!* Dead—*et* Gerard *aussi. Oh, mon Dieu!'*

Panic flooded her. Panic and the first terrible, overwhelming crush of grief. She sucked in a huge lungful of air, then another, fighting off the pain. 'No. You're wrong. You're lying! He can't be dead!'

But *Madame* shook her head and wept, her whole body shaken with sobs, and Annie realised it must be true.

'No… Dear God, no.'

She looked outside and saw the *gendarme* talking to Monsieur Gaultier, both of them shaking their heads in disbelief, and she ran out past them, up to the place where he'd taken her in his arms and made love to her with such passionate intensity just a few short hours before. Such exquisite joy—

'Etienne, no. You can't be dead,' she wept, falling to the

soft, sweet earth where she'd lain with him so recently. 'No! It's not true.'

The sobs racked her body endlessly, the pain tearing her apart cell by cell, leaving her in tatters.

Madame found her there, prostrate with grief, and helped her back to the house.

'I have to go and see him,' she said. 'I can't believe—'

So Madame Chevallier called a taxi, and she went first to the village, but the *gendarme* wouldn't talk to her. Then she went to the town where it had happened, where the hospital was and the morgue, but the information was even less forthcoming.

The only thing she was sure of was that he was gone, but even his death she had to take on trust. She wanted to see his body, to say goodbye, but she was told his family had taken it already, and no, she couldn't be given their details.

'It is gone, *mademoiselle*. You cannot see him. You must go home.'

Home. It was the only thing in her suddenly topsy-turvy world to make sense. She'd go home, to the only people who really cared about her. Liz and Roger would look after her. She went back, packed her things and set off. She should have phoned them, but she couldn't bring herself to say the words, and so she made her way to Calais and took the first available crossing, caught the train from Dover and arrived back at ten that night, going straight to their house.

Roger answered the door, his face haggard, and Annie, even through her grief, could see that something was terribly, horribly wrong.

A shiver of dread ran down her spine. 'Roger?' she whispered. 'What's happened?'

'It's Liz,' he said, and then he started to cry, dry, racking sobs that tore her apart.

'Where is she?'

'In bed. Don't wake her. She's got a headache. Annie, she's dying—'

A brain tumour. Roger told her the bare bones, but Liz filled her in on all the details in the morning, sitting at the kitchen table after the children had gone to school.

'Inoperable?' she echoed hollowly. 'Are they sure?'

'Oh, yes. I've had every kind of scan, believe me.' Liz searched Annie's eyes, and frowned. Even then, in the midst of such agony, she noticed that something was wrong. Her hand found Annie's, gripping it hard. 'Annie, what is it? What's happened to you? You shouldn't be home yet. What's going on? You look awful, my love.'

She swallowed the tears, not wanting to cry about something that must seem so remote to this very dear friend in the midst of her own grief, but unable to hold them back. 'Etienne's dead.'

Liz's face was shocked. 'What? How? Why?'

She shook her head. 'I don't know. All they'd tell me was he'd been mugged in an alley in the town. He was with another man, and he was killed, too. They were beaten to death—'

'Who would do such a thing? Do they know who did it?'

She shook her head. 'I don't think so. They wouldn't tell me much. I just— Liz, I can't believe it. First him, and now you—'

And then the dam burst, and they held each other and wept the raw, bitter tears of grief...

The gravel crunched under his tyres as he drew to a halt, cut the engine and got out, a lump in his throat. He was about to ring the doorbell when an elderly terrier trotted round the corner of the house and came up to him, sniffing.

'Nipper?'

The dog pricked his ears, whined and jumped up at him, his stubby little tail thrashing wildly in apparent recognition, and the lump in his throat just got bigger.

'Nipper, it *is* you,' he murmured. 'I can't believe it! What a good old boy!' He crouched down, and the dog lashed his face with his tongue in greeting, all the time whining and wagging and wriggling furiously under his hands, unable to get enough of his old friend.

'Nipper! Nipper, get down! Bad dog. I'm so sorry. Nipper!'

He straightened slowly, taking in the changes that time had carved in his godmother's face. The lump wedged itself in his throat, so that for a moment he couldn't speak but could only stand there and let the homecoming fill his heart.

'I'm so sorry about that. What can I do for you?' she said, moving closer, and then suddenly she stopped, her hand flying to her mouth, the secateurs clattering unheeded to the ground at his feet. 'Michael?' she whispered soundlessly, and then recovered herself. 'I'm so sorry. For a moment there, I thought you were someone else—'

'Oh, Peggy, I might have known I wouldn't fool you,' he said gruffly, and he felt his face contort into a smile as his arms opened to receive her...

A river of tears later, they were sitting in the kitchen, his godmother on one side, his godfather on the other, catching up on nine very long years while the dog lay heavy on his feet, endlessly washing his ankle above the top of his sock as if he couldn't believe his old friend had really returned.

The dog wasn't alone. Peggy kept touching his face, her fingers infinitely gentle and tentative, getting to know the new him.

'It doesn't hurt,' he assured her quietly. Not much, at least. Not with the painkillers.

'But it did. It must have done.'

He nodded. 'Yes. It did. I'm glad you didn't see it.'

She shook her head. 'We should have been there for you.'

'It wasn't possible. It wasn't safe. I'm sorry they had to tell you I was dead.'

'I knew you weren't,' she told him. 'The flowers on my birthday, the cards. They said you were dead, but I knew.'

'I didn't believe her,' Malcolm said. 'I thought she was imagining it. At one point I thought she had a secret admirer—someone from the local horticultural society.'

'Silly man,' Peggy said with a fond smile. 'As if.' She paused, then went on, 'I don't suppose you can tell us—'

He gave a twisted smile. 'You know better than to ask that. I've told you all I can. It's all over the television, anyway—and all that really matters is that it's over and I'm alive—even if I don't really look like me any more.'

His godfather nodded wordlessly. 'If I may say so,' he muttered gruffly, 'the nose is better.'

He chuckled. 'I agree. The nose is a bonus. The headaches I could live without, and the teeth aren't great. At least they don't go in a glass at night, though, so I should be thankful for small mercies.'

'So—I take it they gave you a new identity? Who've you been all this time?'

'Michael Harding.'

'Oh—like the thriller writer. How ironic. I've read all his books...love 'em. Fancy you having the same name.'

'I *am* the writer,' he said diffidently, and shrugged. 'I had to do something while I was marking time, and I thought I might as well put all that experience to good use. I had no idea it was going to be such a success or that I'd love it so much.'

Peggy's eyes filled again and she nodded slowly. 'I wondered if it was you. I could hear your voice in the words. Oh, Michael, I'm so proud of you!'

Malcolm's hand curled round his shoulder, squeezing tight as he stood up. 'Absolutely. And your parents would have been proud—very, very proud, and with good reason. Many good reasons.'

'Thank you,' he said gruffly, unbearably touched. 'I'm just glad they didn't have to go through what you have done.'

'Amen to that.' He harrumphed and made a great production of clearing his throat. 'Well, I think this calls for a drink,' he said, retrieving a bottle of champagne from the fridge and putting three flutes on the table. He stripped off the foil and twisted the wire cage, just as Michael put his hand in his pocket.

'There's something else you should know,' he said, and pulled out a photograph and slid it on to the table. 'It seems I have a son.'

The cork popped loudly in the silence and, while the wine foamed unheeded over Malcolm's hand, Peggy started to weep again.

CHAPTER TWO

'GOOD morning.'

She looked up, and for a second her heart stopped.

And then he moved, stepped forwards into the room, and as the light hit his face Annie felt the stupid, foolish hope drain away and her heart started again.

She picked up a tea towel, drying her hands for something to do that didn't involve anything fragile like crockery. Crazy. For a moment there— But it was silly. It was just because she'd been thinking about him—

'You OK?' he asked, his voice low and rough and strangely sensuous. 'You look as if you've seen a ghost.'

She nearly laughed aloud, and dragged her eyes from the battered, lived-in face in front of her, staring down in bewilderment at her shaking hands. Lord, she should have stopped doing this after all these years, clutching at straws, seeing him in any random stranger, but there was just something—

'Sorry. You reminded me of someone. Can I get you anything?'

He shook his head. 'You must be Annie Miller. I'm Michael Harding—your landlord. It's good to meet you. I'm sorry it's taken so long.'

He held out his hand, and she dropped the tea towel and reached over the cakes and placed her hand briefly in his warm, strong grasp—a grasp that was somehow safe and solid and utterly reassuring.

She fought the urge to leave her hand there—probably for ever—and tried to remember how to talk.

'That's OK, I know you're busy. Ruth said you'd be coming over,' she told him, her voice unaccountably breathless. She retrieved her hand and found a smile from somewhere, and his lips tilted in answer, a crooked, distorted smile, one corner of his mouth strangely reluctant. It should have made him ugly, but it didn't, something about the eyes and firm, sculpted lips devastatingly attractive—

'Any chance of getting a few quiet minutes with you this morning so we can talk?' he was asking, his soft and yet rough voice doing something weird to her insides. She forced herself to concentrate on his words, and found herself suddenly nervous. Was this it? Was he going to give her notice? Planning to sell up or hike her rent out of reach?

She schooled her voice and her expression, trying to quell the panic. 'It's quiet now that the breakfast crowd have gone. Will this do?'

'Sure. I'd just like to chat, really—have a look round, see it with my own eyes. I haven't been here for years, but Ruth tells me you've done a good job. I gather it's very successful. I just wanted to make sure you're happy with everything.'

She felt the tension ease a fraction and wondered if she was being too trusting. Probably. It was her greatest fault.

'Help yourself, it won't take you long to see it all—the cloakroom's through that door at the back, and the store's out there, too, and the kitchen you can see.'

He looked at it over the counter and nodded. 'Nice, having it in the middle like this. Friendly.'

'That was one of the things Liz and I insisted on, having the preparation area right in the middle of this long wall. It makes it relaxed and approachable, a bit like sitting in someone's kitchen while they cook for you. And you can see everything—there are no nasty surprises, no dirty corners. You know exactly what conditions your food's being prepared under, and people like that. We thought it was a good idea.'

He nodded. 'It's good. Low key, easy. Relaxed. I like it. Who's Liz?'

'Oh—the founder, really. She was my late husband's first wife. She was lovely.'

'Was?'

'She died nine years ago, just after she set it up.'

'I'm sorry,' he said, and for some reason it didn't seem like a platitude. He didn't dwell, though, but moved on, his eyes taking everything in, and she followed him, answering questions, smiling as necessary and wondering what he'd think of her housekeeping.

He went into the store, looked round, checked out the loo, then turned, almost on top of her, and her heart hitched.

'It is small, isn't it?' he said, far too close for comfort and trampling all over her common sense.

Ruth was right. He was broodingly sexy. Very. She backed away, reversing into a table. 'Intimate.'

'It's tiny,' he said, with a lopsided grin that made her heart lurch again.

'Small but perfectly formed,' she quipped, and his eyes flicked over her and returned to her face.

'Absolutely,' he murmured, and she stared into those gorgeous blue eyes and felt herself colour. Heavens. How could he not have been Ruth's type? He'd be any woman's type if she had a pulse—

She turned away abruptly. 'Coffee?' she said, her voice scratchy and a little high, and behind her she heard him clear his throat softly, more of a grunt than a cough, as if he was reining back, distancing himself from the suddenly intimate moment.

'That would be lovely.'

So she poured two mugs of coffee and set them down on opposite sides of the round table by the window at the front, where she could see her regulars coming and get their orders under way.

She took the chair closest to the kitchen area. 'I gather from Ruth that you want to refurbish the place,' she said, meeting those dazzling eyes head-on with a challenge, and he nodded.

'I do. It's looking a bit sad. I hadn't really registered—Ruth's been too uncomplaining, and so have you. The flat needs a new kitchen and bathroom, and with the antique shop empty I was thinking maybe we could do something more with this place—give you a little more room as well as freshening it up a little. If you want?'

'How much room?' she asked, trying to concentrate on the overheads and not his face. 'I can't really afford to pay much more.'

He shrugged, his lips pursing, one side reluctant. 'As much as you need. You could take all of it.'

She shook her head. 'The stairs would be in the way. I wouldn't like it divided into two—it wouldn't feel the same. And anyway, the kitchen's not big enough for all those tables. If you're offering bits of the place, I'd rather have the garden.'

He chuckled. 'How did I know that was coming?'

He peeled back the lid on the coffee creamer and tipped it in, stirring it with deliberation, and it gave her a moment to study him openly.

His hair was short and dark, the temples threaded with grey. She wondered how old he was. Forty? Forty-five? More, maybe, or less, but it seemed irrelevant. Whatever, he was very attractive in a very masculine and hard-edged way.

It was odd that he *was* so attractive, really, because his face wasn't classically handsome, by any means. There was something peculiar about it, she decided. Irregular. The jaw wasn't quite symmetrical, the left side of it etched with fine scars that carved white lines in the shadow of his stubble. His chin was a little crooked, his teeth not quite straight.

And yet it was an attractive face for all that. Interesting. She'd love to know the story behind it, but it wasn't the sort of thing you could ask.

Not yet, anyway. Maybe later, when she knew him better—and now she really *had* lost it! He was her landlord. This was their first meeting in seven years. Once the refurb was finished it would probably be another seven before she saw him again, and at that rate they'd both be dead before she knew him well enough to ask—

'Penny for them.'

She shook her head. No way! 'Nothing,' she denied. 'I was compiling a shopping list.'

One eyebrow arched. 'For a witch's brew?'

'I beg your pardon?'

'You were scowling at me. I don't think I fancy the recipe.'

She felt colour touch her cheeks. 'I'm sorry. I was miles away,' she lied.

Contemplating getting to know him better. Much better.

Oh, good grief! She hadn't done this for years, hadn't felt this devastating tug of attraction since—well, since Etienne.

Perhaps it was his body that had triggered the response? They were the same physical type—same height, or there-abouts, although Michael was heavier than Etienne. Same build, though—lithe and muscular. Powerful. And something about the eyes—

But it was more than that, something not quite physical, some deep connection that went right to the heart of her and tumbled her senses into chaos—just as Etienne had done, but in a very different way, because Etienne absolutely never brooded and Michael—well, Michael was deep as the ocean, and she could get lost in those eyes—

Then he looked up again, fixing her with those very eyes, and a slow, lazy curve tilted the right side of his mouth.

And the chaos just got worse.

Lord, she was gorgeous. Beautiful and defensive and responsive as ever, her skin colouring even as he looked at her.

That went with the auburn hair, of course, the rich, warm red that gave her those amazing green eyes and clear, creamy skin. She had freckles after the summer, just like she'd had in France—

He dragged his eyes away, coughed to clear his throat, hauled his libido back under control. He didn't want to blow it now, when it looked as though he'd got over the first hurdle. His heartbeat was starting to steady, the nerves of steel he'd always had before an op coming back now to help him through, but this was much, much harder, somehow much scarier because it was the real thing.

She'd given him a fright when she'd first looked up at him. He'd been sure she'd recognised him, but then she'd talked herself out of it as he watched. He'd seen the cogs turn, and then he'd just had to deal with her veiled curiosity.

She'd been studying him just now, and it had taken all his self-control not to get up and walk away. He hated looking like this—hated what had been done to him, the fact that he didn't recognise himself any more. And he hated being studied. Normally he would have walked away or stared the person down, but this was Annie, and she needed to be able to live with it. So he'd let her look, pretending interest in the coffee, just hoping it didn't make her want to run.

'So you want the garden?' he said, forcing himself to stick to the game plan, and for a moment she looked a little startled.

Then she nodded.

'Yes—but I know it goes with the flat.'

'Not necessarily,' he said slowly, watching her. 'We could certainly divide it. What did you have in mind? You've obviously been thinking about it—how long have you been here now, did you say?'

'Nine years.'

As if he didn't know that, almost to the minute. He kept his expression steady—not easy, considering. 'So in that time you must have come up with some ideas.'

'Oh, all sorts, but one of the problems is that to gain access to the garden at the back I'd have to lose one of the tables, and I can't really afford to do that. Our summers aren't reliable enough.'

'But you could have a conservatory.'

She laughed. 'I couldn't possibly justify the expense! It would cost a fortune to have one big enough to do any good, and the place doesn't do much more than break even really. I make a reasonable living, but I work hard for it and there's no slack in the system. I wouldn't contemplate taking on any expansion plans.'

'But I might.'

Her eyes snapped back to his, widening. 'Why? Why would you do that?'

He shrugged. Why, indeed? To make her happy? Crazy.

'I've got the money—why not? It would add to the value of the property.'

'Only if you're thinking of selling it,' she said, and he could see the apprehension in her eyes. He shook his head and hastened to reassure her.

'No. It was just an idea. Don't worry about it. But the access to the cloakroom through the store—that's not a very good idea, and it's a bit cramped. There was a doorway on the other side at the back of the stairs, according to my plans. We could open it up and make a store there. Or create an alcove, as well as a store. Take more off the antique shop. There are lots of options. I don't see the cost as a factor. Think about it.'

She caught her lip between her teeth, worrying it gently, making it pinker. He had an overwhelming urge to soothe the tiny bruise with his tongue and had to remind himself firmly what he was doing here.

Helping. Not hindering, not chatting her up or flirting with her or putting the moves on her.

He'd done that nine years ago, and look where it had got them. No. This time he was going to do things right. Take it slowly, give them a chance to get to know each other properly. There was far too much at stake to blow it because of his overactive hormones.

He picked up his cup, dragged his eyes off her and drained it in one.

'Right. Let me pay you for the coffee and I'll go and get on. Lots to do.'

'Don't be ridiculous!' she said quickly. 'I wouldn't dream of taking any money off you—'

He laughed softly. 'No, I insist—because I'm just about to rip out the kitchen in the flat and I intend to pop down whenever I need a drink or something to eat, and if you won't let me pay my way I won't feel I can—'

'Rubbish. Anyway,' she said, and her mouth tipped up into a grin that made his heart crash against his ribs, 'I'll keep a tally and get my pound of flesh. I'm still after the garden, remember?'

He laughed again, and shook his head. 'I won't argue—for now. And think about what I said about the changes you want.'

'I will. Thanks.'

She met his eyes, and the urge to bend forwards and brush his lips against hers nearly overwhelmed him.

Nearly.

He slotted the chair under the table, grabbed his jacket and fled for the door before he got himself into trouble.

Wow.

Annie sat down again with a bump, staring after him. The door at the bottom of the stairs closed softly behind him, and she heard his footsteps running up into the flat above. Suddenly she could breathe again, and she sucked in a great lungful of air and shook her head to clear it.

Wow, she thought again. What *was* it about him? Was it simply that he'd reminded her so forcefully of Etienne? Although he wasn't really that like him. It had just been the initial shock.

But it was more than the looks. He had the same way of concentrating on what she was saying, really listening to her, watching her attentively. Etienne had done that, and it had made her feel somehow special.

Crazy. Michael was just trying to find out what she wanted from the tearoom. He wasn't being attentive; he was just listening to her suggestions for improving his investment.

And any fanciful notions to the contrary had better go straight out of her head, together with any foolish ideas about getting to know him better. This minute.

Now.

There was a thump upstairs, and her attention zinged straight back to him.

Great, she thought. *Kept your mind off him for less than a second. You're doing well, Annie. Really well.*

There was another thump overhead. With any luck he'd be so busy up there he wouldn't find time to come down here pestering her and putting her senses into turmoil.

'You need a life,' she muttered. 'One half-decent man wanders in here and you go completely to pieces.'

She put the scones in the oven, straightened up and saw a coach pull into the square. Oh, no! Just what she needed when her brain was out to lunch. She threw a few more scones into the pan, shut the oven door and refilled the coffee machine as the first of the coach party wandered through the door, peered around and headed for the window table.

Plastering on a smile, she picked up her notepad and went out into the fray.

He'd done it.

Amazing.

OK, theirs had been a brief affair, and nine years would have blurred the memories, but even so he was surprised he'd got away with it.

He shouldn't have been. It was no surprise, really. The young Frenchman she'd loved was dead. She wouldn't be looking for him in an Englishman, especially one who looked so different. When he'd caught her studying him, the look on her face had caught him on the raw. There was no way there'd been recognition in her eyes, just curiosity, and maybe a little fascination. He didn't want her to be fascinated—at least, not like that, but he couldn't blame her. He was no oil painting.

Apart from the nerve damage that had taken away the spontaneous little movements of his lips, contorting his smile, the structure had been so damaged that, even if she'd known, she would have struggled to recognise him. Hell, he sometimes had a shock even now when he caught sight of himself in a mirror. Not to mention the fact that it had aged him more than he cared to admit. He sure as hell didn't look like a man of thirty-eight.

Of course his stupid masculine pride had hoped she'd recognise him right away, and there'd been that moment of panic when she'd first seen him. He'd got away with it, though, brazened it out, and the bit of him that still had any common sense knew it was just as well.

What he wanted—no, needed—was time to build a relationship with her as the people they were now.

No strings. No past. Just the present.

And hopefully the future...

And this place would give him all the time he needed. Whistling softly under his breath, he found a screwdriver and set about dismantling the cupboards.

He hadn't been exaggerating about using her as a kitchen.

He came down for coffee at eleven-thirty, then reappeared at one looking scruffy and harassed and short of caffeine.

'I could do with some lunch,' he said gruffly.

'Coffee first?' she said with a smile that wouldn't quite behave, and he gave her that lopsided grin that creased his eyes and turned her insides out, and nodded.

'You'd better believe it—a huge one—and something substantial to blot it up following not far behind. I'm starving.'

'A pasta bake with roasted vegetables and a side salad?'

'Chuck in a good big lump of bread and you're on.'

She suppressed the smile, but it wouldn't quite go. 'Bad day?'

'The kitchen's fighting back,' he said drily, showing her his hand, and she tutted and cleaned up the scuff on his knuckle with a damp paper napkin and stuck a plaster on it.

'Thanks,' he murmured, then added cheekily, 'I'll get out of your way now—I'd hate to hold up my lunch,' and looked around for a table.

She felt her eyebrows shoot up and a smile tugged at her lips. 'Pushing your luck, aren't you? We're a bit busy—sit by the window with the others. It's my regulars' table—I think you probably qualify already and it's all you deserve after that remark, so I'm throwing you to the piranhas!'

'Are they that bad?'

She laughed. 'You don't know the half of it.'

He chuckled and went over, introducing himself to them and settling his lean, rangy body on the only spare chair. By the time she'd poured his coffee and put the pasta bake in the microwave to heat, he was already entrenched in their conversation about parking on the market square, the current hot topic in the village.

She pulled up the little stool she used for reaching the top of the fridge-freezer and joined them for a few moments, content just to sit there and watch them all wrangling over the insoluble problem of conservation versus trade.

Michael wasn't having that, though. He turned to her and said, 'So what's your opinion?' and dragged her into the conversation.

She laughed and threw up her hands. 'I don't have one. Well, to be exact, I have two, so I don't count. When I'm here, I want people to be able to park. When I'm at home, which is there—' she pointed out her house to him through the window '—I don't want to look at cars. So I'm keeping out of it, not that it will make the slightest difference, because the council will do what they think fit and ignore us all as usual—'

Grace chipped in with her ferociously held views on conservation, Chris complained that there was never anywhere to park close enough to leave a sleeping baby in the vehicle for a few minutes to grab a sanity-restoring coffee amongst friends, and Michael cradled his coffee in his big battered hands and sat back and smiled at her over the pandemonium.

Good grief. How intimate that smile seemed in the crowded room. And how curious that his smile should have become so important to her in such a ridiculously short space of time! The microwave beeped, rescuing her from mental paralysis and any further dangerous speculation, and she leapt up and went back into her little kitchen area and made his salad and sliced him a couple of big chunks of corn bread, her whole body humming with the awareness of his eyes on her for the entire time.

She set the plate down in front of him, warned him that the pasta bake would be hot, and went back behind her counter to deal with a customer who was leaving and wanted to pay the bill.

Then another couple came in and dithered about and changed their order half a dozen times, sat down, glanced across at Michael's meal and changed their minds again.

By the time she'd dealt with them, cleared a couple of tables and loaded the dishwasher, her regulars were drifting out and Michael was left at the table on his own. He wandered over, coming into the kitchen area that was strictly off-limits to customers, and when she pointed that out to him he told her calmly that he owned it and anyway, even if he didn't, she wasn't clearing up after him.

And he put his plate in the dishwasher, refilled his coffee mug and looked round at her crowded little workspace with a pleated brow. 'Poky, isn't it?'

'It's efficient.'

'No, it isn't. It's outdated and cramped.'

'It was the best we could afford,' she said, beginning to bristle and wondering what had happened to that smile that melted her insides, when he suddenly produced it.

'And you've done wonders with it, and you're clearly hugely popular, but that's not a surprise,' he said softly in the low, gravelly voice that finished what the smile had started. 'That pasta bake was delicious. Thank you.'

He sighed and raked his fingers through his hair, the smile rueful now. 'Unfortunately the kitchen's still waiting for me upstairs, so I suppose I ought to go and tackle it before I start rearranging yours. Come and sit and have a drink with me for a minute first, though,' he said, and all the reasons why she shouldn't suddenly went out of the window.

She sat down, pushed the regulars' wreckage out of the way for a moment, and buried her nose in a much-needed cup of coffee. 'Oh, bliss,' she murmured.

'Hectic morning?'

'I haven't stopped,' she confessed. 'It's been bedlam. I was going to have a look through a few recipe books for some new soups, but I haven't had a chance.'

'You do soup?'

She nodded. 'In the winter. I'll be starting it any day now. It's really popular, but I like to do a variety and introduce a few new ones every year. I used to test them out on Roger, but since he died I have to test them on my customers—dangerous, if it bombs!'

'You could test them on me,' he offered, and her heart skittered crazily. Why? They were talking about sampling soups, nothing more. Certainly nothing that should make her heart dance about like a manic puppet!

'You're just after more food,' she said, trying to lighten the suddenly electric atmosphere.

He sat back and chuckled. 'Of course. If I play my cards right, I won't ever have to cook at all. What could be better?'

She was saved the necessity of finding a reply by the arrival of customers, and while she was sorting out their order, Michael left, waggling his fingers at her as he went out of the door and headed up the stairs.

There was a thump and a crash, followed by something she was glad she and her customers couldn't quite hear, and his footsteps came back down the stairs again.

'Got another plaster?' he asked, and she threw him the first aid kit.

'Take it with you—you're obviously going to need it,' she said with a smile, and thus cleverly avoided having to touch him. She was still tingling from the last time!

His finger was sore.

Not that he was any stranger to pain, far from it, but it was just constantly in the way. Everything seemed to require pressure on just that bit of the pad that he'd sliced on the hinge, and finally he packed up his tools, looked around at the carnage and headed back downstairs.

Time for a bucketful of tea, something tasty from her selection of mouthwatering cakes to tide him over until he could be bothered to cook later, and another opportunity to get close to the woman who'd dominated his life and his thoughts for so long.

You're overdoing it, he told himself, but he didn't seem to have any control, and when he walked in her eyes flicked up and caught his instantly and she smiled, and his heart slammed against his ribs and hiccuped into a nice steady gallop.

Nine years, he thought, and he still felt just the same. Time to cool off. Fast.

'I'm going home—I know when I'm beaten. I'll see you tomorrow,' he said and, resisting the urge to hang around any longer, he headed for the door, just as a small boy dragging a backpack wandered in.

'Hi, Mum,' he said, and Annie gave the boy a smile that melted Michael's aching heart.

'Hi, darling. Good day at school?'

Damn. If only he hadn't said he was going—

Whatever. He'd waited over eight years for a formal introduction to his son. Another day or two wouldn't make any difference. He forced himself to carry on walking...

'Mummy, you aren't *listening* to me!'

She jumped guiltily, put down the iron and switched her attention back to Stephen—and away from the man who'd been occupying altogether too much time in her head for the past ten hours.

Heavens, was that all it was? Ten short hours? It seemed—

'Mumm-eeee!'

'Sorry, darling. What is it?'

'My French homework. I can't do it.'

French. She gave a strangled little laugh. Her French was appalling—just enough to get her in trouble, and not enough to get her out of it.

No. Don't go there.

She looked at the book opened out on her kitchen table, and felt a flutter of panic. 'Darling, I'm sorry, my French isn't up to much. Is it easy?'

'If it was easy, I wouldn't need you to help me,' he said in that tone of voice that eight-year-olds reserved for people who were particularly intellectually challenged. 'My father would have been able to help me,' he added with an elaborate sigh.

'Daddy wasn't any better at French than me,' she pointed out, but Stephen just looked at her patiently.

'No, not *Daddy*, my *father*.'

Etienne.

Heavens, how he was cropping up in her life in the last few days! She'd hardly thought of him for years, and now here he was again.

'Yes, he would have been able to help you,' she said, her voice a little strained. 'I'm sorry I'm so useless.' Useless and exhausted and unable to think of anything but Etienne and... inexplicably—the broodingly sexy Michael.

'You aren't useless,' Stephen said kindly. 'Just bad at French. But it's OK, I still love you and you make great cakes.'

She smiled and ruffled his hair, making him duck out of her reach and swat her hand away.

'What's a window?'

'La fenêtre,' she told him.

'Why's it a girl? That's silly.'

But he wrote it down, checking the spelling, his tongue poking out of the side of his mouth as he struggled with the unfamiliar word. 'What's a door?'

'La porte,' she said automatically, getting up to answer the phone and hoping desperately that whoever was ringing was good at French, or at least better than her. 'Ruth—hi! How are things?'

'Great. Fantastic. I should have done it ages ago.'

Annie smiled, pleased for her friend and feeling only a little twinge of envy. 'I'm really glad,' she said, squashing the green streak firmly. 'You deserve a good man in your life.'

'Talking of which, how did you get on today with Michael? Did he come over?'

Her heart did that now-familiar tap-dance on her ribcage, and her mouth kicked up a notch. 'Oh, yes. He's torn the place apart, judging by the noise and the language overhead and the number of plasters he's had off me.'

Ruth laughed. 'So he hasn't put your rent up yet?'

She chuckled. 'No. In fact, if anything, he keeps trying to foist new bits of the premises on to me—the antique shop, more room for a store—'

'Well, let's face it, Annie, you could do with the extra space.'

'Yes, but not the extra cost, which incidentally he's being extraordinarily evasive about. And he keeps pointing out how crowded and poky it is, and I'm beginning to wonder if he isn't right.'

'He is right—and that's part of the charm of the place. Tell him you like it as it is. Have the store, because you need it, but nothing else if you don't want it. Don't let him bully you. Be firm, for goodness' sake, or he'll railroad you into all sorts. I know him, remember. He's like a steamroller when he gets going and he'll kill you with kindness. I should know.'

'I'll bear it in mind. How's your French?'

'Awful.' She hesitated for a second. 'What's the problem?'

'Stephen's homework,' she said. 'He's eight and I can cope now, but I'll be out of my depth in a week! And another thing—now you've moved away I can't test my soups on you,' she added in mock protest. 'Are you sure Tim's so great?'

Ruth laughed. 'Absolutely! And if you want a guinea pig for your soup, ask Michael. Wait till he's pressuring you about the premises and slip it in to distract him. Food's the easiest way to divert him, because he always forgets to eat and he's always hungry.'

'Well, he was certainly hungry today, he had loads—and he's already volunteered for the soup-testing detail.'

'He didn't waste any time, then. I bet you're spoiling him. You don't want to do that, he'll get fat.'

Annie chuckled. 'I'll tell him you said that. And you take care. Come and see me some time.'

'I will. I might bring Tim at the weekend.'

'Do that. Speak soon.'

She hung up and turned back to Stephen, to find him engrossed in a book, his homework forgotten.

'Hey, you, come on. French.'

'Finished it.'

'Really?'

'Really. Can we have ice cream?'

'Not till you've put your books away. Are you sure you've finished?'

He rolled his eyes, and there was such a look of his father about him that her heart hiccuped. Crazy. She hadn't thought about him in ages, and now it seemed she couldn't think about anything else.

Except Michael, and even that was confusing.

She dreamed about Etienne that night, laughing softly in the darkness, kissing her under the spreading branches of the old oak behind the château—but when he turned his head in the moonlight, he had Michael's face, and she woke hot and breathless and aching for something she'd almost forgotten existed…

CHAPTER THREE

HE WAS already upstairs thumping around and laying waste to the flat by the time she opened up at twenty to nine.

Grace was one of the first in, followed by Chris and then Jackie.

'So, what's this with the landlord, then?' Chris asked, her eyes bright with curiosity.

'What's what? He's doing up the flat—you can hear it.'

'Hmm. We aren't blind, we all noticed,' Grace told her, which meant they'd been talking about it at some point since lunchtime yesterday.

She slapped some bacon into the electric griddle and sighed. 'Now look, girls, let's get one thing straight. He's my landlord—nothing more, nothing less.'

'You were being very nice to him.'

She rolled her eyes. 'Grace, of course I was being nice to him. I'm hardly going to alienate myself from him, am I?'

'Alienate yourself from who?' Michael asked, strolling in as if he owned the place—funny, that—and grinning at her, so that there was nothing to do but brazen it out, and serve them all right.

'You. They think there's something going on between us, because they have such sad little lives they have to gossip about something—'

'Sorry, ladies, she's right. Nothing's going on,' he assured them, and then ruined it by adding, 'sadly. However, while there's life…' His mouth quirked. 'Have I just ruined my chances of getting breakfast?'

She could cheerfully have hit him. Her heart, however, had other ideas, and seemed to be connected directly to her mouth, which promptly smiled forgivingly. Her tongue, however, was still her own.

'That depends on whether you're going to sit quietly and behave, or incite this lot to riot, because believe me, they need no encouragement,' she said tartly.

'As if I'd do that,' he said, cosying up to them all and grinning that curiously engaging crooked grin of his.

'So, what are you doing upstairs? Apart from making lots of very impressive noises, that is,' Jackie said, leaning towards him and showing him too much cleavage for comfort. Well, Annie's comfort, anyway. Michael was probably feeling just fine, she thought acidly.

He grunted. 'I'm glad you're impressed. The kitchen doesn't seem to think I'm being in the least effective.'

He held out his damaged hands, and they clucked and tutted and fussed over him like a flock of broody hens until she could have hit them.

'Breakfast,' she said, setting down a huge heap of bacon sandwiches in the middle of the table, followed by a jug of coffee, a pot of tea and a handful of mugs.

The heap vanished in seconds, mostly into Michael.

'Ruth told me not to overfeed you,' she said blandly, and he snorted.

'She's a hard woman,' he murmured.

'She said you'd get fat.'

He laughed then—not the huge, all-encompassing laugh

that Etienne would have laughed, or Roger's dry chuckle, but a quiet huff of laughter that for some reason made her feel sad.

She didn't know why, but something gave her the feeling that he didn't laugh much, that perhaps he didn't know how, or had forgotten.

Silly, really, when she looked at the easy way he was getting on with her friends, but there was just something—

'So how *is* the kitchen?'

'Winning. I might take a sledgehammer to it.' He drained his coffee, pushed back his chair and stood up. 'In fact, I think I'll do that now, teach it a lesson. See you all later.'

'And I need to get back and fight with the washing machine,' Chris said dolefully. 'I know—perhaps I'll take a sledgehammer to that. Solve the problem for a few days, anyway! Perhaps then I'd get to dawdle here all morning like you lot while my daughter's at nursery!'

Annie put the plates in the dishwasher, wiped the table and topped up the coffee before sitting down again with Jackie and Grace. 'Right, you two,' she said briskly, to keep them off the subject of her destructive and altogether too interesting landlord. 'Soup recipes. What works, what doesn't?'

'I like your parsnip soup,' Grace said promptly.

Jackie pulled a face. 'I don't. I like the winter vegetable— it's easier to see what's in it. The parsnip's just a purée.'

'Didn't like the minestrone you tried last year,' Grace continued. 'The broccoli and Stilton was good, though. Try that again.'

'Mmm—yes. I'd forgotten that. What about carrot and orange?' Annie suggested.

'In stick-in-the-mud old Suffolk? They'll hate it, too weird,' Jackie said, instantly damning the entire county.

Predictably, Grace bristled. 'That's unfair and a sweeping generalisation. And anyway, there's nothing wrong with sticking to tradition. I think you should try it instead of doing things differently just for the hell of it,' Grace said.

'Oh, Lord, I've poked a sleeping tiger. Little Miss Let's Preserve It At All Costs is up in arms—ouch!'

'Serve you right,' Grace said. 'I'll give you poking tigers. Annie, if you want to try carrot and orange, by all means do so. Why don't you try it out on Michael?'

'And talking of Michael—'

'We were talking about soup,' she reminded them.

'So we were. I wonder whose idea that was?' Grace murmured.

'Not mine—I can think of *much* more interesting things to talk about,' Jackie replied with a cheeky grin. 'Starting with that very, *very* sexy man upstairs. Any more coffee?'

He could hear the laughter underneath, and it was curiously comforting to know that her life wasn't all just one continuous grind to make ends meet.

Her friends were nice people. Good people, caring, if a little over-curious. They'd look out for her.

And watch him, clearly, like hawks. Well, that was fine. He wasn't intending to do anything wrong, but their courtship was clearly going to be a more public and open thing than he'd anticipated, and when he told her the whole story— well, there'd be the whole village lined up to hear the tale, no doubt, and judge him accordingly.

Damn.

He didn't go down for lunch. Instead he slowly and systematically dismantled the kitchen units, ripped up the carpets and ordered a skip. The rest of the day was spent trekking up and down the stairs with armfuls of rubbish, and by the time he'd filled the skip he was feeling shaky with hunger and he'd got a killer headache coming on.

But he didn't want to go in there until Stephen got off the school bus, and it was nearly six before he accepted that Tuesdays were clearly different.

He was crouched down packing up his tools for the night when he heard a light footfall on the stairs and Annie appeared in the doorway of the kitchen.

'Hi—I hope you don't mind me coming up.'

He turned and sat against the wall, stretching out his cramped legs and sighing. 'Not at all. Come in.'

'I just wondered—you haven't been in since breakfast. I hoped it wasn't because of what I said about Ruth telling me not to feed you too much.'

He gave a wry smile. Well, they all looked wry these days, or awry, anyway, but this one at least was meant to. 'I just wanted to get the place cleared. I didn't really think to stop,' he lied, and she tutted.

'Ruth said you often forget to eat. I wondered—Stephen's at chess club at school tonight until seven, and he's being dropped off by a friend's mother after she's fed them. It'll be about eight o'clock, and I was going to play with a soup recipe. I've also got some leftover bits of quiche that are destined for the bin if they aren't eaten today. Can I tempt you?'

'Don't you want to go home?' he asked, unwilling to admit even to himself how horribly tempted he was, but she flashed him a tentative smile.

'Oh, I am going home,' she said. 'Sorry, I didn't make that clear. I wondered if you wanted to come over—but I expect you've got better things to do.'

He jack-knifed to his feet, dusting off his seat and trying not to look too damned eager.

'Not at all. I can't think of anything I'd rather do.'

'In which case you can carry the bag with all the dishes in it for me.' She grinned, and headed for the door.

Flicking off the lights, he followed her down, locked the door of the flat and slung the strap of the bag she handed him over his shoulder. 'Just lead the way,' he said.

They went in through the back door, over a mat that said 'Beware of the Kids'. That made him smile, till he remembered one of them was his. Then he felt a strange pang somewhere in the middle of his chest.

A large ginger cat was lying on the windowsill, paws tucked under his chest, and he turned his head and studied the newcomer with baleful eyes.

'Nice cat.'

'He's a horrible cat. He rules the house. Stephen's the only one he'll tolerate, and he'll let him do anything. He drapes him round his neck like a collar and the cat just lies there. If I try and stroke him he shreds me, so be warned. Stick that there—thanks.'

He set the bag down, and she put the kettle on, told him to sit down and started putting the contents of the bag away and pulling things out of the fridge.

'So—what's the soup going to be?' he asked, to take his mind off the sight of black trousers stretched taut over a firm, slender bottom that was doing unspeakable things to his fragile self-control.

'Don't know. I'll see what I've got. I like to use seasonal vegetables, but that can be a bit restricting, so I have to put unusual things in, like nuts and spices and stuff. I've made a Stilton and broccoli soup that goes down well, and there are the usual standbys, but I just fancied doing something unusual.'

'How about Jerusalem artichokes?'

'Fiddly to peel.'

'My godmother doesn't peel them; she scrubs them and cooks them in with onions and something else—can't remember what, but it's gorgeous. Spinach, maybe. I know it's green. Want me to ask her?'

Annie nodded. 'Could you? That would be really kind.'

'No problem,' he murmured, stretching out his legs and easing the kinks in his body while he watched her.

She made a cup of tea and set it down in front of him, then started chopping and slicing.

'Anything I can do?'

'Sit there and talk to me.'

'OK.'

But where to start? So many questions to ask, so much he wanted to know. This one he knew, but he thought it might get him other answers, answers to the questions he couldn't ask. 'Why a tearoom?' he said, and waited.

'Oh. Well, that goes back years, to Roger's first wife—Liz. I was telling you about her. Roger was my husband—you met him once. You probably don't remember.'

'Of course I do. He was incredibly generous about my writing. I was sorry to hear he'd died.'

'Thank you. He liked you—said you were very interesting. I was out at the time—you popped in because Ruth had said he liked your books. You brought him a signed copy— it's in his study, in pride of place. He treasured it.'

Guilt washed over him. He'd only done it so he could see the man she'd married, talk to him and find out what kind of man was bringing up his son.

Decent, had been the answer. Decent and straightforward and endlessly kind, and he'd felt relieved and guilty at the same time. Not to mention jealous as hell.

'You were saying about Liz,' he said, dragging the conversation back on track, and she nodded.

'She was a tutor at college—I got to know her quite well during my course, and we became friends. She was fed up with lecturing, though, and since her girls were growing up she felt she could take on something else, with commitment in the holidays.'

'Hence the tearoom?'

Annie nodded. 'She suggested we got together and started a little business, and we talked about it, and then the lease on that one came up. It was ideal, so handy for her, and I wasn't very far away. It had always been a little café, but it had a dreadful reputation and it was in dire need of sorting out. We ripped out the kitchen, rearranged and refitted it and were going to open in the autumn.'

'Not the best time, surely?'

'Well, not really, but with all the work to do on it we wouldn't have been ready for the summer, and I was already committed to going to France for September and October— I'd got a job cooking for the harvest season on a vineyard in the Rhône valley, to get some experience of French country cooking—not the fancy, twiddly stuff I'd done at college but real, proper food. And we thought the winter would give us time to find our feet.'

'And did it?'

'We never got the chance to find out. We decided Liz should open it when school started, working on the principle that business would take a while to pick up and it wouldn't be too busy until I got back, and that way Liz could have the last summer holiday with her children. We didn't realise it was going to be her last summer ever.'

She broke off, not saying any more, and he waited a while before prompting her.

'What happened?' he said softly, and she lifted a shoulder

in the way he remembered so well and carried on, her voice quiet and slightly expressionless.

'She had a brain tumour. She died that February. She'd already opened Miller's, of course, while I was away, and I ended up running it and looking after her and the girls, but it wasn't easy, not when I was pregnant as well.'

His heart hitched against his ribs. Now he was getting somewhere. 'Pregnant?' he said carefully. 'That wasn't on the agenda, was it?'

Her laugh was gentle but self-deprecating. 'Not exactly. France was—a disaster. I fell in love with one of the estate managers, a guy called Etienne Duprés—stupid, stupid thing to do, but I was young and impressionable and he was gorgeous—good-looking, virile, sweep-you-off-your-feet type. He certainly swept me off mine.'

'So Roger wasn't Stephen's father?'

She shook her head. 'No—good heavens, no. He was married to Liz—devoted to her.'

'Sorry. I just assumed Stephen had come along later, after you were married,' he lied, and wondered why he didn't choke on it.

'No. He was Etienne's child.'

And stupidly, hearing her actually say the words meant an enormous amount. Even though he knew—had concrete proof, in fact—that Stephen was his child, to hear her acknowledge it gave him a curious sense of satisfaction.

'So why didn't you marry this Etienne guy?' he prompted, and held his breath. What would she say? What did she know? He wasn't sure. All he'd been able to find out was that she'd returned to England and had a child. His child. So he held his breath and watched her carefully. Even so, he almost missed the flicker of pain in her eyes.

'He died. He and another man who worked with him. They

were beaten up. Their bodies were found a few miles away in the town. I never did know why—I don't suppose there was a reason, but the French authorities stonewalled me when I tried to find out more. They must have known something was going on, I suppose. It was on the news the other day, the vineyard—something to do with human trafficking. I don't know if you saw it.'

He shrugged, wondering what she'd say, how she'd felt about seeing it. He knew how he'd felt—sick, for the most part.

'Rings a bell. What about it?' he said casually.

'Claude Gaultier—he was the owner—was running some kind of slave labour and prostitution racket. He was a gangmaster, I think is the term. I suspect Etienne and his friend must have got themselves involved somehow.'

Clever girl. 'Wrong place, wrong time?' he murmured, watching her carefully still, and she nodded.

'Maybe. It might have been nothing to do with it, of course; I could just be letting my imagination run away with me. Anyway, I never got a chance to see his body. They said it had been taken away by his family. So that was it. For a while I thought I'd die, too, but you don't, do you? You just go on, day by day, on autopilot. I came back, found that Liz was terminally ill and got on with it.'

'And then you married Roger,' he said, and waited.

She hesitated for a moment. 'Yes. He was a wonderful man—a brilliant father, even though he was ill. I never thought I'd get over Etienne, but he helped me to see that there was more than one kind of love.'

'You miss him.'

It wasn't a question, but she answered it anyway, turning the knife a little further. 'Roger?' she said, and smiled tenderly. 'Yes, I miss him. Every day.' And then she added unexpectedly, 'Sometimes I'm so lonely, and I wonder if this is all there is now, all there's going to be—'

She broke off, colouring. 'I can't believe I'm telling you this,' she muttered, turning back to her chopping board. She attacked the vegetables, slicing and chopping them viciously and scraping them into a big pot. Then, throwing in a slosh of olive oil, she turned on the heat and started to stir them, all without saying another word.

He waited her out, nursing his tea and watching her while he dealt with the fact that she still missed this man who'd taken what should have been his place in her life, and after a few minutes she crumbled a stock cube into the mix, poured water over the top and came and sat down.

'I'm sorry. I don't normally dish out personal information like that,' she said at last, but she wouldn't meet his eyes, and with a quiet sigh he reached out a finger and tilted up her chin, forcing her to face him.

'It's OK,' he murmured. 'You've been through hell in the last few years. You needed to let off steam, and it's going nowhere. I don't gossip.'

She coloured again, nodded and found a little smile. 'Thanks.'

'Any time. How old are you, Annie? Late twenties, early thirties?'

The smile faltered. 'Thirty.'

'And you're alone,' he murmured, hearing his voice turn husky. 'That's such a travesty. You should have a lover, Annie—someone to share the nights with.'

The colour returned in force, but she met his eyes defiantly. 'So who do you share your nights with, Michael? I've never heard Ruth talk about a Mrs Harding.'

He gave a huff of laughter. Oh, he shared his nights, all right—with the woman opposite him, in his dreams. But there was no way she was knowing that, not yet. '*Touché*. You've got me there. But I'm different. I'm used to it. It's my choice.'

She studied him thoughtfully. 'Is it? Or are you just as lonely as anybody else?'

He held her eyes with effort. 'I don't see it as loneliness,' he lied. 'I prefer the word solitude. It helps me write.' But she just arched a brow and went back to her soup while the tension hummed between them like a bow-string.

He forced himself to relax, to take a nice, steady breath, to drink his tea.

'Thought any more about the alterations?' he said at last, and she paused in her stirring and tasting and looked at him over her shoulder, spoon poised over the pot.

'Not really. I just wish I knew what your motives were.'

No way, he thought. He was going to hell for this and all the other lies he was telling her just now, but there was no help for it. 'No motives,' he said evenly. 'I just want to keep my tenants happy, and now seems a good time to make changes, with you the only one it affects.'

She gave him a doubtful look, sloshed something into the soup and stirred, tasted again and put the lid on.

'I could do with more storage.'

'OK.'

'And the garden, if I could see a way. And the alcove you were talking about.'

'Or you could move the whole thing next door into the antique shop, fit its store room out as a kitchen and have loads of room, and a door to the garden.'

She blinked and sat down opposite him as if her strings had been cut.

'Move it next door?'

He shrugged. 'Whatever. It's possible at the moment to do anything. That's all I'm saying. Think out of the box.'

Her smile was wry. 'Michael, I can't afford to think out of the box.'

'I could go in with you.'

'What—take turns to make soup and cakes and load the dishwasher? I don't think so.'

'I could be a silent partner.'

'I don't need someone else sharing the profits. I don't make enough as it is.'

'You might make more with more room.'

'It would lose its intimacy. I think that would be a mistake. And anyway, I'm running at full stretch as it is. I only get help for a few hours on some days. I can't afford to expand.'

'You should charge more. You're too cheap. You could add fifty per cent—'

'And lose all my regulars? I don't think so.'

He conceded the point, prodding the issue around a little further just for the sake of hearing her voice. He didn't care what she did about the business. He hoped, rashly, that it would all be academic in a few weeks anyway, if his plan worked out.

She stood up again, tested the soup, poured it into a liquidiser, tested it again, stirred in something that looked suspiciously like cream and set the bowl down on the table between them.

'So what is it?'

She shrugged. 'Winter vegetable medley?' she suggested with a grin, and he chuckled.

'Winging it?'

'Absolutely. Just wanted to try a few new flavours. It's a sweet potato base—that's where the colour comes from. I tell you what, if it's OK I'll let you name it.'

'You'll have to try harder than that to get the garden,' he growled softly, and she laughed.

He held out his bowl to her, struggling to regain control of his emotions. Her laugh had haunted him, a lighthearted ripple of sound that he hadn't heard for years, and it went straight to his heart.

He put the bowl down, watched her as she ladled some into her own bowl and then looked at him expectantly.

'Well, go on then—taste it,' she prompted, but he shook his head.

'After you,' he said, his voice a little tight and gruff, but it was a miracle he could talk at all. He certainly couldn't eat. The soup had to wait a moment until he'd shifted the lump in his throat.

It seemed so odd having a man in her kitchen again. No, scratch that. It seemed odd having a man like this in her kitchen. At all. Ever.

Roger had never made her feel like this, not even remotely. He'd never threatened her physical space, never crowded her, never made her aware of every hair on her head and every inch of her body.

Not that Michael was doing anything to make her nervous. He didn't have to. He just had to sit there and breathe, and it was enough.

Crazy. She'd only ever felt like this once before, and she'd been twenty-one and innocent. Now she was thirty—and only marginally less innocent, she conceded. Still, she dealt with flirts every day in her work, and never had a problem.

Michael hardly flirted, though. He just talked to her, watched her working, focused on her with that *intensity* that was so darned unnerving. And he seemed to have an extraordinary capacity to get her to spill her guts.

She couldn't *believe* what she'd told him. Too much information, she thought. Crazy woman. You'll frighten him away.

And suddenly, she realised that that mattered, much, much more than it should have done.

'Is it OK?' she asked, to fill the deafening silence, and he nodded.

'Excellent.'

He'd seemed reluctant to start eating, but once he had, his spoon dipped rhythmically into the soup and she refilled his bowl twice before he put the spoon down with careful deliberation and shot her a wry grin.

'That was delicious. Thank you.'

'Name?'

He chuckled, making shivers run over her skin. 'You'll have to give me time. How about Annie's Winter Warmer?' he suggested after a moment, his head cocked on one side and his eyes fixed on her face.

She shrugged. 'Could do. Mmm. Yeah, maybe—all I have to do is remember what I put in it.'

No mean achievement considering she hadn't been able to concentrate!

'Quiche?' she suggested, wondering if he'd be able to fit anything else in, but he nodded.

'Please. I'm starving.'

'Still?'

He laughed softly, rippling her senses. 'I've been working hard. There's a lot of me.'

'I noticed,' she said, but she didn't explain which bit of his remark she was referring to, and thankfully he had the sense not to ask.

Instead he looked down at the table, lining up his bowl and mug and knife with careful precision, and she grabbed the chance to move without him watching her and stood up, clearing the table and bringing out the last few slices of quiche.

'There are two sorts. If I put it all out, you can choose.'

'You're not having any?' he asked, but she shook her head.

'I'm full. I had a scone earlier. I need to make some things for tomorrow, but you carry on, please.'

And if she didn't have to sit opposite him she might have some chance of slowing her heartbeat down before it went off the scale...

So what had she noticed?

The fact that he'd been working hard, or the fact that there was a lot of him?

Ego made him plonk for the latter, and he'd had to duck his head to hide the smile of satisfaction.

Always possible, of course, that she was simply talking about the fact that he'd been making a hideous racket overhead for most of the past two days.

In fact, that was the most likely. It had been hard to miss.

His smile faded, and with a quiet sigh he put his ego back in the box and set about demolishing the quiche.

She was busy on the other side of the kitchen, working with swift efficiency born of long years of practice, and he watched her in silence as he ate.

She was still beautiful, her body perhaps a little thinner but softly rounded where it mattered. She could do with putting a little weight on, but if he was guilty of forgetting to eat, he was certain she was, too. Either that or she was often too busy to stop.

There was a clatter at the door, and it swung open, only the coats on the back stopping it from banging against the wall.

'Hi, Mum—oh. Hello. Who are you?'

He felt his palms break out, his heart pick up, and he pushed away his plate and stood up slowly.

'I'm Michael—and you must be Stephen. It's good to meet you—I've heard a lot about you.'

And extending his arm, he waited, his breath jammed in his throat, until Stephen reached out and, for the first time in his eight and a bit years, he placed his hand trustingly in his father's.

Emotion locked his throat solid. Dear God, he thought. He's the spitting image of me at that age. He's got my eyes. She'll see it—notice it instantly when we're side by side.

But she didn't.

She wiped her hands and turned, hugged her son, caught his coat before it slid off the table to the floor and hung it on the back of the door.

'So how was chess club?' she asked him, and he sighed, his face glum.

'Useless. I can't play. Dad was going to teach me some moves, but—'

He shrugged expressively, and Michael's heart contracted. Poor little tyke. Obviously Annie wasn't the only one to miss Roger. There was more to being a father than biology. The acknowledgement was curiously painful.

'Never mind,' she was saying, squeezing his shoulder comfortingly. 'Perhaps we can get a book from the library?'

'I could teach you,' he found himself saying in a strangled voice. He cleared his throat. 'If your mother doesn't mind?'

He looked into her eyes, saw the relief in them and felt the tension ease.

'Could you? Do you have time? You're so busy—'

'Not too busy to do that.' Never too busy for my son.

'Well, that would be wonderful. Thank you. We'll have to arrange a time.'

'We could do it now!' Stephen said, brightening, but she shook her head.

'No. You've got school tomorrow and it's already eight. You need to have a bath and get to bed. Have you had enough to eat?'

He nodded, and she kissed him and sent him upstairs to run his bath.

Michael tucked his chair under the table, feeling for his car keys in the pocket of his jeans, suddenly needing air. 'I should be off—leave you to get on,' he said, and he wasn't sure but there might have been a flicker of disappointment on her face.

Or maybe he was clutching at straws.

'Have you had enough to eat? There's more, if you're still hungry—'

'Absolutely not,' he said, summoning a smile. Any more food would have choked him, but that was nothing to do with the food and everything to do with her and his son and the emotion jamming his throat. 'Thank you, that was lovely, but I really ought to be going.'

'I'm just going to have a cup of tea—stay,' she said. 'We could talk about this chess thing.'

He shook his head. 'Another time,' he said. 'I could do with a bath myself, and a reasonably early night. I'll see you tomorrow.'

When I've had time to let all this sink in, and get over the feel of my son's hand in mine.

He looked down at her, standing so close that if he reached out he could reel her in against his chest and kiss her soft, full mouth until she whimpered. He backed away. No. Not yet. It was far, far too soon.

Thanking her again for the meal, he said goodnight, let himself out and drove slowly home, lost in thought.

* * *

'D'you think he'll really teach me to play chess?'

Annie smoothed her son's hair back off his brow and hugged him. 'I don't know. He said so, but he's busy.'

'Daddy said he'd teach me, but he died.'

'I know. I'm sorry. I know he would much rather have been here with us teaching you to play chess, but we don't always get what we want, and sometimes it's very hard.'

'I miss him,' Stephen mumbled, and Annie sighed.

'I know. I miss him, too.'

'Michael's nice.'

She tweaked his nose. 'Only because he said he'd teach you chess,' she said with a slightly breathless laugh, and tried not to think about Michael. She was thinking about him altogether too much as it was.

'What happened to his face?'

She hesitated. 'I'm not sure. I think he's probably had an accident. It's not the sort of thing you can ask.'

Stephen wrinkled his nose. 'It makes him look kind of funny. His mouth's a bit crooked.'

Like his sense of humour, she nearly said, but that was odd, because surely she didn't know anything about his sense of humour. Not really, not after so short a time. She was just imagining it, filling in the blanks, which was something she really had to stop doing, because she was getting more and more drawn to him, and it was crazy.

She'd done this with Etienne, and look where that had got her? Perhaps it was the way he had of focusing on her that Etienne had had, making her feel special. Important. The centre of his world.

But he wasn't Etienne, and she wasn't the girl she'd been nine years ago.

'Time to put your light out and go to sleep,' she said, kissing her son's cheek and snuggling the quilt around his skinny little shoulders. 'I'll see you in the morning. Night-night.'

'Sleep tight,' he mumbled back, dropping off already, and as she reached the door, he added, 'Ask him about the chess tomorrow.'

'OK. Now go to sleep. Love you.'

She went back downstairs, wondering if it was such a good idea getting Michael involved in Stephen's life. Mainly, she realised, because it meant involving him in hers, and hers, frankly, was involved enough!

It didn't stop him being the last thing she thought about as she fell asleep, though—and the first thing she thought about in the morning...

CHAPTER FOUR

HE FELT as if he'd been hit by a truck.

Carefully, gingerly, he rolled over and flexed his shoulders. Ouch. Not good.

He tried to sit up, and bit back a groan of pain and frustration.

That darned kitchen was out to get him—either that or the tension of the past few days had screwed him up. Both, probably. He tried again, fighting off the wave of nausea as he padded barefoot to the kitchen, fumbled pills out of the packet and propped his forehead against the front of the fridge while he waited for the glass to fill from the iced water dispenser.

The icy draught slid down his throat, reviving him as he swallowed the pills that hopefully would head this thing off before it turned into a full-blown migraine.

If he got lucky.

He opened his mouth, waggled his jaw experimentally and gave up. Damn. He needed to see Pete and get this mess sorted out.

The clock said eight-thirty. Annie would be in the tearoom—expecting him? He slumped at the kitchen table and knotted his fists together, then forced himself to relax. He wasn't going to get anywhere with this headache if he didn't let the tension go.

He sat back, rolled his shoulders and winced.

Maybe let the pills work.

Back to bed for a while—and try not to think about Annie.

It didn't work. He lay there, thinking about her quicksilver smile and the sparkle in her eyes, the freckles that dusted her nose and how good those soft, full lips would feel under his.

At least, under the areas of them that still had sensation.

'Oh, hell—'

He threw off the bedclothes, ignoring the screaming in his head, turned on the shower good and hot and propped himself up under the pounding spray. Half an hour later he was more relaxed, his head had eased with the tension in his shoulders and he felt halfway to being human again.

Now all he had to do was go over to the Ancient House and pretend to be doing something useful there. If nothing else, he ought to set a time for Stephen's chess lessons. The last thing he was going to do was let his son down, and no mere headache was going to get in the way.

Although only a total masochist would describe this demon in his skull as a mere headache. He phoned the osteopath before he left the house, got himself on the waiting list for an urgent appointment, and then he set off for the village. Perhaps he'd feel more human after a huge mug of Annie's coffee.

Or just her smile...

'You look rough.'

The cock-eyed grin he shot her did that thing to her insides again. 'Well, cheers. I feel much better for knowing that.'

'Heavy night?' she asked, and one brow climbed towards his hairline.

'Are you always this sympathetic?'

'You think you deserve it, with a hangover?' she teased, but he shook his head and winced.

'No hangover,' he muttered, and she looked at him more closely and felt a pang of guilt. A little frown pleated her brow.

'Michael, are you OK?'

'I've been better but I'll live. Don't worry, I won't keel over on the premises and compromise your reputation.'

She felt a bigger pang of guilt, and then a flutter of panic. Her reputation? 'It wasn't—you didn't get ill after the quiche, did you?'

He smiled ruefully. 'It's nothing to do with the quiche. You haven't poisoned me, you're safe. I get headaches. It's nothing.'

She frowned again. 'It doesn't look like nothing. Sit down before you fall down. What can I get you?'

'A quiet corner away from your piranhas,' he said with a slow smile, and she gave a little huff of laughter.

'I'll tell them you said that.'

'Please don't bother. A large filter coffee would be lovely. And we need to talk about this bill—'

'Don't be stupid. I've told you about that.'

He sighed and gave her a thoughtful look. 'Is this anything to do with why you struggle to make ends meet?' he murmured. 'Just how many freeloaders *do* you have, Annie?'

She felt herself colouring. 'I don't like to think of them as freeloaders—'

'So, several, then?'

'They're friends.'

'All of them?' he said softly, and she felt her defences crumble.

Her breath eased out on a sigh, and she shrugged. 'OK. You've got me. I'm soft. But it's my choice—'

'Of course it is. You'd mother the whole world, given half a chance, wouldn't you? Mother Teresa and Mrs Beeton rolled into one.'

She turned away, unwilling to discuss this with him. He sounded altogether too damn *right*. And if he didn't want her mothering him, fine. She wouldn't. She was all done mothering people anyway. She'd looked after Liz until she died, then she'd looked after Roger and the girls and Stephen—and all the time the tearoom had demanded attention—was *still* demanding attention. Half the people that came in were lame ducks.

He was right. Sickeningly. She mothered everybody. Well, not any more. She was Stephen's mother, and that was it. The rest of them were off her list. Starting with him. He, of all of them, could afford it.

She turned back with his coffee in her hand and met his eyes defiantly. 'That'll be one pound fifty,' she said, thrusting it at him, and his eyes crinkled with a smile.

'Better,' he murmured, and taking the coffee from her hand, he dropped the change into her palm and headed for the little table at the back, the one she'd have to lose if she got access to the garden.

It wouldn't be much of a loss, she thought. Nobody liked sitting there; it was too much in the way for people going to the loo. But Michael sat himself down at it, turning his back to the window and watching her thoughtfully over his cup, and she realised for the first time that it had a clear view of her working in the kitchen area and he was taking full advantage of it.

Hmph. Perhaps she *should* get rid of that table. Right now. Immediately.

She turned back to the mess, quickly emptying and reloading the dishwasher and setting it off again in an attempt to tame the chaos. It had been hell first thing, a coach party *en route* to the coast pausing for an early coffee hard on the heels of the breakfast crowd. She hadn't had a minute to draw breath, and if she didn't get ahead while she had the chance—

'Hiya!'

She gave an inward groan. Grace and Jackie. Just what she needed.

'Hi,' she said, dredging up a smile.

'Well, don't look so pleased to see us. What's the matter, no Michael today?'

'He's here—over there, by the back window,' she pointed out. 'Leave him alone, he's got a headache.'

'Oh, poor baby,' Grace murmured, and immediately headed over to him. 'Hi. How's the head?'

'Improving.'

'Want some company? You're welcome to join us.'

His grin was fleeting. 'I'm OK. I'm off in a minute, anyway,' he told her, and Annie felt a stupid sense of loss. Crazy. She was letting herself get far too involved with this man—

'So, it's just us, kiddo,' Grace said, coming back to the counter and grinning at Jackie and Annie. 'What shall we have, Jack? Something messy and complicated, like a bacon sandwich and a latte?'

'Or you could just have a scone and filter coffee and keep out of my hair until I've got the place straight,' she found herself saying.

Their jaws all but dropped. 'Are you OK?'

'Just busy. Don't worry. I'll do you a bacon sandwich—'

'No—no. Don't. A scone's fine. I'll have cheese.'

'I'll have fruit. And filter coffee's fine. No rush. Thanks.'

They scuttled over to the big window table at the front and slid on to the chairs, watching her warily, and she gave an inward sigh and took their coffees over. Lattes, as usual, to assuage her guilt.

'I'm sorry. I'm being a bitch.'

'What's the matter?'

She looked at Jackie and shrugged. 'I don't know. I feel—unsettled. I just had words with Michael.'

'Words?'

And of course these were the last people she could tell, since they, largely, were the subject of the argument.

'I was sticking my nose in,' he explained, approaching so silently she hadn't heard him. 'Annie, I'm sorry, you're right, it's none of my business. I'll see you later. I've just had a call from the osteopath. I'm going to get my head fixed. Maybe I'll get my diplomacy back as a side effect, you never know.'

'Want to get me some?' she suggested, sending him a silent apology with her eyes, and he smiled slowly and leant over and dropped a kiss on her cheek.

Just like that. Out of nowhere.

'You'll do. I'll see you later,' he murmured, and went out, leaving Jackie and Grace open-mouthed and her legs on the point of collapsing.

Jackie shut her mouth, opened it again and whispered, 'Wow.'

Grace just shook her head and sighed lustily. 'I smell romance in the air.'

'Rubbish,' Annie said briskly, scooting back into the kitchen and wondering just exactly how high her colour was. 'Two scones coming up.' And no doubt a whole heap of personal and highly intrusive questions!

'Better?'

He nodded slowly. 'Much. I think it was wrestling with the kitchen. I'm OK now, but I could do with a quiet few days. I might devote myself to planning. Had any more thoughts about down here?'

She sighed and shook her head. 'Sorry, no. I haven't had time—and anyway, I can't afford to do anything to it—'

'I thought we'd dealt with that.'

She met his eyes squarely. 'Now who's mothering?'

A glimmer of appreciation flared briefly in those gorgeous blue depths. 'It *is* my property. I'm entitled to improve it if I want to. And I do.'

'And I still don't know why.'

He shrugged. 'Maybe because I'm a perfectionist and I don't like to see things not working as they should.'

'Such as?' she retorted, starting to bristle again.

He shrugged again. 'The store room?'

OK. She had to give him that. The store was woefully inadequate.

'And the kitchen area. It really isn't very well organised. You could have much more storage here—'

'I can't afford it,' she said again, patiently, as if she were talking to an idiot.

It wasn't lost on him. He grinned and shook his head.

'We have dealt with this,' he repeated, just as patiently, and stood his ground, arms folded, looking solid and immoveable and for all the world like a battle-scarred warrior who'd ended up in her tearoom by mistake.

She wasn't going to win.

She chucked the tea towel she was torturing into the bag in the corner and he arched a brow quizzically.

'Throwing in the towel?' he murmured, and she shot him a saccharine smile.

'Very clever. I haven't got time to argue.'

'Good,' he said, his smile widening, and she ground her teeth.

'So much for the return of your diplomacy,' she bit out, and he chuckled. Damn him, he actually laughed at her! A couple entered the tearoom behind him, and grabbing her order pad like a lifeline, she muttered, 'Excuse me,' squeezed past him and tried very hard to ignore the tingle running through her from that fleeting encounter with his lean, hard body.

Impossible. Heat zinged through her, and she couldn't have been more aware of him if he'd been wired up to the National Grid. The wretched man was going to be the death of her!

She wrote down their order and went back behind the counter, shooting him a wary look. 'You still here?'

'I was hoping for a pot of tea, a scone and a few minutes of your time. If that's possible.'

He looked patient, long-suffering and perhaps a little disappointed in her. She bit her lip, took a deep breath and dredged up a smile. 'I'm sorry. I'm behaving like a child. I don't even know what we're fighting about.'

'You're just not used to people doing anything but taking,' he said quietly. 'Well, I've got news for you, Annie. I don't want to take anything from you—nothing at all.'

And he turned on his heel and walked out.

Good Lord! He'd been on the point of telling her just how much he wanted to give her. Starting with his soul!

Idiot. He opened the door to the flat, walked slowly and heavily upstairs and sat down in the wreckage of the kitchen. Well, at least it was clear now. He propped himself against the wall and studied it dispiritedly.

Why the hell were they fighting? They hadn't fought before—not for a moment! They'd teased and laughed and flirted—

And he hadn't been her landlord, and he'd been playing a totally different person, a charming womaniser who'd set about disarming her from the first meeting.

Now they were both different, he because he was actually being himself, and she because she was older, wiser, laden with responsibility and rushed off her feet. And he kept hounding her to make changes when she'd had so many she probably never wanted to change anything ever again!

'Fool,' he muttered, crossing his arms on his knees and resting his aching head on them. He ought to go home to bed, but he couldn't leave it like this—

'Michael?'

He lifted his head and studied her thoughtfully. 'Hi. Have you escaped?'

She laughed, a soft, rueful little ripple of sound that brought a lump to his throat.

'For a moment. Jude's minding the shop.' She came and sat down beside him on the dusty floor, avoiding his eyes. 'Look, I'm really sorry. I don't know what's going on. Can we start today again?'

He reached out a hand, and after a moment's hesitation she put hers in it.

'Truce?' she murmured, and he smiled at her, tugged her gently towards him and dropped a kiss on her startled lips.

'Oh!' she said, her soft voice breathless, and then she smiled, looking suddenly young and innocent and twenty-one again, and his gut clenched.

'I take it that's a yes?' she said, and he smiled.

'That's a yes,' he said, his voice gruff, and pulling her back again, he kissed her once more, then let her go quickly, before he could do anything else stupid to screw this up. He got to his feet, held out his hand and helped her up, then dropped her hand fast before he got too darned used to holding it.

'I don't suppose you want to come back down and have that chat?' she said, meeting his eyes with a certain hesitation.

The smile wouldn't be held back. 'What—rather than sit here on a cold, dusty floor and stare at this lot? I think I could be talked into it.' He held a hand out towards the door. 'After you.'

She turned away from him with a smile, and he saw the back of her trousers.

'Oops. Dust,' he told her, jerking his head slightly in the direction of her delectable bottom. She peered over her shoulder, brushed ineffectually at her seat and then looked up at him.

'That better?'

'Marginally. Here, let me.' And, without allowing himself to think about it, he took his hand and swiped it firmly over her taut, trim backside. 'That's got it,' he said, swallowing hard, and ramming his hand in his pocket where it couldn't get into any more mischief, he followed her downstairs.

'So—tea and a scone, was it?' she asked, and he gave a slightly distracted smile and nodded.

'Please.' He tilted his head slightly towards Jude. 'So—who did you say that was?'

'Judy—my assistant. She helps me out on Wednesdays so I can go and cook, but we've been so busy today I was going to stay and help her clear up.'

'So you don't really have time to talk?'

She looked at her watch, feeling the pressure of all the things she still had to do before Stephen finished school. 'I could later more easily—after I shut? About five-thirty? That would be better.'

He nodded. 'I'll come back then. What about Stephen?'

'He comes here from school. He'll be here about a quarter to four. He's OK, he sits at the table and does his homework if I'm not at home. He'll be fine.'

'Right. I'll see you later.'

She watched him go, her bottom still tingling from the

touch of his hand, and she lifted her hand and traced her lips, still dazed.

'You OK?'

'I'm fine, Jude.' She looked around, seeing the place suddenly almost empty. Typical, just when she'd sent him off. 'Look, I tell you what, why don't I go home and throw together some more pasta bakes? And we'll need scones for tomorrow. Anything else you've noticed?'

'We're low on apple cake. I've just sold the last two bits that were out, and there's only a couple in the tin.'

'OK. I'll do some of that if I've got time. Can you send Stephen over when he arrives, and I'll come and lock up at five-thirty. If Michael comes back before I do, can you give him a coffee and ask him to hang on?'

'Sure.'

She ignored the curiosity in her assistant's eyes, grabbed what she needed to take home and headed out of the door before something else cropped up. It always did.

She was up to her arms in flour when Stephen wandered in, munching an apricot slice. 'Judy gave it to me,' he said by way of explanation, and she nodded and dropped a fleeting kiss on his head.

Fleeting because he ducked the moment he sensed her coming, and shot under her arm and out of the room. 'I'm going to the loo,' he said, vanishing up the stairs.

'Don't be long, you've got homework to do,' she called after him. She knew quite well what he'd be doing—sitting in there with his nose in a book, hiding from his homework behind the locked door. She sighed. Oh, well, at least it kept him out of her hair while she was cooking, and he could always do his homework while Michael was here.

In fact, that would be better, she decided, and left Stephen to it.

* * *

'So how's it going?'

Michael raked up a smile from somewhere. 'Oh, up and down. We had a bit of a fight today.'

Ruth raised an eyebrow and settled herself more comfortably on his sofa. 'About?'

He shrugged. 'Nothing, really. She has this bunch of freeloaders—'

'Her support group. Yeah, I know. Grace and Jackie and Chris.'

'Amongst others.'

'So don't tell me—you called them freeloaders?'

He shrugged again. 'And if I did?'

Ruth rolled her eyes. 'They're her friends, Michael. She loves them to bits, and they love her. She needs them.'

'But they could still pay—'

'They do pay. They just pay less. They don't really cost her anything, they just don't make her a profit. That's allowed, isn't it? Not to make a profit from your friends?'

Suddenly he started to see it from Annie's side, and with a groan he dropped back against the sofa and rolled his head towards her. 'Do you have to be right about everything?' he said wryly.

'Only if you insist on being wrong.'

He laughed. 'So how's life with Tim?'

'Wonderful.' She turned, wriggling round so she was facing him, and gave him a searching look. 'So—I take it she still doesn't know who you are?'

He shook his head. 'No. Not yet. But I'm getting there.'

'And does she like you?'

He thought of the kiss, and the startled, pleased expression on her face, and felt himself colour slightly. 'I think so. I hope so. It's not as easy this time.'

'That's because you're being you, and you're a miserable, grumpy old sod most of the time.'

'Well, cheers,' he grunted. 'With friends like you—'

'Someone needs to keep you aware of reality,' she said drily. 'So when are you going to tell her?'

He shrugged. 'I don't know. Not yet. It's so complicated.'

She worried her lip with her teeth. 'Be careful, Michael. Don't leave it too long. I know your reasons, and I respect them, but you have to see it from her side.'

He nodded. 'I know. I won't muck about. Just as soon as I feel we've got a chance, I'll tell her.'

'You mind you do. What about Stephen?'

He felt his face soften, and looked away. 'He's a great kid. I met him last night.'

'He's lovely, isn't he? Bit of a handful.'

'Is he? Odd, he didn't seem it.'

'She's brought him up very well. They always insisted on manners, so you would have seen the good side of him, but there's a stubborn streak in there a mile wide.'

'I wonder which one of us he gets that from?' he murmured with a grin.

'Either,' Ruth said bluntly. 'There's nothing to choose between you. So when are you seeing them again?'

'This evening—five-thirty. And I'm going to give him chess lessons.'

Ruth nodded. 'Nice one. He'll like that. Roger started teaching him just before he died.'

'I gather.'

'Just don't leave it too long,' she said again, and with a little wave of her hand, she left him there, thinking about what she'd said about seeing it from Annie's side.

She'd understand—wouldn't she? After all, what choice did he have? If he just walked right up to her and said, *Hi, remember me, you used to call me Etienne and for the last nine years you've thought I was dead, but now I'm back, looking mangled and unrecognisable and nothing like that warm, charismatic guy you fell for, and I want you to marry me and let me share my life with you and your son,* he could just see how well that would go down!

And because of the Mother Teresa/Mrs Beeton thing, she'd take him straight back into her life, regardless of her personal feelings, and he'd never know if she'd married him for Stephen's sake or because she loved him.

And there was no way he was letting her throw away her chances of happiness on a loveless marriage.

Even if it was with him.

CHAPTER FIVE

'ANNIE not here?'

Judy looked up and shook her head at him. 'She's gone home to bake. She'll be back at five-thirty to close.'

He nodded. 'OK. I'll go over there. Thanks.'

He crossed the corner of the square, walked up to her front door and rang the bell. He heard a yell and the thunder of feet on stairs, then the door was yanked back on its hinges and Stephen stood there grinning at him.

'Hi. Have you come to teach me chess?' he asked without preamble, and Michael felt his lips twitch.

'Maybe. Depends what your mother says. Do you have homework?'

He picked up the sound of her footsteps approaching, then she appeared through a doorway, a welcoming smile on her face.

'Hi. I wondered if you'd come over. Come on through. I'm up to my eyes.'

Up to her elbows, certainly. He followed her to the kitchen, taking in all the little period details of the house as he went—the pictures on the walls, the antique furniture, the lovely tiles on the hall floor, the smooth curl on the end of the banister rail—it was elegant and welcoming, yet somehow—stifling.

Steeped in the nineteenth century and up to its neck in tradition. Not her at all.

Unlike the kitchen, which was all Annie. Clutter was strewn from end to end—wire cooling trays and pots and pans and the air rich with the scent of cinnamon and apples, coming from a huge shallow pan of what looked like her Dutch apple cake.

It was fast becoming one of his favourites and, without asking him, she cut a slice out of the corner of the tray and slid the plate towards him on the table.

'Here. It's still warm. I'll make tea—do you want cream with that, by the way?'

'No, thanks, it's fine like this, and tea will be lovely. What about Stephen?'

'Yuck, I hate apple cake,' he said with feeling. 'Can I have a scone?'

'No, you've already had an apricot slice since you got home. You won't want your supper.'

'But I'm *starving*!' he said with all the pathos of the young, and Michael had to look away to hide the smile.

'Have you done your homework?' she asked, and he sighed heavily.

'Sort of.'

'Is it finished?'

'Sort of.'

'That would be a no, then. Go and do it now, please, before supper.'

'But Michael was going to teach me to play chess!'

'No, Michael was going to ask your mother if and when it would be all right,' Michael corrected, and earned himself a Brownie point.

'Homework first,' she said firmly, and he flounced out with a sigh and banged the door just the teeniest bit behind him.

'Little monster,' she muttered.

'He's just checking me out and testing you.'

She rolled her eyes. 'Tell me about it. I think bringing him up's going to be a handful. He can be a nightmare.' She set a pot of tea down on the table, looked at him thoughtfully and said, 'So what was it you wanted to talk about?'

He shrugged and smiled. Another wry, awry effort because he could see how busy she was and all he'd really wanted was her company.

So he lied. Again.

'It was about the chess, really,' he said, and she looked at him in puzzlement.

'Oh. I'd wondered—'

She broke off, looking confused, and suddenly he didn't want to lie. He wanted her to know the truth—and he wanted to know what she wondered. So he asked her.

And she sighed. 'I don't know. Nothing. It's silly.'

'What?'

She shrugged. 'Nothing. I'm being ridiculous.'

She turned back to the stove, and he stood up and went over to her, cupping her shoulders lightly in his hands and making her jump.

'Oh! You startled me. I didn't hear you—'

'What did you think?' he asked softly. 'That I wanted to spend time with you?'

She turned in his hands, looking up at him with wide, puzzled eyes. 'Is that true?'

He nodded. 'Yes. The chess was just an excuse. I promised him I'd teach him, and I will. I'd like to. But that's not why I wanted to see you. Why I want to see you.'

He could see a pulse beating in her throat, deep in the warm, soft hollow at its base. He had an urge to touch it, to lower his head and stroke his tongue lightly over it, to feel it beat against his flesh—

'All finished!'

She sucked in a huge breath and stepped back, colliding with the stove, her eyes wide and shocked, her pupils flared. And he hadn't even touched her, except the lightest touch of his hands on her shoulders.

God alone knows what would happen when he did. It would be like a match to tinder. He stepped back, dropping his hands and sucking in a deep, steadying breath of his own before he turned to his son.

'Are you sure?' he asked. 'I don't want to be responsible for you messing up at school because we're playing chess when you should be working.'

'I have done it, I promise,' he said, meeting Michael's eyes squarely without a trace of evasion.

Either he was as good a liar as his father or he was telling the truth.

Michael gave him the benefit of the doubt. 'OK. Have you got a chess set?'

He nodded and ran out, then ran back. 'Where is it?'

'In your dad's study, on the bottom shelf on the left, I think,' Annie said. 'The red box.'

He reappeared a minute later with a faded red box, opened the lid and started to extract the pieces and set them up on the board.

'Well, you're doing that right, so you must know something,' Michael said with a smile, and Stephen grinned back.

'I'm not that useless!' he said, and over his head Michael saw Annie roll her eyes and smile.

'I have to go and shut up the tearoom. Are you OK if I leave you two together for a moment?'

He met her eyes. 'Of course. Take as long as you need. We'll be fine, won't we, Sport?'

'Yeah, we're fine.'

They exchanged grins, and something inside Michael's chest tightened up and squeezed, so that he could hardly breathe or swallow.

'Right,' he said, clearing his throat. 'You're the youngest, you start.'

By the time Annie came back, they were halfway through the game, and even she could see that Stephen was struggling. Oh, dear. She'd rather hoped Michael would give him a chance, but maybe next time—

'You can't do that, you'll put yourself in check.'

'How—oh. OK.'

Oh, dear, he sounded so crestfallen.

'I'm not going to win, am I?' he said soulfully, and Michael shook his head.

'Sorry, son. Not this time.'

Son. Oh, God, if only. Stephen so badly needed a father—and not an invalid as Roger had become, but a vital, healthy, active man who could keep up with his antics and stay one step ahead of that busy and inquisitive little mind—

And she was getting ahead of herself, talking of staying one step ahead. Try ten. *Three days, Annie, and you've got him playing father to your son.*

'Checkmate.'

'What? Oh, no! I didn't see that coming!'

Stephen folded his arms and threw himself back in the chair, a pout on his lips his sisters would have been proud of.

'You'll get there. You just need time. Set them up again. I'll teach you some moves, help you think it through, now I know how your mind works.'

Annie stifled a laugh at that, and Michael lifted his head and met her eyes. His lips twitched, and she had to turn away, biting her own lip to stop the chuckle from escaping.

'What do you fancy for supper, guys?' she asked, and Stephen promptly told her lasagne. No surprises there, then.

'What about you, Michael?'

'Am I staying?' he asked, and she turned back and met his eyes.

'If you like,' she said, not wanting to seem too pushy, too— well, too needy, really. 'I mean, I expect you're busy, but if you're not, there's plenty—'

'I'm not busy,' he said, and she ground to a halt and smiled.

'Good. Lasagne all right with you?'

'Whatever. I'm not fussy. You know me, I'll eat anything so long as I don't have to cook it.'

So she sliced a good three portions from the fresh pan of lasagne she'd made earlier, put them into the oven to heat and turned her attention to the salad.

'Do I *have* to have salad?' Stephen said in his best long-suffering voice, as if he was force-fed it three times a day.

'Yes, you do,' she replied. 'It's good for you.'

'Don't care. Hate it.'

'You don't hate it—and don't be rude, please, or you'll be putting that chess set away instantly.'

He stifled a sigh and turned his attention back to the game. 'OK,' he said heavily. 'I'll eat salad. Michael, could you show me how to win?'

Michael's lips twitched again.

'I think we need to start a little further back. How about some opening moves?'

She watched them as she prepared their supper and cleared up the chaos from the afternoon's cooking fest. He was good with Stephen, she realised. Very good. Patient, explaining things carefully without patronising him, but pitching it just right to stretch him a little and not so much that he gave up.

And then he called a halt, just when she was about to, and she realised he'd been keeping an eye on her, too, and checking her progress so he could be the one to stop the lesson.

So she wasn't always the nag, the scold, the one wielding the big stick.

And she found she was suddenly hugely grateful to him, because being a single parent was difficult and endless and sharing it, even in this small way, truly lightened the load.

Supper was different as well. More fun. She and Stephen often had fun then, talking over silly things that had happened in the day, but with Michael there it was—well, it was more interesting.

And when Stephen had gone up to bed and she'd finished bagging up her pasta bakes in their individual dishes and put them in the freezer outside in the garage, they'd sat down together in the little sitting room at the back and shared a pot of tea in a companionable silence.

Then Michael looked at his watch and sighed, getting to his feet. 'I ought to go. I've got things to do, a couple of phone calls to make.'

She nodded, getting up to see him out. 'Of course you have. I'm sorry, I've kept you too long—'

'No, you haven't. You've been lovely.'

'Not a cross between Mother Teresa and Mrs Beeton?' she teased with only a flicker of hurt, and he clicked his tongue and shook his head and pulled her gently into his arms.

'I'm sorry,' he murmured into her hair.

'Don't be. You were right. I collect lame ducks. Always have. It makes a change to have someone to lean on.'

He squeezed her gently. 'What I said—about not wanting anything from you,' he said quietly. 'It wasn't quite the truth. What I meant was, I don't want to take anything you aren't ready to give me. I didn't mean I didn't want you.'

She looked up, her breath catching at the gruff, husky note in his voice, and her eyes met his and locked. Good grief. She thought she'd burn up with the need in them, but then suddenly it was gone, as suddenly as it had come, and she wondered if she'd imagined it.

He lifted his hand, grazing his knuckles gently over her cheek. 'Goodnight, Annie,' he murmured, and lowering his head, he brushed his lips lightly, tentatively, over hers.

'Goodnight, Michael,' she whispered, and lifting herself up on tiptoe, she kissed him back.

For a moment he stiffened, but then he gave a rough, tattered groan and slanted his mouth more securely over hers and kissed her as if he was dying for her.

Dear God.

It only lasted seconds. Maybe four, five? And then he wrenched himself away and dropped his hands from her shoulders as if she might burn him. He could very well be right—

'Sleep tight. I'll see you tomorrow,' he said, and all but bolted for the door.

She watched him go, then locked up, went back into the kitchen and fed the cat, made another cup of tea and settled down again on the sofa to think about the feel of his lips and the heat of his mouth and the need in his eyes.

Sleep tight?

She didn't sleep a wink.

* * *

He avoided her on Thursday. He had to. Things were moving far too fast.

What the hell had he been *thinking* about to kiss her like that?

'Too much, you fool,' he muttered, wrenching the bath away from the wall without even thinking about what it was doing to his neck. To hell with his neck. He didn't care about his neck. All he cared about was Annie, and kissing her again, and—

'Damn!'

The blood spurted from the cut, and he glared at it in disgust. He'd have to wash it.

Except, of course, he'd taken out the basin already, and the only running water was in the loo. Not a great idea.

Which left him no choice but to go back downstairs and use the basin in Annie's cloakroom to sort it out. And that meant seeing Annie.

Well, his mind might think that was a lousy idea, but his body was all for it. With a grunt of disgust he tugged his rugby shirt down to give him greater privacy and ran down the stairs, his finger clutched in a wad of loo paper.

'Oops,' she said with a knowing grin. 'Want a plaster?'

'No. I think I need a nurse,' he muttered. A psychiatric one.

'I'll come,' she said, picking up the first aid kit and chivvying him through to the cloakroom.

The *tiny* cloakroom, with her pressed up against him clucking and tutting and pulling the cut open and pouring icy water into it—

'Ouch!'

'Baby,' she teased. 'You'll live. It needs to be clean.'

'I'm sure it is now,' he said drily, and handed her another handful of loo roll to dry it.

She stuck a plaster neatly over the cut, told him to apply pressure to it and cleaned up the basin.

'Sorry about the mess,' he said, but she just threw him a smile that made his body shriek with delight and patted his cheek.

'Don't worry. Although I'm going to have to restock my first aid kit at this rate.'

'I'll buy you a new one,' he promised. 'I'll get myself one while I'm at it. Or perhaps a job lot. Wonder if I'll get a bulk discount?'

He was just talking for the sake of it, but she chuckled and shooed him back out, went behind the counter and reached for a teapot.

'Tea? Or are you still on coffee?'

'Tea would be lovely,' he said, giving up on the idea of going back upstairs without a qualm.

Moments later she set the pot down on the table, followed by two cups, a milk jug and a slice of apple cake. 'Here. I expect you need this,' she said, sliding on to the chair beside his and pushing the cake towards him.

'I do. I missed lunch,' he said unnecessarily, and met her eyes.

Only for a second, though, before hers skittered away.

'Um—about last night,' she began, and he sighed.

'I know. I'm sorry. I was out of line—'

'*You* were?' she exclaimed, then lowered her voice hastily. 'No. It was me. I kissed you back. You just gave me a peck, and I—' She floundered to a halt, and he found himself holding his breath.

'You—what?' he coaxed, desperate to hear what she was going to say.

'I pushed it,' she confessed hurriedly. 'Turned it into something it wasn't meant to be.'

'I didn't exactly object,' he pointed out, thinking he ought to be fair about that, at least, and it got a chuckle from her.

'No—I suppose you didn't, but it wasn't fair to move the goalposts. There you were, just being polite—'

'Polite?' he mouthed, and gave a strangled little laugh. 'You think I was being *polite*?' He stuck a finger under her chin, steered her head round to face him and waited for her to meet his eyes. Finally.

'I was not being polite,' he said firmly. 'At all. Not even slightly.'

'Oh,' she said, and gave a relieved little laugh. 'I wondered if that was why you skipped lunch.'

He groaned. 'It was—in a way. I thought I'd overdone it. Pushed you.'

'Pushed *me*—oh, no. No, not at all. It was—fine.'

Fine? She thought his kiss was *fine*? He was obviously losing his touch.

'Um—Stephen said thanks for the chess lesson, by the way. It was all he could talk about at breakfast.'

He smiled. 'He's welcome. When do you want me to teach him again?'

She met his eyes then, searchingly, and he found the contact unnerving. God only knows what she'd see if she looked too hard. 'Are you sure it's OK?'

He forced a grin. 'I'll do anything for supper.'

And she relaxed, at last, and laughed softly.

'Tomorrow?'

'Sure. Same sort of time?'

She nodded. 'Well, no, actually, a bit later,' she amended. 'Come at six-thirty—that'll give me time to sort this lot out—oh, no, Stephen's at a friend's house. Saturday?'

He nodded. 'Sure.'

'Just come round the back and let yourself in. It's easier if I'm busy in the kitchen.'

He nodded again, then stabbed his fork into the apple cake and sliced off a chunk. She was right, he was starving—and not only for the cake. It made a good start, though.

'Hi, Honey, I'm home!' he sang, knocking on the back door as he opened it, and then he ground to a halt and shut his eyes, wincing inwardly with embarrassment.

Great. Just what he needed!

'Sorry,' he said, opening his eyes and greeting the two young women at the table with a sheepish grin. 'I didn't realise Annie had company. I'm Michael.'

He held out his hand, and they shook it in turn.

'I'm Kate,' the younger one said with a curious but friendly smile, 'and this is Vicky. We're her stepdaughters.'

'Ah,' he said, and nodded. 'Of course you are. I can see your father in you both. Um—is she around?'

'She's upstairs—she said something about sorting out the beds. She wasn't expecting us.'

He was on the point of telling them to go and make their own beds when he realised it was actually none of his business.

Kate was still looking at him curiously, but Vicky's look was altogether more searching. 'Are you in the habit of walking in like that?' she asked, her voice less than friendly, and Kate stared at her in obvious astonishment.

'Vicky!'

Vicky was no problem to him. He could deal with her with one hand tied behind his back. But, for the sake of harmony and because it was their house, too, he reined in his temper. 'No, I'm not, actually,' he told them. 'Annie told me to come in, though. I'm here to give Stephen a chess lesson.'

'Really?'

'Really,' he said drily, his grip on his temper slipping a fraction at her arch tone. 'Do you have a problem with that?'

'Only if you're using it as an excuse to get in her knickers.'

He froze, astonished at the unexpectedness of her attack and her choice of words, while Kate coloured furiously and hissed 'Vix!' at her sister in horror.

After a lengthy silence which he did nothing to alleviate, he leant towards Vicky, propped both hands on the table, and said very slowly and carefully, 'If I wanted to get into your stepmother's knickers—which, by the way, is absolutely none of your business—I wouldn't stoop to using her son as an excuse.'

And then he straightened up and went over to the hall door, just as it opened and Annie came in.

'Michael! I didn't hear you arrive. Have you met the girls?'

'Oh, yes,' he said softly, his back to them. 'I've already been warned off.'

'Really?' Her eyes widened, then narrowed. 'Well, we wouldn't want to give them the wrong idea,' she murmured and, going up on tiptoe, she hooked a hand around the back of his neck, pulled him down and kissed him.

It was just a peck, but it was proprietorial and it made him want to beat his chest like Tarzan.

She grinned at him, dropped back on to her heels and moved past him.

'So, have you put the kettle on for Michael, girls?' she said cheerfully, and Kate got up, still clearly flustered, and grabbed the kettle and shoved it under the tap.

Vicky was made of sterner stuff. She gave him a baleful look. 'I'll bring my things in from the car,' she said shortly, and disappeared.

'Stephen's in the study,' Annie told him. 'Why don't you go through and find him, and I'll bring you some tea in a moment?'

He nodded, having a fair idea of what was about to take place, and not wanting to be in Vicky's shoes for anything. 'Don't be too hard on her,' he murmured.

'Hard?' she said, and he realised she was quietly seething. 'I'll give her hard. Don't worry about Vicky. She'll get over it.'

'Annie—she loves you.'

And her eyes softened, and her shoulders dropped inches. 'OK. I won't kill her. This time.'

'Promise?'

She smiled up at him. 'I promise. Go on.'

He went, keeping one ear out for the screams and cries he felt sure would follow, but there were none. She appeared five minutes later with a cup of tea, set it down beside him, glanced at the chessboard and said, 'Oh. You seem to have lost a lot of pieces.'

'Mmm. He's a quick study.'

And Stephen grinned up at her, and he just hoped she had the sense not to say anything else.

'Come on, Sport, thrash me and get it over with,' he said with a sigh, and Stephen turned his attention back to the board and rubbed his hands together with glee.

'Checkmate,' he said with a grin a mile wide, and Michael leant over the corner of the desk, ruffled his son's hair and grinned right back.

'So. Who's going to tell me the truth?' she said, and Kate looked away.

Vicky sighed. 'He walked in, saying, "Hi, Honey, I'm home!" in a stupid voice. What was I supposed to think?'

She could just imagine his embarrassment and confusion when he'd seen the girls. It made her laugh just to picture it. 'Oh, dear,' she said after a moment. 'So you put two and two together, made about twenty-five and warned him off, is that right?'

'Is that what he told you?'

'That he'd been warned off? Yes.' She leant forwards and covered Vicky's hand, squeezing it gently. 'Vix, he's my landlord. And he's a friend. And really, if I wanted to have a relationship with him, there isn't a good reason why I shouldn't, is there?'

She shook her head, looking embarrassed and unhappy. 'I'm sorry. It's just—'

'What?'

'Well, Dad.'

'Vicky, your father's dead, darling—and anyway, you know we didn't have that kind of a relationship. Your mother was the only woman in the world for him, and he'd be the last person to want me to sit about and mope.'

'I'm sorry,' she said again. 'It's just that he's so—'

'So what?' she prompted, when Vicky broke off.

'So—I don't know. Male! Macho. Dangerous.'

'Dangerous?' she exclaimed, laughing. 'Michael's not dangerous! He'd kill me with kindness if I let him. He keeps trying to get me to extend the tearoom and won't take any more rent—'

'Rent? Your *landlord*?' Kate squealed, cottoning on at last. 'He's Michael *Harding*?'

Vicky went pale. 'Oh, my God. I've just told one of the richest and most successful authors on the bestseller list to leave my stepmother alone. I can't believe it. Oh, God, I want to die.'

'I'm sure that won't be necessary,' Michael said gently,

hooking out a chair and dropping into it beside her. 'Anyway, if it makes you feel better, your brother just thrashed me at chess.'

'Good grief, you must be crap,' Kate said with a stifled laugh, and he chuckled.

'Or just a very nice man,' Annie said, smiling at him. 'Don't let him win too often. He'll be insufferable.'

Michael snorted. 'Don't worry, I won't. My ego can't cope with it.'

And, getting to his feet, he headed back out, just a gentle squeeze on her shoulder to tell her—and the girls—that she wasn't forgotten while he was out of the room.

Their eyes met, and Vicky groaned.

'I'm going to have to apologise, aren't I?' she said.

'It might be nice. And while you're on a roll, I've put clean sheets out on your beds. You could make them up to save me a job. Kate, fancy helping me with the supper?'

'Sure.'

And that, she hoped, was the end of that.

CHAPTER SIX

'Look—I'm really sorry.'

Michael looked up at Vicky and his heart ached for her.

'It's OK, Vicky.'

'No. I shouldn't have said what I did. I can't believe I did—'

He gave a grunt of laughter. 'I had a moment's doubt, I must say. Followed by the urge to rip your head off, but what would that achieve? And then I sat down and thought about what you must be feeling—what you're going through at the moment, you and Kate, and it all made much more sense.'

She shook her head. 'It's not about Dad.'

'I know. It's about Annie, and what she means to you, and preserving the status quo. And suddenly a man appears in her life and the status quo is threatened. And my guess is you panicked, just like I did when my mother died. My father had been an invalid for years, and whether it was the strain of looking after him or just one of those crazy things, she got cancer.'

'Oh, God, I'm sorry. I know how that feels. How old were you?'

'Eighteen. She died when I was twenty, and he couldn't go on without her. By the time I was twenty-one I'd lost them both. I don't know if he died of a broken heart or because of his old injuries—he'd been a bomb disposal officer, and got caught in a chemical blast—but whatever, he only lasted months after she died, and I didn't know what the hell was going to happen to me.

'I was at university, the family home had to be packed up and sorted out, and without my godparents I think I would have lost it. As it was I joined the army and ended up in the SAS. Dangerous and messy and exactly what I needed, but my godparents were always there for me, like a safety net, in case it all went wrong. And they still are. And the fact that the house isn't there any more, and I can't just go home and go up to the bedroom I used as a child, somehow doesn't matter. I've got my own life now, as you will, and just because Annie needs to move on with her life doesn't mean she won't be there for you, just as my godparents are there for me. She loves you to bits, you know. Nothing's going to change that.'

Her eyes were sparkling, filling with tears, and as he watched one welled over and slid down her cheek.

'I just miss them both. I don't think I'll ever get over losing Mum. I was only twelve. You shouldn't lose your Mum when you're twelve. And then when Dad died last year—it wasn't exactly a surprise, you know, but—' She broke off, shrugged, and he reached out a hand and squeezed her shoulder gently.

'I know. It's always a shock. Even when you know, even when you're expecting it, there's always that last breath, and then they're gone. And that's never going to be easy to accept, even when you can see a mile off that it's coming.'

She nodded, another tear joining the first, and she brushed them away impatiently. 'Kate seems to be taking it so much better.'

'Perhaps because she doesn't feel any responsibility? I mean, if Annie gets married again—'

Her head snapped up. 'Are you going to marry her?'

He laughed, wondering if it sounded as strained as it felt. 'Good grief, she only met me on Monday. I think that's a little hasty, even by my standards. I was just hypothesising. So, if she were to get married again, what next? Kate would assume you'd sort it. Wherever you are would become her home, her focus, unless Annie's new husband was prepared to welcome you into his home.'

Vicky chewed her lip worriedly. 'And if not? What would happen to this house?'

He shrugged. 'I don't know. It's something you'd have to discuss with Annie if it ever arose. But I can't imagine her making a new life that excluded you; she's not that sort of woman. I think she'd give up her own personal happiness before she'd do that to you.'

She was doing it now, he could have told her. Carrying on with this house, still keeping the home fires burning so the girls felt secure until they'd truly flown the nest.

And it was something he was going to have to take on board. Was he prepared to welcome the girls into his home, as well as Annie and his son?

Yes, he realised in surprise. Even after just one rather eventful evening, he found he was—because if he didn't, Annie would be unhappy, and he couldn't do that to her. Couldn't do it to any of them. God knows they were going to have enough to come to terms with without that.

He shot Vicky a crooked smile. 'I get the feeling we've been deliberately abandoned so we can have this chat,' he said softly, and she smiled back.

'We have. I asked them to. And I really am sorry—'

He grinned. 'Hey, Vicky, I'm cool with it, really. Don't worry.'

He patted her hand, stood up and stretched out the kinks

in his neck and shoulders. 'I need to go home. Things to do. I'll see you round. You take care, now.'

'You, too. And, for the record, I'm really pleased for Annie. She looks kind of lit up inside, you know? And it's been so long since I've seen that, if I ever have. So thanks, if it's your doing. And good luck.'

His grin slipped a little. 'Thanks.'

He went out and closed the door softly, sucked in a breath and let it go, then turned to find Annie standing just feet away, her eyes filled with tears.

'Thank you,' she whispered almost silently. 'Thank you for being so kind to her.'

He ushered her into the kitchen, pushing the door closed behind them. The lights were out, and as she reached for them he stilled her hand, wrapped it in his and cradled it against his heart and with his other hand, he threaded his fingers through her hair, anchored her head and kissed her very, very thoroughly.

Then he lifted his head a fraction, propped his forehead on hers and sighed softly.

'I need to go,' he murmured.

'I know. I need to get to bed. I've got a lot to do tomorrow. Thank you for letting Stephen win—'

His finger found her lips, shushing her silently. 'Leave the kid his moment of glory,' he murmured. 'The next time he'll have to try a lot, lot harder. Right, I'm going. I'll see you on Monday—damn, no I won't. I'm in Norfolk. I'll see you on Tuesday. In fact, what are you doing on Tuesday evening?'

'Tuesday? That's chess club. Cooking, then, until eight.'

'Fancy playing hookey?'

'Hookey?'

He nodded. 'I'll cook for you. I'll pick you up at six. Be hungry.'

And, with a quick kiss to the tip of her nose, he let himself out of the back door and went home while he could still drag himself away.

Tuesday took for ever to come. Crazy how much she was looking forward to it. Grace and Jackie and Chris came in for lunch, Chris juggling the baby, and they took one look at her and sat her down and pumped her for information.

'So, how's it going?' Jackie asked. 'Has he asked you out?'

'Have you asked him out?' Chris said with a grin. 'I wouldn't leave a little thing like that to chance!'

She pulled a face. 'He's had supper at mine three times now—all with the chess in mind, of course—so yes, in a manner of speaking I have asked him out.'

'And?'

'And what?'

Grace rolled her eyes. 'And has he asked you?'

She felt herself colour slightly. 'Um—he's cooking for me tonight.'

'Where? In the flat upstairs? I hope the kitchen's perked up since the last time I saw it—it was in a skip!'

'Jackie, don't be silly.'

They were sitting looking at her expectantly, and she realised she didn't really know the answer.

'His house, I imagine.'

'Which is where?'

She shrugged. 'I have no idea,' she admitted. 'None at all. Can't be far.'

And she felt a sudden flutter of panic. She was going out for the evening with a man who was almost a stranger, to an unknown destination—good grief, there were names for people like her. Starting with naïve, and foolish, and ending with idiot.

And yet somehow she knew she was safe.

And anyway, he wasn't a stranger. Ruth had known him for years and said he was one of the kindest men she'd ever met, and the way he'd been with the kids on Saturday night backed that up.

But nevertheless, a little shiver of something—anticipation? Dread? Excitement?—ran over her skin.

'Are you going straight from here?'

She nodded, and Grace sat bolt upright. 'You can't! You need to go home and freshen up. Shower, change, shave your legs, put on your best underwear—'

'Grace!' she hissed, glancing over her shoulder and hoping all the rest of her customers were stone deaf, but Grace was unabashed.

'I'll babysit the tearoom for you. You go—what time do you want me back here? Four? That give you long enough?'

'Tons—'

'So use it wisely. Right, girls. What's she going to wear?'

'What are you going to eat now, more to the point—'

Jackie shot her an astonished look. 'What could possibly be more to the point than that? He's to die for, Annie. You need to dress up, woman. Glad rags. This needs planning like a military campaign.'

'He's probably planning beans on toast,' she protested weakly, but the girls were up and running, and before she knew what was what they'd got her house key off her and were gone, leaving her with the baby and the mess on the table while they plundered her wardrobe.

'Right,' Grace said when they came back a few minutes later. 'We've put a selection out on your bed. And you will be vetted when I've shut up shop. Here's your key. I need to shoot.'

'What about lunch?'

She flapped her hand at Annie. 'No time. Things to do before four. I'll see you then. Bye, girls.'

She zipped out, leaving Jackie and Chris plotting while the baby waved her arms around and smiled happily.

Oh, to be so young and free, Annie thought wistfully, and it wasn't just the baby she was thinking of…

'I can't wear them!'

She looked at the clothes the girls had left out for her and laughed a little frantically. A clingy dress, a pair of evening trousers and a slinky top, a clingy jumper—what was it with the clingy stuff?—a skirt she'd been meaning to throw out for ages because it was too short, a pair of outrageous little shoes with wickedly high heels that she could hardly stand in, never mind walk—she couldn't wear any of this lot!

She put on the trousers and the jumper, but it just looked like something she'd wear every day. A bit dressier, but nothing special. And suddenly, for no very sensible reason and a lot of rather silly ones, she wanted to look special.

For him.

She pulled off the jumper and trousers, slipped the dress over her head and shimmied it down her hips. She'd never worn it. She'd bought it ages ago for a Christmas do, but then they hadn't gone. It must be nearly two years old. She wriggled her feet into the shoes, turned to the mirror—

And froze.

Was that her? That woman with the sparkle in her eyes and the glow in her cheeks and the soft, full lips that were rosy with anticipation?

The doorbell rang, and she stared at herself in horror. No! He couldn't be here this early! But he was. She looked down and there he was, in the front garden, chatting to Grace, the scheming little she-rat.

Oh, well, there was no time to do anything about it now. She sucked in her stomach, straightened her shoulders and checked herself in front of the mirror, then slapped on the merest touch of lip gloss to complete her make-up and picked her way carefully through the abandoned clothes and down the stairs.

'Coming!' she called and, grabbing her coat, she dived into it and buttoned it before opening the door, bag slung casually over her shoulder.

Grace narrowed her eyes and tilted her head slightly, but then her eyes slid down, clocked the shoes and she smirked. Annie reached out and took the key and thanked Grace, then turned to Michael.

'Ready when you are,' she said, closing the door firmly behind her, and Grace winked and mouthed 'Good luck!', wiggled her fingers and ran across to the car park in the middle of the square.

'Where's your car?'

'Next to Grace's,' he said, and she looked.

OK. Neither of them was the respectable and middle-of-the-road Volvo estate he'd been using all last week. On one side was a grubby but newish off-roader, the other side was a—oh, boy. Something much classier. Gorgeous, in a sleek and sinuous and utterly outrageous way. But which—?

'The DB9,' he said. 'It's my baby—a lunatic bit of self-indulgence. I thought you might like it.' He pressed a plip on the remote and the Aston Martin's indicators flashed. Well, she conceded, if he'd bothered to break out the flash car, maybe Grace had been right about the clothes. And he'd probably had the meal catered. He was always saying how he never got round to cooking. Suddenly she didn't feel quite so overdressed.

He opened the car door, seated her, pulled down the belt

and leant over her to clip it, his face just inches from hers, his hand warm against her hip.

'OK?' he murmured, and she nodded.

She didn't dare trust herself to speak.

He closed the door with one of those clunks that whispered quality, and went round to the driver's side, sliding in beside her and clipping on his seat belt before firing up the engine.

A fabulous, deliciously throaty burble echoed through the bodywork and made her shiver. As he eased out of the car park, through the village and on to the open road, he opened it up and the burble turned to a sexy, full-blooded growl that took her breath away.

He didn't exceed the speed limit, nor did he take her out of her comfort-zone, but the coiled power of the car was there, and somehow that was enough.

Then he eased back on the throttle, turned down a track and guided the car slowly alongside the hedge until they rounded a bend and there it was.

'It's a barn!' she said, her eyes wide. 'Oh, Michael! I didn't know you lived in a barn! Oh, I'm so envious!'

'Your house is gorgeous,' he said, but there was a question in his voice and she answered it.

'It's not my house. It's Liz and Roger's house, their dream, their home, their sanctuary. It's not mine. I feel as if I'm living in a museum sometimes. Someone else's image of the perfect house. But this—'

He opened the door and ushered her in, reached out to touch the switch that brought the lights up slowly, illuminating every nook and cranny of the interior.

It seemed to go up for miles. She shook her head wordlessly, taking it all in. The heavy, twisted oak beams, the steel walkway that crossed the central space and linked the two ends upstairs, the open-plan living area that flowed naturally from the sitting end through to the kitchen—and in the central section a wall of glass on each side that soared all the way up to the eaves of the roof.

Through the one they were facing she could see lights twinkling in the gathering gloom. 'Is that the church spire in the village?' she said, and he nodded.

'Yes.'

'That's just on the other side of the market square to the house, behind the shops.'

'I know.'

'How amazing. What a fabulous view you must have in daylight.'

'It is. It's gorgeous.' His hands cupped her arms gently. 'Here, let me take your coat,' he murmured, and she let it slip from her shoulders into his waiting hands, holding her breath for his reaction to the dress.

She wasn't disappointed. He inhaled sharply and, as she turned, his eyes flared and then were swiftly controlled.

'You look beautiful,' he said huskily, his voice sounding more gravelly even than usual. 'Come on through. You can sit here and talk to me while I cook. We're having beef Stroganoff.'

They were, as well. Properly cooked, with meltingly tender fillet steak and soured cream and onions sweated in butter, served with wild rice and baby-leaf salad.

She perched on a stool at the granite-topped island, propped her chin on her hands and watched him work.

'Here,' he said, pouring a slug of red wine for her and sliding it towards her. 'Taste that.'

'I'm not much of a wine buff.'

'You'll like this one. My godfather gave it to me yesterday. One of his friends owns a very old vineyard that's been in the family for generations, and he sent him a case.'

It was gorgeous. Unbelievable. It slid down her throat like velvet, leaving a wild burst of flavours that brought her eyes wide open then let them drift shut on the experience.

'Mmm,' she said, and he grinned.

'Said you'd like it. It's not commercially available. Friends and family only, and they're pretty good friends, so every now and then he gets a treat.'

'And you're wasting it on me when you're driving me?'

He shook his head. 'I'm not bothered. I don't drink a lot. I can have a glass with you, and if there's any left I can finish it later.'

'If there's any left?' she said with a chuckle. 'I'm hardly going to drink the other however-many glasses, even if it is sublime! I might have two, at a push.'

'Then I'll certainly get to enjoy it later. That's fine. It's quality, not quantity.'

He stirred the onions in the pan, came back to the island and smiled at her. 'OK?'

'Wonderful. But I feel curiously redundant. Can I do anything?'

He shook his head. 'Just talk to me.'

So she did, in between watching the quick, precise movements of his hands as he tore and sliced and whisked. And she found herself wondering what those hands would feel like on her body, just as he dipped his finger in the salad dressing and sucked it, then dipped it back in and held it out to her to taste.

Their eyes locked, and he leant over, holding his finger to her lips in silent invitation.

How could she refuse?

She opened her mouth, closed it round his fingertip and suckled gently. Heat exploded through her, and as she looked up at him she saw that same heat reflected in his eyes.

She straightened up, dragged in a breath, looked away.

'Um—it's fine,' she said.

'Estate-bottled olive oil from the same vineyard, and they also make the balsamic vinegar,' he said, his voice so husky she could hardly hear the words.

Or was that because of the roaring in her ears?

She turned away, clutching the fabulously rare and delicious wine in front of her with both hands, like a cross to ward off evil spirits.

What was it she'd told Ruth about not wanting a man in her life? And yet here she was, just two weeks later, burning for him so fiercely she thought she'd die in the fire.

His hands closed over her shoulders, turning her gently towards him. The wine vanished, and then she was in his arms.

'Relax. I'm only going to hold you,' he murmured, his voice low and soothing, and she let herself lean into him, resting her head against his chest and listening to the deep, even rhythm of his heartbeat.

And gradually her body relaxed, the tension easing, shifting as she accepted this thing that was happening to her—to them—and let herself acclimatise.

'OK now?'

She nodded. 'I'm sorry. I'm not used to this. It's been a while since I've dated anyone.'

His laugh was gruff and warm, and he hugged her. 'That makes two of us,' he said, and let her go, returning to the onions and mushrooms, testing them, then throwing the rice into a pan of boiling water.

'Can I lay the table?' she asked.

'Done,' he said, and she turned and stared.

How could she have missed it? A long, plain wooden table and tall, graceful chairs, set in the centre of the vaulted section, was laid with sleek stainless steel cutlery and slate place mats arranged at right angles to each other at one end, slender white candles waiting for a flame to work their magic.

So simple. So clean, so pure, so unfussy.

So Michael.

And a rose. Just one, in a tall, slim glass, beside one of the places. A white rose, touched with cream, the bud about to burst.

Tears filled her eyes. 'You're really spoiling me, aren't you?' she said, suddenly fiercely glad that she'd worn the dress and not caring if this thing was going too fast for common sense. Since when had that had anything to do with anything?

'I'd like to,' he said, and there was something utterly sincere in his voice, utterly trustworthy and decent and honourable. It made her feel safe—oddly, since she was poised on the brink of a precipice, staring out over the unknown.

He picked up a remote control, and soft music flowed through the room, romantic vocals designed to set the mood. The lights dimmed, he picked up the dishes and put them on the table, then held out his hand to her, his mouth kicking up in that one-sided, curiously sexy smile.

'Dinner is served, *madame.*'

A shiver ran over her. Etienne had called her *mademoiselle*, in just the same way. She was falling for Michael as she'd fallen for him, headlong without thought or caution.

Was that how she was destined to fall in love every time?

She held out her hand to him, letting him take it and settle her in the chair. He lit the candles, lifted the lid on the dishes and she caught the scent of the steaming, fragrant rice and the rich, creamy Stroganoff.

It tasted wonderful. The flavours, the textures, meltingly tender and rich and smooth, the salad a sweet, fresh counterpoint.

She shook her head, smiled wordlessly at him and cleared her plate.

'More?'

'Absolutely. I'll probably put on a half a stone, but who cares?'

He chuckled. 'I'll take that as a compliment,' he said, and piled another helping on each of their plates.

'If you can cook like that, why on earth do you need to eat in my scruffy little tearoom?' she asked in amazement as she set her fork down for the second time.

'Because the food is wonderful.'

'No. *That* was wonderful. My food is wholesome.'

'Exactly. That's what you need on a daily basis. If I ate like that all the time, I'd probably have a heart attack before I'm forty.'

The words stopped her in her tracks, and she looked away, sucking in a suddenly much-needed breath. 'I don't think that's always why people have heart attacks,' she said quietly, and he groaned and put down his glass.

'Oh, Annie, I'm so sorry. I can't believe I said that.'

She looked back at him, smiling to reassure him. 'Don't be silly. I was just feeling guilty because the whole time I've been with you I've hardly given Roger a thought.'

Well, it was plausible, at least. In fact she'd suddenly considered the possibility of losing him and been shocked at the stab of grief that had pierced her heart. It was nothing to do with Roger and everything to do with this man and what he was coming to mean to her.

And suddenly she couldn't lie to him.

'That's not true,' she said, before she could bottle out. 'Actually, it was the thought of you dying—of anything—that shook me. Apparently you're coming to mean something to me—something I hadn't expected. I know you were joking, but—it's just—I've lost two men already. I know it happens. I'm sorry, I'm being silly, spoiling things—'

'Annie, I'm not going to die,' he said, leaning towards her and taking her suddenly cold hand in his. 'I promise you, I have no intention of dying—at least not for a damn long while.'

'What about your headaches?' she said, and his mouth twisted into a wry smile.

'They're just the aftermath of my accident,' he told her. 'I had neck injuries as well as facial injuries. Sometimes, if I do something stupid or get stressed out, I get a migraine. The osteopath fixes it, it's not a problem.'

She nodded, reassured about something she hadn't realised was troubling her. 'Liz had headaches,' she said, and he sighed.

'Of course. I'm sorry, I didn't think about that, either.'

'Why should you? It's over—past. Let's talk about something else.'

'Such as?'

'You,' she said promptly. 'So how long have you got before this heart attack you aren't planning to have at forty?' she asked, swirling the wine in her glass as she studied him shamelessly.

He chuckled and eased back in his chair. 'Two years. I'm thirty-eight.'

Strange. He looked older, and yet not. Maybe it was just because of all that had happened to him, but the touch of silver at his temples and the lived-in face were older than the body.

Vicky was right. He was male. Macho. Dangerous.

But only to her heart.

Their eyes locked and, despite all the things she wanted to

know about him, she couldn't string a single coherent thought together. All she could do was feel—

He pushed back his chair and stood up, holding out a hand to her.

'Dance with me,' he murmured, and without argument or question she stood and went into his arms.

Common sense reared its head briefly. 'This is crazy,' she whispered. 'I have to get back for Stephen.'

'You're quite safe. It's quarter past seven. I'll have to take you back at a quarter to eight. When I make love to you, Annie, I'm going to want more than half an hour to do it.'

When I make love to you.

Not if.

When.

Oh, yes. Please. It's been so long.

Her body seemed to fit so perfectly against his. Their legs meshed seamlessly, thigh to thigh, hip to hip, their bodies swaying together in perfect harmony.

She felt his lips trace a slow, leisurely trail down from her brow, over her cheekbone, across her ear and down to the sensitive skin of her throat. She lifted her head, allowing him access to the hollow where his touch was making the pulse leap.

His tongue stroked it, dragging a groan from her aching, longing body, and with a murmured 'Shh,' he rocked her gently against him, bringing their hips closer together so she could feel exactly what this was doing to him, too.

A whimper escaped from her mouth, and he lifted his head and stared down into her eyes, then slowly, achingly slowly, he lowered his mouth to hers.

That was when she realised she'd never been kissed in her life before. Not by Etienne, not by Roger, certainly, and not even by Michael in that slow, thorough exploration on Saturday night.

Because this kiss was a promise, a vow, a total surrender of his heart to hers.

And hers to his.

Finally he lifted his head, his eyes dark with need and laced with regret. 'I have to take you home,' he said hoarsely.

'No,' she moaned. 'Please, no.'

'I have to,' he said. 'Stephen—'

And that was enough.

There would be time for them. But she couldn't let her son down, and she was shocked at how close she'd come to it.

She took a step back out of his arms, and then another.

'Of course,' she agreed. 'We'll go now.'

While we still can...

CHAPTER SEVEN

Wow.

He'd been *that* close.

He dropped into the sofa, a glass of Antoine's excellent Pinot Noir in his hand, and closed his eyes.

She'd tasted of wine and cream, and honey from the salad dressing, and her body had felt so good—so soft, slender and yet lush, full in all the right places.

She'd changed, filled out. From breast-feeding?

The thought dragged a groan from the bottom of his lungs. He wanted her. Needed her.

He squeezed his eyes tight against the sudden prickle of tears. He'd waited so long, loved her for ever. And it seemed she loved him, too.

She hadn't said so, but he'd felt it. That kiss had said it all, and it was more than chemistry. It was recognition, he was sure of it. Their souls had been reunited in that kiss, and finally, after the agony of the past nine years, he allowed himself to dare to hope.

And it was time to tell her the truth, and hope she'd forgive him for all the lies and deception of the past and present.

'I love you, Annie,' he said softly. 'Whatever happens, I love you. I always have, and I always will.'

He opened his eyes again, staring out over the valley to the lights of the village in the distance. He could see the flood-lights illuminating the church, and just down and to the left was her house. He couldn't tell which room she was in, but if he got out the binoculars he could work it out, even in the dark.

He didn't, though. He just waited, and eventually the lights went out.

'Sleep tight, my darling,' he murmured.

Then, draining his glass, he went up to bed.

'Hi, Sport.'

'Hi. I'm starving. Can we play chess?'

'Maybe later. Haven't you got homework to do?' Annie asked, coming over to the round table by the window where Michael had been for the past half hour and where Stephen was now busy making himself at home after school.

'Not tonight. Mr Greaves was sick, and we had a supply teacher. She let us off. She's cool, I like her.'

'I'll bet,' Annie muttered. 'So did you go swimming this afternoon then?'

He shook his head and pulled a face. 'No. We couldn't. She's not a lifesaver. I told her we didn't need a lifesaver—well, I don't, anyway, but she wouldn't change her mind.'

He looked so glum and crestfallen. Michael had vowed he was going to have less to do with him until he'd talked to Annie, but there was a pool at his house, just sitting there waiting—

'Are you a good swimmer?' he asked, and Stephen nodded.

'He swims like a fish,' Annie said. 'And he needs to burn off energy, so I hope you did something energetic instead?' she added, turning her attention to her son.

'We had to be trees,' he said, disgust in his voice. Michael nearly laughed aloud, and there was a twinkle in Annie's eyes, quickly disguised. He looked away as she spoke, biting the inside of his cheek to trap the laugh.

'I thought she was cool?' she was saying.

'Only because of the homework.'

Michael glanced up and met her eyes again, then glanced at Stephen and jerked his head slightly.

To his relief she understood. 'Stephen, why don't you go and wash your hands before you have something to eat?' she suggested, and with a sigh he slid off his chair and headed for the cloakroom.

Annie cocked her head on one side. 'Why did you want him out of the way?'

He smiled wryly. 'I've got a pool at the barn,' he told her. 'It's heated, it's safe and, unlike the partly cool teacher, I *am* a lifesaver. I could take him over now, let him swim and give him a game of chess, then you could come over when you finish here and we could have supper. Well, if you bring something to eat we could. I've got salad but not much else. And I might be able to find another glass of that wine for you.'

Stephen was coming back, and she hesitated, doubt in her eyes. 'You will take care of him?'

'With my life,' he vowed. 'Nothing will happen to him while I'm looking after him, I promise.'

Still she wavered, and he sensed the struggle in her, and the moment that he won.

She nodded. 'OK. Stephen, do you want to go swimming with Michael at his house?'

The boy's eyes widened with delight. 'You've got a pool? Wicked!'

'So is that a yes?'

'I think so,' Annie said drily. 'You'll need to go home and

get your swimming things. Michael, could you go with him? Do you mind?'

'Of course not. And when you come over, you could bring yours and join us in the pool.'

She looked flustered for a second. 'I have to cook some time this week. I'll be running out.'

'I'll help you later.'

'My silent partner?'

He laughed softly. 'I can't promise to be silent, but at least you know I can cook.'

Amongst other things.

Heat flared in her eyes and she looked hastily away. 'I'll see you guys later, then. About six or so.'

'Can you remember the way?'

She nodded. 'Of course.'

He ruffled his son's hair and stood up. 'Come on then, Tiger. Let's go.'

Annie watched them through the window, her son and the man who was coming to mean so much to her.

He was wonderful with the boy—just what Stephen needed.

Just what she needed—

'No!'

He stopped Stephen on the kerb with a firm hand on his collar, just before he ran out in front of a car. Her heart in her mouth, she was on the point of rushing out to tell him off when Michael shook his head and said something. Stephen hung his head, then muttered what looked like a slightly shamefaced apology; then Michael reached out and took his shoulder—not his hand, because he wouldn't have allowed that liberty—and steered him across the road and in through her gate without any further incident.

'So where are they going?'

'Michael's taking him swimming. He's got a pool at his house.' She turned towards Grace and found the woman eyeing her with unashamed curiosity.

'Indeed?' she said slowly. 'Wicked.'

'That's what Stephen said. Are you on your own?'

'No, Jack's just parking and Chris is joining us.' Grace grinned. 'So how was dinner? I liked the car.'

'What was it?' Chris asked, appearing at her elbow.

'An Aston Martin DB9.'

Chris whistled softly. 'Wow, the guy has class. Can he cook?'

She nodded slowly, remembering the food, the wine, the candlelight and soft music. Dancing with him.

The kiss.

'Yes, he can cook.' She was pretty damn certain he could do everything.

Especially that—

Colouring, she turned back to the kitchen. 'Tea?'

'Mmm. And the rest,' Grace said. 'You don't get away with that.'

Annie sighed. She didn't imagine for a moment that she would!

'So,' Jackie said the moment she sat down with them, 'tell us all. What did he cook you?'

'Don't be boring. What's the house like?' Chris asked, and Grace rolled her eyes.

'You lot! Talk about the trivia,' she said, then lowered her voice to a conspiratorial whisper. 'Can he kiss?'

Annie sighed. 'Beef Stroganoff the proper way with meltingly tender rare fillet steak, served on a bed of wild rice with a side salad, the most gorgeous estate-bottled Pinot Noir from a friend of his godfather that was quite amazing, a lovely,

lovely converted barn with stunning views over the valley towards the village, and yes. Absolutely.'

Grace sighed with contentment.

'Thought so.'

'What?' Jackie said, clearly lost.

'He can kiss. I knew it.'

All six eyes swivelled back to Annie, and she felt her colour mount.

'That was all! It was just a little kiss.'

Like the north pole in January was just a little chilly.

Chris looked out to the car park and watched as Michael backed the Volvo out of a space and drove slowly away, Stephen strapped into the rear passenger seat.

'Interesting.'

'What?' Annie asked, craning her neck and starting to worry.

'He's put him in the back,' Chris explained. 'If you put them in the front without a booster seat the seat belt's too high on their necks until they're about twelve. Not something you'd expect a bachelor to think of.'

'I'm amazed you let him go with Michael.' That from Grace, who'd obviously moved on from the kiss, to Annie's relief.

'I haven't had a choice about letting him do things with other people. I'm in here so much that I either have him here bored to death with me or I let him get on with his life with someone else.'

And worry myself sick the entire time, she added silently.

'He'll be fine,' Chris said gently. 'Michael's thoughtful and intelligent and considerate.'

'And he can kiss, and he's got a great sense of humour, he doesn't smoke and he's got a lovely, lovely barn. So when's the big day?'

Annie laughed and swatted Jackie gently. 'Give me time to breathe! I've only known him just over a week!'

'Nine days, seven hours and fifteen minutes,' Grace said smugly.

Annie already knew that. It said something about what a sad, desperate widow she was turning into.

'If you say so,' she said, and dragged the conversation into safer waters. 'What can I take over there for supper?'

Their eyes locked on hers again. 'You're going for supper?'

'Again?'

'Two nights running?'

So much for safe!

'That was cool!'

Michael grinned and threw the boy a towel. 'Here—you can go and shower and get dressed. We can have a game of chess before your mum gets here, and maybe we can swim again later if she wants to.'

'Excellent!'

He showed him how the shower worked in the wet room off the lobby by the pool, then left him to it. He hovered in earshot, though, preparing the salad in the kitchen, and when he heard the water stop he went up to his room and showered and dressed in record time. He'd promised Annie no harm would come to her son, and although he knew he was taking it to ridiculous extremes, as far as he was concerned that included slipping in the shower.

He'd also promised Annie a swim, but after the exhausting chase up and down the pool and rough and tumble he'd had with Stephen, he was more than ready to slump into a chair with a glass of Antoine's wine and put his feet up.

All that exercise on top of damn all sleep was a killer. Chess was just about all he felt he could manage.

'OK, Sport?'

Stephen nodded. He was standing in the dining room, his hair spiking wildly, peering out over the valley. 'Is that our village?' he asked, pointing, and Michael nodded.

'Yup. See the church spire? Your house must be down and to the left a bit.'

'I can't see it.'

'That might be because the lights aren't on, if your mum isn't at home yet,' he replied, resisting the urge to ruffle the boy's hair for the sake of it. 'You can see it better in the daytime.'

'Can I come and swim again? At the weekend?' And then his face lit up. 'Oh. Can't come at the weekend. I'm going to Bristol with Edward for Tom's birthday! Ed's dad's driving us down on Saturday morning early, because he's got a meeting or something, and we're going to an assault course on Saturday and then we're going to have pizza and go to the cinema, and Mum's bringing us back on Sunday. It's going to be so wicked.'

'In Bristol?' he said.

Stephen nodded. 'Tom lives there now. He moved just after my birthday. I haven't seen him for ages.'

Since July or thereabouts, Michael calculated. Ages? He didn't know what ages was. Ages was Stephen's lifetime. All of it, from the moment of conception—

'Fancy a game of chess?'

'Yeah! Wonder if I'll beat you again?'

'Not if I have anything to say about it!' Michael said drily. 'Being beaten once by an eight-year-old is hard. Being beaten more than that is downright careless.'

'Maybe I'm just dead good?'

Michael snorted. 'Maybe you just got lucky.'

'We'll see, shall we?' Stephen said with a cheeky grin, and Michael allowed himself one masculine and sporting ruffle of the dark, damp hair so like his own.

'Oh, I think I'm ready for you.'

'You reckon?'

'I reckon. Bring it on, Tiger. Let's see what you're made of.'

He was improving, there was no question about it, but he wasn't there yet. He wouldn't catch Michael without cooperation for a while, but then he had a heck of a lot of catching up to do.

Months. Months and months of sitting over a chessboard or a computer waiting for his face to heal, for his ribs to recover and the plaster casts to come off his arms, for his voice to come back to something approaching normal after his throat had been kicked in.

Months when there'd been nothing else to do but lie and watch television or think about David and what had gone wrong.

Months haunted by David's death, by Ruth's long, slow road to recovery, by the memory of Annie's tears when he'd told her he loved her just before he'd left her for the last time.

Months he didn't want to remember or go through ever again—

'Check.'

He sucked in a sharp breath, stared down at the board and frowned. Hell's teeth. He was losing it. Getting sloppy.

He studied the pieces for a moment, eyes narrowed, and then made his move. Stephen would have no choice but to do *that*, and then he could do *that*, and that would be it. He'd have him.

Ego saved for another day.

'Your move.'

The outside lights came on, and he pushed back the chair and went to the door, opening it and standing there, propped against the door frame, watching her approach.

'Is he OK?'

He smiled. 'Of course he's OK. We've had a great time. I'm just thrashing him at chess. Everything all right with you?'

She smiled up at him, her face softening. 'It is now.'

His heart seemed to swell in his chest, and drawing the door to behind him, he lowered his head and stole a light, lingering kiss.

He felt the door open behind him and lifted his head, just as Stephen came out.

'Have you brought supper? I'm *starving!*'

'Mum, you have to see the pool! It's brilliant!'

He grabbed her hand and towed her through the house, past the dining room where they'd eaten that amazingly romantic meal and where he'd danced with her and kissed her oh, so beautifully, through the kitchen and off through a doorway at the end into a lobby. Then on, through the lobby, and into a huge room, another barn in its own right. And there, filling the centre, was a clear, still pool that gleamed in the light streaming through the windows from the floodlights in the courtyard outside.

Michael reached round beside her and touched a switch, and light flooded the room—under the water, up into the beams, through the plants—everywhere, but so subtle, so carefully planned that the sources were all but invisible.

'I didn't cover it—I wasn't sure if you'd want to go in later.'

She did. She wanted to so much it was almost an ache, but she had so much to do, and swimming practically naked with

Michael in this somehow very intimate setting was not one of the things on her to-do list. Her wish-list, however, was a different matter!

'That's my favourite bit,' he said, pointing to a recess, and she saw a huge round whirlpool. 'My treat, after a long work-out, as a reward for being good. And it's brilliant for getting the kinks out when I've been writing hard.'

It looked wonderfully, enormously inviting, and she felt herself wavering.

She dragged her eyes away and smiled down at Stephen. 'I bet you had loads of fun.'

'I did—and Michael says I can come again, but not the weekend because I'm at Tom's, so it'll have to be another time—'

'Hey, hey, slow down! Maybe Michael doesn't want you constantly underfoot. In fact, let's eat and get you home. You're getting over-excited and you've got school tomorrow.'

'He's fine. He's a kid. He's allowed to be enthusiastic. So—does it appeal? Do I leave the cover off?'

She hesitated, and he grinned and dropped an arm round her shoulders, hugging her briefly before releasing her and turning away.

'I'll leave it—keep your options open. Did you manage to find anything for us to eat?'

She nodded, following him reluctantly away from the in-viting water and back into the kitchen. 'I brought some soup and quiche and a few slices of cheesecake. Is that OK? Not quite up to your standard, I'm afraid, but it was the best I could do—'

'It sounds great. I don't suppose you brought corn bread?'

She would have teased him, but he saw the indulgent smile just as she felt it reach her eyes. 'Now, what do you think?'

If Stephen hadn't been there, she thought he would have

hugged her again. Instead he winked, and she felt the impact of it right down to her toes.

'Plates?' she said, getting practical, and he put the crockery out on the central island, retrieved the salad from his huge American fridge-freezer and put it on the table.

'Any of that dressing left?' she asked, and he nodded.

'In the fridge.'

She opened it, and laughed. It was vast—and almost empty. Some cheese, a tired wedge of melon, a few wrinkled grapes and a plastic milk carton—semi-skimmed, she noticed—were about all that was in it, except a few vegetables lurking in the drawers at the bottom and the remains of last night's rice under cling wrap.

'Good job you've got such a big fridge,' she teased, and he grinned.

'I bought it for the water chiller. I love iced water. Drink gallons of it.'

'Can we have one, Mum?' Stephen asked. 'Look, it's cool. You get a glass and push it here, and you get cold water, and if you push it here you get ice!'

She turned to Michael and gave a wry smile. 'You seem to be a big hit with my son. Everything you have is either cool or brilliant.'

His smile was a little wary—or was that just because his mouth didn't move quite right? She wasn't sure, but it didn't seem to reach his eyes.

'We aim to please,' he said lightly, and turned away, but not before she saw a slight grimace cross his face.

'Are you OK?'

He nodded. 'Just ache a bit. We swam for a long time. I might have twinged something.'

She had the distinct feeling he was lying, but she didn't push it, and by the time the soup was heated and the meal was on the table, his smile was firmly back in place and Stephen was chattering nineteen to the dozen to cover any potential silences.

She told herself she was imagining it, but when Stephen wanted to swim again right after supper, he shook his head. 'Only if your mother wants to. It's getting late, and she's got things to do.'

Outstaying their welcome? Suddenly it seemed like it.

She met his eyes. 'I'm sorry. We've taken you over—'

'No. Annie, I didn't mean that,' he said, apparently reading her mind. 'I just don't want you ending up exhausted because you've had to burn the candle at both ends. You're more than welcome, both of you.' He glanced away from her to Stephen.

'We've got a game of chess to finish. Why don't you go and make your move?'

'I did. It's your turn.'

'Right. I'll do that, then while I clear up you can make your next move, and if your mother wants to swim, she can be changing while we finish the game. If not, well, whatever. We can have a cup of coffee and you can go.'

His eyes were back on her again, putting the ball back in her court. Then he went over to the sitting area, stared down at the chessboard on the table in the middle, moved a piece and came back to her, leaving Stephen there to contemplate his next attempted coup.

'I'd like you to stay a while,' he murmured. 'You aren't overstaying your welcome, and I'm not trying to buy my way into your heart by spoiling your son.'

She frowned. 'I didn't think you were. The thought hadn't even occurred to me. I was just concerned that you must be getting sick of him.'

A strange emotion flickered in his eyes and was gone. 'Not at all. Did you bring your things?'

She nodded.

'So, do you want to swim?'

'Is the hot tub warm?'

His smile was slow and gentle. 'No. It's hot. It's gorgeous, and it'll do you good. Go and change and slide into it and wallow. I'll come and join you when I've thrashed the pipsqeak. The changing room's just off the lobby on the right.'

She nodded, picked up her bag and went through to the changing room.

Tumbled stone tiles covered the walls, the floor was warm slate, and there was a wet room that looked as if it had a drenching shower. No expense spared, then, she thought, and suddenly realised just how rich he must be.

How totally out of her league.

What on *earth* was she doing here with him? Why was he interested in her? Of all the women he could have, why her, for heaven's sake? He was gorgeous! A real catch.

Why her?

She changed into her discreet and all-covering black chainstore costume, wrapped her towel around her like a sarong and headed out to the pool room.

He'd turned the lights on for her, and the whirlpool was bubbling gently. She dipped her toe in, sighed and followed it, sinking under the foaming water with a blissful sigh. Stretching her arms out along the rim, she laid back, shut her eyes and let go.

He stood there for a moment watching her. Stephen hadn't wanted to swim again—not once he'd discovered there was satellite TV. He was settled on the sofa in front of a cartoon channel, and Michael didn't think it would be long before his eyes drooped.

He wasn't alone.

He'd brought coffee on a tray, and he set it down at the edge of the tub and slid into the water beside her.

'Hi, gorgeous,' he murmured and, leaning over, he dropped a kiss on her lips.

Her eyes fluttered open and she smiled at him sleepily.

'I'm sorry—I must have dozed off.'

'You're tired. That's fine. I've brought you coffee.'

He handed her a cup, and she sat up straighter and took it from him. He shifted so he was opposite her, watching her over the top of his cup. Their legs brushed, and her eyes flew up to meet his, automatically pulling her legs away a fraction.

He went after them, hooking his heels behind hers and pulling them back towards him, then threading his legs around hers so they were enclosed, all the time holding her eyes with his.

Heat flared in them, and she swallowed slightly.

He put his cup down, reached under the water and pulled her feet on to his lap, then one at a time he massaged her feet and ankles, easing out the strain of standing all day.

'Oh, that's bliss,' she groaned, putting her own cup down and sliding further under the water, her hands locked on the rim to stop her sliding right under. He changed feet, and her toes brushed against his groin, making him suck in his breath sharply. The urge to pull her across the water and into his arms nearly overwhelmed him, but he concentrated on the other foot, reminding himself that her son...*their* son—was just a few metres away and didn't need that liberal an education.

He just hoped he didn't have to get out of the water in front of her any time soon.

'So who won the chess?' she asked lazily, and he gave a strained chuckle.

'Who do you think? I'm not letting him get away with that twice.'

'What's he doing?'

'Watching cartoons on the telly. I think he's nearly asleep.'

'Good. That means I don't need to feel guilty for keeping him up.'

'You could stay here,' he suggested out of the blue. 'I've got plenty of bedrooms.'

Including mine, with a very large, very empty bed just crying out for you—

'No.' She shook her head. 'That's too much. Anyway, the cat will sulk.'

'The cat always sulks. I've never seen that cat when it's not sulking,' he said with a grin.

'Horrible cat. It acquired us five years ago. I suppose at some point I'm going to stop thinking of it as a stray.'

He laughed and rubbed his thumbs lightly over the soles of her feet, his fingers curled loosely over the top of her toes. 'OK now?'

She nodded. 'Lovely. Thank you. They really ache some days with all the standing.'

'I can imagine.' He tipped his head on one side. 'About the weekend.'

She shook her head. 'Stephen's in Bristol with a friend for an old schoolmate's birthday party. I have to drive down on Sunday and pick them up, and I'm open on Saturday. I won't have a weekend, I'm afraid.'

'I was thinking about Saturday night.'

She shook her head again. 'No. I can't do anything. I've got to make an early start on Sunday if I'm going to Bristol and back.'

'That's what I was going to say. If you could get someone to cover you for Saturday afternoon, we could go down and spend the night near there and bring the kids back on Sunday. There's a hotel just outside Cardiff with the most spectacular view across the city and over the bay, and the food's wonderful. This time of year I shouldn't think they'll be too busy, so they should have a couple of rooms.'

'A couple?'

Her eyes were worried.

'A couple. No strings, Annie. I'm not trying to sneak you away for a dirty weekend. I just thought you might like to share the driving, and get away for a night. We could go in the Volvo. It's a piece of cake to drive.'

'I know. Roger used to have one; it was lovely.' She nibbled her lip.

'Penny for them.'

She met his eyes squarely, then came out with something totally unexpected.

'Why me?' she said.

His heart lurched. Oh, this one was dead easy. Too easy, but he wasn't lying to her again. Never, if he had his way. This time, though, he didn't have to. He simply told her the truth.

'Because ever since I met you, I haven't been able to get you out of my head. You make my sun come out, my days worth living. I want you, Annie. I want a relationship with you—a full-on, proper, serious relationship. I want us to have time to get to know each other, to be sure it's what we both want, but as far as I'm concerned, it's the real thing and nothing's going to change that. I love you.'

She swallowed hard, looked away, looked back again, her eyes shimmering.

'That's the nicest thing anyone's ever said to me—but you still haven't answered my question.'

He shrugged. 'I can't. I don't know why you, in particular,

but it is you, very definitely. I've never felt like this about another woman in my life. And I've never told another woman
that I love her.'

She closed her eyes, and the threatening tears spilled over
and slid down her cheeks.

'It's so quick,' she whispered.

He could have laughed out loud. Quick? They'd had nine
years—but they hadn't really, and she was right. It was quick.
It had been quick then, and it was no different now.

No different at all in one respect. She still didn't know who
he really was—and that was something he was going to have
to deal with very, very soon...

CHAPTER EIGHT

THEY went cross-country, avoiding the M25 and the M4 as long as possible. Their journey took them through the picturesque Cotswolds to Cheltenham, then through the Forest of Dean via Ross-on-Wye and down to Monmouth, picking up the M4 at Newport for the last stretch to Cardiff.

It was a beautiful day, and Annie found herself dozing, cosseted in the big comfortable passenger seat while Michael drove.

All the way.

He turned off the motorway just before six, cut through a few back roads and headed north again, then turned into the drive of the hotel and pulled up facing south with the hotel behind them.

And in front of them was the most fantastic view over Cardiff to the Bay, across the Bristol Channel and all the way to Weston-Super-Mare in the distance.

Lights were starting to come on, the sun low in the sky now, and an amazing sunset was streaking the clouds a stunning pink. Michael got out of the car, bent over and smiled at her.

'Come on. We can see the sunset from our rooms.'

'How do you know that?'

'Because I know which rooms we've been given.'

She opened the door and got out. 'How do you know? Have you stayed here before?'

He nodded. 'Several times. Ruth and I used it when we were researching in the area. I've set a book in this part of Wales.'

She remembered it. Remembered the vividly drawn characters, the banked emotions held back of necessity, the wild explosion of heat when those emotions were finally released. Was that what it would be like with him—?

'Come on.'

She went, following him as he picked up their cases as if they weighed nothing and headed for the steps.

'Mr Harding, welcome back. Here you are—your keys. Could you just sign there for me? Thank you. I hope you enjoy your stay. If there's anything you need, just give us a call.'

The receptionist slid the card keys across the desk to him, and he handed them to Annie and led the way through doors and down stairs and round the corner until she wondered why he'd be taking her on a tour of the basement; then at the end of the wide corridor he stopped.

'We've got these two in the corner,' he said, and taking the keys from her he opened one of the doors, ushering her in.

She didn't know what to expect, but it was amazing. Nothing like a basement, but at ground level, taking advantage, obviously, of the sloping site, and the room was stunning. Gorgeous. An enormous room, with a bathroom on one side as she entered it, hanging space and shelving on the other. As the room widened out, a huge double bed sat on one wall, with a sofa and chair beyond it arranged around French doors which led out on to a terrace.

Beyond the terrace the ground fell away again, and there stretched out in front of her was the most spectacular sky she'd ever seen.

'It's beautiful,' she said, unable to take her eyes off it, and he ushered her out of the doors and stood close behind her, his arm over her shoulder, pointing out various landmarks around the Bay and in the city centre sprawling below them.

More and more lights came on as they watched, and then finally the sun sank into the sea, the sky darkening to ink as night enveloped the landscape, broken only by pinpricks of light in the velvet blackness.

She shivered, and he wrapped his arms around her and rested his chin on her head, pulling her back firmly against his chest so she could feel his powerful body reassuringly solid behind her.

'Thank you for bringing me here,' she said softly. 'It's lovely. I haven't been away for so long.'

'When?' he asked. 'When was the last time you went away for a night?'

She shook her head, feeling the rasp of his chin against her hair. 'I don't know. Years. When Stephen was small. Roger and I went to London to a show. Five years ago?'

His arms tightened. 'You need spoiling,' he murmured. 'I'll leave you to unpack and change, then we can go and have a drink before dinner. How long do you want? Do you need to lie down for a while?'

She laughed softly, guilt prickling her. 'Hardly. I'm afraid I dozed in the car. So much for sharing the driving.'

'You were tired. What time were you up?'

'Four,' she confessed. 'I remembered there weren't enough tray bakes.'

He sighed into her hair. 'You work too hard. So what do you want? An hour?'

'Half an hour? How dressy is dinner?'

'Not very. Smart casual.'

She grimaced. She wasn't sure she could do smart casual, but she'd brought the dress. He'd seemed to like it on Tuesday, at least, and let's face it, her choices were distinctly limited! She could dress it up with her only bits of jewellery and the lovely soft cream pashmina the girls had given her for Christmas.

'I'll book us a table for eight, shall I? That'll give you half an hour to get ready and an hour for us to unwind and look at the menu.'

She nodded. 'Sounds good.'

He brushed a kiss on her cheek, and she felt his stubble graze her skin lightly, leaving it tingling.

'See you soon,' he murmured.

He went out, and she looked around at the huge room. It seemed much too big just for her, and she found herself wishing she was sharing it with him.

Still, at least he was treating her with respect. Any other man would have expected her to sleep with him if he'd gone to all this trouble and expense. She should be grateful.

But she wasn't grateful. She was lonely, and tingling with anticipation, and she was more than ready for the next step.

He contemplated a tie, but it was so long since he'd worn one he thought it would strangle him.

Damn. Was it necessary?

No. It was a Savile Row shirt, one of his favourites, and with his navy chinos and a linen jacket he was sure he'd do. But then he thought of Annie, of what she'd be doing now. Hair, make-up, those ridiculous little shoes that were all pointy toes and heels so high she'd need oxygen. And that dress? Please, God, let her wear the dress—

He put on the tie, checked his watch and tapped on her door.

'Coming!' she called, and after a few seconds the door swung in.

He nearly punched the air.

She was wearing the dress, and she looked if anything even more stunning than she had the other night. And she smelt of— Oh, God help him, she was wearing that perfume. The perfume she'd worn in France, the perfume that had haunted him for years.

He sucked in a slow, measured breath, took a step back and groped around for a smile.

'All set?' he said, his voice sounding even more strained than usual, and she nodded.

'I'll just get my things.'

She disappeared for a second, coming back with her bag in one hand and a cream shawl thing in the other. 'Do you think I'll need this?'

He shrugged. 'I don't know. Bring it. You don't want to be cold.'

He knew it wouldn't be a problem for him. Just looking at her was putting him in danger of spontaneous combustion. They went up to the bar, and he turned to her and raised a brow.

'Fancy champagne? To celebrate escaping?'

She hesitated, then that soft, lovely smile lit up her eyes. 'What a good idea. Thank you.'

So they started with champagne—just a half bottle, because they would have something different with their meal—and he lifted his glass and met her eyes.

'To you—for being the most special woman I've ever met. One of the bravest, kindest, least selfish people it's ever been my privilege to know. And to us.'

She swallowed, her eyes sparkling, and lifted her glass. 'To us,' she said, her voice thready with emotion. A tear shim-

mered on her lashes, then slid down her cheek, and he reached
out and caught it with his thumb, sweeping it gently away.

'I love you,' he said gruffly.

She looked down. 'Oh, Michael,' she began, but then the
waitress came to take their order, and the moment was lost.

He didn't mind. There'd be others, and he'd rather hear the
words when she knew who she was saying them to. His jaw
clenched. He was dreading telling her, but he'd have to do it
soon. Tomorrow night?

Not tonight, because they were trapped together, and she'd
probably need time to get used to the idea, and if she wanted
to get away from him it would be somewhat difficult with
two kids in the car and a two hundred and fifty mile trip to
get through.

So, tomorrow night, then.

And God help him.

The meal was wonderful.

Elegantly presented, cooked to perfection, the flavours a
perfect complement to each other.

All of this she noted, the cook in her taking an academic
interest. The rest of her, the woman who was slowly coming
to terms with the fact that she'd fallen headlong in love with
the man sharing this experience with her, wouldn't have cared
if they'd been in a greasy spoon eating beans on toast.

So long as she'd been with him.

They laughed, they argued about education and politics
and advertising, and all the time all she could think about
was being alone with him.

Holding him in her arms. Loving him. Him loving her.

'Was everything all right for you?'

Michael glanced up, smiled distractedly at the waitress
and nodded.

'Wonderful. Thank you. Can we have our coffee by the fire?'

'Of course, sir. I'll bring it through to you. Any drinks?'

'Want a liqueur?' he asked her, but she shook her head.

'I've had enough.' Any more and she was likely to disgrace herself. Her inhibitions were well out of the window anyway.

'Just the coffee, thank you,' he said, getting to his feet and helping her out of the chair, then placing a warm, proprietorial hand on the small of her back and ushering her through to the lounge.

They sat by the window again, so they could see the flames licking through the logs on the fire and the lights stretched out below them, twinkling in the distance.

'All right?'

She nodded. 'Wonderful. Never better.'

'Good.'

His smile was tender, but there was a burning intensity about him that made the breath catch in her lungs.

Suddenly she didn't want the coffee. She just wanted to be alone with him. But it was here now, and he was pouring it and handing her a cup, so she drank it, nibbled one of the sinful little chocolates and wished she knew how to tell him what she was feeling.

'You look tired,' he said suddenly, and put his cup down. 'Come on. Let's call it a day.'

She nodded, got to her feet, walked down to their rooms with her heart in her mouth because she was going to ask him—

'Key?'

She fumbled in her bag, handed him the card, and he slid it into the slot, turned the handle and gave her back the key.

'Are you coming in?' she asked, holding her breath for his reply, but he shook his head.

'No.' He swallowed, his Adam's apple working. 'Don't tempt me, Annie,' he said, his voice low and rough with desire, making her body ache. 'It's difficult enough to be a gentleman. I'll see you in the morning.'

He brushed her lips with his, backing away and closing her door before she could reach for him, and she turned and slumped against the door. She could have screamed with frustration.

'Goodnight, my love,' he murmured through the door, then she heard his door open and close, and she shut her eyes and dropped her head forwards and sighed.

So much for her night of passion.

He stood in the shower under the pounding spray for what seemed like hours. He didn't believe in cold showers. They were just unpleasant and only worked for a few minutes. So the water was hot, and so was he, but at least the tension was gone from his neck and shoulders and he was squeaky clean.

He sluiced the water from his face and hair, grabbed a towel and rubbed himself roughly dry, then put on the towelling robe from the back of the door and went out into the bedroom.

The bed mocked him, acres of it lonely and empty and taunting. When he'd come down with Ruth to research the book set in Cardiff and the Brecon Beacons, he'd imagined bringing Annie here.

Making love to her on just such a bed, in the room next door, where she was lying now.

The result had been the hottest, most passionate and emotional ending he'd ever written. Ruth had cried. Ruth, who never showed any emotion, had cried.

So had he.

And he could cry right now, with frustration.

'One more day. That's all. Just one more day. Hang in there.'

He lay in bed staring at the ceiling, then forced himself to relax. He'd got to drive tomorrow. Make that today. It must be after midnight. He didn't want to crash and kill them all when he'd come this far.

He slowed his breathing, his heartrate, consciously tensed and relaxed each muscle group, and gradually he dozed off.

A noise woke him, just a slight click, but after all the years of training it was enough. Senses on full alert, he opened his eyes a crack and checked the room.

Nothing.

He eased out of bed and padded silently to the French doors. The noise had been outside—Annie's door opening?

And then he saw her, huddled in the hotel's towelling robe, staring out over the twinkling lights. He opened his door and went out, and she turned to him and smiled ruefully.

'I'm sorry—did I wake you?' she said softly.

'I wasn't really asleep,' he admitted.

She walked up to him, placed her hand on his heart, looked up into his eyes.

'Nor was I. I couldn't sleep without you,' she said, and he groaned and closed his eyes.

'Annie, no. We can't do this—'

'Why?'

'It's too soon.'

She gave a funny, brittle little laugh. 'It doesn't feel too soon, believe me.'

He took her hand in his, gripping it like a lifeline. 'We need to talk. There are things you don't know about me—'

'Are you married?'

He shook his head. 'No—'

'No mystery woman stashed away somewhere?'

'Only you.' Only ever you, for so, so long—

'Can I trust you?'

'Absolutely.'

'Then that's all I need to know.' She swallowed, and he realised she was nervous. Her eyes, though, locked with his, and he could see all the way down to her soul. 'I need you, Michael,' she whispered. 'Make love to me—please.'

Dear God, forgive him, he wasn't strong enough—

With a shattered groan he hauled her up against his chest, slanted his mouth over hers and kissed her as if his life depended on it. When he came up for air he couldn't speak, couldn't think, couldn't do anything except scoop her up in his arms, kick her door open and then closed behind them and then lay her on the huge, soft bed and follow her down.

Her robe parted, giving him access to the warm satin skin that he'd longed to touch. His mouth raided it, plundering her body, touching it all—her breasts, full and soft and achingly aroused, her waist, slender and neat, the smooth, taut bowl of her abdomen, the fine, tender skin of her inner thigh—then finally, the most intimate caress of all.

She came apart under his touch, tugging at him wildly, his hair, his robe, pulling him up her, taking his face in her hands and kissing him as the tears poured down her cheeks and the climax tore through her.

'Please—now!' she begged, and he buried himself in her sweet, welcoming body and gave in to the passion that had ridden him for nine long, endless years.

'Annie!' he groaned, then arching up, he felt a great cry rip through him as his body slammed against hers for the final time, the sensation too much as she convulsed around him, her own cry lost in the echo of his as he spilt deep inside her.

As the echoes died away, he felt her body go limp against

him, cradling him in its softness. 'Michael,' she whispered raggedly. 'Oh, Michael—'

He dropped his head into the hollow of her shoulder and struggled for air. 'I love you,' he said.

'I know, my darling,' she murmured, her voice unsteady, her hands stroking him tenderly—tenderly enough to bring tears to his eyes. 'I love you, too.'

Her arms tightened around him as he tried to shift his weight from her, so he eased to his side, taking her with him, and collapsed against the pillows, cradling her against his chest.

She fell asleep almost instantly, but he lay awake, berating himself for his weakness, cursing his stupidity, his lack of self-control.

He should have told her before he'd allowed this to happen. It was wrong. So many lies.

'Forgive me, my love,' he whispered soundlessly. 'Please forgive me...'

She woke to the sound of his heartbeat under her ear, one leg wedged between his solid, hair-roughened thighs and her hand enfolded in his.

His other hand curled protectively over her back, the fingers splayed across her ribs. She moved a fraction, and his eyes flew open and locked with hers.

'Good morning,' she said softly, and he searched her eyes, his face expressionless.

'Good morning.'

His voice was gruff and sleep-roughened, rasping like sandpaper across her senses. And, talking of sandpaper, she lifted her hand and rubbed her palm sensuously over his jaw, revelling in the coarse and very male drag of stubble on her skin.

'Mmm,' she groaned softly, and he rocked against her, tipping her on to her back and following her over, plundering her mouth as his hands explored her body lazily. He lifted his head and stared down at her, his face no longer expressionless, and she felt the surge of passion in his body. Heat coiled through her, and she threaded her fingers through his hair, drew his face down to hers again and took his mouth in a kiss full of promise.

Later, when she'd recovered her breath and her heartbeat had slowed, she smiled up at him and stroked his jaw with her fingertips.

'Wow,' she murmured. 'You can wake me up like that every morning for the rest of my life if you like.'

A shadow seemed to flit through his eyes, leaving them troubled. 'I hope you'll give me that chance,' he said quietly. He glanced at his watch, then sighed. 'Annie, we have to make a move. The wind's picking up—if it gets much worse they'll close the Severn Bridge and we'll have to go the long way round, and we've got far enough to go as it is.'

He was pulling away from her, not just physically but emotionally. She could feel it, feel the chill of his withdrawal, and she felt curiously afraid.

'Michael—you said you wanted to talk,' she said, suddenly realising that she needed to know whatever it was. Needed to know it now—

'Later. Not now. I want time alone with you. Tonight?'

'I'll have Stephen, but that's not a problem. We can talk after he's gone to bed. He won't be late. If they've been up all night he'll be out like a light by eight.'

He nodded. 'OK.'

He stood up, pulling his gown back around him and tugging the belt tight. 'I'll see you in half an hour for breakfast.'

And with that he went out on to the terrace, closed her door behind him and she heard his door click shut seconds later.

A shiver went over her, and she frowned.

Whatever he had to say to her, it couldn't be that bad.

Could it?

He dropped her off at her house at three and headed home. There were things he wanted to gather together before their talk—things he had to show her. And he needed time to get his head in order.

First, though, was a nice long soak in the hot tub to ease out the kinks of the drive. The tension of these last few weeks was killing him, and he could feel a headache starting up, not helped by Stephen and Ed who'd been chattering non-stop in the car the entire way. Oh, well, at least they seemed to have had a good time.

He put the kettle on, took a long, ice-cold drink of water from the fridge dispenser and downed some pills, then stared out over the valley towards her house.

The wind was picking up, bending the trees, the gusts growing stronger by the minute.

Gales had been forecast, and it seemed they weren't wrong. He'd thought it was rough on the way back, the crosswind tugging at the car. The bridge had been open early in the morning, but he'd lay odds it was closed now.

He felt a prickle in the back of his neck, and he frowned.

It was his early-warning system, and he absolutely never ignored it. It had saved his life more times than he cared to remember. His eyes flicked to Annie's house, and the prickling got worse.

Damn.

He was just reaching for the phone when it rang, and he grabbed it.

'Harding.'

Her voice was frantic. 'Michael, it's Annie—Stephen's gone up the beech tree after the cat, and the tree's creaking and now he's stuck and I don't know what to do and I'm so scared it's going to fall—'

His gut clenched with fear. The beech tree was huge—!

'I'm coming. Tell him to stay still. Keep out of the way of the tree, do you understand?' He said it again for emphasis. 'Keep out of the way of the tree. Tell him to stay where he is. I'll be with you in five minutes.'

It took him three, and he nearly put the Aston in the ditch on the S-bend, but then he was there and running into the back garden.

'Where is he?'

'There—' She pointed up into the tree and then he saw him, clinging to a branch, his face white with terror. It was an old tree, and beeches weren't known for their longevity. The roots were probably rotten, and it was creaking ominously with every gust.

If he was lucky, he'd got minutes.

'Michael, get him down, please—!'

'Don't worry. Get back out of the way, Annie. I'll get him.'

There was an old rope ladder at the bottom, attached to one of the lower branches, and he shinned up it in no time flat.

'Don't worry, Stephen, I'm coming,' he yelled over the noise of the wind. 'Hang on tight.'

'The cat,' he sobbed, and Michael glanced across to the end of the branch his son was clinging on to and saw the frightened ginger tom hanging on for dear life. He wasn't alone. As Michael got to him, he could see Stephen's knuckles were white and the boy was shaking.

'It's OK, son, I've got you,' he said, grabbing hold of his

jumper with an iron fist. 'Right. I want you to turn and wrap your arms around my neck. Slowly, now. That's it. Good boy. Now your legs round my waist, and hang on tight.'

'What about Tigger?'

'I can't reach Tigger. Let me get you down first.'

'But you must—'

'In a minute. Hang on, we're going down.'

He glanced down and saw Annie standing, her fists pressed to her mouth, eyes wide with terror.

The wind gusted again, nearly tearing him from the trunk, but he leant into it and hung on as the huge old tree shifted and groaned. He could feel it going, but then the wind eased and he reached out his foot, groping for a branch.

'Left a bit,' Annie called, and he found the branch, swung down to the ladder and slithered down it to the ground.

'You have to get Tigger!' Stephen was sobbing.

'Michael, no!'

'It's OK. Go to your mum, Stephen. I'll get him.'

His son slid from his arms and ran towards Annie, and as Michael turned to go back up for the cat, cursing himself for a fool, the wind gusted again, there was an ominous crack and as if in slow motion the huge tree started to topple towards him.

'Run!' he bellowed and, turning on his heel, he sprinted towards them, throwing himself over them as the tree crashed down around them.

He felt a stabbing pain in his leg, then there was another crack as the branches whiplashed in the aftermath, his head felt as if it had been split open and everything went black…

CHAPTER NINE

'MRS HARDING?'

She opened her mouth to explain that she wasn't Michael's wife, but then shut it and stood up, going towards the doctor.

'How is he?'

'Dazed, disorientated, nauseous—he's had quite a blow to the head, but we're rather concerned, in view of the extent of his previous surgery.'

'Concerned?' she echoed. 'He's not going to—?'

She broke off, unable to say the words, but the doctor shook her head. 'Not unless something changes radically, but we will need to keep him in overnight to be on the safe side. He keeps talking about Stephen, asking if he's all right, and he's asking for you—I take it you're Annie?'

'I am.' She nodded. 'Can I see him?'

'Of course. Come with me.'

She led Annie from the all too familiar relatives' room through into another place that was every bit as familiar. Resus. She'd been here several times with Roger over the years, and the place gave her the creeps.

Michael was lying on a trolley-type bed, wired up to monitors that bleeped and squeaked and frightened the living daylights out of her.

Oh, Lord. Not Michael, too, she prayed. Please, not Michael, too. I can't lose another person that I love—

'Annie?'

His voice was rough and scratchy, but his eyes were wide open and locked on to hers like a laser, and she went straight to his side and took his hand, hanging on like grim death.

'Michael! I was so worried. Are you OK?'

'I'm fine,' he said dismissively. 'What about Stephen?'

'He's OK. He's shaken up and scared, but he's with Ed's parents. They're keeping him overnight. He's got a few bumps and scratches, but he's all right.'

'What about you?'

'I'm fine. We both are.'

'You sure?'

His voice was slurred, but the urgency was all too clear and she hurried to reassure him.

'I'm sure. I wouldn't lie to you.'

His eyes closed briefly. 'Going to be sick,' he said, and turning his head, he retched helplessly.

She reached out a hand and smoothed back his hair, tears coursing unheeded down her cheeks. The nurse dealt with the bowl, wiped his mouth and settled him back on the blood-soaked pillow while she just stood there and tried not to fall apart.

'Don't worry about the blood,' the doctor said, leading her to one side. 'He's got a head wound, they always bleed a lot. We've glued it already, and it's the least of our concerns. I've asked the maxillo-facial surgeon to come down and take a look at his X-rays, because frankly I'm out of my depth. I just wondered if you could tell me where he had his facial reconstruction done, so we can speak to the surgeons there and get any information we might need to read the X-rays.'

'Reconstruction?' she murmured. 'I'm sorry, I don't know.

We haven't been together all that long.' Try two weeks—
'Ruth might know.'

'Ruth?'

'A friend—I've called her, she should be here soon.'

'Got one for me?' a man asked, and the doctor left her
side and flicked a switch, bringing up the light behind a set
of X-rays that even Annie could see weren't normal.

She frowned at them. Good grief. She'd realised he'd had
an injury, obviously, but that extensive? There seemed to be
bits of metal everywhere!

The newcomer was pointing out things on the plates, and
Annie could catch the odd word, but not all of them.

'Replaced cheekbones—massive dental work—jaw—orbit
must be altered—sight affected—contact lenses or glasses?'

'Contact lenses.'

She blinked at Michael. She'd never realised he wore contact lenses, and she'd certainly never seen him in glasses.

'Amazing work,' the man was saying, shaking his head
and turning to look at Michael so she could hear him more
clearly. 'Fantastic result, you really wouldn't know to look at
him—must have been a hell of an injury. I would say he was
lucky to survive, but he probably didn't think so at the time.
I doubt if his own mother would recognise him now. Let's
have a word.'

He went over to Michael, bent over him and smiled. 'Hi
there. I'm Mr Hughes, the maxillo-facial surgeon. I've been
called in to have a look at your X-rays. Can you tell me your
name?'

'Michael—Harding.'

'OK. Can you tell me about your accident?'

'Tree fell on me.'

'OK, Mr Harding. What about before—when your face
was damaged?'

'Armstrong,' he mumbled. 'It's Armstrong...'

Annie blinked. Armstrong? *Armstrong?*

The doctors exchanged significant glances.

But he was slurring more and more, starting to ramble, and Mr Hughes fished out a penlight and flashed in it his eyes. That didn't go down well and Michael turned away with a groan and retched again.

'OK, I think you need to keep an eye on him but his pupils are equal and reactive. I can't see any obvious fractures but I'd like a chat with him when he's feeling better, to make sure there's nothing unforeseen going on. And check the neck again. It might just be whiplash—it's typical of severe facial injuries. Anything that hits the face that hard affects the neck, and the effects can be long-lasting and recurrent. Keep an eye out for a head injury; he's obviously confused, but he's very photophobic. He might be suffering from nothing more than migraine. Has he had pain relief?'

The doctor shook her head. 'Not yet.'

'I would give him morphine—'

'Not morphine,' Michael mumbled. 'Not again. Not going cold turkey again, please. OK now. Just turn off the lights...'

He trailed off, and they dimmed the lights around him slightly and he seemed to relax a little.

'Mrs Harding?' a nurse was saying. 'I've got all his things here that were in his pockets. As we're going to admit him I've got to list them and ask you to sign for them.'

'Of course,' she said, thinking that she really must tell them that she wasn't Mrs Harding—or Mrs Armstrong, come to that. What was that about? Funny thing to get confused about—

'There's just a few things—his phone, his keys, his wallet—that's got £26.58 in it, and three cards, and this ring and chain and a photo—'

'That's my grandmother's ring,' she said, feeling a cold shiver run over her. She reached for it and picked it up, staring down at it in confusion. Why did Michael have it? She'd given it to Etienne—

Tell me where he had his facial reconstruction done— you really wouldn't know to look at him—fantastic result—I doubt if his own mother would recognise him now...'

Or his lover?

She felt the blood drain from her face.

Etienne. He was Etienne.

Or Michael Harding.

Or Michael Armstrong?

She backed away. 'I—I'm sorry, I need some air.'

She turned and ran out, past the nurses, through the double doors and out into the car park, dragging in great lungfuls of air and gulping down the nausea.

Who was he?

'Annie?'

She looked up into Ruth's pale and worried face.

'Who is he?' she asked in a strange, hollow voice that she didn't recognise. 'I don't know who he is, Ruth—what his name is, even. What's going on?'

Ruth swore softly under her breath. 'I knew this would happen. Where is he?'

She swallowed. 'Resus. He's OK. He's got a head injury— they did X-rays—called a specialist down. He'd never seen anything like it—'

She turned away, bile rising in her throat, and felt Ruth's hand on her shoulder.

'Idiot. I told him to tell you—'

'Tell me what, Ruth? What is it he has to tell me? And how much do you know about it?'

Ruth was silent, but her face said it all.

Annie backed away, shaking her head. 'You know, don't you? You know all about it—you always have, right from the beginning. He said you go back years—how many years, Ruth? Nine? Is it nine?'

Ruth's eyes filled with tears. 'Don't hate him, Annie. He loves you.'

'Does he? Which one of him? Etienne Duprés? Michael Harding? Or Michael Armstrong, whoever the hell he might be? I haven't been introduced to that one yet—'

She turned, walking away from the hospital, her legs moving faster and faster until she was running, fighting against the wind that was tugging at her hair and streaking the tears as they fell down her cheeks.

Hands stopped her. Big, gentle hands that halted her progress and turned her, sobbing, against a firm, hard chest.

'Do you want me to take you home?'

She looked up, scanned an unfamiliar but kindly face with worried eyes.

'I'm Tim Warren, by the way. Ruth's fiancé.'

The policeman. Surely he would be all right? She nodded. 'If you don't mind. I don't think I can take any more—'

'Let me tell Ruth what we're doing. Hang on.'

He ran back to her, spoke briefly, kissed her cheek and then was back by Annie's side, his hand under her elbow, guiding her towards his car.

Twenty minutes later she was home, and she held herself together just long enough to close the door on Tim before the dam burst.

She lifted her hand to her mouth to hold back the sobs, and realised she was still holding the ring—the ring she'd given Etienne nine years ago on that fateful night to keep him safe.

But what about her? What about keeping her safe, because nothing now seemed to make any sense.

'Who are you?' she whispered. *'What do you want with me? What do you want with my son?'*

'Idiot.'

Michael winced. 'Don't. Head hurts.'

'Good. It's no more than you deserve,' Ruth ranted at him, then turned away, talking to someone else. The doctor? 'Is he going to be all right?'

'I believe so. Where's Mrs Harding gone? I wanted to ask her something.'

'Home,' Ruth said, and he lay there puzzled and tried to work out who she was talking about. There *was* no Mrs Harding—and why was Ruth saying it was no more than he deserved? He'd been saving Stephen—

'She wasn't feeling well,' Ruth was saying. 'I think she's gone to check on their son. Is it OK if I stay with him?'

'Only if you don't nag,' he slurred, still trying to work it out.

'You wish. I'm his sister,' she lied, and glared down at him.

He grunted, glaring back at her. 'Where's Annie gone?' he mumbled.

'Home. She knows, Michael.'

It took a second to register, then his eyes slid shut and he swore, softly but fluently, in French.

'Go after her.'

'Tim's with her. He's taking her home.'

'Good idea,' he mumbled. 'Going home. Want to go home.'

'Sorry, we have to keep you in,' the doctor said. 'I need to monitor you—'

Pretty little thing. Couldn't have been more than about twelve. He tried to smile at her, but his mouth wouldn't work.

'You'll have to duct-tape me to the trolley,' he mumbled. 'I'm going. Get me the forms.'

'Mr Harding, it really isn't a good idea—'

He sat up and swayed, glaring at the cot sides. 'Let me out of here,' he said firmly and much more clearly. 'I know the risks. I don't have a head injury—I've got a migraine. Got pills at home. Going home—Ruth, get me out. Oh, hell, sick again—'

He retched into a bowl shoved under his face in the nick of time by the long-suffering doctor, and glowered at her defiantly. 'Just let me go.'

'I can't. Why don't you lie down and—?'

'Because I'm going home,' he said clearly. 'Either with or without your approval.' His gaze swivelled to Ruth. 'Where's your car?'

'I'm in Tim's—and he's taking Annie back. Stay till tomorrow, Michael, be reasonable.'

But he couldn't, because he had to get out of here and talk to Annie—and he couldn't do that pinned out like a butterfly and wired up to God knows what. And anyway, he didn't trust them not to pump him full of morphine, and he'd had enough of that to last him a lifetime.

'Now, Ruth,' he pleaded. 'Get me a taxi. Get me out of here.'

Annie didn't know what to do.

All she knew was that she was afraid. She didn't know who he was, or what he wanted, but she knew—she just *knew*— that he was in some way involved with Claude Gaultier.

And that scared the life out of her.

And Ruth? She was involved, too, but she was marrying a policeman. Did that make her one of the good guys? And what about Michael? Was he a good guy or a bad guy? And how could she tell? Oh, God, how had she got herself *involved* in this?

And then she thought of Stephen, and her fear escalated. Michael had been around for years, lurking in the background, somehow contriving to own her tearoom, with Ruth installed in the flat overhead monitoring every detail of their lives.

Befriending her. Spying on her, for heaven's sake! And on Stephen—babysitting him, of all things. And she'd told them in words of one syllable that Stephen was his son. Etienne's son. Michael's son.

The same thing.

Except Etienne had been a playboy, a charmer, a gentleman in his rather lighthearted way. She'd never taken him seriously, but she'd loved him anyway.

But Michael. What kind of man was Michael?

More to the point, *who* was Michael?

What did he want with them? Was he working for Gaultier? Surely not. Gaultier had been killed—unless he wasn't the real boss? But why would any of them be interested in her? What did she know that meant she had to be stalked for nine years? Or was he just after Stephen?

She closed her eyes, breathing deeply to quell the panic. She could feel the wind shaking the house, rattling the glass in the windows. There was a draught under the study door, and she went in there to see if the sash had slipped with the howling gale and something crunched under her shoes.

She flicked on the light and stared in horror. The window had gone, the glass exploded all across the floor, and the hole where it had been was filled with broken branches. One of the bookcases had been knocked over, and Michael's book, the one set in Wales, lay open on the floor at the title page, signed with his bold scrawl.

For Roger, with every good wish, Michael.

He'd been here, met Roger. Infiltrated her family when she'd been out—with Ruth's help? How many times had he been here while they'd been out? How many times had he seen Stephen? With every good wish? She didn't think so. She didn't think so at all, but then she didn't know what to think.

She lifted the phone, staring at the mess, not knowing whether to cry or run. Who could she phone? The police?

Why? They'd ask her questions she had no answers to. The only person who had the answers was Michael, and she had no intention of asking him anything.

She cradled the phone, picked it up again and called Grace.

'Help me,' she said, her body shaking. 'I'm so scared—'

'Annie? My God, what's happened? Where are you?'

'Home. The tree fell down. Michael's in hospital, but it isn't that. He isn't—'

'I'll be right there.'

The line went dead, and she clutched the receiver until the message to please hang up and try again finally penetrated her daze. She put it down and stared at it.

She thought of calling the girls, but what was the point of worrying them? Surely they were safe? Unless he was part of the human trafficking thing?

No. She knew he wasn't. The way he'd made love to her—nobody involved in trafficking prostitutes could be so gentle, so passionate—could they?

'Annie? Annie, open the damn door!'

She opened it, and Grace swept in and hugged her tight.

'Sweetheart, tell me all. What's happened?'

She didn't know where to start, so she began with the most important thing, the thing that somehow drifted to the top.

'He's Stephen's father,' she said.

Grace stared at her. 'But—he's dead.'

'No. He's Michael—but I didn't know. His face is different—his voice. His injuries—'

She remembered the X-rays, and shuddered. What must he have gone through? *No. Don't think about that. Don't let yourself feel sorry for him. Not until you know—*

'Annie? Annie, let me in, I need to talk to you.'

The knocking on the door was relentless, insistent, and they turned towards it uncertainly.

'Ruth,' she said, looking at Grace with fear. 'I don't know if I can trust her. She knew all about it—'

'I'll get it,' Grace said firmly and, pushing past her, she opened the door. 'What is it?'

'I want to see Annie.'

'Maybe she doesn't want to see you.'

'Please, Grace. I need to talk to her—to explain.'

Grace snorted. 'It had better be good—and who are you?'

She heard a low murmur, and Grace stood back. 'OK. You'd better not be a bad cop. I'm a journalist.'

'I'm not a bad cop,' Tim said firmly, pocketing his ID, and following Ruth in; he closed the door and met Annie's eyes. 'Annie, please listen to Ruth. At least hear what she has to say.'

She swallowed hard and nodded. 'All right—but just five minutes.'

'Where's Stephen?' Ruth asked.

'Somewhere safe,' she replied, not even questioning her choice of words.

'Good. He doesn't need to hear this. Tim, could you take a look outside at the tree and make sure the house is OK?'

Annie laughed raggedly. 'I should start in the study. Half of it's in there.'

She turned away, going through to the kitchen, retreating automatically to the room where she felt safe. 'OK, fire away.'

Ruth glanced at Grace. 'Could we have a minute?'

Grace hesitated, then nodded. 'I'll be just outside,' she promised, and closed the door.

'May I sit down?'

Annie nodded, then pulled out a chair and sat down herself. Quickly, before she fell. 'OK, start talking. Who is he? Why is he spying on me? And why are you spying on me? For umpteen bloody years, pretending to be my friend, coming into my home, babysitting my child. How could you, Ruth?'

'Because he asked me to keep an eye on you, to make sure you were safe and that everything was all right.'

'It was—until he came along!'

'That's not fair.'

'How do I know that? I don't even know who he is—and, as for keeping me safe, I've never been so terrified in my life! Ruth, what the hell is going on? Who is he—and come to that, who are you?'

'Me? I'm who I am. You know me.'

'I don't think so. And Michael? What's your connection with Michael? Is that his name, by the way?'

Ruth sighed, and started talking. 'His name's Michael Armstrong. He was in military intelligence. When you met him, he and David were working undercover, trying to get evidence on Claude Gaultier, the owner—'

'I know who Gaultier is. It's Michael I'm having a problem with—and your connection to him. And who's David?'

'You knew him as Gerard.'

'The man who died?'

Ruth nodded, and something that could have been pain flashed in her eyes and was gone. 'David and I were lovers. We were in the police together, in immigration. He was seconded to the task force to work with Michael, because he was bilingual. I was working in London, with the prostitutes. I was—raped. I was in hospital when it all went wrong in France. The first I heard, David was dead, and Michael had survived. Just. They stuck him back together again, gave him a new identity and sent him into the military equivalent of retirement under witness protection.'

No wonder she'd been unable to get anything out of the police in France. They must have been hushed up in a big way. And Ruth's David had been Gerard, the dead man. And she'd been raped. Poor Ruth. *No. Don't feel sorry for her, she's in this up to her lying little neck,* she told herself. But that didn't explain everything anyway, not by a long chalk. Not the years after that night.

'So why did he come here?' she asked, refusing to back down because she *needed* these answers. 'Why did he buy the Ancient House, and live so close, and put you in the flat? Don't tell me it was coincidence.'

She shook her head. 'Oh, no. It was quite deliberate. And he had to pull some pretty impressive strings to be allowed to be here and work with me while we watched you. I still don't know how he did it, or why he bothered with me.'

'But why did he want to be near me? Was it just because of Stephen?'

'You'll have to ask him that. I've told you all I can—all that's mine to tell. All I know, really—except that he would die for you and his son.'

That was true. He'd nearly died that afternoon, throwing himself over them to protect them from the falling tree, shielding them with his body, and the horror of that moment would be with her for ever. But that didn't explain his secrecy.

'Why didn't he tell me who he was?'

'He couldn't. He's bound by the Official Secrets Act. So am I. As long as the case was ongoing, there was nothing he could do. Until Gaultier was arrested.'

'But it all came to a head just over two weeks ago,' Annie said slowly. 'That's when you moved out—when he came into my life.'

'Because he could, at last.'

'And yet still he didn't tell me who he was,' she said, still puzzled. 'Why didn't he, Ruth? Why didn't he tell me then who he was? Was he trying to gather evidence for custody or something?'

Ruth looked horrified. 'No! Nothing like that, I promise you.'

'So what, then?'

She shook her head. 'You'll have to ask him that. I told him to, warned him. He had some crazy idea about getting to know you from scratch. Go and talk to him, Annie. He's a good man. The best. He's only ever had your safety and happiness at heart.'

'And Stephen's? What about Stephen?'

Her face softened. 'He adores Stephen. It's killed him having to watch him from a distance.'

'But—he couldn't have known he was his son. Not for certain. Not until I told him.'

Ruth looked away, and Annie felt the icy chill of betrayal. 'How did he know?' she asked, her voice cold.

'DNA,' Ruth confessed. 'I cut a little bit of his hair one night when I babysat for you.'

She stood up, backing away from the woman she'd thought was her friend. Her legs were shaking, and her voice wasn't her own, but she couldn't take any more. She just wanted Ruth out, wanted this to be over.

'OK, that's enough. I want you to go.'

'Annie, talk to him. Give him a chance to explain.'

'I don't know that he can. He might be a national hero, Ruth, but he's lied to me, deceived me, cheated his way into my life, my bed, my heart—and I don't think I can ever forgive him for that, whatever his motivation.'

'And me?' Ruth asked, lifting her head and meeting Annie's eyes, her own tortured. 'Can you forgive me?'

She couldn't speak. Instead, she simply turned away, and after a moment the door closed softly and left her in silence— a silence broken only by the sound of her own weeping.

CHAPTER TEN

THE next hours and days were hell. Afterwards, Annie didn't know how she'd got through them, but somehow she did.

Tim was wonderful. He took Ruth back to Michael's, then returned with a saw and a hammer and some nails and dealt with the tree, weatherproofing the house with tacked-on plastic sheeting and some old boards as a temporary measure until the morning.

He didn't say much, and Annie was grateful for that. He just worked quietly and steadily, securing her home, clearing up the broken glass in the study, righting the bookcase and returning the books to it.

At least the wind had died down, so the plastic sheet was secure enough to weatherproof it, but the boards across it wouldn't have held back a determined intruder, and Annie was afraid.

'Do you want me to stay?' he asked, but she shook her head.

'No. I'm being silly. I'll be all right. It's Michael I'm afraid of, and he's too ill to be a threat at the moment.'

He hesitated, then said, very gently, 'Michael won't hurt you, Annie. He saved Ruth's life. She tried to kill herself a few months after David died. He wouldn't let her. He kept her going, looked after her, made her feel safe. Without him she wouldn't be here now, and nor would a lot of other people. He's a good man. A really decent man, and he's been through hell. Give him a chance.'

He patted her shoulder awkwardly, then left her with Grace.

Grace, who hadn't left her side since Ruth had gone, who'd held her and let her cry and fed her tea and biscuits and refused to go home now.

'I'll stay with you.'

'I'll be all right.'

'Will you? I don't think so. You look like hell, Annie.'

She started to cry again. 'I just can't believe he didn't tell me. You know, Vicky was right. She said he was dangerous.'

'I don't think he is. You heard what Ruth said about him, what Tim just said.'

'But—military intelligence? Working undercover for the government? He must have killed people—that's what they do. Dog eat dog. I don't think I can spend my life with a ruthless killer, no matter why he did it.'

'But he's Stephen's father, Annie. Don't you think he has a right to see him, at least? That Stephen has a right to his father? They're wonderful together—you've seen them. And he might be a killer, but only because he had to, because someone has to do the dirty jobs to keep us all safe. That doesn't make him a bad person.'

But what Ruth had told her was still sinking in, and she couldn't think clearly. And until she could, until she could be sure that there was no threat whatsoever to her son, she had to keep him safe.

'I want to phone him.'

'Michael?'

'No! Stephen. I need to talk to him, make sure he's all right.'

He was, but he was very worried about Michael, and Annie had to struggle to reassure him. Even to say his name nearly choked her.

'He's gone home,' she told him. 'He's all right. He just had a little cut on his head.' And a face full of metal plates, and yet another name to add to the list—

'I want to see him.'

'I don't think that's a good idea. He's resting. You can see him next week, maybe. Look, Stephen, I want you to stay with Ed for a few days, OK? I'll drop some things over there for you in the morning.'

'But I want to come home.'

'The house is damaged,' she told him, sticking at least a little to the truth. 'Until it's mended you can't stay here. Your bedroom window's broken.'

Well, cracked, anyway, and the guttering was hanging. It was near enough, and it would have to do. Ed's mother had swallowed it, at least.

'I could sleep with you, in your room at the front,' he said, but she was adamant. She wasn't having him anywhere that Michael could find him—not until she was sure.

'Just stay there, darling. You like Ed—what's the problem?'

'I want to see Michael,' he said, and started crying. 'He's hurt, and it's my fault.'

'Nonsense. It's the cat's fault.'

'Is Tigger dead?'

She didn't know. She hadn't given the cat a moment's thought in all this, but Stephen needed to be reassured. And so she lied, cursing Michael for bringing her to this, making her lie to her son when she'd never lied to him in his life.

'No, he's fine,' she said, crossing her fingers and hoping it was true. She'd got enough to deal with without a dead cat.

'I'll see you in the morning—I'll pick you up and take you to school.'

Finally she prised him off the phone and went up to bed. She put Grace in Vicky's room, lent her a nightie and found her a fresh towel in the airing cupboard, then shut her bedroom door and stood there, not knowing quite what to do.

She didn't dare undress. Crazy, probably, but she didn't feel safe enough. Instead she unpacked her case, hanging up the dress she'd worn last night in Cardiff—so long ago. Lifetimes. She couldn't bear to think about it. He'd even toasted her, his eyes shining with sincerity.

'To you—for being the most special woman I've ever met. One of the bravest, kindest, least selfish people it's ever been my privilege to know. And to us.'

What us? Her and who, exactly? Some tough, ruthless undercover agent with a pretty line in lies? So much for his sincerity. She wrapped the pashmina around her shoulders and curled onto the chair by the window, wide, restless eyes watching the market square for signs of life.

There were none, but at about four in the morning she saw Tigger slinking nervously through the undergrowth in the front garden, and she went down and let him in. He was unscathed, and for once seemed pleased to see her.

'You have no idea what you've done,' she told him unsteadily, but the cat just rubbed himself against her legs and purred and then settled himself on the windowsill and washed.

She made a pot of tea, thinking as she drained it that so much caffeine on top of all the drama probably wasn't good for her but not caring one way or the other. She had to do something, and sleep wasn't an option.

She checked the plastic over the window in the study, and

it was fine, but her moving around disturbed Grace who came down and kept her company.

'What are you going to do?' she asked, and Annie shrugged.

'I don't know. I want to run away, but how can I? I've got the girls to think about as well as Stephen, and the tearoom, and this house—I don't know where to start.'

'You could start by talking to Michael—in front of the police, if necessary, if that makes you feel safe? Or me. I'd come with you, if you want. Tim? Ruth? Maybe all of us.'

'And who can I trust, apart from you? I don't even know for sure about Tim. How do I really know he's a policeman?'

Grace sighed and sat back, hugging her knee to her chest. 'You have to start somewhere, Annie. You have to trust someone. I've seen his ID, but if you want proof phone the police—ask about him.'

She nodded, and reached for the phone book. 'I'll do it now.'

She did, and it seemed Tim was, indeed, a policeman. A detective inspector in the CID. A trawl on the internet revealed that DI Warren was very highly thought of. He had commendations for bravery, and he'd worked with victim support groups and on numerous rape cases.

And he thought Michael was a good man. Thought she should give him a chance.

She felt the threat recede a little, but the hurt and suspicion remained. She had to talk to Michael, she knew that, if only to thank him for saving Stephen's life.

Just not yet.

He had to see Michael. He knew there was something his mum wasn't telling him. She never lied, but she didn't always tell him everything. She hadn't when his dad was dying, and she had that same something odd in her voice, and he didn't know why.

He just knew he had to see Michael, to know he was alive and not badly hurt, because it had all been his fault and there was a sick lump in his chest that wouldn't go away.

So on Tuesday, when everyone went to lunch, he told Ed he was going to the loo and slipped out of the gate when the dinner lady wasn't looking and ran down the road.

He knew the way to the barn. Down the hill, over the bridge and through the wiggly bends, up the hill and then along the track to the right. But it was further than he'd thought, and it was raining, and he was cold and his legs were aching by the time he arrived.

He reached up and rang the doorbell, and nothing happened for ages. He must be dead, he was thinking, but then the door opened slowly and Michael stood there, staring down at him, and all he could do was cry.

He couldn't believe it. The kid was standing in the freezing rain, tears coursing down his cheeks, and fear ripped through him. He stooped and gathered the boy into his arms, and he burrowed into the space between Michael's neck and shoulder and whimpered, and the fear grew tenfold.

His arms tightened. 'What's wrong, Stephen? What's happened?'

'N-nothing,' he hiccuped. 'I thought you were dead. Mummy wouldn't let me see you, and I thought you must be dead—'

He felt tears in his own eyes, and blinked them savagely away, his hand finding and cradling the cold, wet head burrowing into him. 'It's all right, son. I'm fine. I just had a headache for a bit. Come on, let's get inside and tell your mum where you are.'

'She'll kill me,' he sobbed.

'No, she won't. She'll be worried, though. We don't want her to worry. Why don't you go and dry off and I'll ring her? There's some towels in the wet room by the pool.'

He put the boy down, squeezed his shoulder for reassurance, and then as Stephen headed for the door, he picked up the phone and dialled her number.

She answered on the first ring. 'Stephen?' she said frantically, just as the sirens sounded outside his house.

'I've got him here,' he told her. 'He's—'

'What do you want with him?' she cried, her voice panic-stricken, pleading. 'You can have anything—I'll do anything, but please don't take him—'

He was stunned. 'Annie, I'm not taking him anywhere. What kind of a monster do you think I am? He just turned up, wringing wet and miserable—'

He glanced over his shoulder as the police burst in, and closed his eyes.

'He's through there,' he told them heavily, just as Stephen wandered back into the kitchen, rubbing his hair with a towel. 'Stephen, come and talk to your mother.'

He held out the phone, and the WPC took it and handed it to the boy, as if he couldn't be trusted to give him the receiver himself. She couldn't stop him looking at his son, though, and Stephen kept his eyes on Michael as he spoke, as if for moral support, and his lip started to wobble again.

'I'm sorry,' he said. 'I didn't mean to scare you, Mummy, but I thought Michael was dead, like Dad and my father, and I didn't want him to die too—'

Michael closed his eyes, squeezing them tight to hold back the tears. Poor little bastard. God, he loved him so much it hurt—

A hand landed on his shoulder.

'We'd like you to come down to the station with us, sir,' a voice said, and he turned and stared at the man in disbelief.

'I have done nothing wrong,' he said. 'Ask him. Ask the boy.'

He shook his head. 'Sorry, sir.'

'Ask DI Warren, then. He'll vouch for me.'

'We'll talk to him at the station.'

He resisted the urge to swear in front of the child, but there were some choice words running through his mind as he picked up his wallet and his keys.

'What about Stephen?'

'You let us worry about the boy, sir.'

'I'm not leaving him here with strangers. He's scared enough. When that tree fell—'

He looked across at his son, identical blue eyes meeting across the chaos, and Stephen ran to him.

He caught him in his arms, cradling him against his chest. 'I have to go, son,' he said gruffly. 'You'll be OK. Your mum'll be here in a minute.'

He heard the skid of tyres on gravel, and Annie ran through the door and stopped dead, staring at him.

For a long moment he met her eyes, reading distrust and fear and the soul-deep pain of betrayal, and knew he'd done this to her. He'd gambled, and he'd lost. When he allowed himself to think about it, the pain would kill him, but for now he had to go along with this farce.

He unwound Stephen's arms from his neck and handed him to his mother without a word, then turned back to the policeman who was waiting less than patiently.

'OK. Let's get this over with.'

'Why did the police want to talk to Michael, Mummy?'

Annie shook her head. 'I didn't know where you'd gone. I

thought you might have gone there.' That he might have taken you, the most precious thing in my life—

'But why the police? Why didn't you just come and get me?'

She couldn't give him a proper answer, not without going into things she couldn't even begin to discuss with him, so she just hugged him again and said, 'I'm sorry. I overreacted. I was just frightened for you.'

'But Michael wouldn't hurt me,' he said, puzzled. 'He likes me, I know he does.'

Such innocence. 'Just promise me you won't do it again,' she said, holding him at arm's length and looking searchingly at him. 'Promise.'

'I promise,' he mumbled. 'But I want to see him. He said I could swim and stuff.'

'He said that today?' Bribing him? She'd kill him—

'No. Last week. I told you.'

She relaxed a fraction. 'I'll think about it,' she said, the stock parental response to anything too difficult to deal with immediately. 'But you must promise me you won't leave school like that and run off ever again.'

'I already promised,' Stephen said, his bottom lip sticking out.

'And if he comes to the school to see you, you aren't to go with him.'

'Why would he do that?' he asked, clearly puzzled.

'I don't know. But you mustn't go anywhere with anyone unless I know about it, OK?'

'OK. Am I in trouble at school?'

She shook her head. 'No. You're not in trouble, darling. We were just all worried about you.' And they won't let you out of sight ever again if I have anything to do with it, because I'd die if anything happened to you, but only after I'd killed anyone who would harm so much as a single hair on your precious head—

'Mummy, what did Michael do wrong? Why are you so frightened of him? I thought you were friends.'

Oh, Lord. The perception of the child.

'He lied to me,' she said.

'But he wouldn't hurt me,' he said again.

What kind of a monster do you think I am?

'I'll talk to him,' she promised.

'Today?'

'Maybe. Do you think Ed's mum would let you stay again tonight, so I can go and talk to him?'

He nodded. 'She said I could stay there till our house was mended, if I like.'

'I'll do it tonight then.'

If I can find the courage...

'Michael?'

He opened his eyes and stared at her, wondering if she was really there or if he'd conjured her up out of his desperate imagination.

No. She was real—and she looked scared to death. He sat up slowly, dried his hands and reached for the remote, turning off the music that was threatening to blow the barn apart.

The silence was shattering, broken only by the bubbling of the Jacuzzi, and right on cue even that fell silent.

'I rang the bell. I couldn't make you hear,' she said, her hands twisting together.

'Sorry. I had the music on.' Idiot. She knows you had the music on. Oh, Annie, don't look at me like that—

'I'll get out,' he said and, reaching for the towel, he stood up, turning his back so she didn't start accusing him of anything else.

He heard the sound of her indrawn breath.

The scars. Damn. He hadn't even thought of it, but no doubt seeing them in the oblique lighting of the barn would just enhance the horror of the livid ridges and corrugated flesh. That was why he'd kept his robe on at the hotel.

He turned slowly to face her, the towel wrapped firmly round his waist. 'I'm sorry. I'm not a pretty sight.'

'That tree could have killed you,' she said, and he realised she wasn't talking about the scars at all, but about the bruises that he hadn't even looked at.

'I'm fine, Annie.'

'It could have killed all of us if it wasn't for you. I wanted to thank you.'

He shrugged into a robe, walked through into the kitchen, took a glass and filled it with iced water, drained it. 'For what?' he asked bitterly. 'Saving my son's life?'

There. It was said, and it vibrated in the air between them like some kind of emotional gauntlet. Would she have the courage to pick it up?

Annie swallowed. 'Ruth said I should listen to you—hear what you had to say. Tim said I should give you a chance. But I'm scared, Michael. Or Etienne. You see, I don't even know who you are—'

'My name's Michael Armstrong,' he said, his voice flat and expressionless. 'I'm thirty-eight, I left school at eighteen and joined the army. My mother died when I was twenty, my father a year later. I was recruited into military intelligence. My mother was French—the wine we drank the other night came from my uncle's vineyard. That's how I knew so much about wine, from staying with Antoine in the summers when I was growing up. I was raised bilingual. My godmother's name is Peggy, my godfather's Malcolm. They're the nearest thing I have to parents, and until three weeks ago, they thought I was dead. They now know I'm alive.'

She stared at him, taking it all in slowly, wondering how his poor godparents must have felt all that time. No. She knew how they'd felt. 'Do you still work for the military?'

He shook his head. 'No. I was invalided out. They gave me a new identity—a new start.'

'And you came here. Why?'

He sighed and rammed a hand through his hair, wincing when he caught the bump with his fingertips. 'I wanted to make sure you were all right. You'd told me where you were going, what you were going to do. It made it easy to find you.'

She shivered. Even then, all that time ago, he had been following her—

'Did you use me, as part of your cover? In France. Did you use me to give yourself more credibility?'

He shook his head, but his answer wasn't what she'd expected. It was far more chilling. 'No—although it wouldn't have hurt my cover at all. I kept close to you because I didn't like the way Gaultier was looking at you. I knew what the bastard was capable of, and I wanted to make sure you were safe. Falling in love with you was a complication I could have done without, though.'

She flinched at the brutal honesty of that remark, but he was obviously done with lies. He went on.

'I came to find you once I was out of hospital, and discovered you were married and you had a child. But the register of births didn't show a father's name, so I didn't think it could be Roger, or you would have put him down. And besides, you called him Stephen. Etienne is French for Stephen, and I was vain enough to imagine you might have called him after me.'

He looked away. 'I bought this barn and started converting it. It helped my mind work, helped the writing. Gave me some kind of physical outlet. And I could watch over you. I had a motorbike, and I used to ride through the market square and try and catch a glimpse of you. And then the Ancient House came up for sale, just after I sold my first book, and so I bought it with the advance, and moved Ruth in there.

'She needed somewhere to live, she'd been through hell and was still not right, but she wanted to live alone again. She'd been here with me until then, roughing it on a building site but preferring it to being vulnerable. Did she tell you what happened?'

'She said she was raped.'

He snorted. 'She had a system—when it all got too tight for comfort, when it looked as if the punters were going to get serious and she needed to get out, she'd press her pager and an officer in a car would cruise round the corner and pick her up, pretending to be a customer. Then one night the car didn't come. It was held up in traffic, some stupid shunt. He came running on foot, just in time to see her being dragged into a car.'

A muscle worked in his jaw. 'I saw the forensics. There were twelve men, at least. She nearly died. They had to do a hysterectomy to save her. She'll never have children, but I think it's a miracle she can have a relationship with a man at all. It says a lot about Tim and the kind of man he is.'

She felt her eyes fill with tears. Talk about above and beyond the call of duty. So much sacrifice. She began to get a feel for what they'd all been through, but still, she couldn't understand why he hadn't come clean as soon as he could.

She searched his face, looking for clues. For the elusive truth. 'Why didn't you tell me who you were? I mean, I know you couldn't before, but when you could? Why didn't you say something then? Why carry on the lie?'

He sighed, dragging his fingers through his hair again,

wincing again as he forgot the bruise. 'Because I wanted to know if you could love me. Me, Michael—not Etienne, not the father of your child, but me, the man I am now, the real man, not the man I was pretending to be, the man you thought you loved. And I wanted to know if I loved you still, loved the woman you'd become. The wife, the mother, the business-woman. You were just a girl. You might have changed—but you hadn't.'

His voice softened. 'You were still Annie, and I knew the moment I spoke to you that nothing felt any different. I still loved you. I still do. More now than ever. And I'm sorry I blew it. I was going to tell you on Sunday night, but the tree got in the way.'

She wasn't going to give in. Not yet, not when there were still things she needed to have answered. She wrapped her arms round her, hugging herself. 'You spied on me for nine years, Michael. Do you have any idea what that makes me feel like? To have been stalked, all that time?'

'No,' he said harshly. 'I wasn't stalking you, Annie. I was keeping you safe. If Gaultier had come after you to get more information on me—I'd seen the way he looked at you. He wanted you, Annie. As long as he was alive, I didn't think you were safe, and I couldn't watch you myself, so Ruth did it for me. To keep you safe.'

She shuddered, not wanting to think about Gaultier. 'And Roger? You set up a meeting, deliberately, while I was out. Why did you need to meet him?'

He looked away. 'You were married to him. He was bring-ing up my son. I wanted to be sure he was kind to you. When I came after you, I was hoping you'd still be single, that this business with Gaultier would be cleared up in a few months. But you were married, and there was a baby, and months turned to years. It looked as if I might never get a chance to be with you, but I could still keep you safe. And then Roger died.'

'And if he hadn't?'

'Then I would have come to you when Gaultier was out of the way and told you both the truth. Asked for a chance to get to know my son, to have a part in his life. I knew from Ruth that you'd told Stephen about Etienne, that he knew Roger was his stepfather. But I swear, I would have done nothing without talking to you. I don't want to harm any of you, Annie. I just want a chance to take care of you. To make you happy.'

'But you *lied* to me, you and Ruth!' she said, her tears of anguish and betrayal welling over. 'You made a fool of me, when I should have recognised you. Why? You should have trusted me—you should have known I'd love you.'

'I did trust you, but I didn't know any such thing. I knew you collected lame ducks, and I didn't want to be one of them. I just didn't want your pity.' He swallowed and turned away so she couldn't see his expression.

'I needed to know that you could still want me for myself, and not just because of some misplaced loyalty to Stephen's father or because you felt sorry for me—'

'Sorry for you? Why should I feel sorry for you? You're hugely successful, you've got vast amounts of money, you could have anyone you wanted. Why should I feel sorry for you, for God's sake?'

'Because you *didn't* recognise me. Because *I* don't recognise me. Because of this face—'

'But your face is fine,' she said, confused. 'OK, it's not your original face, but it's all right. It's just a face. What's wrong with that?'

He turned back to her, his eyes anguished. 'What's wrong? It's disfigured, that's what's wrong. It isn't me, Annie. Not only am I not called my proper name, but I don't even look like me any more. And I know you well enough to know how kind you are. I didn't want to wake up one day and find you'd married me for the wrong reasons, that it was pity in your eyes and not love. And so I lied, to give you time to fall in love with me, and it backfired. Well, Ruth warned me. She said it was stupid. She told me I'd blow it, and she was right.'

His voice cracked and he turned away abruptly. 'I can't do this any more, Annie. I've done all I can. You're safe now, both of you, that's all that really matters. Stephen's got the money, you've got this house—'

'What money?' she asked, confused. 'What house?'

'The trust fund. That legacy from a cousin who didn't exist.'

She felt her stomach drop. 'That was you? You gave Stephen nearly half a million pounds, just like that?'

'I didn't want you to have to stay with Roger if you weren't happy. I thought if you had financial independence, you could start again somewhere else. There was provision for it to be used for housing you both. And this house—it's in your name. You can do what you like with it. Just give me a few days to pack up and get out. I did it all for you anyway—I thought you'd like it, because of the barn in France you said you liked that day.'

'Up in the hills,' she said slowly. 'You remembered.'

'I remember everything about us,' he told her, turning back to face her, his eyes ravaged with pain and regret. 'Every last, incredible moment. And Cardiff. Another one for the memory banks. I shouldn't have done it. Shouldn't have made love to you, either time. But I wasn't strong enough to walk away from you, and wrong as it was, I can't regret it. France, because it gave the world our son, and Cardiff—how could I regret anything so beautiful?'

He reached out, picked up a bunch of keys, held them out to her.

'Here. The keys of your house—with my love. I'm sorry it didn't work for us. I hope you'll both be happy.'

The keys fell through her fingers, and she stared at him, searching his face and finding what she was looking for. At last.

'I did know you,' she said in wonder. 'When you came in. My heart nearly stopped. You said I looked as if I'd seen a ghost, and maybe I had, because it's all still there when I look closely. I just wasn't expecting it, because I knew you were dead, so I reasoned it away.' She stooped and picked up the keys, put them back on the side, let out her breath on a rush.

'I'm sorry,' she whispered, tears spilling down her face. 'I've been such a fool. I was just so scared. This thing's so big—it isn't every day a person like me gets tangled up in some international incident. I didn't know who to speak to, how to know if Stephen was safe. I should have known you couldn't hurt him. I'm sorry. Forgive me. I shouldn't have doubted you—not for a moment. You promised I could trust you. I should have listened to you.'

For an age he stood there staring at her, then with a ragged groan he folded her against his chest and held her tight.

'Oh, God, I thought I'd lost you,' he said unsteadily, and his lips found hers and he kissed her as if he'd die without her. Then he lifted his head and stared down into her eyes, the tears clumping on his lashes. 'Marry me,' he said. 'Please. If you want to. Let me be with you. We can live wherever you like, do whatever you want. The girls can come, too, if you like. You don't even have to marry me if you don't want to. Just say you'll be with me, all of you.'

'Even Vicky?'

He laughed, the sound music to her ears. 'Even Vicky. She's lovely. I'll even put up with the cat if I have to.'

His hands slid to her shoulders, held her away so he could search her eyes. 'Answer me, Annie, for pity's sake,' he said, his voice now shaking with emotion.

'Yes,' she said. 'Oh, yes, my darling. I'll marry you.'

'Thank God,' he said raggedly. 'Oh, thank God.' He drew her back into his arms and held her close. 'What are we going to tell Stephen?'

'The truth,' she said. 'That you were hurt, that I thought you were dead, that you've been waiting for us until it was safe. He loves you, Michael. He knew you wouldn't hurt him—and it took him to tell me.'

'We'll go now—bring him back here, where he belongs.'

'Perhaps you need to get dressed first.'

He gave a strained chuckle. 'Give me five minutes.'

'You're my father? My real father? The Frenchman?'

Michael nodded. 'Yes.' It was all he could manage. The emotion was choking him, and after shutting it all down for so long, there was a hell of a lot of it to deal with.

'But I thought you were dead?'

'So did I,' his mother said gently. 'But he wasn't. He just couldn't tell us.'

'Why?'

He drew Stephen closer. 'Because in the army there are some things that have to be secret, even from the people you love,' he explained simply.

'But you're allowed to not be secret now?'

He nodded. 'That's why I'm here.'

'Why didn't Mummy know you?'

'Because I look different. My face was hurt, and it's

changed the way I look. But my eyes are still the same as yours. See.'

He took Stephen's hand, led him to the mirror in the hall. 'Can you see?'

They met each other's eyes in the glass, and Stephen nodded. 'They're the same.' And then he smiled and said, 'So— can I call you Daddy?' and Michael thought his heart would burst.

He couldn't speak. He just nodded, and then Stephen was in his arms, and Annie, too, and he forgot the pain. Forgot everything except the future, and that was going to be just fine...

It was hours later, and Stephen was finally asleep, out for the count in the guest bedroom at one end of the suspended steel walkway that linked the two upper rooms at each end of the barn. Annie and Michael lay naked on the huge bed in the master bedroom at the other end, the lights on full as she traced the network of scars on his body with her fingertip. Learning him, his history, charting every single nick and graze that had ever happened to him.

Her finger hesitated over a puckered line along his ribs. 'What's this one?'

'A gunshot. I got it the year before I went to France.'

'And this?'

She drew her finger along the length of the great, curving scar that went from spine to navel around his waist. 'That was France. I had a ruptured kidney, they had to remove it.'

'And this?'

'Liver. They sorted it. It's fine now.'

She touched his face again, her fingers gentle, seeking. She touched his chin, opened his mouth, looked at his teeth, finding tiny scars in his mouth to show how the surgeons had done their miraculous work on his face. It must have hurt so much. 'You were very lucky,' she said softly.

He laughed with only a trace of bitterness. 'I didn't feel lucky at the time.'

'In the hospital, you were talking about morphine.'

He couldn't suppress the shudder. 'I got a bit hooked,' he said. 'Coming off it was hell, but it was better than the alternative.'

Her eyes filled with tears, and she kissed him gently, her lips touching every wound, every mark and nick and scratch on him, healing him inside as well as out.

'I'm so sorry. You must have been in so much pain.'

He shrugged. 'It happens. It's called collateral damage. David's death, what happened to me, what happened to Ruth—we all know it's out there. We just have to hope it doesn't get us. At least it's over now and we know it's finished.'

A shiver went over her, and she snuggled closer. 'Tell me about that night,' she said, curling into his side and resting a hand over his heart, so she could feel the deep, steady, even beat that told her he was indeed alive.

'It was stupid. Things like that so often are. Somebody told David about Ruth when he checked in to report something, and he went out of his mind. He grabbed me and dragged me to one side, and muttered something to me in English. I thought we'd got away with it, but then I realised we were getting funny looks. Our cover was blown. I told him—said we had to get out that night. We should have gone straight away, but he didn't want to arouse any more suspicion, and there was one more thing he wanted to check.

'I should have said no. I was in charge, and I should have just got us out, but it gave me time to say goodbye to you—'

He broke off, grazing her cheek gently with his thumb.

'I knew there was a good chance we'd die that night, and I couldn't bear the thought of dying without making love to you just once before I said goodbye.'

'Au revoir.'

'You noticed.'

'Oh, yes. I thought of it later, realised you must have known something was going on, but I had no idea.'

He gave a humourless laugh. 'You wouldn't. If you'd known anything your life would have been in danger, too. But I couldn't resist spending those last hours with you, making love to you. And you were so incredible—so responsive, so tender. It broke my heart to leave you. I really thought I was going to die that night.'

'I knew something was going on. That's why I gave you the ring.'

'I wore it—right up until three weeks ago. I'm afraid I lost it on Sunday.'

'No. I've got it in my bag. It was in your things at the hospital. That was how I knew.'

He rolled his eyes. 'I wondered.'

'Well, that and calling yourself Armstrong. That was a bit of a give-away.'

'I can't believe I did that.'

'I can. You had a head injury. So what happened then, after you left me that night?'

'We went to town. He wanted to phone Ruth, to talk to her before we did anything else. There was a call box. We were dragged out of it, hauled down an alley and kicked to death. At least, they thought so. Something must have spooked them before they had time to finish me off, though, and I had just enough time to find my phone and dial a number that would bring in reinforcements before I passed out.'

'So someone from your team rescued you?'

He nodded. 'We were wearing tracking devices. I don't know what was said. I just know I woke up in England in a haze of morphine and stayed there for weeks—and that was the good bit. Then I set about finding Ruth, to make sure she was all right.'

'But she wasn't, was she? Tim said something about her trying to kill herself.'

'Mmm. Guilt. Someone told her that David had been informed about the rape, so she thought it was her fault he'd died. It wasn't. It was mine. I should have got us straight out, but—'

'He was a grown man. It was his own fault he blew his cover. Don't forget he nearly got you killed, too.'

'But I was his boss.'

'I think you've paid your debt,' she said softly. She touched his face again, her fingers trembling against the tortured flesh. 'I'm so sorry,' she whispered, swallowing her tears.

'I'm sorry, too. Sorry I lost you, sorry that by the time I'd found you, you were married to Roger and beyond my reach.'

She sighed gently. 'Poor Roger. He was a lovely man, but he was Liz's husband really till the day he died. Our marriage was only ever in name, you know.'

He went still, then lifted his head from the pillow and searched her eyes, his puzzled. 'In name? You didn't—?'

She shook her head, her fingers stroking him still. 'Not once. There was never any suggestion that we should. We had separate rooms.'

He swallowed, his Adam's apple jerking convulsively. 'If you could know how many times I've lain here and tortured myself with an image of you with him—'

'No. There's only ever been you, in thirty years.'

He stared at her again. 'What?'

'In France—that was my first time. And Cardiff was the second.'

'And third,' he said, his voice gruff with emotion. 'Oh, Annie. I don't deserve you.'

'Oh, I think you do—but I want the truth from now on.'

'And nothing but the truth, so help me God.' His smile was wry and uncertain. 'You do trust me now, don't you?' he asked, searching her face for any last trace of doubt, but there was none.

'Yes, my darling. I trust you. I'd trust you with my life. I might as well, as it seems you've been looking after it for nine years anyway.' She pressed her lips to his jaw, over the scars. 'It's my turn now to look after you, and I intend to devote every waking minute to it—well, when I'm not working, anyway.'

'What about the tearoom?'

'What about it?'

'Do you still want to run it? You don't need to. We've got enough money, after all, you hardly need to work. You could sell it.' He hugged her gently. 'Your regulars could come here for coffee and have a swim. I wouldn't mind if it meant I had you.'

'Don't you mean my freeloaders?' she teased, and he groaned.

'OK, I'm sorry. Your friends.'

'Better. I don't know. It all depends.'

'On what?'

She lifted her face, met his eyes. 'We didn't take precautions on Sunday. If I'm pregnant—'

He felt a giant hand squeeze his heart tight. 'Is it likely?'

She shrugged. 'Maybe. And if not, we can always keep trying—if you want to?'

He felt tears well in his eyes, but he didn't care. This was

Annie, and he had no secrets from her. Not now. 'Oh, yes, I want to. It ripped me apart not being there for you when you had Stephen. Missing his babyhood—' He broke off. 'I know I won't get that chance again, but another baby, that would be incredible. Maybe a sister for him—'

'Or two?'

'As many as you like. There can't be too many. I love kids. I love you. How can I be too happy?'

She laughed and snuggled closer. 'You can't—and you'll deserve every second of it. Even the dirty nappies.'

'Oh, joy,' he murmured, but he was still smiling, and he didn't think he'd ever be able to stop.

* * * * *

CLASSIC

Harlequin® *Romance*

COMING NEXT MONTH
AVAILABLE JUNE 12, 2012

#4315 THE TYCOON'S SECRET DAUGHTER
First Time Dads!
Susan Meier

#4316 THE SHERIFF'S DOORSTEP BABY
Teresa Carpenter

#4317 THE REBEL RANCHER
Cadence Creek Cowboys
Donna Alward

#4318 PLAIN JANE IN THE SPOTLIGHT
The Falcon Dynasty
Lucy Gordon

#4319 SECRETS AND SPEED DATING
Leah Ashton

#4320 THE SHEIKH'S JEWEL
Melissa James

REQUEST YOUR FREE BOOKS!
2 FREE NOVELS PLUS 2 FREE GIFTS!

◆ Harlequin®

Romance

From the Heart, For the Heart

Harlequin *Romance*

A touching new duet from fan-favorite author

SUSAN MEIER

When millionaire CEO Max Montgomery spots
Kate Hunter-Montgomery—the wife he's never forgotten—
back in town with a daughter who looks just like him, he's
determined to win her back. But can this savvy business tycoon
convince Kate to trust him a second time with her heart?

Find out this June in

THE TYCOON'S SECRET DAUGHTER

And look for book 2 coming this August!

NANNY FOR THE MILLIONAIRE'S TWINS

Saddle up with Harlequin® series books this summer
and find a cowboy for every mood!

*The legacy of the powerful
Sicilian Ferrara dynasty continues in
THE FORBIDDEN FERRARA
by* USA TODAY *bestselling author Sarah Morgan.*

Enjoy this sneak peek!

A Ferrara would never sit down at a Baracchi table for fear of being poisoned.

Fia had no idea why Santo was here. He didn't know.

He *couldn't* know.

"*Buona sera,* Fia."

A deep male voice came from the doorway, and she turned. The crazy thing was, she didn't know his voice. But she knew his eyes and they were looking at her now—two dark pools of dangerous black. They gleamed bright with intelligence and hard with ruthless purpose. They were the eyes of a man who thrived in a cutthroat business environment. A man who knew what he wanted and wasn't afraid to go after it. They were the same eyes that had glittered into hers in the darkness three years before as they'd ripped each other's clothes and slaked a fierce hunger.

He was exactly the same. Still the same "born to rule" Ferrara self-confidence; the same innate sophistication, polished until it shone bright as the paintwork of his Lamborghini.

She wanted him to go to hell and stay there.

He was her biggest mistake.

And judging from the cold, cynical glint in his eye, he considered her to be his.

"Well, this is a surprise. The Ferrara brothers don't usually step down from their ivory tower to mingle with us mortals. Checking out the competition?" She adopted her most businesslike tone, while all the time her anxiety was rising and the questions were pounding through her head.

Did he know?

Had he found out?

A faint smile touched his mouth and the movement distracted her. There was an almost deadly beauty in the sensual curve of those lips. Everything about the man was dark and sexual, as if he'd been designed for the express purpose of drawing women to their doom. If rumor were correct, he did that with appalling frequency.

Fia wasn't fooled by his apparently relaxed pose or his deceptively mild tone.

Santo Ferrara was the most dangerous man she'd ever met.

Will Santo discover Fia's secret?

Find out in THE FORBIDDEN FERRARA
by USA TODAY bestselling author Sarah Morgan,
available this June from Harlequin Presents®!